THE BRIDGE OF EVON
The Taste of Riverwater

THE BRIDGE OF EVON

The Taste of Riverwater

Written by
Marshall Cunningham

Noble Theme PS.45

Published by Noble Theme Publishing

Book Cover by Alexandra Allden

Map Illustration by Jenna Warren

First Edition 2025

To Bo

My Foxlaris

PREFACE

"Unto whomsoever much is given,
of him shall much be required."

Since I have the ability to write great things, I should write about Him and share the writings.

I wrote those words in Mrs. Howell's sixth grade class in response to what Luke 12:48 meant to me. On August 22nd, 2013. Two years after I got the idea for *The Bridge of Evon*. Half a year before I started drafting it in earnest. Twelve years until the world would finally read what it was I wished to share.

This book has been my life since I was nine years old. I write this now at twenty-three, on the eve of twenty-four. My story parallels the one you hold in your hands. You needn't this tale to understand the one of foxes and jackalopes, dwarves and raccoons. But it is the journey behind the journey. The reason I spent so long living in this quirky little world.

God has blessed me with this story. I intend to tell it.

My passion for the fantasy genre began in third grade in the aftermath of one simple agreement: my father would buy me the box set of *Harry Potter* books (which I'd been begging for after seeing them in the Scholastic catalog), but only if I promised to read *The Chronicles of Narnia* as well.

An easy choice.

At that point in time I hungered for any page I could get my hands on, so its no wonder I hoarded the books around me like Smaug with his dwarven gold (who I'd yet to meet, mind you). As I read, I found myself loving the world, characters, and magic of C. S. Lewis' Narnia more than that of J. K. Rowling and Hogwarts. It imbued me with a genuine passion for wonder and adventure that fueled many dreams and stories of my own. These feelings expanded when I discovered J. R. R. Tolkien and *The Lord of the Rings* a few years later, devouring *The Hobbit* in the weeks leading up to the launch of the first film (*now* I knew Smaug). These two men became my heroes and helped open the gateway towards my love of fantasy. From them I jumped to Brian Jacques and the Redwall series, the cosmere of Brandon Sanderson and duchies of Robin Hobb, and deeper into the classics such as Robin Hood and King Arthur. No story was safe from my grasp.

As I grew older, however, I began to scrutinize the books I read and found myself burdened with a burning conviction: none led me down a road that strengthened my Christian faith. Only Tolkien and Lewis managed to do so. While what I poured into myself was always fun, enjoyable, and a great escape from the world around me, I knew deep within that it lacked the challenge needed to truly transform me into someone better off because I read the book. My faith is the most important thing in my life—every pursuit I lend myself to, even that of reading, should be a venture that helps me mature as a Christian.

I tried seeking out works similar to those of my two heroes. No treasure came from such a quest. The Christian fiction at the bookstore was nothing but plain, Amish romances. The few stories that did stand out were plagued by theological nonsense that failed to present correct Biblical truths. Past that, Christian storytelling in other mediums like film came off as cheesy, preachy, and a disservice to the faith they represented. Stories no longer filled my grasp—only disappointment.

As someone who craved fiction that would teach and test my faith, as well as fulfill this inherent need to explore new worlds and experience fresh ideas, my heart broke. Where could I go to find what I needed? Were Christianity and fiction just too different of ideas to properly mix?

It was amidst this very questioning that true work on Evon started. I took the fledgling ideas scraped together in fourth grade and formulated them into something new, something *meaningful*. The world I imagined would become that missing piece of strong Christian fiction and fun, enthralling adventure. I realize now that my original conviction to seek out fulfilling fantasy was not to find it in the world, but create it and put it out there myself.

I outlined and wrote *The Bridge of Evon* throughout my middle and high school career. The first draft was completed on July 19th, 2019, a month before my senior year. It sat in that state—a mismatched collage of 250,000+ words written from age eleven to seventeen—until I unearthed it in college a few years later. There, it became the core of my Honors College Capstone Thesis about how to properly create true, meaningful Christian Fiction. I again visited Lewis and Tolkien, only this time as a student of form and technique instead of a reader of fervor and love. With them joined Flannery O'Connor, George MacDonald, G.K. Chesterton, Andrew Peterson. Through a study of their writings I formed new knowledge in the realm of Christian Fiction, creating terminology and graphs that synthesized my research and, for the first time that I could find, made this genre into a field of study.

My findings brought me back to Evon. I dusted off the original manuscript and rewrote it from the ground up, incorporating what I'd learned. It blossomed into a 330,000+ word behemoth, a work larger than all of *The Chronicles of Narnia* combined. Before it was a miracle for a high schooler to write; now it rivaled that of my mentors.

God works through Christian creativity. If I've only learned one single truth through these past years of writing, it's that. I've seen His hand move in ways I once thought impossible. Just thinking about the plot alone tingles me with excitement, not because it looms over *The Lord of the Rings* in terms of greatness or anything, but because I can see exactly where God intervened. *He* shaped this, not Marshall Cunningham.

I remember one specific night while I stayed in a Missouri cabin during Christmas break. A single lamp glowed in the corner, painted my face a warm gold clashing with the silver blare of my screen. Winter winds howled outside. My uncles snored in the room behind me. The chapter's outline scrolled over my eyes again and again and again, and each time I knew it wasn't going the way it should. It didn't click. The scenes lost their balance in weaving from one to the other. I physically had no way to say what needed to be said.

So I prayed. Head bowed, eyes closed, grandfather clock ticking towards 1 AM. I asked God for guidance, that what needed to be shared to my readers, whoever they may be, would come across and affect them the way He wanted. I didn't want a single one of my ideas near this book. Only His.

And God replied.

I won't say the specifics of the scene to save you from spoilers (it will be revealed later, promise), but in that moment, the entire novel connected. I was gifted the way to explain how becoming a Christian works. It showed God's plan, truth, love, and open gift of salvation that waits for us all—all in a point I never saw coming.

After I finished the chapter I went back to those lines in the outline and left this little note:

This right here was NOT me - ALL GOD!!!!

Examples like this happened continually. It built a reliance on God I hadn't encountered before. My faith deepened, and the way in which I wrote focused solely on my Lord. The end result is a novel with which I am exceedingly happy beyond what words here can describe. However, letting God tell His tale through me presented a challenge I ponder now: I can write these stories, but can I live them?

Is the trust seen throughout just words on a page? Or will I take it to heart and become as active in obeying it as these characters are? I've tried to with this novel, but what about in my own life? In the mundane, the ordinary, the times where I don't think of God at all? I don't believe I can put this message out into the world while rejecting it myself. What good is a chef who doesn't like his own food? These lessons *must* permeate my own heart before they have a chance to encounter others. Being given this project comes with it a great deal of responsibility. The words reflect me, and I reflect God. Thus, I have to trust. I have to choose. I have to be an example of what living out the morals of *The Bridge of Evon* looks like. It's what separates Christian fiction from the rest of literature. A romance author who writes about "love at first sight" yet doesn't believe it isn't all that important, yet a Christian writer who forsakes the key tenets of his faith saps the novel's proof of work. As I said before, God's given me this story, and I intend to tell it. And I'd be a fool not to live it too.

My reflections on this book have shown me that I'm only at the beginning of where God wants me. I've so much to learn on every possible level, from trusting, writing, teaching, creating, all of it. Christian fiction fits right into that. *The Bridge of Evon* is only one book. The genre still needs work far and beyond what I've accomplished here. Through these experiences, however, my passion for the subject *exploded.* I want my career dedicated to fixing this broken, barren, bleeding section of literature, and that extends further than the mere creation of new works.

As of the publishing of this book, I have created my own Christian fiction publishing company, Noble Theme Publishing (taken from Psalm 45:1). The company has three core modes of operation—reviving the past through the publication of lost, out-of-print works of classical Christian fiction; rescuing the present by signing currently working authors who feel homeless in the bookstore for being too Christian for regular publishers and too secular for the modern Christian presses; and writing the future via the creation of new works, teaching the next generation of Christian writers, and firmly establishing a true foundation of Christian fiction no different then I did in my Capstone. I see Noble Theme expanding past the production of books. There's potential to host workshops, teach at events, create online lessons, dip into film production, and show the world how powerful a genre Christian fiction can actually be.

Along with this, I opened a bookstore called Bean's Books on July

1st of 2024, a month after graduating from college. It sells both new and used books, and when it comes to the Christian fiction section, I hand-select only the *best* this genre has to offer. The store has not only become my career, but I've been able to use it as the grounds for many local literary events, Christian and secular alike. Promoting the importance of literature does just as much good as writing it. This will go hand-in-hand with Noble Theme by completing a type of "vertical integration" for Christian fiction. I'll be able to write, publish, sell, and teach within the genre. A combination like brims with potential. If I want to see change, I need to be willing to take the steps to see it happen.

Don't get me wrong, I understand how huge an undertaking this is. It's not like the average twenty-three-year-old to open two wildly complex businesses right after graduation with the hope of changing an entire literary market. But it's also not typical for one to write a 850+ page, 330,000+ word fantasy epic with a decade and a half of developed lore behind it *twice*. It is only through God that I've accomplished such a feat. So too is it by His power alone that these other two goals see the light of day.

Now, a year and a half after college, I sit here writing this preface a few days away from sending the manuscript off to print after a successful Kickstarter raised over $7,000 to see this book (split into four parts, thankfully) come to life. I could conclude by droning on about how I implemented what I discovered in my college research, or recap the challenges I faced to get this book to you now, but, honestly, I'd rather not. *The Bridge of Evon* and its story is important to me for reasons beyond that. A reason that's been with me since the very start.

What is to happen to the kids like me?

Once they finish *Narnia* and flip the last page of *The Return of the King*, what should their next step be? Many may gravitate towards the darker, riskier worlds like I did. That is not to say there is anything wrong with traveling to Martin's Westeros or Sapkowski's Continent.

I implore all fantasy lovers to get lost in such rich and inviting lands. However, I can personally attest to the morals, impressions, and lessons found there as paling in comparison to what springs forth from the Bible. Sacrificing life-saving truth for the thrill of escapism should never have to be an option.

I want the next third-grade Marshall Cunningham to have the same choice my dad gave me: *Harry Potter*, and the rest of the secular fantasy world on one hand, and *Narnia* on the other. But *Narnia* should not be where that choice ends. There ought to be a massive genre waiting for him, dying to grasp his hand and guide him through world after world, land after land, and, by the end, delivering a message that is exciting to the mind and comforting to the soul. That is the end goal of this book, of this mission I've set myself on. While it may take years, decades, or centuries, I plan to devote myself to fulfilling it one way or another.

I felt the calling in my heart to write *The Bridge of Evon,* so I wrote it. Now I see that path—and calling—stretching beyond to further influence Christian fiction in ways completely apart from writing. And I'm gonna journey down it. It will be difficult. It will break me down. Creating this novel did just that. But what I have in God, that beautiful trust filling my heart with a peace everlasting, joy sweet to the taste, *that* matters infinitely more than any pain this world can muster.

To rephrase what I scribbled down in that sixth grade classroom, I'm His writer. He's my Author. And I will go wherever His story takes me.

— Marshall Cunningham
November 2025

ACKNOWLEDGEMENTS

I've what feels like millions of people to thank for their contributions toward this book. You don't write something for close to fifteen years without bringing it up every once and a while (and I've done it more than once, and *definitely* for more than a while). I want to highlight all of the following people and give them the deepest, most sincere love and thanks I can muster.

God, first and foremost. My Savior, my Life, the only reason I breathe here and now. Let my words always be Yours. I thank you so dearly for everyone below.

My parents, Scott and Sherry, for reading me *Goodnight Moon* as a babe, buying me books as a kid (and adult), and building my bookstore now. I'd be nothing without y'all.

My brother, Bo, who I was blessed to share a childhood with, one filled with the Lego playing, forest exploring, and video making that created the foundation of this book. Love you, Passa.

MoMo Kessie for her endless, ceaseless love, and for giving me the notebook that I wrote the first inkling of this book within. *I love you!!*

MoMo Mary and PawPaw George, in whose home I typed the official first chapter, and who supported my writing wholeheartedly both on earth and in Heaven now.

Abbey and Emma, my cousins, and the very first eyes to ever read this story.

Bean, my reading and writing buddy, my schnauzer girl who never left my side and made the many, many hours of writing all the less lonely.

My girlfriend, Caitlyn King, for her dear love in the final days of finishing this project, and for being the only person actually happy I put my dog above her.

Garrett Bullock, my longest friend, Employee of the Year, and Evon's biggest fan. How hollow this story would be without you always by my side.

Matthew Gilleran, the most decorated audiobook narrator—and friend—I could ask for. (Aww shucks, Marshall, what an incredibly nice thing to say, I'm totally saying this from my heart and definitely not reading it out from the book) ;)

Mrs. Jenna Warren for her *astounding* work on creating The Map of Evon, and for letting me beat her in *Lord of the Rings* Trivia Pursuit.

Ava Bramlett for beta reading this series literally as I write these very words.

Mrs. Rhonda Robinson, Mrs. Mary Nabholz, Mrs. Shandi Summers, and Mrs. Laura Shelton, my high school English teachers, for allowing me to express my creativity in poems, projects, and plays. I wouldn't be here with the chances y'all gave me and the literature y'all opened my eyes to.

Drew (Coach) Miller, my eighth grade Bible teacher who I promised to name a character after. He'll appear in the second book.

And he's awesome.

Dr. Hawkins for being my mentor during my Capstone project and enriching my life by introducing me to Christian writers I can now call my new favorites.

My college friends of Braydon and Caroline Bivins, Kristína Coggin, and Chloe Emmerling for their unlimited uplifting and support for anything I write. Few people have purer hearts.

John and Clive. My heroes. I hope I do y'all proud.

And, finally, to everyone who supported *The Bridge of Evon* Kickstarter! We raised over $7,000 to fund the publishing of these four books in July of 2025. Just thinking about it now, many months after the fact, brings me to tears. Thank you, thank you, thank you. All y'all made this boy's dream come true. ***Thank you!***

Joe and Stacye Austin, Scott Austin, The Barron Family, Heath Besowshek, Loren Biggs, Carol Bradford, Ava Bramlett, Kelly Brogdon, Garrett Bullock, Katherine Burns, Jaxon Charlton, The Cole Family, Bo Cunningham, George Cunningham Jr., Greg Cunningham, Malcolm Cunningham, Sherry and Scott Cunningham, Jackson D. McDonald, Essie Decuir, Jon Dor, Ron Duggins, Tierney Earnest, Josh and Brooke Evans, Madison Evans, Nick Flesher, Florentina, Ftost-Frame, Lauren Grasso, Olivia Henry, TJ Johnston, Jared Jowers, Kylei Keever, Samantha Keil, Andrea & Ben King, Jace Kramer, Claire Lee, Topanga Leslie, Kristy Linville, Kevin and Donna Lyon, Drew Miller, Katherine Malloy, Matthias720, Durgan Maxey, Megan Mercer, Mary Nabholz, Rebecca O'Neill, Grace Olivia Martin, Linda Petit, Ringmaster, Rhonda Robinson, Anna Samons, Karen Samuhel, Melissa Seme, Tara Shuster, Christine Sterling, Drew Strickland, Giselle T., Michael Taylor, Tonia, David Trotter, Corrina Van Brunt, Georgann Whitley, Thomas Williams, Marti Wilson, Ben Wrobbel, and Julie Wynegar.

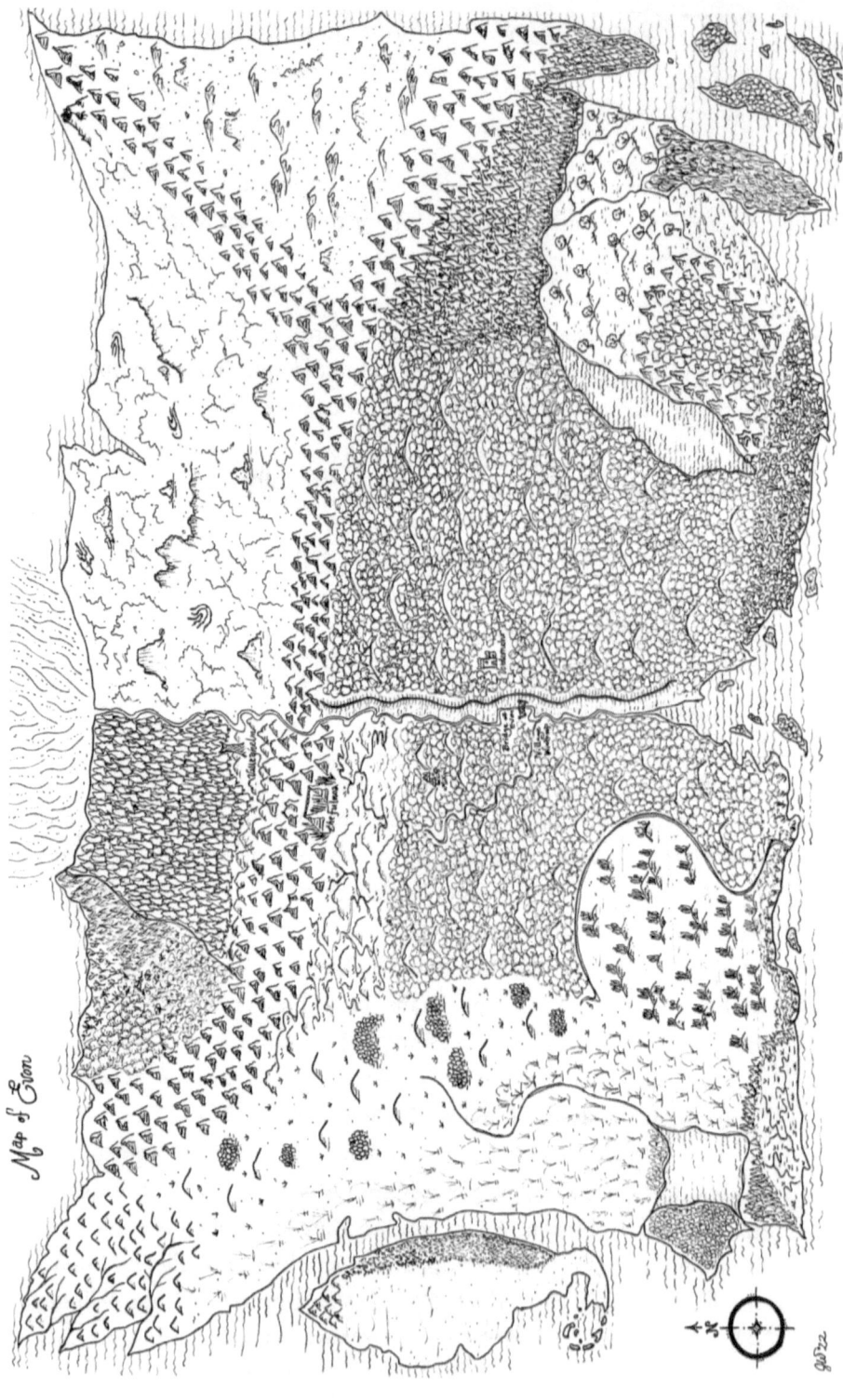

Map of Eron

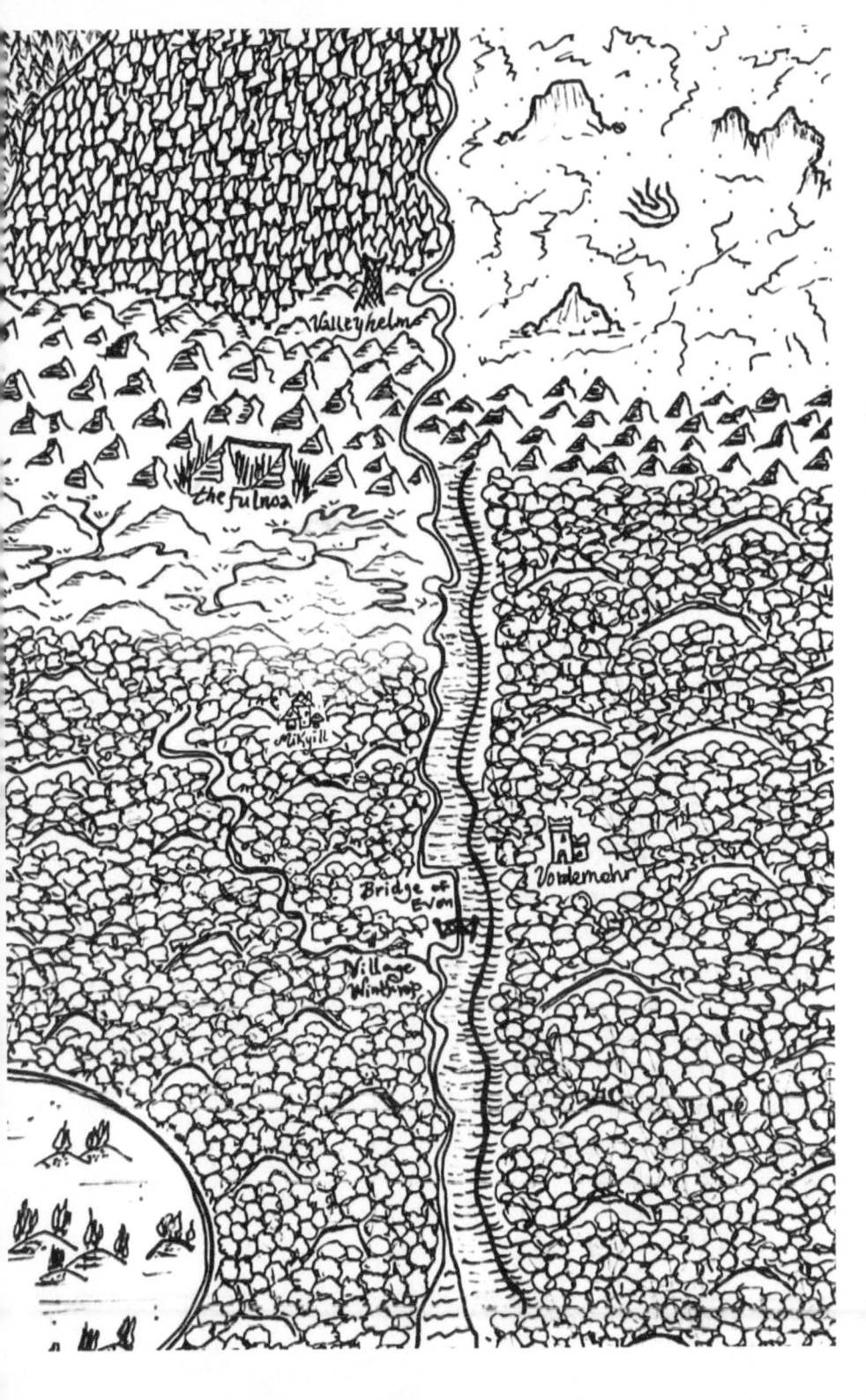

Pronunciation Guide

Acirema: *uh-SEER-uh-muh*
Adalgiso: *uh-dahl-GEE-soh*
Aisar: *AYE-sar*
Cammont: *cuh-MONT*
Dubyr: *DOOB-yer*
Enaled: *eh-NAHL-ed*
Evon: *ee-VOHN*
Feiht: *fee-HET*
Foehn: *fane*
Foxlaris: *FOX-ler-iz*
Foxtamas: *FOX-tuh-mus*
Fulnoa: *full-NO-uh*
Garona: *GUH-ron-uh*
Getophry: *get-OFF-ree*
Ghroat: *gr-OTE*
Gniw: *new*
Gregabbit: *GREH-guh-bit*
Hucksubtle: *HUCK-sut-ul*
Iota: *eye-OH-tuh*
Lordell: *LORD-ul*
Losrym: *LOZ-rem*
Mechmilne: *MEH-chuh-milne*
Mikyill: *MEEK-yill*
Nohsis: *NO-sis*
Omaya: *oh-MY-uh*

Ratatoskr: *ruh-TAT-oh-sker*
Reinden: *RAIN-den*
Roihelm: *ROY-helm*
Rokanoe: *ROW-ken-oh*
Ruel: *ROO-ul*
Tarasque: *TAYR-usk*
Tauronon: *TAR-oh-non*
Tirsol: *TEER-sul*
Tywyll: *TIE-why-el*
Velvedier: *vel-vuh-DEER*
Vordemohr: *VORD-more*

PROLOGUE

Splash!

The young fox leapt into the ready river waters. They rose like glistening glass an inch above his ankle, welcoming the boy and his joy kicking and spraying through the waves. His fellow friends and village-mates joined further downstream. Together, they doused the bright, cloudless morn in a misting of brisk, lively fun, spanning the River Nohsis from shore to shore.

It flowed down the entirety of Evon, splitting the land in two like a mighty blue vena cava. Past the boughs lurching from forests, beneath the shadows of looming ridges, through the stale air guarding the wastelands, the ripples ran long, passing now between the playing of children at the land's center. Swaths of green arose on either side. The waves ebbed along the long stretches of sand coating the Western shore. They waded back to grass that eased to woodland, a striking viridescence prancing in the sweet, cooling gales. On the opposite side, dozens of yards away in the East, a mirror image emerged. If the mirror was cracked. The reflection jagged.

A pebble beach scattered its coast. Low, smooth rocks jaunted upwards into sharper stones tangled between the thick ropes of roots slithering out from the dim underbrush. All the trees were an envy green. Hushed, muted bark twisted like petrified smoke. Even the village children skipping stones from its shore couldn't see but a few feet in. Shadows hid the forest like a curtain. Miles into the interior, a ridge bolted up into the sky, high enough to become the start of a mountain. The rest of the East lay blocked behind. It cast a violet shade over the

River at sundown, and in the late morning, a sweetened shade.

Thus lay Evon. Two brother sides, splintered down the center, yet each equally resting against the drifting, redeeming waves slipping along their dichotomous shores.

But something else connected them. Something unexpected in the roar of a river, unique from all the other magics and mysteries hidden within the land—a tree. A *golden* tree. Square in the middle of the world.

The fox hopped along its bright, bulbous oak roots. They dove in and out of the water like a sea monster, sprawling and anchoring itself into both shores, sand and stone alike. The poor boy barely kept himself from crashing into the waves. His hand shot out and gripped the golden bark. It felt smooth, not jagged, frigid like steel's sting. He figured he could wrap his arms around the trunk at *least* fifty times and still not clasp his hands. It might take even more to touch the branches above. Despite how far they dipped down—their gilded shimmer flashing off the sun in a dazzling gleam—none of the villagers had ever been able to reach them. Poppa always said they wouldn't be able to pull a leaf off them even if they succeeded. But they still could shake like the other oaks, bending in the breeze? It never made sense to him.

A funny thought. Because for everyone else, *he* never made sense to *them!* His fur didn't burn the color of a crimson sunset or the trickle of a newborn flame—it blared blue. A fierce shade, one of fresh-sliced sapphires cutting light with slashes of azure. It covered him from head to toe. Licked his ears, made his tail flutter off him like a hyacinth. Had he not been dressed in brown overalls and a tattered tan shirt (the only shirt Momma let him go river playing in), the leaves above would've been unable to tell him apart from the waters. They kept their peace, though. If foxes aren't usually blue, then trees are certainly never gold.

Yet despite the uniqueness without, within, the boy was indistinguishable from the others around him. He proved it by hopping from the roots and participating in an activity no child of Evon could resist: digging.

His knees sank into the loamy riverbed. Giggling, he clawed away the dirt beside his fellow excavators, a squirrel and a gnome. The root beside them parsed away the waters and left just enough room amongst the shallows for them to explore. And what were they after? Nothing less than the end of a golden root.

Lord Cammont poisoned their minds with the thought the last time he took them on a day out to Nohsis. He told them how a certain few roots burrow far into the earth, hundreds and hundreds of miles down into the heart of Evon. However, if one was to reach their end, they'd uncover a tunnel. A tunnel leading to distant lands never before graced by the presence of an Evoneer.

The rich earth stood no ground against the speed of the blue paws raging through it. Dirt spluttered and splattered and sprayed over the trio. Amidst the digging, the gnome's knuckle suddenly crashed down with a wide and sudden *THUD!*

The youngster reared back, hugging and shaking the pain from his fingers. As he did, the other two shoveled away the murky dirt to see what he'd hit.

Anxious, excited breaths rose their chests up and down, up and down, the potential possibility seizing their hearts with an unbending grip. The object was planted deep.

Felt thick to the touch.

Rugged.

Wooden!

And…square?

All three deflated as the hopes of a golden root melted into a bland box. No gold. No earthy fibers. Just a plain, simple chest, stained dark by mud, eroded with lichen, and just large enough to fit in their grip.

But far from a loss.

What could be hiding inside!?

The children erupted in speculation. The squirrel bet elf treasure. The gnome (now recovered) bet gems from the Fulnoa dwarves. The fox bet gold, the root still on his mind. *Pirate* gold, more specifically. A long-lost bounty buried in Nohsis by runaways all the way from the Sea of Evon. Oh, what a thought! It had the squirrel and gnome ripping the box from the tomb and trying to chip off the overgrowth to pry it open, all while the fox jaunted off, hoots and hollers thrown to everyone he could find.

"Poppa! Poppa!"

The cry flicked up a single ear from the older fox snoozing on the Western shore. Compared to his son, his fur *did* burn the color of a crimson sunset and the trickle of a newborn flame. Most, though, lay covered by his layers of tunics and buttons, joined by the book resting upon his face. A newer one, from some start-up Mikyill press, the fresh scent of ink just strong enough to lull him to sleep. He hadn't *meant* to pass out while watching the children. If the other parents knew, they'd rob him of his precious chaperone privileges. But with warming sands at his neck, the waters caressing his bare toes and rolled slacks like the gentle hug of a mother's love, he found the words blurring and sky darkening as the novel tipped over his nose.

It also hid the East. Sometimes the sight still brought him back there. Even all these years later. The ridges scarred his vision. The waves against that stony shore ebbing with their blood...

But the blue brought him back. Skipping and waving, panting and shouting for his father to rise from his reading.

"Poppa, get up!" the boy shouted as he approached. Chuckling, the older fox set his book aside and hugged his knees, sharing the giddy smile of his son.

"What's up, buddy?" he asked.

"We found a box!" His words twinkled with excitement. "It's all nasty and stuff, but it's pirate treasure!"

"*Pirate* treasure, huh?"

"Yeah! Buckil says it's elf treasure but Dawny thinks it's just some part of the tree, but I know it ain't either 'cause it ain't all that old lookin' and it ain't gold at all."

The father fox beamed.

"Sounds like we're fixin' to be rich!" he laughed.

"We need you to come open it! The top's rotted on." Before he could reply, his son snatched his arm and tried dragging him with every ounce of his blue, blistering might. "Come on, hurry!"

"Gotta pull harder than that!"

The blue fox took up the challenge. He lifted hard and ground his feet deep within the sand until a stiffened groan puttered out from his rising Poppa (serenaded with a few stray pops of his back). How he envied the energy bubbling in his boy.

Together, the duo waded hand-in-hand across the shallows. The older fox pondered what could've been buried beneath the Roistrom. Some memento maybe? Or a chest left behind in the days prior? The rest of the children had already flooded in to take a peek of it themselves. But upon seeing their guardian, their ranks parted and let the duo through.

"Let's see here, what did you kids dig up, huh?" he asked while kneeling amongst the roots, letting the ripples sprinkle through his morning trousers. Very rarely did his orange legs show. Those closest knew of the scars he hid and, worse, the missing tail. Such history had no place on a fine, now *thoroughly* exciting day.

He took the rugged ark in his paws and scraped away the crust along its seal. With a little wiggling, he broke through and eased open the lid.

Everyone clambered over him at once. The blue fox leapt on his shoulders like climbing a tree while his friends poked their little heads closer to get a view of the bounty. All held bated breaths. Burgeoning wonder. Giddy, grandiose glee.

The fox pulled the top all the way back for everyone to see inside.

Four treasures were within. Resting on a soaked velvet mat. A threadbare handkerchief bearing splats of ancient stains; a golden yet corroded tiara, flowered by ruby petals and fit for the head a child; a long-rusted throwing star dulled by decay; and a kitchen knife, dainty, with a single silver glimmer outshining the corrosion around it.

The children reared back in disappointment. This wasn't pirate treasure at all! Not even close! Where were the gems, the Tops, the gold!

But the father stayed still. Eyes planted. Quivering with tears.

His trembling hand lowered and graced the blade. Each finger wrapped around the handle one after the other, unable to fully tighten. Choking it choked him. Made the roots at his side feel like tendrils sneaking up to drag him back down, to the feelings, the fright, the faces and their fates lurking below the surface.

No.

Not again.

It was too real. He couldn't go back, it couldn't happen again.

Stop it! No, no, stop! Not them! Please, stop, not him, not him—

"Poppa?"

Azure eyes peeped over his head as his son woke him from the memories. Steps pattered on his shoulders. Not danger. Hands held tight to his neck. Not fear. "You okay?"

Softly, his father placed the knife back down. A single tear dripped from his eye, rolled down his cheek, and disappeared into the river waters flowing at his side.

"Yeah, I'm good, buddy. Just, um...brought back some memories."

"Whatcha mean?" questioned the boy.

A weak yet genuine smile spread across his face.

"I just so happen to know who buried this here treasure."

"No way!"

"Yup!"

"Whose is it!"

"You'll have to wait and see."

With that, he rose chuckling from the riverbed, wooden box in hand. "Alright kids," he yelled to the others. "Let's head to shore! I gotta real good story for y'all."

"Is it about elves?" the squirrel shouted.

"Or dwarves!?" added the gnome.

"No, dragons!" a squeaky rabbit hoped.

The father fox laughed to himself.

"A little bit of it all!"

Yips and yays overpowered the winds and waves as the pack scampered to the Western grass. Their leader lagged behind, drifting through the shallows, saying his farewells to the mellowed flow wading on about its day. And for a moment, he paused to uplift his head. So too did the billowy clouds roll by in a morning sea all their own.

It was time…wasn't it? To tell them the full story? Already his chin curled, heart thumped, thumped, *thumped* thick as a bleating drum. Everything—everyone—still clear as the day gifted around him. Yet he couldn't forsake what the story had taught him. Had *made* him.

It lay evident at every corner. In the chest dripping in his hands, the blue grip tugging at his side to hurry, the waters bubbling at his feet, the sky livening the morn, the ability blessed within to rise above himself on wings not his own.

It was time.

Time to pass along all he had learned.

The kids hastily washed their mucky hands and dried off their soggy feet and sped to gather around the father. He took a seat upon an aged stump (again with grunts and pops) and rested the box by his side. His son sat closest. Eyes wide like sapphires.

Once everyone sat eager and ready, a dozens of grinning faces hungry for the tale, he began. Smiling.

"Now, this story starts off like all the good ones do: a long, long time ago…"

BOOK I
THE TASTE OF RIVERWATER

I

"THIS LIFE: HOW SWEET, HOW SWEET."

The frozen forest of Pradifore bundled itself against the winds of winter. Spiteful they swept. Thorns of snow and ice blistering the air, shredding bark and snapping boughs. Ghastly howls lurking in the shadows echoing like war cries. The kind of cold lungs refuse to breathe. But the staunch Wood parlayed the storm. Not a single leaf, of which few still held, split away to flutter across the hazy, clouded northern sky, darkened by the early night. The monstrous trunks boasted their freshly grown layers of ice, shielding their bodies like moss stitched upon a moistened stone. The blue, crystalline armor endured the bruising and kept the inner tree stable and warm, forcing the creeping cold to mold into a summer breeze. Every stalk in Pradifore Wood assembled in such a way. No gale nor axe could mar them.

Deep within the forest, lone from all others of its kind, one squatty giant stood out. It wore the same frozen coat as the rest. The branches drooped close to the snow gathered ankle-high, and its roots rippled far. The true significance, though, lay inside.

Carved into the tree was a lovely, cozy home. It housed only two stout rooms joined by a central staircase. Neither were dingy nor brittle like a fallen log. They had the inner looks of a cabin, with smooth brown rings painting every surface and a musk scented with the earthy notes of maple. Its wooden walls were decorated with an honest meeting of little means and big heart. Heirloom portraits, hand-weaved tapestries, clay vases bearing nettles and branches for medicinal teas—the entire structure radiated warmth. It felt no different from the other northern families' homes in Pradifore. Burrowing into the trees was the only way to survive. The ice without kept those inside toasty. Where there came a grove, there sprouted a village. And where they lay sparse, a single family home came to be.

Flickering firelight danced to the tune of a perfected chopping thumping within the kitchen. A female fox, dressed in her usual nightly gown of pink and purple, worked to finish off the last few chunks of a potato. Finding one hadn't been easy, but the preparation became no task at all. Her rich blue eyes gazed up from the far-too-tiny kitchen towards the tattered table only a few feet away.

Still gone.

She shook her head. It scrambled the thoughts of worry about her husband and son. The wrinkles drawn deep into her young, thirty-year-old face only widened. Had it really taken this long? The storm was nasty, sure, but…no, they could handle it. They always did.

As she worked, a beady pair of brown eyes scanned down from the winding stairwell that partitioned the kitchen's meager bar and table from the roaring fire and rocking chairs of the den. They crept along with her every movement drenched in the flames of the hearth and oil lamp. She dumped the potato chunks into the stew pot on the counter beside her, joining the sparse carrot ends and mushroom bits.

The stalker's stomach sank.

A grumpy fire rose in his soul. Oh, how he wished to holler throughout the whole house a booming "*Omaya Scottsworth!*" just like she did to him. But he knew the repercussions for such an offense. His mother would surely leave him out in the snow this time.

"Foxlaris!" Omaya called from below. "They should be back soon, get on down!" His dark orange paws shook with anger just thinking of the meager dinner waiting for him. The entirety of his snug, rag-covered, eight-year-old body prickled.

"Momma, I ain't eating what they bring! I'm tired of that stew!" he proclaimed, whisking away from his hideout and down to the table. He bolted his paws to his hips. A strong stance. One the mother fox didn't have the time to notice. Instead, she tossed scraps and skin of the spud into the readied cast-iron pot. The very same her grandmother worked with to make the very same meal. It always had more than enough room for whatever was to come.

"You don't even know what they've got," came her answer.

"Yes I do! Just a buncha roots, an' berries, and, and, a whole lotta nothing!" the young boy rallied again. Still, no reply.

Foxlaris Scottsworth moodily plopped into this usual seat at the table and snuggled his head beneath his arms (conveniently with his back *away* from the kitchen). The hard wood beneath wasn't helping his sour attitude. It hurt to hide his face upon it. He watched as Omaya carefully hung the pot above the back wall's fireplace. The stupid thing always made his secret lurking spot (the stairs) too hot. It could fit nowhere else though, as the bottom floor of the Scottsworth Tree barely fit what they needed. A simple bar, table, chairs, and fireplace; the bare essentials to make a house a home.

"Why's Poppa always gotta bring him out there? You know I'm the best!" Foxlaris started again. "Every time I'm out, we always find the good stuff!"

"He invited you, didn't he?" his mother shot back, stern blue eyes finally breaking down to her son. "Said you were too tired if I remember right. So, he took Foxtamas instead." She added a scoop of snow and stirred it until it melted down to broth. "You don't need to be out there anyway, honey, recovering from being sick an' all. I know you don't want that coming back, right?"

The boy's eyes rolled. Yes...he *was* given the offer. But he was too tired then! Really! He and Foxtamas had just finished a fresh game of house-climbing before they left. What kid had the strength to go out gathering after such a match? They'd run around the yard at *least* a dozen times. His little lungs still wheezed from it.

Foxtamas' probably didn't. They never did. Even after he fell face-first from the high branches. His year-younger brother just *had* to take the *one* job he'd mastered. His stomach rolled with malice. And hunger.

"It ain't my fault Foxtamas doesn't get sick!"

"I know it's not, hun." Omaya made the short trek back to the kitchen, wiping down the wooden bar with a rag. "But it gives you more time to work around here with me, don't it?" She offered him a soft smile. He tossed back a disgusted scowl.

"Cooking and cleaning ain't fun at all!"

"But it's gotta be done."

"Why can't Foxtamas do it then?"

"He has and he will. Just like you've gone out with Poppa and stayed here with me. We all got jobs to do." She cleaned her bony hands off and took a seat opposite her son. Kindness radiated from her, like a peek of sun after the thralls of a winter's rage.

Inwardly, though, she ached. Her poor, poor son. The fire behind her cast shadows long, drawing out the frailty of his cheeks and bags beneath his eyes. It was coming upon two years since the last time a healer saw him. They just had too little to take him into town—if they could even show their faces there. Mother's remedies still did him well. But for how long...only Roihelm knew.

"You better cheer up about something or you won't get a lick of supper. I know you're better than that," she told him, her words backed by the motherly power of persuasion. Foxlaris kept his stare pinned to the ground. Why did she have to be so controlling and...*right*...all the time?

"Fine," he pouted. "...When's Tidingsdale gonna start then?" Just thinking of the annual event slowed his angst. Pradifore always felt so mystical in those waning winter weeks.

As Evon shifts to spring, a special fifth season called Tidingsdale emerges. All Evoneers gather their local lavender and purple plants, wring them into dye, and pour them at the roots of the local forest giants. As the first leaves blossom, they arrive not with a bright, lively green. Instead, they weave together and form a canopy of glittering purple to cover the land, displaying Evon's magic, wonder, and bliss in the arrival of a new year. The Scottsworths always held the traditional Feast of Thanks upon the bloom. Such remembrance kept them humble, especially towards their Author, Roihelm. But this year, the snows had yet to slack. Each night fell darker than the last. Past springs would have shown their flowery heads by then on the brighter days. Now…nothing. Bitter cold marching through lingering nights.

"I can't really say, baby," she replied with a soft, sinking tone. "The winds won't let up, and the dye'll take a bit to grow back. I'm not sure we have enough saved to color our own tree."

Another, grumpier rage beat upon Foxlaris, kneading into his soul a righteous rampage. First he was sick. Then he couldn't go out and gather. And now a late Tidingsdale!? This wasn't fair! Why couldn't things go right for once? Why couldn't he have *control?* Why couldn't he—

SLAM!!

The front door catapulted open and slung a wintery wave into the household. Its splash soaked the mother and son, froze their hearts in place from frost and shock. Their heads whipped over in fear.

The looming figure choked the doorway. Heavy blackened strips of torn coats and tunics wound over his stern body, a mix between suffocation and mummification. The thick pounds of snow coating his shoulders began to drip down as he stepped in and tossed a loose burlap sack upon the table. Slowly, he stripped away the rags iced to his face. Sprigs of light orange fur tinged by rosy cheeks bounded out until the full face of a father showed.

A face marked by an inkling of worry. No different than a pebble lodged in the sole of a boot, but noticeable to a loving wife.

"Foxperch, love!" Omaya cried, rushing over to her husband, forgetting all about the cold brandishing his attire. The ragged soul smiled and pulled her tight. Her warmth thawed the numbness biting his fingers. It took all he had not to succumb and let his entire weight fall upon her.

"Longer than usual, I know," he whispered, breath cold upon her neck.

"No, you're just fine, just fine."

As the two reconnected, a second, smaller figure slid in. It quickly shed its white giveaways contrasting the same black fit as the father fox and stomped towards the table. A solid *thud!* rang through the house, rattling Foxlaris to the point of squeaking. He looked to the younger fox, who was giggling to himself and admiring the prized possession he slammed down.

A jar.

His bulbous blue eyes watched its contents swirl. Within flew a pack of gigyants wild, glowing bugs bright as sapphires and native to the spacious Pradifore Wood. How gorgeous did they shimmer, filling the glass with smoky blue haze. Foxtamas had snatched a few on the smaller side, though. He knew how the tales went, of the folks claiming to see ghosts or spirits only for them to be gigyants the size of *actual* dwarf-mined sapphires. But he didn't give such notions a second of his joy. He only cared that they were caught.

"Momma, momma, come see!" the youngest Scottsworth shouted. He turned around to see his parents still embracing. Warmth long exchanged. Greetings long past. As keen as his ears were, the boy made out nothing apart from the normally bellowing voice of Foxperch mumbling something into the ear of his wife.

"Should we leave?" Omaya asked, breathless.

"No, I bet it's all talk, always is."

"You sure? You don't think they'll come here?"

"Don't let it worry you. We'll be fine."

Nodding, she broke away, giving him one final stare for reassurance. Her blue eyes met his brown. No words needed to pass between them.

"What was that, honey?" She turned back with a puffy grin and found Foxtamas, her youngest, buzzing with joy beside his catch.

"Gigyants! I got 'em for you while Poppa got the food. Lookit, this one's big, just like the stories! Wanna name them?" probed the boy. His entire face twisted with glee. Everyone could tell when Foxtamas had been out exploring. The seemingly endless spans of the forest, even with their tree still in view, made him as rambunctious as the ice was cold. However, Omaya could only nod at his response, doing what she could to catch her breath.

"What a great gift! How about you and Foxlaris go on up to the room and name them? Me and Poppa gotta start getting dinner ready with all the stuff you two brought in."

"Okay!" shouted the fox, already snatching back the jar. "We'll save one for you!"

Never had he darted so quick to the stairs. His fur was a lighter shade like his father's. Shedding his patchwork cloak revealed a spry young body, hopping up the stairs one after the next. He moved as fearless as the wind.

Yet from below he caught the silent eye of older brother staring him down from the table. Really? *Another* mood? He never liked the sight of his pouty lip and darkened eyes. They'd both been having the time of their lives just a few hours earlier. Maybe it was his sickness still. Momma said he always caught the bad attitude bug along with the colds. Perhaps naming the gigyants would heal him a bit.

"Come on, Foxlaris! Let's go!" Foxtamas rambled while rushing up the steep wooden climb.

The oldest rolled his eyes.

A mistake.

He felt Omaya's beady glare before he saw it. Fine. He'd go. But before taking off, he shot one last glance back to the table and gathering bag. His slander had become prophecy.

Nothing but roots and berries.

"Giggy! Oh, and Giggo! That's what I'm naming mine. You can get the big one, Foxlaris!"

Foxtamas refused to separate his gaze from the blue vortex planted upon the single nightstand of the shared bedroom. It sat between the two sets of looming bunked beds on either side of the cramped bedroom. The soft light ebbed away the usual darkness. Hearing the screaming winds outside had made for terrible company thus far; the bugs and their brightness were much more welcome.

Foxlaris shared no such sentiment. Sitting on his bottom bunk, the fox kept his focus out to the flurries whipping past the window. Irritation consumed him. Roots! Really!? Oh, if he could just have the chance, the time to go out on his own, to not be stuck in the house sick, or tired, or weak. He just wanted…more. And the foolery of gigyant naming didn't quench such a thirst.

"Come on, what's his na—,"

"Shut up!" squawked the boy. "I don't care about some dumb name." Foxtamas jumped back from the jar. He turned a furrowed brow his brother's way, his face pale in the moonlight.

"Why don'tcha? Is there something wrong with them—""No," Foxlaris spat, "it's all dumb, and, and *stupid!* They're just a buncha bugs, Foxtamas. Get over it!"

The younger fox stared into his heated brown eyes. Never had they seemed so sick, so inflamed—worse, never had he felt so hurt. He was only trying to share the fun. Craft small stories. Do things with his brother that made them happy.

Slowly, his peppy smile drooped away, and he glared back to the three buzzing bugs. They flew around so joyous. Carefree. What did he have to do to join them?

"Oh…okay. I just wanted to play, that's all," he murmured. With a heavy heart, the boy pushed the jar further upon the stand and sulked out of the room.

Foxlaris watched, smirking. A shiver of triumph rushed through him from bringing his brothers' high spirits down to his level. It wasn't fair that Foxtamas got to enjoy himself so easily.

"See how it feels?" Foxlaris grumbled to himself as he crossed his arms and flopped on his side. He glared at the glowing jar in front of him, its blue light burning away the orange of his fur.

It wasn't fair… but it wasn't Foxtamas' fault, either. It wasn't Foxtamas' fault that he got sick, that he was cooped up all the time, that he was weaker than his younger brother.

Foxlaris' ears drooped and his arms slackened as he thought on all the ways Foxtamas tried to cheer him up over the long months.

A shout for dinner met his ears. He expected his distaste for the meal to consume him once again. But it didn't. It was the last thing on his mind as he crept down the stairs and towards the kitchen. The taste of guilt filled him more than stew would.

Something inside Foxlaris changed.

The soup didn't last long. All four foxes sipped in silence, ignoring the bitter taste of grimmelroot and grimacing through chews of carrot leaf. Foxperch rarely looked up from his bowl. His wavering hand brought the spoon to his lips where it stayed too long, resting on his quivering lip. When he glanced up, he saw past his sons, into the flames of the hearth dancing at their backs.

Omaya reached over and held his hand beneath the table. Even her warmth couldn't quell the tremors. Thankfully, neither boy noticed, too invested in trials all their own.

Once done, the worn, wooden bowls were stacked beneath the kitchen window and the family dressed down to their oversized gowns. Usually, Poppa would tell them about his day in town if we went, or Momma would recite a Roihelm parable she knew from her childhood spent further west in the depths of Pradifore's hinterwood. None felt the need that night. The rattles of the storm brought enough excitement to lull them to sleep. A sleep some longed for more than others.

The fireplace trickled out. Doors locked. Quilts gathered. And the steps creaked as the foxes ascended. Though, before any dared adorn the bunks, Omaya called to her sons.

"Boys, come on, say your prayers. You won't sleep well if you don't!" She spoke faster than usual, but it didn't bother Foxtamas. Momma just wanted to get to bed after all that cooking.

Now with higher spirits after the meal, the youngest slumped down to his knees and rested his clasped hands on the edge of Foxlaris' bottom bunk. He always loved being the one to say their nightly prayers. Just thinking about Roihelm —the Blue Phoenix, Author of

Evon— filled him with a silly, giddy joy. Momma's stories made him sound like an *actual* legend, one he could *talk to!*

Before bowing his head, he gave a firm, blue glance to his mother. She clung to Foxperch, clawing at the edges of his burlap shirt. Hiding her worry wasn't an option. But his father pulled her closer and nodded for his son to continue. He obeyed. What good was there to give into such fear?

"Dear Roihelm," he began, smile bright upon his lips, "let us have a nice night and get a lotta sleep, and let us have a good breakfast and morning tomorrow. We love you! Bye!"

"Foxtamas…" his father's low, raspy voice spoke. "What do we say instead of *bye?*"

"Oh, right! Meki Cunery, the Scottsworths." Much more formal. The closing came from Old Evonian, meaning something close to 'Your Family'. Few prayers had the same ending. For them, it worked well enough to connect them to the big blue phoenix in the sky. And to give them peace, even for a single breath.

The family of four bundled themselves against the winds of winter. Even with the ice outside their stubby wooden home, the frost crept close, its sharp claws rubbing against the window with teasing rattles. Foxtamas, though, felt right at home atop his bunk. He wrapped himself up in his fraying quilt like a caterpillar entering a chrysalis. Poppa did the same, sleeping on an equal plane. Momma tucked Foxlaris in below before lying down across from him, curling into a tighter ball than normal. Everyone looked exhausted, the gigyant trio of Giggy, Giggo, and Sir Unnamed already asleep. It only felt right to join them.

Thus, bidding goodnight to his day of tree-climbing and gigyant-hunting, and promising to *actually* sleep instead of tickling Foxlaris with a blanket or staring wide-eyed in the thralls of his imagination, the little fox pulled the covers tighter and drifted gently into the blistering, black night. Tomorrow Foxlaris would be happier. Join him and Poppa. And Momma wouldn't be so scared. All calming thoughts.

But thoughts can only get you so far.

2

"IT WILL BLEED LIKE TEARS THAT CLING"

The storm refused to lighten up. Flurries continued flying past as the clouds above grew heavier, dark. None of the brilliant Evonian sky, with its silver clusters and streaks of lavender, could peer through as it often tried. Snow replaced the stars. Yet even so, one light did remain pulsing within the Wood.

Little cinders tossed and wavered amongst powdery flakes. They verged on being mistaken for the lost stars, vagabonds beneath the impenetrable canopy. Nonsense, really. The embers had a home. A nice one at that. They hailed from the singular pillar of light piercing the mask of darkness, blinding Pradifore Wood. It was no sun. No fallen constellation.

It was the burning husk of the Scottsworth Tree.

The choking woke him.

Foxtamas bolted to life as a cough roared through his frail frame. It jolted him up in his bed, forced him to *gasp* for any breath of clean air. His senses stumped up from their sleep, and, sluggishly at first, revealed the hell erupting around him.

Fire and smoke consumed his home. The once tranquil bedroom conquered by the dance of flames crackling and cackling and climbing from floor to ceiling. Leaps of orange and flares of red burned every corner of his vision. Worse were the bellows of black smog pumping into his chest and mind. He could only make out the bunk across from him amidst the chaos. Right as the outline became clear, it collapsed into a roaring pile of sparks.

"MOMMA!!" erupted the fox, leaning upon the edge of his bed. The true state of the danger dawned on him.

He sucked in a jagged breath that wailed into another nasty cough. It brought him away from the railing, gasping for any air that didn't burn his throat. But a noise overpowered the cough. Over the crackling cackles came a semblance of shouting voices from outside. One sounded like…Poppa? It had his brashness. The others didn't. Nothing close. No, they were cruel, backed by the hot, striking clang of steel.

"OW! *POPPA!!*" Foxtamas shrieked again as pecks of embers leapt across his fur. The cry did nothing. Outside, the voices of his family continued without any notice of him. The burning bedroom raged on. Black and red closed in.

Suddenly, with an ear-numbing *CRACK!*, the wooden beams supporting the bunk snapped. Down came the bed and, with it, the fox. All tumbled into the fiery depths below, catapulting sparks into the choked air.

Poor Foxtamas wheezed. His once-orange face was smeared with soot, forcing a burnt, bitter taste into his mouth. Part of his bunk pinned his bottom half to the floor. Pain seared through his chest as bruises spread down his body. He watched the cuts from the splinters ooze his very own blood. Never had he seen it; now, he wished he never had.

"M…Momma," he murmured again, "F-F-Fox…Foxlaris…" Through the smog he could still make out the staircase on the room's other side. Great stalks of flame guarded it, but if he could move from beneath the bed then—

Another eruption cut him short. Part of the ceiling hurled in front of him. Mortified, the fox squeezed out the last of his energy and scrambled from under the bunk, barely in time to avoid being crushed. A black, wiry mess of branches and sizzled leaves had broken through. Blocking the way to the stairs.

It was at that moment, staring at the ashen tree, feeling his fur singe, flinching at the flames, the weight of the situation buried Foxtamas.

His family was gone. They had to be out there—somewhere—with others, while he…wasn't. He'd been trapped. Left to burn. The dancing fires around him two-stepped closer with each short, wavering breath. His stinging eyes couldn't bear to look down. The burning blood of his home covered his body. It…it wasn't right! Why was he hurting? Why was he like this? The blood, the gashes, the bruises, the burns; it wasn't him. It couldn't be. Th-this wasn't his home! What did he have, who had him, where would he go, what would he do, what was *he!?* His home was gone…his family was gone…he was…

Alone.

Hopelessly,

and utterly,

alone.

BOOM!!!

Breached! Breached! The gates deep within him had been breached!

Unsplintered, unchecked, now decimated to ash. How! How was it even possible!? *Other* forces apart from his own? And one so vicious, so warring and devastating? No, stop, it couldn't be! Such horrors were just stories, or lessons, or, or—

The time had passed to ask such questions. Invasion consumed the boy's existence. The fierce, foreign army conquered every nerve in his body, every want of his heart, every thought thundering within his head. Oh, how deep they drove their flag! A strike hotter than the flames and waving bold for all to see. They made their claim. No going back. The castle succumbed to the enemy's claws, and all peace, love, and hope fled. Joy left.

For the first time in his life, Foxtamas Scottsworth knew fear.

"No, stop! Stop! Help, please, help! *Help! HELP!*"

He dropped to his knees. His tears burned as they poured down his ashen cheeks. Foxtamas covered himself with his hands as best he could, but it did little to stop the fire from lapping up to his body. It wouldn't stop! There wasn't a thing for him to do. Not a clean gasp of air remained; the smell of smoke gagged him. Everything became an unavoidable and inescapable pain branded both inside and out. The fear choked him worse than the smog, stabbed at his heart with a blade made from every horror his mind could conjure. He wouldn't be getting out. He'd die here. He'd never see his family again.

Oh, it was too much!

"MOM-MA-A-A!" The boy's last effort. One final cry to the outer world. "MOMMA, *HELP!*"

"FOXTAMAS!"

It came muffled, it came quiet, but sure enough his keen ears lapped the reply like water for his parched throat.

"MOMMA!?"

"WHERE ARE YOU!" shrieked Omaya, icy with fear. Foxtamas spun around, trying to find where she could be. The voice came from outside. She sounded just as stranded as her son.

Still, it told him she lived, just enough comfort to make his heart race instead of slow, the pain ease instead of flare. Drops of hope surged through him.

"I, I…I'm coming Momma!"

Foxtamas rose. He waved away the smoke as best he could, clearing some room to see. It stung his eyes to peer out. Tears mixed with the ashes and embers, stabbing him with pricks and pokes. But he fought through.

There, amongst the terror, the single window of the bedroom still lay unblocked. The fire had stained it a dull gray and cracked away the edges. Foxtamas knew what he had to do. Had he not done it so many times before? Heights were his friend, the high branches his playground, and the window the doorway to fun. That was before the nagging in his chest, though. The inner army of fear controlled him now.

His feet refused to move despite the lapping burns. A horrid tremble took over his hands, made his eyes dart left and right as his heart roared to a wicked, raging beat. He…he couldn't. He, he'd get hurt, a-a-and the fall, the feeling, it, it would—

Another part of the roof crumbled down beside him. The sparks exploded into a singed heap of brambles. A part of him, the fledgling defense of reason, felt the pain and counteracted the worry. It couldn't be any worse than this! Out there was hope, this…this was *death*. Momma was out there. His whole family might be. It would hurt, but…he had to.

But, what about—

No!

But—

NO!

"AAAAHHHH!!!"

The fox ran without question. His unguarded feet raced right across the red-glowing ashes of his home. They burned. But not enough for him to stop. Through the smoke, through the flames, through the crackles and crashes Foxtamas shot, heading directly to the window. To his family. To hope.

Outside the burning tree, Omaya and Foxlaris bundled against a bank of snow. The mother tossed together a lopsided burlap bag for her eldest while belting cries of rescue for her youngest. Between it all, her voice trembled to whisper calming words as Foxlaris gasped amongst the billows of smoke. She pressed him against her heaving chest. Wrapped him in her shawl. Anything to keep him warm, distracted, oblivious to the night. But he couldn't stop watching the battle behind her.

Foxperch fought in the distance. Hooded figures, all dark and cloaked, swung their curved swords towards him. The fox stood his ground as best he could, brandishing his axe and chopping down whichever attacker dared get close. Screams broke louder than the collapsing home illuminating the horror of their battle. Their shadows whipped around them like sharpened obsidian blades forged by the flames.

Foxlaris didn't know how to pull his eyes away. He should be doing something. He should help, but what could he do? What difference could he make? He felt the horror searing itself into his memory. The swings, the blows, the blood…all of it consumed him.

CRASH!!

Without warning, the window above them shattered, and out flew the lost Scottsworth. He burst overhead like a shooting star. Foxtamas flailed with a horrific cry as he tumbled down into the snow.

"Foxtamas!" shouted Omaya. She leapt towards the singed body of the boy, lifting him into her arms. "Foxtamas! Baby, are you okay?"

He didn't know how to act. The sudden blistering of the storm came as a welcome relief to the hellish burns scourging his fur, but after a few seconds, the cold turned unbearable. The air, however, tasted fresh. Breathable. He took one long drag before slowly lifting his lids and falling into the arms of his mother.

"M–Momma…" he sighed, on the verge of going limp.

"I got you baby, I got you," she whispered. Omaya forced him into the firmest hug she could muster. Her tears stung his wounds.

Foxtamas struggled to hug her back. As he did, he gazed over her shoulder and caught a glimpse of the battle. A pang of fear stabbed his stomach, pushing him away from his mother and into the freezing pile of snow.

"P–P–Poppa—"

"Shhh, it's alright," soothed Omaya, trying to find a smile. She wiped the soot from her son's eyes with a small handkerchief. In the same moment, a cry split from the father fox behind her. It pushed her hand harder against her son, hastened her words.

"Listen, both of you," their mother commanded. Her shaky arms pulled both brothers close. "You have to run away from here, do you understand? Take the path to Dallowridge. It's where we went for Calmas, and to see the shops, remember?" Their faces were too petrified to move. Tears leaked out, chins warbling with terror. "Babies, please! *Do you remember?*"

"Y-Yes," Foxlaris finally admitted with a wheeze.

"Go there and don't look back! We won't be far behind." She tightened the sack upon Foxtamas's back and stuffed the handkerchief deep within his pocket. "Do you understand?"

"But Momma!" the younger fox cried, falling into her with a shivering hug. "We can't go alone! We need you!"

"I know, but you have to, okay?" She quickly embraced the boy before setting him back to his feet. "Be brave, Foxtamas. We won't be gone for long." Omaya pulled back from them and found her words robbed from her tongue. The equal fierceness of the storm and the situation froze the mother fox, leaving her overwhelmed as she gazed on her boys. All her world lay before her. She'd given everything she could for them, raised them despite the harshness of the frozen forest. Now they stood burned. Bruised. Beaten by choices not their own. Yet they still lived, and as long as they did, all would be alright.

It had to be.

"I love you, babies." Her voice cracked and gave way to the trembling of her chin and glistening of her eyes. "Go! *Hurry!*"

Omaya covered them in one last hug before forcing them away and towards the ice-covered Wood. Both wanted to protest. Both just about tried. But, when they looked into the blue eyes of their mother, they knew what had to be done.

Foxtamas and Foxlaris shouted back words of love and bound away, hand-in-hand. Omaya watched the two twinkling dots of orange flutter away from the crippled nest. They trickled further, further, further, further...

Then gone.

Out of her hands and into the wide, wide world of Evon.

"Roihelm," the heartbroken mother gasped between staggered, burning breaths. "Be with them.

"Please."

The brothers obeyed. Both knew the little snow-laden trail that wound around towards the main road. A "road" in name only, being nothing more than a clearing through the enormous pines and oaks that ruled the land. Traveling down would lead them, eventually, to Dallowridge. They rarely took it with their parents and never without them. The children tried to recall what they could of the town. They were warm memories—the only warmth either would feel for some time.

The storm could not care less. Swathes of merciless winds sheered through rags and fur. Their growing bones ached in the throbbing pain of the cold. The thrashes of snow grew stronger, building a wall of never-ending white no matter which way they looked. The Wood seemed the same at every turn.

When they did come upon the road, it stood out solely from the light dousing of gravel still sticking out past the powder. The boys followed it closely. It twisted under roots and curved around the giants. Still, the lack of moonlight made Pradifore an endless array of trees and snow. The Dallowridge way could be forward, or backwards, or somewhere to the right or left—they had no way to tell.

As they pressed forward, Foxtamas noticed his older brother starting to lag behind. He slowed his pace, letting Foxlaris catch up and brutally gasp for the frigid air.

"You okay?" asked the younger fox while Foxlaris hunched over in exhaustion.

"Y-Y-Yeah," he muttered. "I'm…I'm just cold."

"S-So am I," replied Foxtamas. Though, a part of him saw through his brother's lie. He'd never been one to easily catch his breath. A wound from being a victim of sickness. It was one thing to see him tucker out while playing around the house, but this…

The army of fear grew in number as his blue eyes watched on.

Soon the path became impossible to find. Tree after tree they passed, all locked away in their slick, icy confines. They dared not help the children on their way. These were soldiers, not Samaritans. Foxtamas' gaze dizzied at the midnight Wood. The terrain grew tougher the further they went; roots and thorns sprang from the ground, harsh frozen groves locking together to form great shields of ice. Every turn wasn't a way forward but a trek deeper into the unknown.

"Fox...tamas..." Foxlaris suddenly sighed. "I...can't..."

The older boy's lanky orange body collapsed into the snow with a soft, effortless plop.

"Foxlaris!" Foxtamas fell right alongside him and shook him back and forth until his limp neck flung from chest to back. "Come on, wake up!"

Nothing.

Under his snow-caked rags and shivering chest Foxtamas could still make out breath. Light and wheezing. The running and exhaustion had finally reached him.

Panic took over. He scanned the surrounding trees fierce and fearful until finding an alcove large enough to prop his brother within.

"Come! On!" he coughed, dragging the limp Foxlaris. It took all the strength still in the child to haul him away from the path and around to the crude shelter. Once there, he propped his brother up and unfastened the pack Omaya strapped to him.

"Please," muttered Foxtamas. "Please!" He sifted through the contents, begging for something to wake him. What had Poppa used when they'd fall from the house? Salts? Or cold water? Or, or just something, anything!

His hands shook. One part freezing. One part fear.

The fox dumped the bag out into the snow. Their poor mother hadn't the time to meet every possible need in her scramble to leave the house. It was just enough to reach the small village. If that.

He sorted out a small sack of berries, a few gold Tops (the Evonian currency imbedded with a gem) used for spending, the threadbare skeleton of a worn quilt, and a lone cutting knife from their kitchen. Foxtamas jumped at the final provision. He'd never been allowed to touch such a weapon, and for good reason. Carefully, he pinched it by the handle and stuffed it far into his pocket, well and away from any use.

"Foxlaris," he called again, shaking him against the tree. The pushes almost made the unconscious fox slide off the tree's shield of ice. It didn't do a thing to wake him. "Oh, goodness," squeaked the boy, scrambling to find some other solution. He unfolded the messy brown and tan quilt (nothing more than a scrap that had laid about the house) and tucked it around his brother. He made sure to go under the feet and legs. Just how Momma always did.

"There, is that good?" Foxtamas glanced up as if genuinely awaiting a response. His brother only gave a soft, jagged huff, barely visible in the sharp breeze.

There wasn't a thing left to do. The crushing cold of the snow finally begun to numb the fox. His shivers started fresh and uncontrollable; his lungs coated with ice like the forest around him. Only the mocking gusts of wind made any noise.

All lay still.

Frozen.

"P-P-Please wake up," the child mumbled. He pushed himself closer to his brother, wrapping himself with the burlap sack and tucking his feet into the bottom. "I-I don't wanna be here, Foxlaris. I'm scared. R-R-Really scared." Tears dripped down from his eyes. The bite of the air began to freeze them upon his cheeks. "I don't know what I'm doing w-w-without you. Don't leave me…please don't…I'm scared. I'm…scared."

It was the only thought left inside his head. Strong was the night in sapping away his hope and strength. He warded off more assaults of worry until, after long, his weary lids slipped down to hide the darkness. The army within subsided. Listening to the hidden hymn of the wind lulled the boy into a restless sleep.

3

"CLOSE TO A MOTHER'S CHEEK AS SHE HOLDS"

Foxtamas' heart leapt. He'd never been a light sleeper, but the volleys of fear within kept his already keen ears on high alert. Gradually, he clued in on the sound that had awoken him in the night. On the opposite side of their tree came the unmistakable crunch of footsteps. Hardy ones, tracks that pushed deep into the packed snow. He knew the walk from a single step.

Like lightning, his little limbs scrambled up and darted towards the savior. The fox wound around the slick trunk, jumping out into the white-washed lane with relief and a childish grin finally rising past the cuts of his face.

"Poppa!" he bleated with glee. His arms flung open and he darted towards the man. As he did, he took in one good, full look at the figure.

His cloak was dark. Face hooded. One gnarled, clawed hand reached out towards the boy while the other carried a curved sword dripping the last few drops of hot, crimson blood.

All lay in shadow apart from the gleam of yellow eyes. How sickly they looked, vivid with burning, beating veins and black holes that hardly held a soul.

"There y'are!" the cloaked beast snarled, his voice tinny and muffled by the sound of a hard-pressed gargle. He leapt forward at the boy. Foxtamas halted his run right as the edge of the blackened claw scraping the loose threads of his shirt.

"GET AWAY!" cried the fox. This was no Poppa. His legs tripped backwards in his effort to escape. Again, the villain swiped, and again he nipped the corner of the rags. Through his scurries and tumbles, Foxtamas found footing in the snow and enough will to sprint hard until a ringing blared in his ears. He ran straight into the navy wilderness. Twinkling glints from the ice and snow glowed just bright enough to save him from crashing into the trees.

"Get over 'ere, boy!" the brute's shout echoed as the pair shot into a thick pine grove. The small trickles of moonlight extinguished at the entrance. Above, the branches hung low, iced edges like meat hooks, with the trunks below growing mere inches apart. Foxtamas collided with the solid walls of ice springing up at every turn. The crashes further bruised his body and sent him spinning into a tunnel of darkness. He ran no different than with his eyes closed, dodging through a living nightmare.

Suddenly, his foot caught on a wide, frozen root buried beneath the snow. His body flipped over, breaking into a breath-snatching fall against a pine.

"H...He..." The breaths wouldn't come. Foxtamas rolled himself over, clutching at his throat. He couldn't shout, couldn't breathe. Horrified, the fox tried to clamber against the bark at his back, but the ice refused to give a grip. There would be no getting up.

"...help..."

Foxtamas flipped back around. His pursuer had yet to slow. The haunted gleam of yellow eyes the only ounce of light pouring in. Oh, the poor fox tried to scream again, he really did. But a vision of blood silenced him as if the blade had already fallen upon his throat. What more could he do? He'd already escaped death too many times that night. Now it finally caught up to him, sickly glare and all.

But death tripped.

Right as the hooded man went to raise his sword, the tip of his boot fell victim to the same root as his prey. His throat let out a messy yelp as he launched forward. All Foxtamas could do was cower.

THUNK!!

Down went the villain. The top of his head *smashed* above the fox and into the immovable shield of the tree. A grunt slipped from his mouth before falling limp upon the boy.

"GAHH! GET OFF! *GET OFF!*"

The force brought him a new wind. Stinging tears burned down his cheeks as he extended every muscle to wiggle free. But no matter the force, the murderer weighed too much. Nothing worked to lift him.

Foxtamas panicked. This is how he'd die, beneath the unconscious body of the man who killed his parents. In the scramble to escape, however, a new sensation shot through him: pain. A hot, pulsing pain beating from his side.

Shivering, the boy rushed and twisted out his arm. Blood dripped from his singed fur.

"No, no! Stop it, stop!" his wails mingled into a mess of sobs. He never imagined this would be the feeling of a blade plunged into his flesh. The stories made it seem honorable, or brave, or–or a good way to go. This hurt. It felt like a part of him had been crushed from within.

The boy kept up his wiggling until he slipped out from beneath the body. Gasping, he crawled away, a maroon trail staining the snow behind him. His trembling hands grappled at his side.

There, protruding out, was the kitchen knife from his mother.

The blade, at least. Its silver edge pierced through his pocket and into the frozen air. On it glistened gobs of darkened blood that dripped down his side.

He patted the supposed injury. It didn't feel like a cut, but more like a...bruise.

Foxtamas scrambled up and rolled the body away from him. It had yet to move. A greater pool of red bubbled from its chest, congealing and settling to freeze.

The knife had stabbed *the attacker*, not the fox. Both the strike against the tree and the shank of the blade sealed his fate. Despite his demise, his yellow glare still glowed like the sizzling coals of a dying fire, stare pinned to Foxtamas. The boy couldn't move.

He...he killed him.

He'd murdered.

Him, just a child, just a lost, lonely kid…

"I…I…I'm s-sorry," whispered Foxtamas, stepping back and away from the twisted, bleeding corpse. He hadn't the capacity to process such a sight. Fear's ashy taste rose in his mouth again, and instead of facing it, he ran, springing out of the grove and back towards Foxlaris. There wasn't time to think. He just needed to find his brother.

"Foxlaris!" he shouted as he arrived back. Still tucked inside the alcove, the elder Scottsworth looked just as alive as the cloaked man Foxtamas left behind. The quilt's pattern had long been covered in a rising layer of white, and a gentle paleness started to wash over the fullness of the fox's face. "Foxlaris!"

"Mmm…" Quiet as it was, a sound still stirred.

"Hey, hey!" His brother spat, shaking him and tossing away his covers. "Are you okay?"

"What…who, who screamed?" Foxlaris' voice lagged in between his careful wheezes.

"N-No one, it's okay! Come on, we gotta keep running!"

"B-But—"

"Come on!"

Foxtamas hauled his brother up. He leaned him on his shoulder as Foxlaris found his balance, careful to throw together the bag while he did. Once set, they started off again. This time with the blue eyes of Foxtamas incessantly checking their backs.

Pradifore grew worse. The billows and volleys of snow and sleet slowed the pace of the brothers inches away from a halt. Icy thorns crawled over their feet. Branches blocked path after path. Their shivers worsened their already poor vision, shaking the slits of light into a headache. Hope faded fast. Foxlaris' legs kept collapsing and throwing him into the snow while he himself barely held onto consciousness. As much as he tried to avoid it, Foxtamas nearly succumbed to the same fate. The constant ups and downs wore his body as threadbare as the quilt across his brother's shoulders. A few steps forward felt like a year of progress.

"You gotta stay up," the young fox said, helping Foxlaris to stumble over an over-sized root. "We...we can't keep falling—"

"W-W-What's that?" the boy suddenly spoke. He held out a stammering hand edging on frostbite. Its end pointed to a trickle of soft, blue light ebbing from a thicket further ahead. The glow painted a gentle pattern upon the snow, waving like water but leaping like flames.

"I d-d-don't know," Foxtamas replied. "Let's s-see." He couldn't be sure if what they saw was real. Too many of his dreams had been filled with the same wild stints of magic. Perhaps this entire night had been one of them. No fire. No murder. Just an overblown nightmare drawing on the foraging adventure he and and Poppa had the day before.

Such a want was but a dream within itself.

The pair hobbled towards the grove whilst leaning upon each other. Had it been any further, poor Foxtamas would have had to carry Foxlaris in his arms. They pushed past the brambles and thicket until the sapphire light burst out, blinding them.

Winter disappeared. The air within mellowed, warming the brothers as if they'd walked into a shimmering spring day. From their feet flowed a field of flowers tucked inside the stout circling of trees (all of which had shed their ice). Each blossom was the same blue hue as the light. How fierce they looked! So inviting yet mysterious, otherworldly but right at home. Roses twisted upon silver vines, daisies and tulips hugged the ground like picnic blankets, poppies danced to the whistling melodies hummed by the cooled rush of wind. All melded together to form an earthen sea of crisp, sapphire waves.

Planted among the flowers rested a massive vestige of stone. Once they may have served as pillars to a shrine or home. Robust, towering, carved from a porous granite, there thrived within them a beating blue light. Yet they'd fallen to ruins all the same. Still, they bore carvings that time found impossible to erase. Most were of Old Evonian words and symbols lost of all meaning to the modern Evoneer. They trailed up and across the ruins, joined by sections of intricate yet faded winged carvings. Feathers and quills made random appearances whereas entire wings were sculpted at the tops and bottoms.

A real, vivid history radiated from the stones. Part of them lay dormant, like they waited for a specific time to rise once again. The children couldn't quite place the feeling. Still, it stirred within them a prickling excitement that fluttered their hearts.

"Woah!" Foxtamas broke the serene silence. He leapt into the grove, sweeping the ruins with his hand and frolicking amongst the flowers. "It's magic! Lookit!"

"Hah!" laughed Foxlaris. To his surprise, a burst of energy flowers through him. His chest warmed as if he'd downed a piping autumn. Giggling, he rushed further in and joined Foxtamas to play with the magic.

The boys couldn't contain themselves. How they laughed, how they climbed, how they smelled the sweet scents of the petals. Their frolics stirred a glittery dust into the air. It sparked like an ember but with the same azure hue as the flowers. The blazes whisked past the roses and under the stones, catching the attention of the foxes.

"What's that?" asked Foxlaris, jumping up to touch it as it flew above him.

"I told you, it's gotta be magic!" his brother replied. Foxtamas wasted no time joining in on the fun of catching the embers.

"No way. Magic can't look like that!"

"Sure it ca—woah!" Suddenly, the dust dispersed and multiplied itself, forming around them a misty, sapphire haze. Their laughs turned to gasps. Wistfully it twisted over itself, spreading past them like a midnight sky whose lights burned a feverish glory. The stars had returned!

For a moment Foxtamas wondered if his brother had been right. This wasn't some spell like the stories. It buzzed like a gigyant, only too fast and fine to be one.

Before he could decide, the sparks wrapped around each fox.

"It tickles!" squirmed Foxtamas between laughs, swiping away at it.

"No, it don't!" Foxlaris chuckled. Somehow, the dust soothed him as it raced across his weary limbs. The cold lingering in his fingers subsided; the tightness of his lungs slackened. "It feels good!"

Foxtamas then felt the same sensation. He glanced down and watched the soot melt away and burns, cuts, and scars heal in a blink.

"Hah! It does!" The embers worked while the fox danced around laughing. His cheeky, infectious smile spread the same sense of joy towards his brother. The fear retreated! Both boys leapt in the tranquility. Pure, kindred simplicity beat through their shared hearts. They'd had nothing before and could want nothing more now. This was it. This was...everything.

What did the world look like outside this grove?

Where...where had they come from?

And why did...did he feel so...so...tired?

Foxlaris slowed. He grappled towards part of the pillar, clutching at a wing before sinking down to his knees.

"Why'd you stop!" his brother called, bounding over to him. "What's wrong?"

"I'm just, just...just, uh—" his lids sagged down before a firm sentence could find him. With a smile on his lips, Foxlaris drifted away. This time with a snore instead of a wheeze.

"Don't be like that! Wake up, come on!" Foxtamas couldn't shut off his giggles as he shook him. They tightened his cheeks so high they covered his eyes. It was just like Foxlaris to stomp out all the fun! Oh, he was just being silly! He couldn't be tired. Tiredness didn't feel right. Only this, only joy!

The laughs sapped away his breath.

Only ease!

He brushed his hands across the flowers as he chuckled.

Only comfort!

Gripping his sides, Foxtamas stumbled over his brother.

Only...sleep.

The boy released one last laugh before collapsing atop his kin. It didn't bother Foxlaris one bit. His snores continued. Joined by his younger brother but a moment later.

Together they rested in perfect harmony as the glowing blue embers faded away from them and dispersed back into the grove, sighing as they did. A job well done. Easier than anticipated.

Now things could *really* begin.

Foxtamas peeked open an eye. Gone was the grove. The luscious blue bed. A rough cot tickled his bare back instead. Crackles of a roaring fire echoed somewhere nearby. Tinges of warmth flooded near his feet. His mind stared blankly at an array of fuzzy details from the night's events flashing across the dark ceiling above him. Something about a fire, and...blood. And flowers. The images waded in and out. Laps of water against his mind. They slowed, though, as a shadow loomed over him. He couldn't make out the creature apart from a pair of antlers. How...odd. The fox felt the waves beckon again at his shore. He might just wade out to them. Flow...flow far and away.

Had not the creature's voice pushed out with both calm and grace to anchor him to land.

"Come now, laddie, wake oup!"

4

"HER BABY BEFORE HE JOURNEYS HOME."

4 Years Later

The dawning sun crested over the ridges and treetops of central Evon. Prickly licks of light made bright the greenery, tickling awake the drooping, dreaming heads from the night's slumber. Up perked the branches, tight tossed the wind, and the magenta waves of sky melted into a newborn blue. The world never looked so beautiful.

As for the village planted within it…that was a different story.

Village Winthrop sprang awake like gasping from a nightmare. Stout, rattling windows pushed aside their sackcloth curtains while doors creaked open to the day's start. Half a hundred homes made the hamlet. All were withered with straw roofs sogging from the spring showers and peeling gray paint fallen like dying petals. Some of the wooden shacks were homes, others shops. Struggling gardens grew behind most. The poor buildings wound around the front half of a knoll cleared in the thick of Mechmilne Wood. From the forest's edge wound a gravel path that snaked through the village's center and up to the very top. There, bearing down over the houses, gleamed what the Winthropains called "the Palace"—the only structure *not* struck by disrepair.

It was a longhouse, formed wide with whole logs and large enough to hold at least a dozen families, especially those with older children who'd off and left the poor excuse of a town. The golden roof atop always caught the sun at the right angle, stinging the eyes of the passing villagers below. Just another reason to avoid looking at it as far as they were concerned. But King Aisar oft provided a well enough reason for that.

A door opened at the exact opposite of the Palace, at the edge of the village, at the last home of Winthrop situated between the gravel path's end, forest overgrowth, and graveyard rounding past their yard and almost behind the hill. They called it the Cammont Household. A thatched hay roof, greasy white paint soaked into boards held up by rusted nails, a garden of carrots, basil, and garlic fending off tendrils of ivy, drooping stone steps stacked up to the entrance, and a circular chimney that always spurted out a little warmth—the embodiment of the village, but home for the boy rubbing together his hands and shutting the door behind him.

A smile parted the sea of his orange cheeks. The crisp air ruffled his sackcloth garments (stitched from spare flour bags) and tickled his toes poking from the holes of his sandals.

Foxtamas Scottsworth gazed up the Main Road. His heart pumped when he caught the gold glimmer of the Palace. A miniature journey awaited him—one he'd become all too accustomed to taking.

Up the boy went. The gravel road was busier than he expected due to the party Mrs. Cammont hoped to pull off tonight. His scurrying avoided the otter, Mr. Jillengilch, hauling down his wheelbarrow to gather berries further in Mechmilne (alongside his youngest, Rilli, poking her head out with a giggle). The old Dr. Wardly followed past and stopped into the shop of his begrudgingly "good" friend Sir Penst, the merchant badger. So too came Dovely Writ, grabbing a few supplies before her son, Tolocove, left for his trip south. Brother and sister duo Dafton and Sheshly Minnel passed by the fox with a nod. Had it been Dafton and Ramuckster, the squirrel's older brother, juvenile words may have replaced the kind gesture.

The further Foxtamas traveled the thicker the crowd grew until he passed by a member of seemingly every family, seeing Frannie Hilsk, Poppiara Celty, Ilu Vontari, Berry-Don Mussen, Sepwing Safatoll, the

Faunorado twins, all *five* Kobochaun children, and Nore Makin, snoring in an alley between homes. All met him with smiles or quick chats, especially those closer to his age. Everyone ensured he'd feel welcome at all times—a promise they made to Mrs. Cammont the day he and Foxlaris arrived that frigid winter night. Rarely did Village Winthrop ever see outsiders move in. If they did, they were of the lowest class, desolate as the rest. No other town would take them in apart from Winthrop. It's why, despite the pressure King Aisar put to their necks, few ever left. Evon seemed to have little for them.

The Main Road lurched left before taking one final push up to the Palace. It forged past a small grove of birch trees wherein Foxtamas finally gave himself the chance to breathe, far and away from the business below. How'd he not spotted Foxlaris in all the commotion? He and Bunns liked to get a head start, yes, but the younger fox couldn't be *that* far behind, right?

As he meandered between trees and took in the lovely morn, a *SMASH!* shattered from further up ahead. His keen ears perked and chest slammed into a tree. Just the thought of being seen near such commotion stirred his heart to a frenzy.

Carefully, he peeked out from the trunk. The noise came from a broken hanging pot placed outside Miss Tilly's flower shop. A scuffle ruffled inside the baby blue building until two armored men emerged, one a leprechaun and the other a wolverine, carrying a sobbing groundhog between them.

"Please, please!" the elderly woman begged, trying to rip her cotton sleeves from their arms. "I-I didn't know! I'll pay, I have the Tops, please!"

"Enough!" the wolverine roared. Both he and his partner bore the same leather and bronze dressing with a maroon "W" etched into the center. The protection would do little in a real battle, but few Winthropians were known to fight, let alone rebel. He hiked her up further. The intense dragging knocked over another pot, this one a growing bouquet of asters, to the ground. The hem of Miss Tilly's dress drug through the dirt. "That's for the king to decide."

Foxtamas hid. Slid down, hugging his chest, heart beating and lungs panting.

Winthrop Watchers.

The village's local militia. They served as Aisar's hands and feet, finding those who didn't pay their monthly dues and guarding the Palace from any unwanted visitors (also known as *the villagers*). Few if any joined the guard willingly. Every so often the king declared a conscription. It gathered what local men it could find, be they young or old, and forced them into the guard. Many years had passed since the last, taking with it Mr. Gregabbit Cammont and his eldest son, Reinden, a year or so after the Scottsworths' arrival. It tore the poor jackalope family apart.

But rumor had it that Aisar planned another gathering. If Winthrop knew one thing of their Watchers, it was that they'd aged—rapidly. Young blood would be needed before long. Either that or let the fat raccoon of a king feel the wrath of those he oppressed. As if they had the might to make that happen.

But Foxtamas couldn't focus on such details at that moment. He tucked his hands under his arms, but the rattles wouldn't stop. Neither would the pace of his heart. The birch felt, it felt like…like ice shielded it. The grass prickling his feet stung like snow, and the sound of the Watchers marching away no different than, than…than the killer.

The guards would get him. They'd pull him up and try him for some crime and chain him to the dungeons in the darkness alone and scared and alone and alone and alone—

Within, the army of fear snickered. Another job well done. Nothing the boy did could shake the worry trembling through his body. It had conquered him that night in Pradifore. Nothing could overtake their lands now.

Slowly, as the winds hastened and memory of his journey returned, Foxtamas found the strength to rise and continue up. He couldn't let them down by being scared. Not again, anyway.

The houses began to rear back and leave room for the approaching Palace. The small, gilded detailing upon the building came into view the closer the fox approached. They swirled through the Northern timber, making the bark look like it bled gold. Columns like miniature trees wound around the entire hall to hold up the roof. Always they reminded the boy of Pradifore…of home. His last memories of the forest were just as blurry as when he'd arrived in Winthrop. One moment they trudged wearily through the snow, and the next Mrs. Cammont shook them awake, hundreds of miles south without any explanation.

The Palace's entryway pointed directly at the end of the Main Road that stopped left of the center. It didn't view *exactly* over Winthrop since the knoll twisted at its top to a point that, while hidden from most homes, gave a direct look over the village. It was one of the few particulars Aisar let slide. Thus, why Foxtamas headed that way.

Two Watchers, halberds in hand, guarded the oaken doors leading in. The carved details of Winthrop's founding history pressed hard into the smalls of their backs. Past their low helms they watched the fox, whistling and wandering past houses like he was searching for something. One of them, a rabbit, thought he looked familiar. The other, an aged sparrow, didn't mind. He'd given up knowing anyone outside of their ranks years ago. Plus, sleep called. It had lulled his lids for an hour now.

Foxtamas *was* in fact searching for something—an opportunity. The only way behind the Palace and to his rendezvous was past the left side where an entanglement of unkempt grass spread out from the creeping forest edge that tapered up the village's back. When the Watchers switched shifts, they left a gap of time just small enough for the boy to scamper into the lawn and crawl through it to the overlook.

The plan worked dozens of times before, and it would again. He bent down near a small patch of yellow tulips sprouting at the corner of the Deffmire's Estate, peeked at the path, and felt his heart plummet to the depths of his chest.

They…they were trimming it. Some coyote Watcher, clasped in

sweat and overalls, whacked away with a hoe, buzzing down to the roots. The mess of weeds and moss would be gone, nothing but a straight clearing to the hill's edge.

Panic returned.

He couldn't get through *that!* The hoe would cleave right through his neck if the gardener saw him trying to shuffle past! Or he'd *actually* be in the dungeons this time! Oh, just standing this close was bound to land him in a disaster. He had to do something, he had to—

CREeEeEaAaAaAk!!

The Palace doors edged open. Both the rabbit and sparrow sighed and turned to head in.

The clock ticked. Foxtamas had a mere few seconds to make his move. How every muscle in his body tried dragging him back to the Household, to his bed, his books, anything of comfort rather than *this!* They'd be fine without him. He wouldn't even need an excuse with the evidence being cleared and kept up right before him. But...

But...

No.

But...

No, he couldn't let them down. They'd do the exact same for him.

Foxtamas Scottsworth blinked, and the decision was made. His body did all the work while his mind cowered in the back of his head.

In the three-second gap before the next set of Watchers arrived for their shift, the fox, sackcloth clinging to his shaking skin, *leapt* through the sliver of space between the doors and fumbled into the Palace.

The inner shaping of the Palace worked as one long, royal hall. A red carpet rolled from the doors, past the columns matching those outside and holding up the upper story, all the way down to the throne seated on a stone stage. Such a chair had been dwarven-crafted from alloys of gold and silver. The dreamy bright luster of the gold had faded, however, where the arms rested and back scratched. So much so the inlay of rubies on the headrest forming a "W" lay surrounded by a patchy, exposed silver.

Hallways departed on either side, one to the kitchens, the other the barracks and, to everyone's horror, the dungeons. Before them two staircases rose, placed a few yards away from the throne. They led to the railings of the second story which wound across the entirety of the Palace's throne room. On each side lay a room over the wings: one for the king, and one for his daughter, Princess Acirema.

It was only after scurrying into the shadows of the left corner that Foxtamas finally regained consciousness. Thankfully, the columns and upper level created a darkened side for him to slip into, stuffed with cobwebbed pews, tables, and other relics from Aisar's former High Council withered to mindless decoration. His breaths quickened and heartbeat staggered in his ears. The fox tried to push himself through the wall only for splinters to poke through his shirt, pricking him like the fierce pangs of fear searing his mind.

Why had he done this! How was he supposed to get out? For all that talk of avoiding the dungeons, the entrance lay within that very room, waiting, jeering, begging to snatch him right up!

As the thoughts churned, the two Watchers replacing the rabbit and sparrow passed by. Foxtamas ducked beneath a bench and held his hands close to silence his panicked whimpers. Their boots didn't stomp louder than his heart.

Once through, they closed the oaken doors and left the rest of the Palace silent apart from a few murmurings out of the kitchen. The fox gulped. It rang like a bell.

He popped up from under the bench, sweating. Now *had* to be his chance. Any longer and Watchers would crawl through the place like starved ants at a picnic. From what he could tell, the darkness he hid in extended all the way to the opening of the westmost hall. Beyond that point rose one of the staircases cut into the wall's side. It led to the second floor's railing that looked roughly one Scottsworth away from the wooden beams latticed across the ceiling. They crossed *just* enough times to reach the circular stained-glass window propped high at the Palace's peak—a lovely rendition of intertwined lilies untouched from earlier reigns.

Foxtamas didn't like the plan. Hated in, in full honesty, despite what Momma would warn of such a word. But did he have any other option? Under the benches. Up the stairs. Onto the beams. Slide out the window. Four steps. Just four. Just…four…

It was a thin balm, but a working one. The fox dropped back to his knees and crawled through the darkness. His still-raspy gasps sucked up the dust and webbing. They crunched in the back of his mouth—getting up and gagging, though, was out of the question. He kept up the pace until he lay just feet from the stairwell. Already one step down, a fourth of the way. It would be easy. A quite literal hop, skip, and jump.

Before he could hop to the stairs, the ground beneath rumbled. Or, more appropriately, shuddered, as the form of King Aisar Feiht approached from the hallway.

The rosy aroma of the Palace soured. The torchlight rubbing the walls darkened. The raccoon's form filled the frame, lurching forward with one squeaking *STOMP!* after the other. Such force rippled through the rolling fat body like the casting of stones into a lake. He wore over his size a light morning gown, still bearing crumbs from his breakfast, and freshly extended to cover the gray lump of fat peeping from above his trousers. It was thick and patterned, a sparkling burgundy that made every shimmy of his body glow. Surprisingly, despite the weight pooled at his ankles and tugging down his body, the king's face stood rather slim. His eyes beamed a misty hazel that glistened through the black stripe rounding over his head. Both cheeks were gaunt, and a line of thin yet parted lips gasped through his pushes forward. Unlike others his size, Aisar seemed disconnected from his weight, like a man simply wearing a suit. Something more worked behind the ceaseless jiggles of his saunter, signaled by his proper posture and words whispered breathily to himself.

"Yes, yes," the raccoon heaved before mounting the throne like a slug inching up a wall, "how many today, then?" he asked the Watcher who followed behind.

"Reports say four this morning, five from last night," the elderly hedgehog surmised. Aisar finally found his spot and relieved the mounds of their tension. He looked no different than an overstuffed flour sack.

"Bring them in," huffed the king. He reached from the throne's spire and put on the crown. It barely covered his ears. "Any order. Don't care to dally in details this morning."

With a nod, the Watcher made his way to the eastern hall, the taps of his boots echoing as he descended to the dungeons.

And there, Foxtamas sat. Just him and the king.

His face had lain inches away from Aisar's slippers when he passed. It felt no different than being a worm dangling in a fish's pond. He'd be caught. There was no way around it now, not with the apparent omnipresence the king possessed. Whispers of hatred villagers made against him felt like screams, even within the confines of their own homes. If he could hear those, then any shuffle upwards Foxtamas made would be an earthquake.

But the fox still moved. Better to be caught closer to the exit than dirtying on the floor.

He took one last look both ways before leaping up to the stairs. No squeaks came from the landing. Despite Mrs. Cammont's best efforts, Foxtamas rarely if ever put on more than his bare skin and bones.

The wall at his right gave him just enough cover to slither up. He eased up one limb at a time, forming a meticulous crawl. Up and up and up the fox moved. Below, the kitchens grew louder, the thumps of the returning Watchers fast approaching. He didn't have long.

Right as he neared the top, just three steps away, his sandal snagged a splinter, and his knee crashed down, echoing.

"Acirema!" the bombarding voice of Aisar called from below. It already sounded dry so soon after his meal. "That you, darling? Come down, let me see you this morning!"

Foxtamas' body pressed flushed with the step. What was he to do *now!?* Impersonate the princess? Lay still until he was found? If he moved, he'd surely cause another noise, and with the king already alerted—

"Darling?"

Oh, anything but *that!*

Panic took over, and the fox forced himself to breathe. As he did, the steps from the dungeons grew louder. His keen ears made out two heavy stomps of Watchers and the dragging of a third. They crossed from the hall and stood before the throne where, with a cough, the elderly hedgehog spoke again.

"Yarly Tilly, sire. Late tax payments of roughly, um, two weeks."

"P...Please," the groundhog murmured with a rasp.

"Silence!" demanded Aisar. "You'll speak when spoken to. Two weeks, you say?"

"Yes, Your Grace."

"And did the men search her house?"

"Yes."

"And?"

"Enough Tops to cover nine days and the late fee."

Foxtamas heard the floor beneath the throne creak as Aisar reclined, grunting. Now was his chance. With the king distracted, he hopped up the remaining steps and dropped to his knees against the railing. Large gaps filled in between the poles. Anyone with a wandering gaze would see a stain of orange peeping through.

"I-I-I do have enough!" the old woman pleaded with a warble in her voice. "I promise, I promise—"

"What did I *say!?*" Aisar roared in return.

Above, the fox finally caught a glimpse of the florist. The Watchers had spliced tears through the gray of her morning gown, it's bottom shredded to threads. Tears carved rivers into the wrinkles of her cheeks. Her small, squinted face clearly had yet to stop crying ever since she opened her door.

However, to the fox's shock, he recognized the second Watcher holding her up beside the hedgehog: Mr. Gregabbit Cammont, his "adopted" father. Like barren branches, the jackalope's antlers poked high through the top of his helm. Both his brown eyes cast low at the carpet, and the unkempt moustache that always covered his lip like a sweater had grown gray. Watcherhood never suited him. It suited very few, truthfully.

Mr. Cammont's appearance pushed Foxtamas along, crawling alongside the railing with haste. He'd *certainly* be recognized and called out if he saw him.

Halfway there. Moreso, really. The barking continued below, fueling him like wind to his sails. Miss Tilly didn't deserve that. No one did.

"And you intend to pay this *how?*" the raccoon asked. He rubbed the longer strips of fur along his chin. Plucked one on accident.

"M-My garden! Under the petunias, I've a stash, I swear it!" Miss Tilly shouted.

"Consisting of…?"

"Ten green Tops! Take them, please!"

The hazel gaze of the king glanced at Gregabbit and the hedge-hog.

"Will that be sufficient?"

"Yes, Your Grace," the older Watcher nodded.

"Fair is fair, then," said the king. Miss Tilly dropped weightless with relief. "Have Hazelhurst dig them up once he's done with the weeds. And have her in a cell for a week."

The groundhog rose. Mortified.

"What! No!" Her shriek echoed off the walls. Foxtamas covered his ears.

"I'm sorry, Your Grace?" asked the hedgehog, he, too, concerned.

"A warning," sighed Aisar, rolling his eyes and readjusting himself as if in casual conversation. "A reassurance to me that you *won't* have this problem again."

"Wait, please, you can't do this! I'm paying!"

"And how I wish that was enough." His lumpy hand flicked with a bounce. "Take her!"

Again, the young Scottsworth looked away. He'd scooted right beneath the closest beam, and with the florist's screams below, never was there a better time to start step three. He hated to use the kind woman's terror as a distraction, but…he had to. The thought made his heartbeat evident through his sackcloth.

The jump to the rafters proved easier than expected. Fear plagued him, of course, but the instinct from climbing his family tree in Pradifore took over, balancing him on the railing and leaping up to the flat, squared platform. The fox breathed a bit easier up there. Even with all the dust. By the time he made it to his feet, the groundhog had gone, leaving the king alone yet again.

"Acirema!" came his call. "You ready now?"

Foxtamas inched closer to the back wall, a few yards from the window and his escape. If Aisar did glance at her door, he'd find nothing. The thought made him snicker. Softly.

"If she's running with those street rats again, I'll have bars hammered to that window." His threat cut quiet under his breath, but the fox still heard it. He couldn't help a gulp. Being one of the rats in question, messing up now would land him a broken back, dungeon time, *and* the princess' imprisonment within her room. The closer the finish, the more dangerous the stakes.

Gregabbit and the hedgehog returned. This time, in place of the fanfare of screams, there came only chains dangling across the floor. Foxtamas was just about to the wall when the sounds reached him. He paused to take his final look.

On one hand, he gloated, taking in the Palace from above, with its golden throne, burgundy carpet, and gilded pattern filed throughout. The boy felt like a victor standing atop the spoils conquered from the gluttonous king. On the other, he tried to take one last good look at Gregabbit. If Mrs. Cammont caught wind of his antics, she'd first reprimand him, then ask what news came of her husband.

But he couldn't focus on him. Instead, his blue eyes were torn away by the prisoner kneeling at his left and before the smirking king.

"Opel…" muttered Foxtamas. He barely recognized the jackalope. Dried blood crusted over a cut slashed over her right eye. Bruises littered her body, purple splotches through her rags. Bits of her antlers had been butchered off, matching the knicks cut into her ears.

The niece of Mrs. Cammont, she'd only been around a time or two between traveling to the larger cities and trying to leave Winthrop behind. Yet she always returned. Little was ever spoken of her, and when it was, the conversations were kept short. How long had she been *here?*

"Now, this is one I've been waiting for!" Aisar chuckled and rubbed together his paws. "The rebel, yes?"

"Opel Myre, sire," nodded the hedgehog. "Caught in the act of co-conspiracy and open rebellion against your lordship with intention to kill."

Opel didn't say a word. The green of her eyes stared lifelessly at the king. Beside her, Gregabbit's head fell. He held his own niece in chains. Powerless to do anything for her.

"Not the first, not the last," he started again, a giggle escaping like a case of hiccups. "Tell me, who all were you with? What was your plan? I love these kind of stories—reality turned fiction in the blink of an eye."

She stared.

He grinned.

"Nothing? *Really?* Now's your chance! You're here *inches* from me. This is your dream, girl! I bet you hoped I'd be crying when you got this close. Not, well, not laughing!"

Aisar gripped the throne as a laugh chugged through him, his belly and gown rising like the start of a tsunami.

She stared.

"Go on, I don't bite. I know you think I do, big as I am."

From above, Foxtamas crept closer. He dropped to his chest and slid right above the throne, fueled by a passion that overpowered his fear in a war that could be won within the blink of an eye.

Oh, with one pounce he could end the monster. Just like Sir Qualdinclaw had against the Vollowbeast, or when the Wizards Yil and Knir slew the Fell Queen with the sharpened ends of their staffs. The king's mockery would end in one good swipe of the boy's hands. His claws seemed sharp enough. Down he'd topple, freeing the village from his clutches. Foxtamas would be storied like all the rest.

Suddenly, in his daydreaming, he caught Opel watching him with widened eyes. Neither Aisar nor the Watchers noticed, all too focused on the king's monologue. Her mouth pursed with words ready to pounce.

Shhh! the fox barely mimed the signal in time. He didn't need her death on his already full plate of consequences. Yet it was in that attention that the fear regained control. He saw where he was, thought of what he wanted to do, and felt the shivers ripple through his hands and knees.

He needed to leave.

Fast.

Why had he ventured so close! The window had been an arm's length away and he ran from it! *Ran!* What was he supposed to do, *save her?* Aisar practically had his greasy hands around her neck. One fox couldn't do that. One scared, little, lonely fox watching from above.

With a hop, he made it back to his feet and inched to the window. Hopefully Opel didn't stare, but he couldn't control her. The stain-glass lilies were right there. Their light painted him a warming gold and mauve, a sharpness like harp strings pulling him closer. He could almost hug them.

Foxtamas crossed to the beam nearest the window and took the final steps, placing himself no more than a yard away. Excitement showered him as he rushed to the end, only for his foot to dangle too close to the edge. His leg fell. And the rest of his body followed.

Opel jumped.

Aisar noticed and cut his words short. He twisted his head, confused.

"What's wrong? Scared now—"

"If Ah mae, Yer Grace."

To the king's surprise, Gregabbit Cammont stepped forward in front of his niece. The lip under his moustache twitched with fear.

"Um...yes, Cammont?" His striped eyebrows lowered in a look of suspicion.

"Well, uh...Ah'd like tae vouch for her, Yer Grace. She's mah niece, Ah've known her since her mum swaddled her." Beads of sweat trickled down from beneath his helmet.

"If only they could *stay* children we'd live in a happier world," snickered Aisar.

"Y-Yes, but wha' Ah mean is Ah've seen her grow, an' Ah know she ain't the monster yer thinkin'. Just, em...misguided, yer could say."

"And as her uncle you had no chance in guiding her?"

"Ah did, or, Ah tried. Weh all did. B-B-But et's ah long process, an' Ah assure yer tha' if yer spare her now tha' mah wife'll work with her, Ah promise yer." Gregabbit's hands pressed together, shaking. "She was the late Queen Anlana's handmaiden, s-served her well. She's good, Ah swear et."

"Mmm," came the king's reply. His eyes shot away at his wife's name, behind to the darkened hallway behind the prisoner. "I remember her service, Cammont. But I'm also too aware of your *son* that she raises and the hellion he's become."

"Aye, but he's just ah wee lad, Ah promise yer. Opel here is—"

"No, that's enough." Aisar returned his focus to the jackalope. The Watcher barely had time to wick away the sweat that pooled on his chin. "I hear your plea. And I will spare the girl's life."

"Yes, Yer Grace, thank yer," whimpered Gregabbit as he dropped to his knees, equal beside his teary-eyed niece. "Ah thank yer, truly, Ah do."

Nodding, the raccoon turned his attention to the hedgehog. A certain darkness grew over his eyes as he spoke, as if the notion of rebellion or sparing a criminal or hearing Anlana mentioned or any twisted concoction of such triggers forced him to live up to his reputation.

"Nail her."

Spoken like thunder across a winter sky.

Opel sank into the floor. Nailing. Anything but that. Every Winthropian feared it. Just the image made the slosh of porridge and warm water gurgle in the pit of her stomach.

Two metal spikes. Blunt. Driven into your knees and crippling you for life.

She gagged.

"W…Wha', Yer Grace?" asked Gregabbit, rising from the floor.

"You heard me, and three months in the dungeon alongside."

The jackalope could hardly blink or talk or breathe. The command had turned him into a statue petrified by horror.

"But, but yer said yer'd spare her!" he cried. The hedgehog tried to lift her up, but the cut of Gregabbit's glare turned back at him, damp with tears, stopped his hand.

"And I *am*. But a rebel is a rebel and deserves justice no matter how soothing the mercy." The words rolled off his tongue without a second thought, followed close by a yawn. "Now, get her up and—"

"But—"

"One more word and you'll join her, Cammont!" His pithy bark echoed to the Watchers standing guard outside. "Now *GO!*"

Opel didn't need their help. She jumped to her feet and leaned as far to Aisar as her chains would allow. Fiery spit rained hell from her mouth.

"Yer'll have yer day! Yer'll die with fear in yer eyes and live all the horrors yer bestow! Weh'll dance on yer grave, dance 'till our feet turn tae nubs and cackle like crones over yer miserable waste of ah life yer *fat, pathetic, wicked waste of breath!*"

The hedgehog whipped her back until she stumbled to the ground. However, the king laughed. Giggled, even, at the remarks. He slapped his knee and sent a jiggle through his legs, kicking up his slippers in glee.

"Good! Dance, child, dance! Let me live in your minds! You'll never be rid of me, *never!* Give me that life eternal! *HA!*"

His chuckles serenaded her return to the dungeons. Only once did her cold yet defeated glare leave the blob melting into the throne. It was to look back at the rafters and back to the fox, dangling from the beam.

He'd watched the entire scene unfold whilst wedged between two intersecting rows. Each arm caught a different side, forcing him to grip both lest he drop upon the king. The predicament burned. What little climbing strength remained from Pradifore exhausted itself in the first few minutes. Neither leg was long enough to swing up and grapple on a side. When he tried, the grip of his fingers slipped, inch by inch. It overextended his shoulders to the point of a searing pain rising in the joints.

Gradually, Foxtamas sank lower and lower and lower and the sweat leaked quicker and quicker and quicker. He didn't have a choice—it was act or fall. Right as Aisar pardoned the girl, he swung his entire weight rightward and slapped his left hand on the beam. His claws sunk in not even an eighth of an inch, but he needn't anymore. Scratches bore deep and breaths huffed sharp as the boy clambered up. Neither hand held enough traction to fully pull him up. Instead, he enlisted his legs to kick back behind. They caught the edge of the opposing beam and shot him just in reach of the other side.

Foxtamas hugged the wood tight and rolled upon it, landing on his back. Whooped.

Yet through it all he still witnessed the encounter. He almost fell at the nailing's mention. Nightmares of the practice haunted him for weeks after he first heard about it. Now, to see the command be given to someone he *knew*, it...it...

No.

He had to move. Not out of disregard for Opel, but for the pending bawling and passing out the idea would cause.

The fox rose, pushing to the window with a careful placing of steps. The lilies again warmed him. All the dust he kicked up sparkled like gigyants. He skirted over the beam until his paws finally touched the glass, heated by the sun behind. Through the lavender panels he saw the outcrop of Mechmilne. It rolled out for miles beyond Winthrop, the ridges springing up like frozen waves. The leaves were colored as if

Tidingsdale was still upon them. It made Foxtamas smile.

The window tilted out just enough for him to climb through. He'd be down in one final climb down the Palace's side. The fox sipped the Palace's rose-tinted air for the final time and slipped out.

Step four completed.

***

Bunnclar Cammont had been throwing, catching, and throwing again a stone into the air, letting it fall plump in his paw for what felt close to a good three-and-a-half centuries. The birch on which the jackalope leaned rubbed tough against his plush white fur, sneaking through the many holes in his tunic he refused to let his mother fix. He scrunched his nose until it pinkened and rolled his rich brown eyes—*another* annoyance. As if the waiting hadn't been enough to devastate one morning. Already he faced the heft of his antlers that just *appeared* overnight. Both Da' and Reinden had warned him of the sudden growth spirit. "Et'll bog yer down," they said, "Won't bae tossin' them toys like yer been." Oh, why'd they have to be right! If he leaned too far back, he'd end up rolling all the way back down home, and too far forward would crash him into the back of the Palace, right into that big fat back of Aisar.

Maybe they *weren't* so bad, then.

But he'd get used to them. He had to. A heavy head never stopped a warrior from honing his skills. And their being elk, a finery amongst his kind, well, it was a *duty* to take care of them!

The rock finally fell between his fingers, and he turned his exhausted attention to his partner in crime—the princess. Dawning a freeing, luscious gray and golden dress, Acirema busied herself by surveying the morning sun. Its reflection sprang out like pin pokes from her silver tiara that twisted in a thin band over her ears. One more polish and it would've been a halo.

Every feature of the girl sculpted her as the epitome of royalty, poise, and perfection. Her back stood straight, hands clasped, eyes dark and awake, smile mellow but not frowning. Aisar would be proud—the Winthropians prouder. Even in her sneaking out and joining with her friends, Acirema Feiht still glowed like the golden hope they knew she'd be. Her ascension would mark a new era for the poor village. One of vivacity. Of purpose. Of *life!*

"Ah'm convinced the laddies done forgot!" the Cammont boy proclaimed with his uniquely jackalopian accent. He yanked himself off the birch and proceeded to mope around the Palace's back lawn with a careful eye on the princess. He made sure never to leave her thinking alone for too long.

"Bunns, *you* said you saw them get up," the raccoon responded. She broke from her thoughts and glared at the irritated hybrid.

"*Gettin'* oup, not out the door!" He flung his head up as he spoke, and the antlers hauled him to the wooden back wall.

Acirema rubbed her temples. The sigh following came out all its own. It was times like these she counted it a blessing that she now had other friends apart from Bunns. He was the first villager she ever truly met. When Mrs. Cammont would rise early to attend to her mother, she'd bring along her newborn, a boy that walked at three months and ran at four. Acirema never matched his energy. That didn't stop them playing in her room or skipping between the Palace columns in little games all their own. When the Scottsworths arrived, they folded right in. Except that day, it seemed.

She gently took a rest at the birch's roots and watched Bunns steady himself.

"Well, I don't think they're coming the usual way," the princess said with a nod to the cleared Palace grass to their right. The old coyote Hazelhurst narrowly avoided finding her and Bunns before starting his work. "Think they're lost?"

"Eh, maybe. Should weh go an' find 'em?"

"You can, I've got to stay here."

"Aye, *suuuuuure* yer do!"

"You know the rules, Antlerears," her crisp voice peeped behind a giggle. "Go on, hop on back down there."

The boy groaned.

"Et's *always* meh, ain't et?" bemoaned Bunns as he twirled in a circle of self-pity. "Lil' lad'll never get ahead. Woe is meh! Stuck tae Queenie's boot like ah mashed mushroom." He leaned up against the Palace's shrubs and planted a trembling paw over his *very* wounded heart. Acirema squeezed her lips to contain any trickle of a laugh. "When will Ah finally have mah peace!"

GAAAH!!!

Acirema blinked, and a rush of yells, crunches, and blur of orange jumbled before her.

"Bunns!"

She bolted to the foliage and found, twisted amongst broken branches and fluttering leaves, the tangled body of Foxtamas Scottsworth suffocating the yelping Bunnclar Cammont.

How the princess howled! She stumbled back to the ground and grabbed her ribs to stop the laughs from squeezing the breath out of her. The squeals came closer to overpowering the boys' back and forth bickering as they wrestled their way from the bushes.

"Wha' is Mum feedin' yer!" grunted Bunns.

"Less than she's been feeding you!" Foxtamas retorted, twisting up a leg and accidentally smacking his adopted brother.

"Watch et, Scottoh!"

"Get your antlers outta my face!"

"How 'bout yer get yer *body* offa mine!"

They both suddenly felt a pull at their sackcloth collars. Their bodies flung out from the shrubs, battered and bruised, and they looked at the upside-down figure of Acirema staring them down. Gone were the giggles, and in their place a motherly scowl that forced the boys up to their feet.

"Foxtamas Scottsworth!" yapped the raccoon, finger pressed to his chest. "What in *EVON* were you doing up there! Were you *trying* to get yourself killed!?"

"Aye, an' tryin' tae kill *meh!*" added Bunns. He tossed out a loose branch from his antlers.

"I-I-I can explain," he replied with a nervous laugh. "I tried to go around the usual way but they were cutting the grass, a-and I kinda just freaked out and snuck on in when the Watchers changed out, and—"

"Did Father see you?" Acirema asked quickly. Wide-eyed. The twitch of her bottom lip signaled her fear to the fox.

"I don't think so. He was, uh, um…busy." For a moment he almost revealed what he'd seen. But Acirema dealt with the complaints of her father daily, and to hear what he'd done to Bunns' cousin, well…he couldn't. This was a fun day for them. One she'd planned out. He didn't dare ruin it.

"You *sure?*"

"Yeah. He would've said something if he did."

Relieved, she stepped back and took in a breath of the passing wind.

"Yer made et all the way tae the window?" asked Bunns. "How'd yer manage *tha'?*" Before the fox replied, he picked one final leaf off the jackalope's head. His antlers only rose to Foxtamas' neck—he the shortest and the younger Scottsworth the tallest of the four friends.

"I almost didn't. I hid under the columns and crawled to the stairs when Aisar came through, and when I crawled up *those* he kept calling and asking if it was Acirema up there."

"Oh, no…" groaned the princess. "Did he get suspicious of me?"

"Just a bit worried. But then I hopped on the railing and crawled out the window, and I tried climbing down, but my foot slipped and—"

"And yer tried tae kill meh." Bunns scoffed and turned up his nose. "After all weh've done for yer—"

"Maybe I would've spared you if you *woke me up!* I could've been crawling through the grass right beside you and not risking my *life* in there!"

"You said you saw them up, Bunns…" added Acirema.

"Oup stirrin' in ah dream! But sure, make et mah fault again."

"Or you could've gone around."

The trio whipped towards the forest's edge. There, leaning against a tree and outfitted in his gray rags, bearing both a bag and walking stick, was the smirking Foxlaris Scottsworth. He stood the same height as his brother, only with his ever-darkening red fur and brown stare that squinted with his grin. Even for his young age he gave off the aura of an adult. His stature held tall with an uplifted head—a blossomed rose amongst the seedlings.

"*There* yer are, Rizzeh! Worried yer followed the murderer here!" chuckled Bunns, causing Foxtamas to toss his hands in the air. When the boys first arrived, he couldn't keep either of their names straight. Thus, Foxlaris became "Rizzy" and Foxtamas, lacking any good morpheme to mold, got "Scotto" from their last name. They fit well besides Acirema's "Queenie." That didn't come by necessity like the others—he just wanted to remind her of who he served.

"But look, still took you longer!" the younger brother spat back.

"Nope. I woke up maybe ten minutes ago." Foxlaris' sneer grew tighter, and Foxtamas squinted until the blues of his eyes looked like narrow rivers.

The older fox feared he'd been caught in his lie.

He left well ahead of Foxtamas, charting his trek and taking on the climb a few steps at a time. Any faster and he'd choke on the gasps his brittle lungs refused.

The wilderness behind the Village was steep. Sickly boys such as himself weren't meant for its rocky steps, overgrown snares of roots hidden by leaves. But Foxlaris went anyway. He *had* to. He wouldn't let his weaker form stop him, hold him back when he had the chance to prove he could *do* something.

No one could know, though. Already he faced their worries for his weakness—the more he quelled such suspicions, the better. He was the eldest of the group. The sternest, the most *adult*. That's what they needed to see.

"Did you *really* sneak through the Palace?" Foxlaris asked back, shifting the conversation away from himself.

"All the way."

"Didn't it scare you?"

"Only a bit," lied Foxtamas.

"Mmmhmmm."

"I'm serious!"

"When are we gonna go, Acirema?" Foxlaris asked. The princess had been leaning on the birch and dozing off at the boys' constant complaints. Some days they just didn't deserve her.

"Right now. You three go on ahead and clear out the spot, I'll go back and grab the box." She turned to head back inside the Palace, but flipped back last minute. "You *did* bring your items, right?"

"Yes ma'am," said Foxlaris with an indication to his bag. The other two patted themselves down and nodded.

"Aye Queenie, Ah'm all set!"

She breathed a bit easier and then turned the corner.

Before Bunns and Foxlaris could start into the woods, Foxtamas hissed at them both, motioning for them to stay put.

"Hey, wait a second," he whispered. His brother's ear cocked up and he glanced back, confused.

"What now?"

The younger fox gulped. His hands clawed at one another.

"I didn't want to tell y'all this when she was here, but...I saw something while I was in there. Something bad. *Real* bad."

Foxlaris and Bunns exchanged worried looks. When Foxtamas spoke in that low, warbled tone, they knew danger lurked on the other end of his words.

"Spill et, Scottoh. Wha' was et?" The jackalope regretted asking the question when the fox's eyes fell to his feet.

"I...I saw Opel."

Bunns swallowed hard.

"And?"

"Aisar had her all chained up, and, and your father was the one that hauled her to him. She was gonna be killed, but he intervened and talked Aisar out of it."

"Tha's Da' alright," he tried to chuckle as if the story had ended. But the single tear hiking down the fox's orange cheeks told him otherwise.

"But…but…"

"But what?" Foxlaris pushed closer with a furrowed brow.

"He ordered her nailed and locked away for three months."

Bunns' white fist balled to the point of cutting into his hand.

"Tha' *BASTARD!*" he roared into an echo that carried down the wooded hill.

"Shh, don't say that!" warned Foxtamas.

"Ah'll say whatever Ah want about tha', tha' *beast!* Now *MOVE!*" He tried to push past the brothers, but they held him back. Foxlaris' snatched his hand away from the pocket he knew hid his weapon. *"Ah'll cut his fatty heart out! Ah'll pluck out his eyes one by one!"*

"Cut it out," demanded the older fox. "There's nothing you can do about it."

"Oh, tha' so, Rizzeh? Give meh one good look at him an' Ah'll—"

"Bunns."

The cool word of Foxtamas sprayed him like a splash of water. He turned and saw his friend, equally distressed, but content in his fury. Any rash move would land him in the same spot as his cousin. Yet within, the rage still flourished. He needed justice for such cruelty, action taken to protect those he loved. But his little fluffy fist just wouldn't do.

It fell to his side. Defeated.

"Don't tell Acirema, okay?"

"Aye," Bunns replied low and somber. "Ah won't. Et's not her burden to bear."

The trio sat in silence for a moment until Foxlaris stepped into Mechmilne with an awakening *crunch!*

"Come on," he said with a wave of his stick. "Let's go."

The boys followed, journeying down the back of Winthrop's hill, into the thicket of the forest, cooling them on the spring day, away from the Palace's shadow and the sniffling little raccoon who, hidden around the corner, had heard every word of her father's wicked ways…

5

"Too will it heal, as wishes blossom"

It wasn't long until the mood of the three boys improved by way of their romping through the woods. They settled on hosting at one of their newer "forts" in Mechmilne's north, only a short walk from Winthrop. The upper branches squatted low from their stumpy trunks circling the clearing. A chilling wind swished and swayed through them, shimmering the speckles of morning light across the four stumps, gathered rocks, and cleaned branches lining around the roots like a wall.

It didn't take long for Acirema to find them. In her paws she carried a stout, gilded oaken box crafted for Palace jewelry. She rested it in the crunchy layer of last autumn's leaves and took a seat on her stump.

"What's this for again?" asked Foxlaris, sitting at the corner opposite her.

"It's supposed to be kind of like a time capsule," she replied, checking her satchel for her item. "But instead of just random stuff, we put in things that represent our wishes. Once we grow up, we can look back to see if they came true." The corners of her mouth spread. She'd thought up the idea between her lessons with Ol' Smetty, the one Watcher learned enough to tutor the princess. It felt just perfect for them. Not a story they could act out per say, but a chance to blend their hopes with imagination and make it…more.

"An' weh're wishin' for…wha' exactly?"

Maybe a story would've been fine after all.

Through her hands, Acirema mumbled out, "Did a single one of you listen when I explained it last night?"

"Well, et was hard tae in the middle of playin' Archers," replied Bunns.

"I listened," Foxtamas said. "If that makes you feel any better." His brother groaned beside him.

"Of *course* you did."

"What, that a bad thing?"

"No, it's not, and very appreciated, Foxtamas," thanked the princess, winking. "But what you do, *Bunns,* is you take an item—which I all *hope* you still have—and make a wish upon it. Something like…a goal, or a promise, or something you want in the future, anything like that. Then we'll store it in the box and check on it down the line. Got it?"

"Right as rain, Queenie!" Bunns answered with a nod and salute. Another gesture the princess avoided smirking at. "Yer want tae do yers first?"

"Oh, no, one of you can go—"

"No, go ahead!" urged Foxtamas. "I'm still thinking of what I'm gonna say. And you might need to show Bunns the ropes."

The jackalope's jaw dropped. But before he could toss out some insult, the princess obliged and scooted to the box. Carefully, she eased open the top to reveal the velvet mat lining on the bottom.

From her satchel she withdrew a miniature golden tiara. It hardly fit the center of her palm, but was no less gorgeous because of it. Elegant cuts of emerald, diamond, and rubies picked up the rays and sparkled like captured stars encrusted on a golden ribbon. It looked fancier than any the boys had seen her wear. Such beauty halted the angst built in their hearts; they could watch the sparkles pirouette in the light of the sun and moon alike.

"This is the first tiara I was ever given," started the princess. Her words, as always, flowed with a smooth assurance to pace out her rushing thoughts. "I believe I was only three. My mother gave it to me for my birthday. And…a few months later she, um…she passed."

Their blissful wonder dropped to bitter silence. The friends nodded in the Queen's remembrance. Bunns was the only one of them to truly remember her and her death, whereas the Scottsworths picked up what little details Acirema shared. Only raw images appeared for him: his mother mourning at his bedside; a gilded coffin carried down the Main Road; storms lasting the entire summer; it's all he had of her legacy. His brown eyes glanced over to Acirema who, despite the pressure of the memories, continued. "I don't remember a lot about her, but there's one thing I've kept in my heart—she said I would make a great Queen. She would...would always tell me I'd meet a lovely prince and rule Winthrop together. I'd always shake my head and snicker at her saying that. Her death...it sort of changed that."

As hard as she tried to keep her veil of confidence unfurled, it crumpled. Water stung her eyes.

"The stories say she and father got caught in a riot at Mikyill. Before they knew what was happening, she...was down." She gulped and overturned the tiara in her hands, gone clammy. "This is all I still have of her."

Trying to preserve her gracefulness, Acirema stiffened her back and rested the golden crown on the velvet lining. She looked it over. Let only one lone tear fall on the velvet and darken like a bruise. "I want to rule with grace and mercy. I want to be good...not like my father. As much as I try to love him I-I-I can't end up like he did. I just wish to be like her. Not him."

The boys watched in silence. When the princess turned back, all three nodded with cheery grins, proud of her vulnerability. She smiled back. Hundreds of questions burdened her head, about her mother, her father, how she'd accomplish any of the goals she set forth. But she knew her friends. They had her.

Her wish would be enough.

Acirema seated herself, and Bunns didn't waste a second hopping up to parade about the grove.

"Now, lassies, listen here!" proclaimed the boy, fiddling with his pocket. "For mah wish, Ah'll bae placin' et on this here beaut!" A flash sparked across their eyes. Bunns' stump *cracked!* out, and a thin sheet of metal, etched out in the shape of a five-pointed star, lodged into its bark.

"This here's mah Da's spinnin' star. Et's one of the first Ah got as ah wee young'un ah few years back." He put his finger through the hole at the center and tried to pry out the throwing star.

It didn't budge.

"When Ah hold et, Ah feel the power tae bae a warrior surgin' through meh! Et's mah callin' Ah'm, eh, Ah'm sure of et." His confidence waned as the strength of his pull waxed. With one final pull—and a toss back of his antlers—the weapon wedged free, sending the jackalope into a spiral, but one he recovered from with a chuckle. "Ah wanna bae the stealthiest, keenest fightin' jackey y'all've ever seen! Everyday Ah'll march through this land with mah stars an' weapons ready tae face all the evils tha' try tae hurt us."

A tremendous show built while Bunns spoke. He spun the metal star over his knuckles, flipping it into the air with a snap of his fingers. It rolled along his arm and spun on the opposite hand. The kid made it known he'd mastered something...something that still squeaked a few snickers out from his friends. They couldn't help themselves! Watching the little jackalope fiddle around like a festival act *begged* for a chuckle here and there.

"Ah wish tae bae the bravest an' bestest warrior in all of Evon! Watch et, they'll bae namin' books an' cities after meh. Yes, Ah can see et now! The City o' Bunnclar, dedicated tae the greatest of Evon!"

That sent them over the edge. Foxtamas rolled off his stump from pure laughter; the low-hanging branches swayed up and down to match the giggling fits of Foxlaris and Acirema. They left the war-rior-wannabe furrowing his brow and tapping his foot, a spitting image of how Mrs. Cammont stared when disappointed.

"Oh, I can't wait to live in the City o' Bunnclar!" the eldest fox howled.

"Neither can I! How about you, Foxtamas?" asked Acirema be-tween gasps for air.

"I'm already packing!"

"Aye, an Ah'll make sure yer livin' in the slums!"

Thus concluded the wish of Bunnclar Cammont. As the jeers died down, he tossed the star at the box, lodging it in the red sea.

Foxlaris rose third. Only the wind moved while he fished out his item, quiet, tempered. It ruffled the back of his fur. Made flashes of home strike his mind as his hand gripped what he sought.

"So, um, this here is my wish, I guess," said the fox. "I didn't think it was s'posed to be like a *really* big dream or wish, but, um…" He pulled from his bag a kitchen knife. Any edge once sharpened upon the blade had long faded, replaced by rust building down the side.

Both Acirema and Bunns cocked a brow in confusion. Foxlaris never liked to cook. Avoided it, really. Why'd he chosen this?

The blue eyes next to them, however, blinking to hold back tears, knew the answer.

"It's one of the knives from our kitchen back in Pradifore. I didn't pay any attention to it or anything but…our mother did." His worn sandals kicked about the fallen leaves at his feet. Maybe if he cleared a large enough spot he could lay down and bury himself beneath them. Anything other than standing there and speaking his…his *heart.*

"On the night we were attacked, she stuffed it in a pack for the two of us. It must've been to protect us or something, I dunno. When we ran, I passed out, and Foxtamas, he, he, um…used it. One of the attackers followed us and caught up when we stopped."

In the corner of his eye, he caught the image of his younger brother, leg shaking upon the stump and wiping away an assault of tears. Foxlaris forced himself to look down. "All he had was this knife. When the brute saw us, Foxtamas ran and got him away from me, and then that…thing…tripped and landed on it. But I think Foxtamas got him."

A pale laugh coughed from his dry, dry mouth. Without realizing it, he'd picked away most of the rust. A single blade of light twinkled across the freshly cleaned sheen.

"He saved me that night. So, um…so that's what I wanna do for him. Repay him, help him, something like that. Like I said, it's not some big thing, but that's the wish I could think of, um, so—"

It hit him like one of the trees above falling on his chest. Foxlaris' breath sapped from his body as he felt his brother's paws wrap around him and head lock over his shoulder. Their hearts beat in sync.

"Thank you," whispered Foxtamas.

Foxlaris patted his back. Then hugged him in return.

"Of course."

Bunns and Acirema smiled softly from behind. Rarely did the boys speak about their past, and even rarer did they embrace so publicly. The love between them grew in that moment. Not bright, not showy, with petals unwinding at the dawn of spring. No, their love deepened. Roots burrowing out of sight and into an untapped well of kinship.

Finally, with the hug over, tears shed, and elder brother back at his seat, the time for Foxtamas Scottsworth arrived. He shook the trickles of emotion off and pulled from his pocket a faded, frayed, and slightly torn handkerchief. Black dots of blood long dried colored the bottom, matched by streaks of soot across the top. They covered the right corner where an emblem of sorts lay stitched. Two foxes, blistering orange and back-to-back, uplifting their arms with the word "Fox" unfurled and fluttering on a scroll above.

"I got this that same night," he began. His face looked stern, striving to keep the same countenance as his brother. "Momma wiped my tears with it and said she and Poppa were gonna meet us somewhere. They never did." The words faded with a hint of despair. Slowly, the fox traced the ash marks as he tried to continue. He held the last remnant of his home. Burnt. Blackened.

"B-B-But I think something better came along...y'all."

A grin shielded his teary eyes as he kept going, knowing his friends and brother were slightly shocked by what he'd said. "Not that they weren't great or anything, of course, I'll always love them, but ever since I got here y'all've been my new family. You've treated me well, been with me, played with me, made me not feel all lonely and stuff. The Cammonts even adopted us. I'm...I'm...well I'm just so dadgum happy to have y'all." The boy took one last look at the handkerchief. New tears started to stain it. "My wish is to just repay it back, y'know? Like, I dunno, with a big ol' cake, or a big gift, a surprise or something.

Y'all deserve it, really. Y-You really do."

With that, he let loose the cloth. It swayed down like the sleepy glide of a maple leaf, landing over the tiara, star, and knife.

Not a dry eye remained in that Mechmilne fort. The wind cooled the tears pooling at their cheeks, but the warmth inside, kindled by the fox's words, won out. Acirema clasped her hands tight and grinned. She looked at Bunns who chuckled to avoid crying; at Foxlaris, head low, but smile still rising; and Foxtamas, taking his seat before leaning over to his brother and patting his back.

"Sorry it was close to yours," he said through the warble of his voice.

"No, you're fine. It was...good," Foxlaris nodded.

"It was, Foxtamas," added the princess. "But you already do so much for us. You make up the stories, you direct the games—"

"Woah, calm et down there, Queenie." Bunns hopped up and winked at the trio. "Yer keep talkin' an' weh'll never get tha' cake!" Where Foxlaris laughed, Acirema groaned.

The raccoon eased the box shut and plucked it from the leafy floor, careful not to rattle the contents inside. "*Anyway,* where should we bury it? It's the last step in making the wishes come true."

Deep, heavy, troubling bouts of thought whirled through the children's minds.

"The Palace?" offered Bunns.

"Eh, would be too hard to find a spot."

Groans, then nods. The reddish ears of Foxlaris jumped to attention.

"The backyard free?"

"Nah, Rizzeh, Mum's startin' tae expand the garden."

Another idea uprooted.

"What about the River?" Foxtamas suggested. "We can use the shallow part where we play."

"True," his brother replied.

"That's not half bad," said Acirema. "Think it'll get washed away?"

"No way, current's too slow."

"Sounds like ah plan tae meh!" Bunns sprang to his feet with the rest following behind. "But let's stop by the house an' get ah quick snack. Can't head tae the River empty!"

Bushes shook, branches swayed, and the waning morning sun of the day guided the friends back home.

***

Bunns popped open the creaking door only to be slapped upside the head. Not by his mother (though she was close), but by the aroma of the thick, boiling broth bubbling over the fireplace.

Mrs. Corlawn Cammont had practically chained herself to the kitchen that morning. Bits of carrot, mushroom, and parsley lay scattered about the well-worn counter running along the wall of the meager Cammont Household. The Scottsworths initially found it so homey because, well, it looked no different than their tree in Pradifore, just without the upper room and boughs groaning outside.

Its kitchen bled into the living room. Corlawn paid particular care to having a clean table and well-swept rug covering the graying wood floor. From the walls hung potato sacks stained red and mounted as curtains. They draped around as decoration, hiding both rotted planks and gaps needing repair before autumn. But that would be for Gregabbit...if he ever returned. Dust coated his mantle-side rocker. The kids knew not to disturb it. Whenever a light breeze broke through, the chair rolled, like the jackalope's ghost had nodded off looking above the flames at a clay vase holding a fresh cut of Miss Tilly's tulips, a spare stack of books Foxtamas left lying around, and a painting of the Cammont family made during a Tidingsdale festival two years prior, costing three weeks of Gregabbit's pay.

Corlawn wicked the sweat from her forehead between pulls and pushes of the stew. Already she'd dirtied her apron with fresh stains from the radishes Mrs. Pineleaf had gifted her. It was either that or candy them, and the hedgehog hadn't the time with both Hedgemis *and* Hedgarkin just now starting to walk.

All of Winthrop knew the jackalope a stellar cook. She even looked the part, with a flaring pink nose wading through scents, the many dishes and ingredients watched by her bulbous brown eyes, and her lips, thinner than the wrinkles weighing down her brow, humming a tune to keep her focused. No one dared test her talents. Her motherhood, on the other hand...

"Mum!" yelped her youngest, hopping up and hitting the door-frame. "Weh're back!"

"Wha' did Ah tell yer 'bout smackin' tha'!" she shouted from the fireplace. "Yer do tha' one more time an' Ah'll wring yer like a wet rag—"

Mrs. Cammont spun around at the very moment Acirema floated into the house. Her eyes widened. The ladle *plopped!* into the soup, and Corlawn curtseyed her ragged brown dress and stained, graying apron. "M'lady! Welcome in! Apologies for tha' an' all this mess, just been busy with cookin' for tonight an'—"

"Oh, Mrs. Cammont," Acirema said, nodding a quick thank you, "you know you don't—"

"Nae m'lady. Yer mum would never forgive meh if Ah didn't. Yer deserve the same respect an' then some." Her voice thumped loud, thick enough to fill the entire home. It made sure Acirema knew *not* to question her fealty. She could cry, protest, throw her in the dungeons like her father, and still the jackalope would bow and honor the girl.

Instead, the princess lifted a smile towards her, puffy like a dande-lion. Mrs. Cammont never failed to be the mother she lost. Stern and strict, caring and kind, she gave whatever the young raccoon needed.

"But wha' are y'all doin' back here? Thought yer had ah big day planned."

"We're just stopping by for a snack," said Foxlaris as he and Foxtamas shuffled up behind.

"Aye, have tae head tae the River tae bury our wishes."

Corlawn chuckled.

"Sounds like fun. But Ah ain't got much. Ah'm usin' et all for the feast tonight."

The *feast!* How could they have forgotten! As far as the children knew, it wasn't for any special occasion. After a brutal stretch of taxes or an abundance of crops, the Winthropians would lay aside their work and gather together. They'd eat, sing, trade stories, play games—the kind of joy Aisar couldn't steal. He could have all the Tops he wished. Their happiness wasn't for sale.

"Wha' about tha' loaf yer made last night?"

"Senessa Solberry is makin' sandwiches out of et."

"Muuuumm," Bunns begged as he spun around.

"Oh, shut et, mister. Go see if weh got some mushrooms an' pickings in the cellar. Yer can have those," Corlawn replied, stern eye glaring down. Her son grinned. Without looking back, he leapt to the door, racoon and foxes close behind.

Yet Foxtamas took the chance to branch off as the others scurried to the cellar. He stopped by his room (more accurately the room of him, Foxlaris, and Bunns), darting straight for the corner. Along the peeling wood sat a black shelf tilted and snuggled into the wall. It matched the two bunked beds and battered wooden wardrobe settled into the small space. Cramped and rugged, it felt like home.

Pages, pamphlets, and books far beyond their prime clustered within the tiny nook. The fox beamed as he rummaged past the titles he collected over the past four years. Every Top he earned went directly to buying some "new" book for the shelf from whatever vendor or merchant passed through. Epics of dwarves, assassins, travelers, wizards—all memorized to the point of recitation. Even folktales from village elders made their way in, jotted on the back of loose parchment he scrounged up while listening.

But nothing ever fully scratched the itch within his soul. Foxtamas wanted to *be* with these characters. With the closing of his eyes he could stand atop the Fulnoa, sail around the Isle of Asda Fraye, camp on the rolling hills of Plentis Plains and let the allurement of the starry sky lull him to sleep. Only to wake up. Gone from it all.

Just once he'd like to see Evon like that, to take a journey, nay, *adventure* across the land. But what if he encountered thieves? Or ran out of water, or food? Or got lost and never made it home? Dying in the dark woods away from his friends, his family, lost, lost…lost and…alone…

Fear slammed the gates and kept them well-guarded and well-shut. The fox would never be freed from the army's clutches.

His blue eyes scanned the layers of novels and pages. If the friends were heading to the River Nohsis, then play was sure to follow, and with it a story to draw from and reenact. As he reached for a tome, a voice called out from behind.

"What are you grabbing?"

"Not sure yet, but I'm thinking knights," replied Foxtamas, turning to see his older brother looming over.

"Again?" he sighed. Foxlaris crouched down beside him.

"*Yes*, again. It was really fun last time."

"Do we even have to do a story today?"

The younger fox stopped shifting and stared at his brother, confused.

"Yeah, why not?"

"Just…just," stuttered Foxlaris. "I dunno, what about catching up on our chores? Doing stuff to help Mrs. Cammont with the feast?"

"Come *on!* That's no fun! We have later today to do that."

"But it's *useful* and what we *should* be doing."

Foxlaris looked away. He knew his brother wouldn't like the suggestion, just *knew* it. With such a big night coming up though, he…he needed to be doing something. Something worthwhile. Something that showed people he…he *mattered.*

When he looked back, Foxtamas had yet to take his blue eyes off him. They sat still. Watering.

"Foxtamas, I didn't mean—"

"I'm sorry," he mumbled out. "I don't know how you figured it, but I'm real sorry."

"No, don't—"

"Not about this." Foxtamas set aside the book in his hand and curled his knees to his chest. "When…when you said your wish, and you said I ran off to save you, I…I…oh, please don't get mad!"

Foxlaris, visibly confused, pushed closer and held his brother's trembling hand.

"Get mad about what?" he asked, soft and quiet.

"I ran 'cause…I was *scared,* Foxlaris! Yeah I got the bad guy away, but I tried saving myself. I'm real sorry, I promise. Being scared like that wasn't what I shoulda' been doing. I'm just—"

Foxlaris held him close before he could finish. Small sobs pattered against his shoulder like a calm evening rain.

The older fox wasn't sure what to think. Of *course* Foxtamas was scared. He had been ever since that night. And if he hadn't been lucky enough to trip the killer, that fear would've left poor Foxlaris dead in the snow.

That stirred his anger. His own kin would rather leave him frozen to death then stand and fight. Of *course!* How could he trust someone like that? Waste an entire *wish* on him!

Foxlaris held tight those thoughts until his eyes fell on the open book beside his brother. He knew it without even seeing the cover: *Sir Brandishwill of the Mount.*

Foxlaris' favorite.

"Don't be sorry," he finally whispered to Foxtamas. "I don't blame you. I ain't mad. It all worked out, didn't it?"

The younger fox pulled back, eyes a tad puffy, fur slightly slick with tears. He nodded.

"Yeah…it did."

"Then don't worry."

"What about your wish?"

"Doesn't change it. Nothing in Evon could."

The pair shared a smile. A warm, warm smile. The kind only found between brothers. Between true kin.

"Do you still not wanna play then?" asked Foxtamas. "'Cause I was gonna add some dwarf stuff you like to it." With that, he tossed over a copy of *Sir Brandishwill of the Mount*, illustrated with the armor-clad dwarf overlooking a sunset. Surprisingly, Foxlaris' face seemed to glow, with raised cheeks and bright eyes.

"Yeah, we can do that. Just don't let it be you-know-what."

Foxtamas instantly caught his brother's hint.

"River Raiders?"

"River Raiders."

They sighed in unison. Defeat crumpled between each syllable.

"If he brings it up, I'm gonna—,"

"I'll stop him," Foxtamas cut in, trying to hide his giggles. The older fox nodded with a stern stare and headed back to the kitchen. Foxlaris did love the play of their imaginary games, no one doubted that. But taking it as far as pretending to be some overpowered, unrealistic knights from the East that crossed the River was just too much to take. *Especially* for a pending fifth time.

Before following, Foxtamas took a last glance at the book. It felt good to unhook that secret from his chest, better even to know his brother didn't hate him for it. The relief let him admire the cover of *Sir Brandishwill* with fresh, renewed eyes.

The flares of flaming pink sizzling beside stripes of orange and blue bathed the Guardmont horizon. The outlines of both the jagged cliffs and the Fulnoa, the twin mountains making up the Dwarven Kingdom, were a black dark as dreams. *That* was adventure! It called to him, ignited his passion and made the fox fly high as a lantern. He hugged the title tight to his chest. His claws poked teensy holes in the cloth cover. Fear faltered in the fight against such a power.

Before long, the four reconvened in the kitchen, ready with the box, book, and basket of undesired goods.

"Don't bae gone tae long, yer hear!" said Mrs. Cammont as they entered, cutting up another round of onions.

"We won't be gone too long," Foxtamas replied.

"Ah hope not! Yer won't want tae bae missin' the feast. Oh, and Ah caught wind of somethin' y'all might want tae hear." Her rosy cheeks blossomed. "Sounds like ol' Dr. Wardly is bringin' a special 'sweet' treat for the lil' bonnies."

Gasps! Cheers! Jumps of joy!

"Butterswath!?" Bunns hopped so high his antlers threatened to scrape the ceiling.

"Guess yer'll have tae see—so *bae back!*"

"Yes ma'am!" Both he and the Scottsworths saluted the mother. That sweet, creamy, caramel-inspired drink, oh it deserved all the boys could muster.

"Will yer bae makin' et, m'lady?" "I don't think so, Mrs. Cammont," Acirema replied, "I doubt Father would like me going out because, well—,"

"Trust meh, Ah understand. Ah'll make sure tae get one of these rascals tae bring yer somethin' oup. But go on, shoo! And have fun!" With that, the motherly jackalope flashed a final smile and turned back to her chopping.

The friends waved goodbye and headed out. Except for Bunns. He hung just beside the door, leaning back and forth and causing the floor to squeak below him.

"Oh um, say, mum," his squeaky voice called to her. The news of Opel had been buried inside him for too long. He had to tell her. She needed to know about her niece, about what that…that *monster* did to her. The pain ate away at him. If he didn't say something, he might just combust.

However, that thought dissipated as he watched his mother. The over-worked woman, grin glued to her cheeks and a tune fluttering from her lips, dumped the onions into the simple stew. It wasn't much. It never was. Yet happiness bloomed in that crooked kitchen. Not hurt.

And he was about to ruin that?

No.

She deserved that joy more than he did.

A warrior protected such a feeling—a thief robbed it away.

"Yes, hun?"

Corlawn wiped her hands and glanced over to the door. Only a sliver of light broke through the open, swinging crack.

The ruddy, gray gravel melted to leaves of bygone ages beneath their feet. Having the last house in Village Winthrop gave direct access to the Mechmilne trail. The Scottsworth boys brought up the back (picking and plucking the best scenes from the book), and Bunns dragged beside Acirema. The princess couldn't help but cast a worried look towards him. Between his skips, the usual, boisterous grin had faded. She knew what slowed him. A lump rose in her throat.

"Um, Bunns…are you feeling alright?"

His eyes shot to her as if she'd read his mind

"Oh, er, Aye! Never better."

"You sure?"

"Why, are mah ears floppy?"

"No, nothing like that. Just wanted to make sure."

The jackalope winked her way and bounded off further into the woods, hollering for the rest to follow. Acirema wished she could take him at his word. Maybe he really did feel fine and had kept the news of Opel far from his mind; or, maybe, he blamed her for the misery that befell his father, brother, and now cousin. Why didn't she do more? Why didn't she stand up to Aisar and defend her people?

Before she journeyed too far from the village, she took one look back, tracing the winding path past the shambled shacks and up to the glinting, golden top. They were there. All of them. All the eyes of Winthrop staring her down. Waiting for her move.

***

Every worry drifted away beneath the sways of Mechmilne Wood. The fellowship of four traveled down a dirt trail twisted around the rotting remnants of logs and over knolls breaking into quiet patches of meadowlark slicked back by the breeze. The trees waved as they passed. Maples shimmied with excitement, elms crawled overhead to gain a better view, ashes stood straight at attention, oaks laughed with burly breathes rumbling from root to canopy; the forest joined the quest, a chaperone watching every step of the way.

Mechmilne always felt as such. Even those far in Mikyill or the smaller towns of Kinsdale or Woodburrow described the Wood as warm as a mother's hug. It was a secret guardian of sorts, one too often forgotten by the protected. What they *didn't* forget, however, was the River Nohsis and how it came to be. Every Evoneer knew the legend—at least, what still got passed down.

Long ago, close to thousands of years, a terrible civil war consumed Evon. The origin remained shrouded in mystery. All that scholars and talespinners knew for certain was the finale. During the battle, Roihelm, the Author of Evon, cast bright his blue wings through the center of the land and split it into two halves. The West housed his supporters, and the East those who stood against his name. From the Phoenix's home in Roimohr, far north and beyond what any Evoneer could seek, the River Nohsis flowed. It filled the gap and created a barrier to forever distance both sides. Thus concluded what came to be known as "The War that Split the World." No one's dared cross the River since. West Evon and East lay as two separate worlds. Once whole, now broken. Separated until the dusk of time.

The grand adventure of trail-trotting and leaf-crunching came to an end as the rushing call of the Nohsis rang clear. Foxtamas burst out from the ferns and shrubbery cluttering the tree line, grinding to a halt on the sand of the shore. His eyes glazed over; heart thumped in the back of his throat.

Monstrous. Elegant. Bold.

The lifeblood of Evon.

Sunlight dove deep into the clear, blistering splashes of the river ripping and thrashing down its land. The waters twirled in and around each other all fifty yards across from one side to the other. They fought like siblings, like children rolling lost in the commotion. Wave after wave shocked the sky with how blue its flashes. Through them, the long bank and soil—pebbled, deep and loamy—glowed, empowered and still remarking on the miracle that formed its creation.

Everything roared, everything ran. The River Nohsis beamed like the masterpiece it was.

And all the fox could do was stare. He felt powerless compared to the River, but in a good way. A comforting way. He hadn't the need to fight against the rapids or shout louder than its belt. It flowed as a living wonder guarding from the looming shadows and ridges of the East. How could the stories feel any more real?

"Hurry, Foxtamas!" The giggling, bright-eyed princess shouted to him. It broke his focus, and he turned to find the trio bounding towards the waters. "We're eating on the bank!"

Bunns wasted no time rummaging through the basket he'd snatched from the cellar. With the help of Foxtamas, the two pitched their patched quilt over the shore and began preparations. The outlining trees of Mechmilne tried to offer slips of shade. Sadly, the open size of the Nohsis bank proved too expansive for the wrinkled black hands to reach.

The boys sliced mushrooms and scrapes of cheese and plated them atop thin cuts of bread. As they worked, Acirema and Foxlaris strode along the lapping edge of the water in search of where they could bury the box.

"I oughta be the one setting up the food," Foxlaris moaned. He eased into the slippery waves to test how scoopable the sand was beneath.

"I know, but you know the rules. Foxtamas and Bunns claimed it first," replied Acirema, checking through the wooden chest one final time. The tiara, star, knife, and even handkerchief all shimmered in the midday sun.

"Mm. You're right. But I don't have to like it."

"Oh, I knew you wouldn't."

"Come on."

"What?"

"Give me the *chance* to like something."

"Trust me, we have," Acirema snorted.

"I just like things how I like them."

"I know. And I'm the same way."

"How? Keeping your dresses pretty?" Foxlaris snorted that time. In response, the princess kicked up a splash of water that stained his clothes like coal.

"Hey!"

Giggling, Acirema turned away as if nothing had happened.

"What, you fall in?" she peered back and asked.

Foxlaris scowled. If she wasn't holding the box, he'd toss her in. *Far.*

But, instead, he kept up his surveying, doing what he could to not fully soak himself. The trail from Winthrop led to one of the Nohsis' shallow bends, perfect for the children's play. The turns at the North and South of Evon spanned miles, the Eastern edge long hidden behind the horizon. Near the center, some places measured fifty yards to the East, if not less, giving them an up-close view of the foreign world.

Foxlaris finally found a suitable spot further into the shallows and began digging out scoops of dirt, slinging them to shore (and close to Acirema). As he did, his brown eyes darted to the darkened land. The trees along the broken, rocky bank grew gnarled, foul, and, as the friends often put it, ugly. Leaves were a dying green, upturned roots sharp and gray like driftwood. No eye could peer past the first row or so, locking the rest of the land behind an oaken gate. The forest rolled like a choppy sea back to a ridge that ran down the entirety of the East. If the shore was the gate, this was the fortress wall. Foxlaris craned his neck fully back just to see the top. In the evening, the sun would dip behind and cover all of Nohsis and the Western shore in shadow. No one ever saw the other side.

Stories, as with all things shrouded in the fog of mystery, sprouted like weeds as to what lay beyond the ridge. It was nothing but an endless swamp birthing dragons every full moon; a burned forest desolate and void of life; an entire civilization of trollfolk that spy on the children playing too long in the River (a favorite of every Western mother); a world of shadow beings, all created to mirror life in the West; and, the one oft repeated by the Village Oldheads and written down by Foxtamas, that it was filled with riches beyond all comprehension and reigned over by a wise, sagely king. However, whoever crossed would only be able to look upon the wealth and never take it lest they spark the king's wrath—thus why the Westerners steered clear of such temptation.

Foxlaris saw right through the fable. He never bought any of the tales as convincing. One time Poppa claimed that Momma's mother came from a creature from the East and he *knew* that to be false. Still, he found the whole land terrible. Just terrible. There was a reason nobody crossed.

"Acirema!" he called back to shore once the hole was dug. "It's ready!"

The princess waded her way over and eased the box into the hole, mindful not to wet *too* much of her dress. Once set, she and the fox patted it down with the loam to create a small hump in the riverbed. The waters rolled over it like wind to a hill.

"So, what we got?"

Foxlaris and Acirema arrived at the "camp" just in time for Bunns to swallow his last bite. "Ah present tae yer perhaps *the* bestest River snack weh've ever had!" The jackalope hopped up and grabbed two small sandwiches off the burlap sack. The pair took them and looked them over. They knew to be weary of Bunns' offerings.

"It's a mushroom and carrot slider," added Foxtamas, winking. "It's good, promise."

Bites were taken, bites were swallowed, and nods followed between the four.

"Not half bad," said Foxlaris, taking his seat.

"Maybe Mrs. Cammont's cooking is finally starting to wear off on you!" the raccoon joked. Instead of rolling his eyes, Bunns took it as a compliment.

"Aye! Can't help but tae learn from the best."

"Did y'all get it buried?" asked Foxtamas.

"Yup," his brother nodded. "Right in the shallow end. Our wishes shouldn't be going anywhere."

"Perfect."

"Say, Queenie, wha's the timeframe for these wishes, eh? Ah year? Decade? *Century?*" asked Bunns. The princess shrugged her shoulders and took another bite.

"No clue. Whenever they get around to coming true, I guess." Suddenly, her eyes grew wide. The sandwich slipped from her fingers. "Wait!" she cried, reaching back for her satchel and clawing through it. "I forgot the surprise!"

"Surprise?" Foxtamas asked. Acirema grinned and winked his way.

"Surprise indeed!" With a sling of her wrist, the raccoon revealed the treat of treats, delight of delights, the drink to forever conquer all drinks—

"Cherry Sugar Fizz!" cried, nay, *bleated* Bunns. His entire body leapt over the blanket to snatch the glass bottle from her hands. Acirema let him have it. She rolled away in a fit of laughter as the boys wrestled for the drink. Inside, the velvet liquid danced. Bubbles swung side-to-side, hand-in-hand, lapping and sizzling and waltzing a tingling, fruity scent out from the cork. *Perfection!*

"H-H-How'd you get this?" Foxlaris stammered, eyes still glued to the glass.

"I sneaked in early this morning before the kitchens fired up. Father just ordered a new crate full, so I don't think anyone will notice one bottle missing. Today's a special day anyway, so I thought we should celebrate!" "Oh lassie, celebrate weh *shall!*" Bunns, quicker than a snap of fingers, flung a star from his pocket deep into the cork and popped it out. Steam and fizz wobbled out. The children kneeled by it as if it holy.

The bottle passed around only twice before it lay empty by the pot-bellied friends. Their stomachs churned with air, and the burn of the bubbles seared their throats with the sweet, tangy taste of the citrus-soaked cherries.

It was bliss.

"Thank…you…Acirema," Foxlaris croaked.

"It was so good…so…so good," added Foxtamas between struggles to burp. Beside him, the jackalope couldn't move. He looked dead. Hopefully just asleep, but with how plump his belly…

"You're welcome. Just…just remind me not to drink so much next time." She rolled over on her side and sighed into the sand. The grime clinging to her dress hem was the least of her worries.

The day carried on. Sailing on calm waves towards the East, the sun sparked out across the waters, warming the bodies recovering from the indulgence. Foxtamas, feeling his sickness wain, called over to the others strewn about the shore.

"Y'all…still wanna play? I brought a book."

"Aye!" The words suddenly brought Bunns back to life. He dusted off the sand from his fur and wiggled the rest off his ears. "Ah was just thinkin' tha' same thing, Scottoh."

"I suppose so," the princess replied, "and I still have my veil if we want to continue our knights game."

"Nae nae, lassie, Ah know somethin' *far* better than tha'."

The hair on Foxtamas' neck froze. His eyes sped to the rising Foxlaris. A twitch of his brother's eye told him all he needed to know before jumping to action.

"Uh, um, D-Dwarves! Yes, I got the book right here, Sir Brandishwill, a good one, right?" he shot out, stammering along the way.

Bunns cocked his ear and stared him over. Those bold, brown eyes pierced right through his trembling soul. Foxtamas held out the sunset-crossed cover like a shield. Every beat of his heart sounded like an arrow thumping off the side.

Come on! He had to agree! They didn't need another fight, especially not today!

"Eh, tha' sounds fun. Better than the Raiders."

One clean swipe took all the sweat from the fox's brow. He shot a quick wink to his brother, receiving a sly smile in response. Foxtamas did the impossible—he saved the day.

While the others went scouting for sticks, rocks, and long leaves for hats, the orange hero stayed back. His search concerned looking for any female role for Acirema, as was her preference. Usually, she would play some damsel in distress, but that had gotten old, especially with Knights. Still, she never minded it since she got time with her friends instead of stuck alone in the cold, empty Palace.

Scanning the lines of heavy ink began to reveal his answer: Brandishwill's sister, Flourishmind. He turned the page to read more about her heroic exploits when a lead piece fell out, followed by a loose sheet of parchment. Surprised, Foxtamas grabbed the pair and looked them over.

What were they doing there? His paws unfolded the sheet and revealed an old slice of schoolwork (always taught by Mrs. Cammont) stashed away for some safe keeping. The fox brushed it off. He tucked both parts near the back cover and focused again on the dwarf.

And yet the spotted brown paper peaked out from the top.

His blue eyes wandered over the scene around him. They landed on the swaying leaves and blooming petals of the Mechmilne edge so enrapturing they threatened to turn his pupils green; they floated along the wide open sky, beautiful crests of cornflower flushes peaked by the powder of clouds; they cascaded down Nohsis' ripples and the flares and flows far and far to the turn of the bend where the waters said their farewells and forwarded on their journey; and, finally, they landed amongst his friends, practicing with their sticks, tossing up the rocks, and giggling at their own antics. What a mystery they all ended up together. The princess, the peasant, the orphans—all playing as one.

That did the trick. Though he could not say it verbally, his heart felt the stir and pushed the lead piece into his hand and paper upon his knee. Right as the trio ventured back to the quilt, he read over his work.

To WHOEVER THIS MAY COME TO:

TODAY IS VERY BEAUTIFUL, WITH ME AND MY FRIENDS BURYING A CAPSULE WHICH CONTAINS OUR DEAREST WISHES. THE THING I WISHED FOR WAS TO HONOR MY FRIENDS IN SOME WAY. THEY ARE VERY CLOSE TO ME, AND I WOULD DO ANYTHING FOR THEM. I HOPE WHOEVER FINDS THIS MAY ONE DAY HAVE FRIENDS SUCH AS I DO. I AM WRITING THIS SMALL NOTE TO SAY THANK YOU TO THEM FOR ALL THEY HAVE GIVEN ME. I ORIGINALLY WAS GOING TO WRITE THIS AND SHOW THEM, BUT ACIREMA HAD AN EMPTY BOTTLE, SO WHY NOT SEND IT ON DOWN THE RIVER? ONCE WE SEND IT OFF, I'M SURE THEY WILL BE SMILING. HOW COULD THIS RIVER BRING ANYTHING OTHER THAN IT? THANK YOU FOR READING THIS, WHOEVER YOU MAY BE!

~ FOXTAMAS SCOTTSWORTH

"Scottoh! Weh found some real strong ones. Yer got tha' lass?" asked Bunns, hopping over and tossing down a fat pile of sticks. They'd make the perfect sword/axe/lance/spear.

"Oh, eh, right!" Foxtamas replied. He hastily rolled up the letter, careful to not smudge the writing, and slipped it into the empty bottle of Cherry Sugar Fizz and replaced the cork.

"Oooooh, wha' yer got there?" pointed out Bunns, "ah letter for lil' miss Aster?"

As hard as he tried, Foxtamas knew he couldn't hide his blush. Instead, he tossed the book over and pushed the bottle behind his back.

"Stop, I-I-I don't even like her."

"Mhhhmmmmm. Who's tha' for then?"

"No one, it's a secret. But look," he pointed the attention to the book and away from himself, "Acirema can be Flourishmind, Brandish-will's sister." Bunns nodded, but his smirk refused to fade.

"If yer say so. And Ah'm gonna bae ol' Brandywilly?"

"Yeah. Me and Foxlaris will take the dwarf lords, Eobin and Bwayine Wolverton." Foxtamas adored playing such a role. The Dwarven Lords of the Fulnoa, the twin-mountain stronghold and capital of dwarven culture, sent thrills through his rags.

"An' wha' do they do?"

"They're the ones who hire Brandishwill after his victory at Castle Oldekrag. He goes out to stop an assassin that's trying to kill the Dwarf Lords. But it turns out to be his sister!"

"Hah! Meh and Queenie warrin' then, eh?"

"Yup! Now go and get them so we can start!"

With a salute, Bunns bounded off with hollers. It bought the fox just enough time to slip the bottle from his back and into the River. It bobbed deep before bouncing to the surface and tumbling its way along the waves. Away sailed his wishes. His hope. His endearment for the moment he lived within. Even at such a tender age, the fox knew that the joy pounding in his chest needed to be shared. It had nowhere to go but out. And around the River's bend.

He waved goodbye.

The war of sibling dwarves rang loud and clear. Brandishwill crossed his "sword" with the "axe" of Flourishmind. The pair battled in the sandy court of Eobin and Bwayine where both Lords overlooked from their "thrones." Funnily enough, they resembled two jutting rocks beneath the forest's edge. They whispered back and forth secrets of Brandishwill's mission. Had they *known* of his sister's true identity? Was it all a set up from the start!? Why, if he caught word from the fight below, he'd certainly turn his weapon upon them! But Flourishmind gave him enough worry with her flails and fury. The cracks of their clashes snapped over the River's waters. It blared like the chopping of a tree, the sizzling rise of a cicada buzz in the summer heat.

All Evon stirred around the four. The waters trickled. Branches swung. Hearts surged.

So, too, did the bottle. As it jumbled down the watery road, only but a few miles south, it slunk past a crooked wooden sign beaten into the Western shore. The stamped white print across it shouted out its message:

LAND SURVEYED AND RESERVED BY THE CITY OF MIKYILL

CONSTRUCTION SOON UNDERWAY

6

"INTO A THRONG OF HEARTBEATS GATHERED"

Hot Stew! Hot Bread! Hot Drinks!

The rising bustle and boisterous jostle of the Winthropian feast couldn't be a pinch more festive. Family after family wiggled their way in, minding the creaking door and sullen planks, packing the Cammont Household fuller than grits overflowing out a cornmeal bag. The rowdy Minnel Squirrel Bunch had arrived early to stir the pot (as usual); though, Mrs. Kobochaun's growing number of relatives made *quick* work outshining them. Dr. Wardly avoided attention by sneaking through his Butterswath casks that just about toppled the star-crossed skunk lovers of Wrinkle Deffmire and Elisha Toffleton twirling about the tables. Mrs. Elnin Quiver and the old Madam Olfstone were already consumed in conversation about the pair. Mr. Lozno Quiver, though, that sporadic jackrabbit, ordered all three Solberry sisters on where to place their cakes and puddings. They barely fit amongst the loaves baked by Dovely and Lilliana of House Writ. It wasn't as if the doves were going to eat what they'd brought—within the hour they'd be gone. The last remnants of such a once-prominent house needed to keep up appearances one way or another.

More pouring of folk, more smushing inside the broken home. By the time the party was *actually* meant to begin, so many smells, songs, and shouts consumed the cabin that no one knew *what* to think! All that mattered was that the party had begun. And a party it would be!

"Gonna be a real lively one tonight, Corly!" joked the otter Mrs.

Jillengilch as she passed by Corlawn. The jackalope finished serving the first taking of stew to the Faunorado Twins before turning to her, laughing.

"Aye! Ah hope Ah made enough!"

"You'll be fine, hun, promise. Say, your boys here? I know Jest and the girls'll probably wanna see 'em."

Oh, she could've slapped her antlers off. The *boys!* After the trio arrived home from battle, she sent them to wash the mud and sand from their fur and make their room at least *appear* decent. Having little means didn't mean they had to have little decency, too. But once the guests started arriving and food needed serving, she lost track. Were they still locked in the midst of chores? Did they even make it back!

"Boys! Boys!" Corlawn shouted, weaving her way to the room. "Yer in there—"

The door swung open to an empty room. A tidied one, thankfully, but still void of her children who'd already scrambled off and into the fray of the feast.

The boys swam through the ocean of Winthropians. They darted past badgers and shimmied around doves and just about crashed into the conversation of a clurichaun and mole. All three smelled the freedom hung thick in the air. One part an aroma of mildewed wood and upturned dirt; the other simmered sugar pressed into a drink.

The casks of Butterswath looked just as golden as they remembered. Bunns snatched up a wooden tankard from the barrel's side and dipped it in, waves of white fizz bubbling around the scoop. It tasted better than the last feast the Wardenson's held. Carmel coated his mouth and stung his gums with sweetness. Like honey right off the comb.

"Hurry oup laddies, get your fill! Ah reckon they'll drain this barrel before weh can get tae eat!" said Bunns, tossing over their cups.

"Ho ho, I'm certain you'll get more than plenty, Mister Cammont."

The boys whipped around and found the elderly goat chuckling from behind. His graying fur and unremarkable waistcoat matched his soft, squinted eyes and smile spread wide. Few faces beamed meeker than that of Dr. Wardly.

"Weh'll bae seein' 'bout tha', Doc. Ah ain't even had a lick o' stew yet!"

"Same here. I bet the three of us could drain the whole keg if you let us," popped in Foxlaris, finally sipping the wonders of Butterswath. While not as pompous and rare as Cherry Sugar Fizz, the drink quenched the same spot.

"I wouldn't doubt it, no, not at all. But, um, guessin' you fellas heard the news today, yes? 'Bout Yarly—or, um, Miss Tilly?" A deeper wrinkle creased over his forehead. News of Aisar and the Watchers always stayed far from his tongue; at least, until the moment demanded it.

Foxtamas paused his drinking to glare at the goat's black eyes. The commotion around him cackled about as clearly as the vase smashing on the road. He'd left the thought of Miss Tilly and Opel behind with his wishes. It felt like bad luck to think about them again.

"Um, yeah, I did," he squeaked. "I...I was walking about and saw them take her. W-Wasn't pretty, Doc."

"Mmm, so I've heard. Rattled us older folk for certain. All we've been talkin' 'bout. But, see, I ask y'all 'cause it seems to have hurt one of your other friends." His mug pointed over to the window corner. Beneath the peeling paint sat three younger girls: the otter Jest Jillengilch, the clurichaun Hopewell Kobochaun, and, with her head low and tears hot, the fox Asterlyn Carventon. "I reckon she's taking it harder than the rest of us, Tilly bein' her guardian an' all. I'd try to say somethin', but..." The Doctor nodded to the three and winked. "Y'all might be of better help."

Foxtamas' heart clenched. But not as tight as his fist.

"We will," he said before bustling to the corner. Foxlaris and Bunns leapt after him, wading through the waves of the crowded room.

The girl swept away another volley of tears. Mangled, rashy tracks had burned down her peach-colored cheeks. Although her friends spoke words as soothing as balm, nothing stopped her crying. She glanced up anticipating their smiles. Instead, she got Foxtamas. Blue eyes blazing with passion, but body frozen to inaction by the fear of the situation.

"Oh, leave her 'lone, Foxtamas, she don't wanna talk right now," Jest shouted to him. Hopewell threatened to push him aside.

"I-I know, b-but I saw it. I saw her." They were the only words the poor fox could mutter. His tail tucked between his legs. What kind of a thing to say was *that!*

Still, it made Asterlyn's ears perk and green eyes, still misted over, focus on the boy.

"Y-Y-You...saw her? Miss Tilly?" asked her hoarse, croaking voice. A whole day of weeping had eroded much of her usual sweet sound.

"Uh, yeah, yeah I did. A-And they didn't hurt her, I swear it. They just took her up to the Palace and into the dungeons for a bit, no nailin' or stuff like that. I remember him sayin' it's just a week in there, nothing more."

His foot shook and hands twitched and teeth rattled at the end of his words as Asterlyn's quivering face took everything in. Deep scarlet hues flushed through the pink of her coat. Though wrapped in sackcloth like the rest of the kids, nothing detracted from her rosy cheeks, quiet smile, and long ears that folded in on themselves.

Foxtamas found himself distracted by her the more he spoke. Bunns and Foxlaris could make their jokes, but he *did* like her, and he would die a painful death if either knew it. To him, she was perfect. Her upbringing, well, a little less so.

Her father, Foxryn, fled from the Grand City of Mikyill after having been the prime suspect of his wife's murder, a crime never solved. He found a job as a Watcher and took the chance to lie low and rear his girl. But the post didn't last long. Only a few months in, a warring band of thieves left Foxryn dead west of the village. His babe fell into the custody of Miss Tilly, the first to claim her. Asterlyn found a home with the groundhog. She raised her like a flower (no different than how she raised her son before being drafted as a Watcher). Watered by love, pruned for the best growth, given the whole of Winthrop to bury deep her roots. Without her, she'd have been chaff flailing in the wind. A free-falling feeling she'd felt the entire day.

"How'd you hear all that?" Aster finally asked back.

"Oh, uh, you're not gonna believe me, but—"

"Don't you lie to her, Scottsworth!" Hopewell threatened.

"Tell me." The fox sniffled and tried to focus on the boy's face. The edge of her smile returned.

"Well...I snuck through the Palace this morning. I didn't mean to, but it was that or be late to meeting Acirema and Bunns and I was gonna feel bad so I just, um...slipped in. I crawled under the benches and heard Aisar talking to the Watchers who brought her in, and—"

Without warning, Asterlyn's face twisted again. Not to cry, but laugh. Foxtamas and two girls exchanged worried looks.

"*You* snuck in the *Palace!* I-I-I can't believe it!" she squeezed through her giggles.

"I did!"

"No way!"

His cheeks burned.

"I can try and be a bit brave sometimes, y'know!"

"Sure you can!" Seeing her smile, the weight and fear of such a daring excursion lifted from Foxtamas' shoulders.

It paid off. The risk was worth it.

"I don't think she'll be in for a week." Foxlaris popped up from behind his brother. He bolstered up his posture and wiped the foamy moustache from the Butterswath off his lip. "Dr. Wardly said he, the Old Boys, and Miss Tilly's friends'll be raking up some funds to try and free her tomorrow morning."

How Asterlyn jumped at such words! She sprang up from the corner and wrapped her arms around both Scottsworth brothers.

"Oh, goodness, goodness me! Are you sure?"

"I just talked to the Doc about it."

"Come on then!" She pulled back and grabbed their hands instead.

"We gotta go thank him! And Foxtamas, you can tell me all about the Palace after." Before they sped off, however, she cut a look back at the pair. "He *did* go in the Palace, right?"

"Hundred percent," Foxlaris replied. "Saw him fall out from the window myself." He winked at his brother. His brother winked back.

Brotherhood spoke its hidden words.

While the foxes traveled off, Bunns caught sight of his mother topping off bowls of soup for the Celtys, the elderly skunk couple.

"Mum! Mum!" he called out. His floppy feet and growing antlers knocked past two of the Solberry fauns. "Mum, are Dah and Reinden going tae make et?"

Just hearing that name made her ears fall limp. She set the empty pot down on nearest table and turned to Bunns, but it was too late. He read the news off her face.

"Oh, mah baby, Ah'm so sorry. Et ain't lookin' like et. He ain't sure when they'll finish their watch."

"Yer sure?" His voice petered out, wobbly and soft.

"Ah am, baby. Ah wish they were here tae."

Her peppy-stepped son flopped into a chair. Months had passed since they got a night off duty. It felt like none of the Watchers did anymore. Would the only way of seeing him be to join the guard when he came of age? Then would he be with his family? Then would he finally stand up against the tyrant? Or would he have to—

"But don't bae givin' oup hope, hear meh?" Corlawn's voice pulled him up from his spiraling thoughts. She bent down and looked him right in the eyes. Paw pushing up the limp ears. "They'll bae back. Roihelm'll look down after 'em an' have 'em back 'fore yer know et."

"Promise?"

The mother smiled and planted a kiss on his forehead.

"Promise. Now go have some fun, y'hear?"

Nodding, the jackalope slumped off. His feet dragged; his eyes kept low. Back to the barrels he went.

The Scottsworths found the poor soul on his third pint of 'Swath, belly bulging out. Bunns took another swig without care. He didn't need to tell the boys what happened. They knew. They always did.

Instead, the three refilled their tankards and watched the raving dally on. Buzz of this, noise of that, and an endless shuffling of sounds sloshed through Household. Nothing much worth hearing unless they were inclined to learn more of Wardenson's garden renovations or the trouble Missla Privvy got into on her journey back from Tresbotton. Bunns listened only to his own voice.

That fat, stinking, worthless *rat!* He nailed his cousin. Stole his father and brother. Jailed Miss Tilly. Pressured his own daughter. Robbed countless sons. Oppressed the entire village. Evil bubbled up from that Palace like a sick sludge and poisoned every Winthropian. Were they just supposed to take it on the chin? Another punch beside the bruises inflicted by poverty, hunger, cold, and death?

No!

They'd so easily forgotten their worth. Aisar could stride in right now and tell them his plans to slaughter them and most would offer up their own knives! That point would come soon enough. Bunns knew it.

He had to fight back. Opel, Gregabbit, Reinden, Miss Tilly, *Acirema,* all of them deserved more than the lives they led. His first instinct told him to take a pair of stars, march through the Palace doors, and fling them at his eyes, but Winthrop would only fall to chaos—and he'd fall dead, no doubt. Bunns needed something else. Something to make the rest of the Village wake up to the nightmare haunting their lives.

And it was at that very moment a string of notes trickled in his ears as the cold Butterswath went down his throat.

Bunns flipped around and saw Tihrio and Driftlok, two vagabond falcons stationed in Winthrop, starting the feast music. A simple tune on their fiddles and snares livened the occasion to a grander, more flavorful degree. Gave the ceaseless noise a comforting hug from behind.

For Bunns, it slapped him like Corlawn tanning his hide.

"Laddies!" He screamed through a gurgle of drink. "Get tae the room, hurry! Ah know wha' weh're doin' next!"

"You gonna sing?" Foxlaris asked, topping off his mug before heading out.

"Better. Ah'm goin' tae *perform!*"

All the work tidying up the room became history long forgotten. The three boys twirled in a swirl of upturned sheets and quilts slung from bunk to bunk as Bunns fired off commands.

"Scottoh, grab mah pillow, nae, mine *and* yers. Rizzeh, mah blanket for the cape."

"Bunns, what in *Evon* are you planning?" Foxlaris asked, tying the wool sheet around his friend's neck.

"Ah'm thinkin' of callin' et an "Ode" like them fancy peddlers do. Et'll bae about our ol' friend—Mr. Kingy!"

Giggles escaped the trio as Foxtamas stuffed the pillows snuggly under his tunic. Puffed out as their liege, Bunns *did* make a striking resemblance to Aisar.

"I think you look the part alright," started the younger fox, "but don't you think it's still a bit, well, mean? It's still Acirema's dad and all—,"

The smile slipped off Bunns' face, replaced by a still, somber countenance. He looked up at Foxtamas' blue eyes with a stare firm and cold.

"Ah don't give ah rip, lad. Tha' brute's taken mah Dah, mah brother, Queenie's freedom, Miss Tilly from yer Aster, *everything* from these folk. Ah'm takin' ah stand for them, lettin' them see wha' they've gone blind tae. Da' tae the Queenie or not. And Ah *know* yer ain't blind tae et either."

"N-No, I'm not—"

"Then weh got tae do this. Who else will?"

The fox, more so than ever before, felt Bunns' pain. He knew their sparse meals. The stale taste in the air without Mr. Cammont home. When he looked into the jackalope's eyes, he didn't see some kid wanting to pull a fun joke. He saw fury.

"I know...I do." Foxtamas tried to hide his snort. "But I think you could use a *bit* more than that."

A couple strokes of the lead piece left the jackalope a whole new boy. Bulging gut, flowery, faux cape, scraggly, sagging stripes, and a belt crown holding up two soggy paper ears—was Aisar *actually* in the building!?

Bunns rattled from glee. He snatched up his Banjalope (an altered fiddle passed down the Cammont line) and headed for the door, beaming at what the crowd outside would think.

"Wait, what about the song? You got one?" Foxlaris asked before they left. The new ruler cocked his head back over the pillows and winked.

"Yer King's got et covered."

As the drifters finished up their rendition of "Lepstro's Lament" upon the main table, a small scurry was underway. The Scottsworths did their best to try and hide Bunns as he squirmed to the "stage." They caught stray glances that turned to scoffs from Madam Olfstone and Mrs. Elnin, yet sent the baby otter Ttey Jillengilch into a rolling fit of laughter. Once close, the jackalope leapt onto the table and shouted to his audience.

Shock, awe, laughter, and cheer all sprang up at the sight of Bunns—or, rather, King Aisar. He strutted about, staring down at his subjects with dainty eyes and a prowling gaze.

"Wha's all this! My peasants havin' ah feast without *meh!*" the sovereign declared while trying to stifle his jackalopian accent. "No invitation! No request! Not even my *Watchers* knew! You can't do tha' to me! No tellin' how much food I've missed out on!" The roaring laughter rattled the very foundation of the Cammont Household. "Just got *one* pot of stew, eh? Whip up ten more an' I'll have a fine start to breakfast!" He made sure to jiggle the pillows like a rumbling gut. That move made even the straightest of faces break.

"Well, I can *not* let this go on any longer! To feast without your King? Horrid! Horrific! One may even call it an *Aisar*-ry sight!"

"You can't do that!" shouted little Morely Kobochaun. The little clurichaun tried jumping up to the table. In response, the king bent down with an exaggerated bow and gasped in pure shock.

"What's this? You *dare* disobey your *liege?*"

"This *our* party!" the boy rebutted.

"But this is *my* Village!"

"Nu-uh!"

"Uh-huh!"

"You ain't 'vited!" Morely fired off (to the cackles of the adults surrounding him). Aisar tumbled back as if struck by an arrow. His hands folded atop his bulging belly, head shaking to the point of the crown unbuckling.

"I could have y'all nailed for such inorbordination or whatsyacallit! But the smell of that soup and bread and 'Swath makes my tum beat louder than my brain. So, I'll join your 'festivities'. In fact, I've got here a song tha' y'all just might like. They kept singing it in the dungeons so much I learned it in my sleep!"

The chuckles and hollers continued, and the dutiful Banjalope emerged. With strings tightened and the whole village clapping, the jester jackalope started his jig with a tap of his foot and flash of his grin.

> Who's the one who'll make ya' run to pay?
> Aisar! Aisar!
> This big ol' slug ain't moved all day!
> The obese King of Winthrop!

> Who's the one who'll tax an empty keg?

Aisar! Aisar!
I heard him call f'eight turkey legs!
The glutt'nous King of Winthrop!

Who's the one who'll nail ye right on through?
Aisar! Aisar!
Remember all those foes he "slew"?
The lying King of Winthrop!

There's just one man who could make me cry,
Aisar! Aisar!
Just shoot an ar'rer right in me eye!
The wor-er-er-rst King, of, *Winthrop!*

Glorious!
They called it.
Stupendous!
If the soup had made you sick, the drinks had run dry, the con-versation had turned sorry, well this, why, it could *only* make you jump for joy! The entire night lit up with praise abounding. Bunns hopped down, bowing time and time again, unable to free himself from the hands and hugs grabbing at his quilted cape. It seemed that Winthrop had finally taken a liking to his antics. And their king.

Before Foxtamas could reunite with the boy, Mrs. Cammont ap-proached with a basket and golden flask.

"Foxtamas, dearie, Ah promised Lady Acirema ah plate from tonight. Would yer mind bringin' et oup tae her?" she asked, her face a mix of concentrated exhaustion yet palpable energy.

"Oh, yes, will do, Mrs. Cammont."

"Thank yer so much, laddie. Don't stay too long, yer may miss the dance!"

The fox nodded and headed towards the door. Before slipping out, he took one last look at Bunns. Never had he smiled like that. Cheeks high enough to blind him. The jackalope knew what he'd done. He could touch the moon and not feel as accomplished. The people saw their ruler for what he was, dancing and singing of his own sins on stage. That's all the raccoon was—a joke. And if they could push back against that, then…

Nothing could stop the citizens of Village Winthrop.

Foxtamas cut through the waning evening air. The speckled twilight behind him cast a murky shadow on the road above. At first his frantic feet darted amongst the houses out of caution. However, the further he went, the quicker he realized no Watchers were making their rounds. Perhaps they all knew of the party and only dared watch from afar; some may have gotten jealous and recalled voluntarily. Regardless, they were up, and the fox's job became plenty easier.

With the guard withdrawn, Foxtamas approached the oaken doors for the second time that day. This excursion would be *far* less invasive. He shimmied to the fresh cut grass on the Palace's left and caught sight of a small bit of rope dangling from an upper window. Both his grin and pace hastened.

There, sitting amongst the wispy, waving grass, feet dangling off the edge of the hill, gaze engaged with the bleeding sun cascading down the horizon, was Acirema. She looked almost too peaceful to bother with a meal dedicated to her father's downfall…

Almost.

"Pssst, Acirema," Foxtamas whispered, sneaking over with basket and flagon extended.

"Foxta—why—oh! Yes!" Her hands graciously reached out and grabbed the food, looking through the tasty selection prepared.

"Mrs. Cammont said she promised you a plate." "I'm glad she did! Her cooking's my favorite, you know."

"And they say y'all live like kings up *here!*"

The pair giggled on for a bit. Foxtamas found him a soft seat next to her on the cliffside. Its point overlooked the entire village, hiding the tarnish and worry. Life up there felt so, so separated to the fox, elevated past what he knew. The same could be said from the view below.

"So why are you outside? If your father knew you were sneaking out, he'd—"

"I know. But he called all the Watchers in and is dealing with some Ratatoskr business. I needed a place to, um…think, and practice my poetry, and there's no better spot," she replied, tearing off bits of the flaky bread before biting in.

"Poetry? Mind if I hear it?"

One sip of soup later and Acirema produced her inked draft, penned in flowery font on the Palace's gilded parchment.

It seeps down from space's palette,
covered in colors of sky.
Slowly it crawls on the evening,
with every dweller ne'er questioning why.

Beautifully it is setting,
not seen until early morn,
it kisses the earth with evening rays;
the nighttime moon soon to be born.

The claps of Foxtamas boomed just about loud enough to alert the Watchers inside.

"Acirema! That was great!" the fox proclaimed. He couldn't help but laugh as she blushed and rolled up the work.

"Why thank you. It was just some throwaway stanzas I was working on, though. I've still got so much to learn."

"Well, I'll tell ya', you got a real knack for it."

Acirema smiled softly. While she finished the last of her soup, Foxtamas leaned back and took in the inspiration for the poem.

He thought she nailed the sight. The sunset spanned across the entire sky, puffed by the streaking clouds spread like violets mixing on a palette. A broad staunch of trees guarded its bottom edge mere feet past the pulsing lights of the Cammont Household. Their blazing canopies reminded him of how campfires consume pine needles in a crackling spit. Beyond, he glared out at the pale blue hum of ridges rising against the horizon. They encircled not only the hill upon which Winthrop sat, but the whole of Evon, Nohsis just a silver tear between them, glinting hues of pink and lavender.

Yet…the beauty only reminded him of what Bunns' had said. Was he, too, about to get distracted from the larger issues at hand? He saw *firsthand* what Aisar did, both the crime and its effect. How much longer could it go on?

His head sunk low. Things had to get better…right? Somehow. Somehow they had to. He wanted a force to dethrone Aisar. He wanted everyone to be safe again. He wanted every day spent with his friends and family in perfect peace. What could get them there? Who possibly could? He had no way to help. He couldn't fight, he couldn't lead, he couldn't even stand on his own. It couldn't be hopeless…it just couldn't be.

"Why can't you be queen now?"

The words blurted from his mouth without him even realizing. Acirema, thoughts also wandering, was ripped back to reality.

"What?" she asked.

Foxtamas didn't know what to say.

"I-I mean, things would be so much better. We would have feasts for you, not against you. We'd be happier, people wouldn't be hurt—,"

"But Foxtamas," she began, staring into his blue eyes darting everywhere but her face, "I'm not ready for that. The only way I'll ever reign is if my father steps down or dies, and I don't think that is happening soon. Until then I'm just a…a mixed up, small, little anxious princess that doesn't know what she's doing."

"Hey, don't say that! You're taller than Bunns—"

"No, I mean it, Foxtamas." She tucked her knees tight to her chest and rested her chin upon them. A quiver rumbled up to her lip. "I…I heard what you told them. About Opel."

Foxtamas felt his face pale.

"Oh no…Acirema, I—"

But she turned away, out of reach from his hug. Foxtamas tried to shuffle closer, but she wouldn't allow it. "It's not your fault! I just didn't want you getting upset about it, y'know, a-a-and Bunns, he's not mad! He said it wasn't your burden to bear—"

"But it *is*." The princess, tears dripping down her stripes, whipped back around. "I'm that monster's daughter. My friend's cousin won't ever walk again because of *him!* What's that make me then?"

"It makes you our *friend*." Foxtamas finally stole her full attention. He crept closer and put both hands on her shoulders. "We know you're not like that. I saw him today with my own eyes and I can't even believe y'all are related."

"Aren't you ever scared I'll *become* him, though? That evil, or sickness, whatever's inside of him, that's inside me too. It has to be."

"I'm scared of a lotta things," the fox chuckled. "But that's not one of them." His hands fell, grasping hers. "You're gonna be the best queen this village is ever gonna have. You aren't sick like him. You aren't evil like him. Even if you nailed everyone down there you still wouldn't be on his level, got me?" Acirema again tried to look away only for Foxtamas to squeeze her palms tight. "And the best part is you still got time. You get to plan and get ready all you like, so when you do wear that crown and sit on that throne, you'll have been doing queen stuff for *years!* How good's that!"

"Pretty…pretty good."

"Exactly!"

His enthusiasm caused her to giggle and finally glance up at his eyes, slick and sparkling in the fading sunset hues. "So don't get too worried about it. We'll be right here with you. All of Winthrop will be. Okay?"

"Okay," mumbled the princess. She pulled herself free from the fox's grip and, in return, hugged him.

Close. Swaying. Foxtamas worried they'd swing right off the cliff's edge. "Thank you."

"Of course," he replied. Both pulled away and smiled at the other.

"You're right. We do have a lot of growing up to do. All of us."

"Some more than others," he chuckled, nodding down to the Cammont Household.

"*You* included," Acirema laughed. "Who knows what it's gonna be like when we're adults."

"This place'll be much better off."

"Besides that. Like who will we be? Who will we meet?" Flurries of the violet light on the wind pushed through her fur. They turned the white above her eyes a pale mauve, like dawn setting a fire a dew-dripped field. She'd give anything to stay warmed by the glow. "What will happen?"

"I dunno." Foxtamas replied with wonder in his voice. A quiet, terse sound. He too stared off. Not to the sun, but to the ridges, the River, the expanse hidden behind the veil of the horizon. "But it'll be a good story. That's for sure."

The princess nodded.

"Yeah...it will be. As good as Brandishwill and Flourishmind?"

Smirking, the fox pinched his nose at her, cheeks rising past his eyes.

"*Way* better than that!"

"But we haven't finished playing it all out yet! Flourishmind's still in hiding after leaving her brother for dead."

"Just you wait. It'll be good, but I think we can do better."

"Better than warring dwarves?

"*Easily!*"

The friends fell back into the grass in a fit of laughter. Their conversation turned to the details of the story, of Brandishwill's revenge, the hidden scheme of Bwayine, the even *more* hidden scheme of Eobin, all of it. Slowly, it phased into plans for another fort and a summer outing to the pond, one with all the Cammonts when they had time off. The sky phased too. Purples sank first to periwinkle, and in a blink, navy. The clouds disguised themselves. Stars blinked, awoken for their day.

Once night fully took over Evon, the pair knew it time to depart. Foxtamas gathered up the bowl and plate and made his faux curtsy to the young majesty.

"Goodnight, Acirema," he waved before heading off.

"Goodnight to you too, Foxtamas. And thank Mrs. Cammont for the meal!"

Like an orange whisper, the fox slipped behind the Palace and into the crisp blanket of nightfall.

The boy arrived back to a soft fiddle song warming the home. The guests were all slow dancing with one another in a memorial for Opel and the rest who'd been taken and tortured that morning. He took his steps quietly so as to avoid interruption, seeking his friend and brother through the swinging folk. As he skirted along the wall, he noticed far across the room four figures in particular. Two were Mrs. Cammont teaching Bunns how to dance, hushing him not to grow angry at his mistakes. The other was Foxlaris. Holding Asterlyn in his arms, swaying to the strings.

An arrow pierced Foxtamas' heart. A sword impaled his gut. The executioner's axe fell swift on his orange, furry neck, dropped by his own kin.

But he knew he shouldn't be upset. Was Foxlaris not the stronger of the brothers? Didn't he keep his cool and offer *real* help when need be? Of the people he'd just wondered about, who'd go on to make Winthrop a better place, Foxlaris topped the list. Aster needed a fox like that. Someone stable, firm. Not someone who just stood by, or…or got scared by every little thing.

Foxtamas admired his brother. He always did. He'd do anything for just an ounce of his stoicism, passion, drive. It's why he knew then, watching the melody drift over their closed eyes and beating chests, that he had no right to interrupt that peace.

The jealousy stung his throat like expired Cherry Sugar Fizz. To think, only moments earlier he'd imagined such a bright future. One where he and the rest of his fellowship would grow into something better than themselves.

But Foxtamas…he couldn't. He wouldn't.

In the face of trials, he saw the real him emerge. One of fear and envy.

He was nothing. Not to Asterlyn, not to himself. Just a scared, little fox.

The wall ended at the edge of his shared room, and Foxtamas Scottsworth chose to retire for the night. No one noticed him gone. As the Quiver's and Rattly's left, followed shortly by the well-worn Minnel squirrels and skunk lovers and Dr. Wardly rolling the bone-dry kegs, he preferred it that way. No good tidings or goodbyes. Just the damp quiet of sleep.

King Aisar was keeping himself busy. Usually that was the job of such a feast, especially when word spread of it being held in his dishonor. Watchers may be called, arrests certainly made. But tonight was different. He only knew the Cammonts were putting it on, the very same Cammonts dear Acirema ran around with. Terrible place to find friends, just terrible. But Aisar tried not to mind. He wanted his daughter happy, after all. Despite his reservations.

Though, was that not his own ambition? To find happiness in his place and squeeze prosperity from it? Father said it best himself, that Roihelm had given them this spot in life, and failure to make use of it was failure to Evon. The command stuck with him. So much so that it was what directed his attention away from the malice of the miscreants and towards the visitor behind him.

"Shall I read it again, Your Grace?" asked the nut-brown squirrel standing in Aisar's lavish quarters. The whicker of lantern light revealed his short, agile stature. He bore an acorn cupule upon his head (most likely from a seed cluster of northern trees) large enough for a cap. The tips of his ears, a bright silver, poked through while his long, chestnut colored tail lay tied through a small hole in the back. Running his blistering paces over the ridges, creeks, fields, towns, and streets of Evon required it, but when off the routes, he kept it up to complete the composure of his attire.

Two long sashes adorned his body. Both were covered with parcels, letters, and scrolls, and the larger bag at his side carried the more important, fragile cases. No part of the squirrel was without purpose. As part of the Ratatoskr—the legion of squirrels employed to carry news and mail from one corner of the West to the other—he didn't have a choice.

"No need, Ruel. I can only be subjected to one reading of Gniw's 'eloquence'. Paraphrase." The king continued staring out his window. His seeking gaze lingered at the Cammont Household. Too many lights. Too loud.

"Yes, Your Grace. He asks for certainty in your Bridge Pledge. Says it will take plenty more than your current offer to put you at the level of ownership you asked for. Other larger contributions have already been made."

"From individuals?"

"Yes."

"Not collective?"

"No, Your Grace. No village nor town." Ruel Burrowfoot had only been made Parcelage a month prior. It got him off going door-to-door to deliver letters. Instead, alongside leading the Central Evon troupe, he entertained any and every important leader from any and every important place. Aisar included.

"Tell me if I'm wrong here, Ruel, but it seems to me that feather-brain thinks we're, what, too small to help?"

"Seems so," the squirrel nodded. He did his best to agree with those he served rather than ruffle feathers or fur. "See? Only needed it once." The king's obese, wobbling mass moved from the view and started to strut, finally allowing the drops of moonlight to trickle in. "Too small, though. Too small, too small, too small. What a notion." His night gown barely scraped past Ruel, carrying with it a half-hearted lavender meant to conceal his smell. "Be honest—do you think me evil?"

A hard swallow from the squirrel.

"Oh, um, well, Your Grace, I've only known you a bit, so, I—"

"No, no, none of that, Ruel. You hear what they say. You carry their words, after all! Out from here and to all those who've escaped my vitriol, my thick, wicked grasp. I'm not blind. They feel they live beneath a tyrant. And who can blame them, hm?" Aisar continued his stroll with stingy picks at his chin. He rounded the curtained bed and leaned against his desk, creaking. "I'm no peach. Never tried to be. You don't get where I am, keep the peace like I do if you are. But this bridge…it changes things. Changes *everything.*" With a push, he launched back upwards, back to burying Ruel in shadow. Every step rattled the many shelves of prizes and ornaments forming his collection. Whatever he deemed too precious to keep in the vaults he stored upstairs instead.

"May I ask how so?"

"Read back what Gniw promised of the East. In his *own* words, this time."

The Parcelage scrambled through the pages of parchment for the passage.

"Right, he says…riches, vast in glory and scale, untapped resources used in the growth of currently recognized domains alongside the prospective lands conquered in name of Pledge progenitor, establishment of trade with locals of Eastern affiliation with direct influence within the central access to such lanes—"

"Yes! All that and more," said Aisar, cutting him off. "It's a feast for the starved inches from his face. Just imagine it! Rivers of gold, legions of followers, fields bursting with fruit and crop to shame all of Efeters. Think of what that could do for us! For Acirema! She'd never want again. Her life would be perfect, Ruel, perfect!" The king shook his fists. One in glee. The other fury. "What kind of father would I be to deprive the one joy of my life such splendor? How…how can I look my baby in her eyes and say I did everything to give her the life she deserved? I'm king! I've been given this village, and now I've been given the chance for a new life altogether. And I can't let that slip through my fingers."

Aisar breathed. His lids fell, and his arms relaxed. Gentle steps led him back to the window where he rested along the wooden sill. The air fluttering by carried a chill.

"Gniw won't have it all. I'll get my new kingdom. I'll rise above every downcast glance this land's ever given me."

He glared out over his subjects.

"And I need them to do it."

Ruel's silver-dipped ears perked up all their own. He couldn't believe the King's words, yet they came with no laugh, no grin to ease the tension. Aisar believed it. He'd planned it all out.

"P–Pardon, Your Grace?" asked the Parcelage.

"Come here," he motioned with the flick of a finger. "See for yourself."

Ruel crept close to the window and looming king. A light stutter quaked through his leg.

"I can tax all I want," started his speech, low in register, lost of all prior glee, but not without a prowling slick to his words. "I can arrest, I can fill the dungeon, I can nail every day I breathe. But those times have to die if we're to live the life we're destined. They're tactics to keep order, not make something of these people, or my *self*, for that matter.

"It feels like I bend to *their* will. We pick them up as stragglers, Ruel. The desolate, the downcast, the peasants no village wants. Who knows what I could've been had I not been burdened by them. A feckless question. I implement what good I can and reap only insurrections, plots for my downfall. See that house right at the bottom?"

Ruel paused his shaking to peek out, passing the murky, shadowy shapes of empty huts to the one breathing with light. He recognized the house—the Cammonts, and those two little fox boys. They were nothing but lovely, the whole lot of them. If he and the rest of his boys weren't careful on their routes, the kids would snag them and force a story or two about their latest adventures. Ruel couldn't help but embellish a bit now and then.

"They feast in my ruin." Aisar's sneer brought the squirrel back into focus. "Just earlier I had one of their relatives nailed for an assassination plot. And they're just *one* family. Think of the others. These tensions, they're far too high for my liking."

"So...you'll ease up on them, then?" asked Ruel.

"Hah! That's a word for it. But yes. I see why you got that position now." Aisar once more left the window, this time wading to a small corner table to spread a raspberry jam over his nightly toast. "Read back the other pledges. What have the others planned to do?"

"Yes, Your Grace. It says Mikyill will fund the actual construction, and the two newer Fulnoa Lords look to be supplying the builders. The other pledgers will just be more funds."

"For...?"

"Says, um...lumber costs, travel expenses, the plan for a new village Bridgeside with Inns, taverns, shops—"

"There!" shouted the King. He demolished the toast in a single bite and huffed the flakes in the direction of the squirrel. "That's our in, Ruel, that's our in! We'll give Gniw the hands to build it all." He spat, rolling back to the window and thumping the glass. "It'll give everyone down there a job, and a *real* one at that. Not whatever grain gleaning they get on with."

"Jobs as in...getting paid?"

"A fair wage—fair to me *and* them. They'll know it comes from this deal that *I* wrought. That's how we get them on my side. Yes...yes! That's it right there!"

You'd have thought Aisar mad in that moment, what with his spins and rubbing of his hands. He looked no different than a kid opening a birthday gift, or a grandfather seconds from holding his one and only granddaughter. Everything connected in that moment. For the first time in years, Aisar Feiht had a plan larger than Winthrop. Larger than *himself.*

"But, Your Grace," interrupted Ruel. The squirrel didn't find it in him to lie—the plan made sense, and if all parties agreed, would work. But the people played like pawns within it...his stomach hurt worse. In some effort to aid them, he extended part of the letter to the giggling raccoon. "President Gniw specifically requests a Top offering for a

Pledge. And if you're wanting to rub shoulders and bring Winthrop, or, um, your position to his level, well—"

Aisar scoffed.

"He'll get his Tops. That greedy bird. I'm not thick enough in the head to think he'll willingly pay these people for sole labor in return. I'll keep our taxes going. Up them, even, but ever so slightly. Then I'll pay him back his change and keep the rest—storehouse of profits to spruce up this place and prepare resources for Winthrop's second coming. *That* satisfy you?"

"Of course, Your Grace, of course. Just wanted to make sure you covered your corners with this." He bowed with a tip of his acorn cap.

"And I appreciate the sentiment. You're wide-eyed, I can see it. You get a plan like this where others wouldn't. But it's a plan that will take time. Time, I believe, we have."

Grunting, Aisar made his way to his bed and finished off the few cold drops of his nighttime tea. It came bitter to his tongue. Licks of lavender sticking to his teeth.

"Much to work through. I'll need to cut any Watcher draftee plans and reroute the program to seek joiners. The rest of those young'uns to be carpenters, stonemasons, whatever Gniw needs. Figure that means a change in tax policy too, and what that means if Winthrop grows, and oh, the prisoners!" The thoughts were too much. His striped head collapsed back onto his three-tiered pillows, aching with it a squeak from his bedframe. "Thus the life of a king, I suppose. My burden to bear for their lives, my success. And as for you, dear Parcelage. Are you commanding this area?"

Ruel nodded and replied, "Yes, Your Grace. I'm over the wider Ratatoskr grouping but serve here, in Central Evon."

"Good. I want you to be my direct line with all Bridge Pact business."

"Oh, um, I'm not sure I can—"

"Like I told you, I like you. You're bright. I need you for this to work. Your boys'll have more provisions than any other town you stop at, and, if Gniw agrees, I'll have you all a cut of Tops with it. I'm certain you'll need them to start your Eastern force. Deal?"

A flutter rose through the squirrel's chest, the same that arose from a freefall from the top of one tree to the bottom of another. Yet often that came less from the fall and more from the fear of what would come if you happened to miss.

"I...I..." The stutters drew a heavy brow from the King. "Yes, Your Grace. I'll ensure it happens."

"Good!" chuckled Aisar, clapping together his hands. "I knew I was right about you. Now go, hurry, onward, onward! Write up my response to the matter and get them to that birdbrain, *quickly*. Winthrop's future is on the line! If, say, Dink, B'Bonrey, Vawdege beats us, we'll never get off this hill. You understand?"

"Perfectly, Your Grace," shot off Ruel. The message was already tucked into the satchel dangling on his left and the knot holding his tail undone, all before Aisar lifted himself up for a better view.

"Good, good. I having a feeling, deep in this gut of mine, this Bridge will only lead to greatness. A greatness not even the brightest are ready to face. But enough of this. Fly, my boy, fly! Let this brotherhood begin!"

A deep, hopeful glimmer twinkled within his aging brown eyes. It looked of splendor, of power, outshining the waning Cammont lights below. Without it, there'd be only a barren pit. Void—an abyss. A chasm no one could clamber across.

Ruel Burrowfoot sped off into the night. With the moon as his guide, he shot past the empty houses, darting into the darkened Mechmilne Wood. The letter in his bandolier weighed terrible on his usually light chest. Even with the knowing of it being passed along and far out of his sight, the sensation remained.

It...burned.

The rest of the Ratatoskr boys followed his lead off to Mikyill, bounding faster than the wind.

A wind robbed of its sweetness.

7

"AROUND THE UNION OF TWO LOST LOVES."

10 Years Later

Tap...Tap...Tap...

If he hit the roof any harder, the slumbering faun beneath would wake. Any lighter, the thatching and wooden boards would slide right off. A fine line not to cross. But he knew what he was doing—it had been his job for quite some time.

With every fling of his mallet, Foxlaris took in a wide breath of the dawn's rising air, fresh from painting the blades below with dew. The usual pastel hues, cascading and whirling in wishing the night away, melted down the overhead sky and over the horizon. A few early-bird clouds got to work like himself. They rustled their fluffy feathers and flew, soaring soft along the pink and periwinkle paths. Every angle exuded beauty, but none greater than the one from right beneath. That was partially why the fox had woken long before any other Winthropian; the other half was more practical.

Nothing stirred. Nothing worked. Nothing bustled or hustled or ran or poked or prodded every which way.

It was quiet. It was peaceful. It gave Foxlaris the right mindset to finish the fixing of Mr. Ochet's roof. As another nail dug in, the first gleam of morning's light burst out over the land. Hot and velvet, the ray shot through the fox's brown eyes, glittering like the unearned crown atop the Palace.

Such radiance danced between the gilded pillars and doors of the immaculate building, celebrating a new day through hops on the golden roof. No one disagreed on its magnificence. But that didn't mean Foxlaris had to like it.

Everything, Palace included, had evolved in Village Winthrop. The gravel road looked white and neater; the houses were repaired, shacks renovated; new outward, ornate wooden fencing, a sign, and proper gate stood commonplace on the fringes. And it all stemmed from the Bridge Pact. Yet, despite what his fellow villagers reaped, the king sowed the seeds. Foxlaris saw right through the scheme years ago. Even after he'd taken a job from it, even after the Cammont's own house had been patched and better mannered, he looked through that grayed, bloated racoon like a fresh-wiped window. He couldn't watch the dawn until the sun plucked that ray-wrought crown from his head.

Foxlaris hated to dwell on such things, though, and kept on, moving further down to a larger, rottener hole. First, he took out the molded plank, secured the new one, and began thatching over. Simple. He did it again, and again, and again, and, once at the edge, scurried to the second row and did it again, and then, of course, again.

He *had* been at work for a while, and the repetitiveness fades the longer you're at it. Really, he came to love it. The years to build up the strength paid off, working his weaker limbs and oft sickly self. Foxlaris would take the repetition over another day spent bedridden.

But he'd been at work not just on this project. Ever since the Inn job finished down at Bridgeburrow, he, Foxtamas, and Bunns had begun their oddball carpentry gigs. Was the goofing around they would've otherwise done more fun? Every time. In fact, he missed it, craved it, even. But the effort? The pay? The, well…the worthwhile-ness? The meaning? The making something better, the rising up?

Every *Tap!* slammed down with his usual, sinking feeling. He was a single handyman among many in the smallest town in the land. The jobs only lasted because of Aisar's Pledge bringing in the extra Tops. Once that ran out, what then? He couldn't do anymore for himself, let alone his family. Yet again the fox would be stuck.

There had to be more in Evon, nay, in his life than repairing roofs and tending turnips. He *had* to make something of himself. Look at Reinden—the lad moved out to Mikyill, found a wife, and has plans for a kid last he heard. Oh, what a *dream!*

Deep down he knew he had to move on from the peasantry he was born into. He had skills scholars studied for, the practicality kings lacked. Foxlaris Scottsworth could be something.

But beyond that. A fact like the fox never liked to face…

Everyone around him, his friends, his family, were drowning in dreams. They wanted adventures that would never happen. They craved expanse and wonder, magic and silliness found only in the ink of a page. No one more so than his own brother. Foxtamas always had his health and his charm, but what did he do with it? Read? Play around? Even now, grown and working, he still lived within his own head, content with the poverty of his life. He'd rather hear about Mikyill than see it with his own eyes. He never needed the purpose or usefulness his elder brother craved.

What folly to live a life like that! Where were the workers, the doers of this world? Being amongst the dreamers only slowed him down, like tar tugging him to the bottom of their pit! He needed to break free. Get out of their grasp. Foxlaris had worked too hard to overcome his weakness, both physical and mental, to fall short now. It was time to show the world his worth.

It was time to…to…to…

Leave.

BANG!

The hidden angst powered into a culminating smash. The board beneath split to a smattering of splinters beyond any notion of repair, and the nail had been driven through ceiling. But the real trouble wasn't with the roof, nor the fox's troubled mind; it was with the waking faun below.

"Oh no, oh no, no no no…," Foxlaris gasped. Like stirring from a haunted sleep, he grappled back the pitiful thoughts he let pour out and rebuked himself for even thinking them. The sound of his pound *had,* in some way, forced the fox's eyes open. He shook his head and gazed over Winthrop a second time. By now, folks had awoken and started the hustle and bustle and running and poking and prodding every which way (Mr. Ochet included, his gruff, squinted stare angled upwards).

Something, though, was off. Their faces, they…they were giddy. Smirking, no, smiling, and smiling wide. Some laughed! Not the children, but the parents! The elders! Hugs from door to door and hurrying from house to shop to back to house.

The poor fox froze. You'd have thought him an orange chimney planted atop that roof. In his escape from the bother of Winthrop, it seemed he'd forgotten the importance of the dawn he and all the others had spent a decade desperately waiting for. Today…today was…

"Grammo Day!" cried Foxtamas, springing up from his cot, wide-eyed, drooling, ears perked up in shock. He'd, why, well, he'd slept in, but, b-b-but how!? Today was *THE* day! The only day that mattered as far as he was concerned!

The cloudy veil of dreams and sleep began to clear, welcoming back his memories of the night prior as he threw off his quilt and stumbled towards the wardrobe. He'd gone long picking the beets from Mr. Ochet's garden. The moon crept well past midnight once he'd finished. Usually around this time the elder faun would hire the trio of boys for a larger summer harvest job. Always easy work for easy pay. That is, easy if everyone showed up…

The beds of both his brother and best friend lay empty. Still.

What else could Foxtamas do but sigh?

Neither had showed up last night. Foxlaris promised to work on roof work before dawn, and Bunns, well, called in an early night on the premise of "training." It was *always* training. Foxtamas had given him a list of at least ten other excuses to use, but he never budged. Hopefully he'd made sure to get his share of the work done—'hopefully' being the one word the fox clung to for dear, precious life.

No matter, though. Today was *Grammo Day!* Such flushes of excitement and zeal couldn't be trifled by a one-off job. Foxtamas slid into his patched-up pants, stomped down into the thick, unbreakable work boots, and tossed on his favorite blue overcoat, the one with golden buttons and faded lines of patterning across the shoulders. Fashionable? Not quite. Better than his average dress? Absolutely.

In a single bound he leapt from the shared room and into the company of Mr. and Mrs. Cammont. Ever since Gregabbit's retirement from the Watchers (and Reinden's departure from Winthrop altogether), a new life swept through the Cammont Household. Holes were patched and doors greased, floors stained and walls painted. Little lanterns hung from rafter to rafter and brightened where the fire failed to reach. A new table—oblong instead of round—lay in the kitchen, a present from the boys for Mr. Cammont's retiring. Their carpentry skills came in handy. Foxlaris rethatched the roof and Foxtamas constructed new shelves and a desk for Corlawn to manage the finances. The craftsmanship warmed the home. Almost as much as Gregabbit's returned presence to his chair in which, as usual, he sprawled.

"Finally awake, eh?" The father jackalope called over in jest. He'd beaten Foxtamas to getting ready. His "slimming" green vest fit him well, joined by his lopsided cap and a fresh trim to his moustache. Gray hairs sprung up through his spread of brown and white. They matched his hue of antler perfectly.

"You know how it is working with those two," the fox replied. He slid towards the kitchen and plopped a small sack of Tops on the table, "Late nights and later mornings!"

"Oh *nae* yer don't, laddie!" came the war cry of Mrs. Cammont. She grabbed the back of Foxtamas's collar the moment the money fell, pulling him back to the point of a choke. "Yer ain't givin' us ah lick, *especially* today!"

Corlawn aged like a weathered statue. Her wrinkles deepened, set in stone, and beady (yet motherly) glare hardened. But her cheeks still carried a blush. They rose and pinched up her crow's feet when she smiled, the kind that roped the sun through a cloudy day. Never had Foxtamas seen her so spruced up. She wore a cornflower blue dress bare of any apron. Little twinkles of silver chain necklaces complimented it, sparkling like the sole, worn wedding band over her finger.

"Mrs. Cammont," the fox pleaded, "you know it's the least I can do to pay y'all back—"

"Nope! Ah won't bae hearin' et!"

"But—"

"Gregabbit!"

"Foxtamas…" Mr. Cammont needn't say much. "Ah don't think yer gonna win this." He added with it a wink from his left eye, the one half blue and half brown.

"Yer heard him, now take yer Tops an' get goin'!" Mrs. Cammont placed the sack firmly in his coat pocket and pushed him towards the door. Though, in doing so, she let her grin poke out. "Spend 'em how yer want, just *not* on us. Yer earned et, workin' like yer have."

"Fine, fine, I hear y'all. And I will. Promise." Foxtamas repaid her smile with a tilt of the head the pair always shared. Little did she know that, behind such kindness, he brewed a plot—one to go against each and every one of her orders.

"Tha's ah good lad."

"Oh, and is Foxlaris still at Mr. Ochet's?"

"Should bae," hollered Gregabbit from the chair. "He ain't been back here."

"Alright, I'll meet him there. Happy Grammo Day!"

"Happy Grammo Day!" Mrs. Cammont hugged him, then pushed him out the door.

Out jumped the fox from the Household, diving with full jubilance towards the Main Road. As always, being the last house before the mighty walls of Mechmilne gave him the perfect view up at the thriving Village and its bustling villagers. Droves of otters, hedgehogs, clurichaun, and other creatures of every sort dotted amongst the houses, shops, and gardens of Winthrop. Never had the gravel path been so full, both of excitement and people.

Foxtamas practically skipped his way up. He passed by the Deffmires sweeping out their house, the Solberry Sisters going through the final rounds of shopping, the new arrivals of Miss Adia Emsie dressing her young daughter Addi-Mae, and, near the edge of old Ochet's place, the vacant window sills and barren plot of the late Yarly Tilly. Between the houses patches of immortelle and inpatients bloomed, gardens grew thick and tangled, and the birch wood trickling through Winthrop's western side reached long like some thriving offspring of Mechmilne. Every turn of the head revealed some corner of the village rejoicing.

How could it not?

Grammo Day—taken from the Old Evonian word for "open"—would finally join the East to the West. A homecoming. The whole world of Evon united once again, not by land, but by the single source for all the overflowing life and wonder pulsing through the world, the key project that put Tops in pockets and smiles on faces: the Bridge of Evon.

Today Foxtamas would step into a story, witness the birth of a myth. He wanted nothing more. Just thinking about the moment fulfilled him. He'd no need for the future, with its endless jobs around the Village, the coming and going of faces old and new. In time he'd welcome back that steady life, but not today. Today…today the dreamer would be wide awake for his fantasy.

Tap…Tap…Tap…

Foxtamas had arrived. Shielding his blue eyes from the blaring sun and clear-skyed day, the younger brother glared up at the oldest, still slaving away on the roof.

"Foxlaris! *Foxlaris!*" he shouted up with a wave of his hands. To his surprise, the calls were heard, and the brown eyes of his brother peeked over the edge of hay and wood.

"What do you need?" the fox called down, crass.

"Did you wake Mr. Ochet up?"

"Kinda."

"What do you mean *kinda*?"

"He got up. Didn't say it was my doing," Foxlaris smirked. Foxtamas didn't.

"I *told* you to get it done last night."

"It's fine, everything worked out."

"Mmmhmm."

"Go ask him yourself."

"He's over at Brae's. Did you even talk to him? *Especially* about Sir Penst?"

Foxlaris paused his hammering. He cast a sorrowful look towards his brother as thoughts of the badger passed over him. He and Ochet were the last of the Old Boys. They kept the tradition of yarn-weaving teatime at dawn going after Dr. Wardly and Mr. Finchuck passed a few years back. But now…their employer was the last one standing. An entire generation of Winthropians gone, buried on the edge of the fence.

"He said he's doing fine. That's it." Foxlaris held back, however, the faun's mention of today already lightening his spirits. Just one slip of a mention might provoke the worst possible question from Foxtamas.

"Well, that's good, y'know. They were real legends around here. Did a lot for us."

"Yeah…" nodded Foxlaris. "And he said if the weather stays good through the rest of the summer, he'll hire us out to build a new ale cellar for the fall." The cheeks of his younger brother grew wide and rosy, pushing Foxlaris' to do the same.

"No way! Really!?"

"Yup."

"But I thought he was done with all that?"

"Guess Brae talked him into it, especially after this incident. Figures bottling ale will be easier than jarring jams."

"Why, less burned ceilings and roofs?"

"Probably."

"Of course Brae did it, though. They're technically kin now."

There was his chance. The elder Scottsworth set aside his mallet and swung his feet over the edge, full concentration on Foxtamas.

"How's that?" he asked, acting engrossed.

"Little Ochie married his daughter a few months back. Off over in Fornrose, I think."

"Huh. Didn't know Brae had a daughter."

"I'm pretty sure. Least that's what Acirema told me."

"And she's *never* wrong."

Both brothers laughed—genuinely.

"Well," said Foxtamas, "we gotta start thinking up plans for the cellar. I'll try and ask him later today how he wants it done."

"Could be how we did Cupin's, or the Rattly's

"Think he wants it that big? It's only him now."

"Wouldn't hurt."

"True."

"We'll just have to ask him ourselves," said Foxtamas with a stretch, wicking away the last lingering licks of sleep. "Oughta be at Grammo Day I figure. Speaking of which—"

Foxlaris' ears drooped.

There went his plan.

"Think he'll be there?" the younger fox asked.

"I, um...yeah, should be."

"Good. No promises we can track him down, but we'll try. You just about done?"

What was there for Foxlaris to do in that moment? Pretend? Lie? He chose instead to look straight down at his brother. Hoping for the best.

"No."

"Better pick that hammer back up then and—"

"And I'm not going."

A snort shot from Foxtamas.

"It won't take you *that* long, come on. I'm going to look for Bunns and we can make him—"

"No, Foxtamas," the elder said, stern, "I'm not going at *all.*"

His brother's face contorted. First to confusion, then to a scrunch of his eyebrows in a manner fit to bargain away the news. Foxlaris would rather throw himself from the roof than see such disappointment consume him.

"What in Evon, no, Foxlaris!" replied Foxtamas, shocked. If the ladder to the roof had been outside instead of in, he would have climbed up and dragged him towards the River Nohsis. "W-W-What are you even *talking about?*"

"Foxtamas, I—"

"No, you're gonna miss the biggest event in the entire *history* of Evon! Of our *lives!* J-Just think about everyone that'll be there! Leaders, dwarves, Efetes, unicorns; we've dreamed of seeing these things for years!"

"Yeah, and they were *dreams*, Foxtamas." How bitter those words sounded—even worse did they taste rolling off the tongue. "It's...it's time you grew outta all that. I have to finish this up so we can get more jobs and make more Tops to get us going somewhere. Okay? I just don't have time for...that."

Maybe he should've thrown himself off the roof. If not for retribution of his sheer stupidity, then to grab his kin and haul him away from the brink of sadness his words pushed him towards.

But no. Foxlaris was right. He had to set up that boundary. Change was going to hurt.

But why couldn't it hurt him the most?

Downtrodden, Foxtamas nodded and tried to keep his eyes dry. He knew Foxlaris couldn't have meant that. And if he did...no. It's just an early morning for him, and you know how he gets cranky with so little sleep, and, um, and...oh, he didn't have time to think on the words. That would end the excitement of Grammo Day before it could properly begin. Instead, Foxtamas gazed back up at his brother, aiming at some comeback.

"Well, you could at least go to see the Inn," he said with drooping words. "Don't you wanna see it all furnished? All our hard work from the winter'll finally be paid off."

Now this caught the fox off guard. He laid aside his mallet and gazed over towards the East. Foxtamas was right: they had worked seemingly forever on the framework of Bridgeborrow Inn and only to be let go during the furnishing process. Had all the work been for nothing? Yes, the town would continue to thrive after Grammo Day, but to be the first to see it, to live in the opening glory?

"Fine. I'll think about it. But *no* promises."

His brother's smile returned.

"I knew you'd come around."

"I didn't—"

"Nope, you did!"

"Don't push it."

With a wink, Foxtamas strutted backwards up the road.

"Don't start dreaming about all the sweets, the drinks, the games, shops—"

"*Foxtamas,*" he growled.

"The *girls!*"

Down shot a spare plank from the roof, falling mere inches from the

giggling younger fox. Foxlaris didn't dare throw his hammer—Foxtamas would *certainly* have him in his grasp then.

"Good one!"

"That was just a warning."

"Keep throwing them, not coming outta my wages!"

Foxlaris grunted and turned back to the roof. Before he could properly start again, his brother shouted one last time.

"Say, know where Bunns ran off to? I'm gonna smack him for leaving me last night."

"Check Ruel's camp," he replied as he gathered a fresh set of nails. "I thought I saw him headed there."

With that, Foxtamas bid his brother adieu and headed to the next leg of his journey, though a part of him couldn't shake the disheartenment still lingering from Foxlaris' earlier denial. Did he really *not* want to go? Even after everything they'd put into it?

He felt fear's pangs begin to claw away inside him. A nagging, begging to burrow through. But he quelled it, at least for the day. Too much was on the line to be scared or worried about Foxlaris. He'd come around—he always did.

Foxlaris, meanwhile, hung his head low and continued pounding away. He knew what he said. He knew how it made Foxtamas feel. It was true, of course, but...but how he *hated* his words, his speech, his sullen demeanor when he knew the pain it brought.

Why...

Why couldn't he just *change?*

"Nae, laddie, yer got et all wrong! Stars are the *future!* Look, Ah'll teach yer and the boys, an—"

"You can't join us, Bunns," chuckled Ruel, walking in tandem with the jackalope. What was this, the third time they'd circled camp? Fourth? Small tents both grounded and slung amongst the trees dotted the fringe beyond Winthrop's fence. The duo wove between the rest of the patrol engaging with other Village squirrels. Some hoped to woo Sheshly Minnel, others tried to recruit her brothers for the job.

Ruel, now a richer brown with the occasional flake of gray popping up behind his ears, needed the company. Today was *the* day. The very one he'd brokered for a decade. So many of the details always felt like some dream ushered back and forth from Mikyill to Winthrop to the Fulnoa, but now, well, here he stood—gilded sash and all.

And that wasn't the reason why he'd been so eager to walk the trail around the Ratatoskr base. For the first time since their founding, the boys just...didn't have work. No mail. Deliveries. Parcels.

Nothing.

Would make the surest of squirrels queasy.

With every leader and their subjects funneled into Bridgeburrow, it made the Ratatoskr practically useless, even for just one day. Of course, they'd begin the entirety of their new route scouting and implementation once the Bridge was crossed and settlements began, but until then, Ruel walked restless. So too did his shaky leg.

"Nae, tha's not what' Ah'm askin—"

"*Sure* it's not."

"Yer just cannae see the vision!" Bunns threw up his hands in disbelief. In all the years of talking to (and only slightly berating) the Parcelage, he'd gained hardly an inch on him—and half of that came from the antlers. What the jackalope lacked in height he made up for in his tenacity. The Bridge Pact's constant need for Aisar's approval meant Ruel's section of the Ratatoskr frequented the Village. Every time they touched down, Bunns would be there, ready to either train, talk, or a little bit of both, even at the cost of his work. A great skill for a budding warrior; horrible for an already faltering Inn employee. But Bunns needed it. *Craved* it. Just missing one chance to be amongst real fighters, well, he'd almost never forgive himself. It's why he never left the Cammont Household without his dangling pouch of throwing stars strapped over his black tunic.

"The *vision* is that our daggers and bows do just fine. Most we run into are the occasional bandit type."

"But yer could have them all in *one*! And *Ah* could be right by yer side tae train yer!" The ever-eager jackalope practically bounded in his begging.

"It's a great offer, Bunns, really. But I figure you got more to worry about right now."

"Wha'? Nae, Ah'm free as ah fish in the sea!"

"Sure about that?"

The squirrel lifted a finger to the figure approaching the camp. Bunns' wide brown eyes followed it, then froze.

"*BUNN.*"

Oh no.

"*CLAR.*"

Oh *no.*

"*CAMM.*"

It was over.

"*ONT.*"

For certain this time.

Foxtamas approached with a shaking head, and the once proud, upstanding ears of the jackalope fell. He tried hiding himself behind Ruel, but those dastardly antlers poked right above his acorn cap.

"Funny seeing you here," said the fox, crossing his arms. Bunns slid out from behind, a cheeky grin wobbling between cheeks.

"Uh, aye, hilarious," he replied stilted.

"Have a good morning then?"

"Yup, fantastic."

"Rested? Refreshed, even?"

"Had tae bae! Was an early morn givin' mah lovely, warrior advice tae our brave Ratatoskr workers. Ain't tha' right, Ruel?"

Trying to conceal his laugh, Ruel nodded towards the fox.

"Oh, absolutely."

"See? Mah time is being used wonderfully!"

"Well, it *should* have been used to help tend Mr. Ochet's radishes last night. Remember that? Our little job that, oh, y'know, *pays us?*"

"Laddie, laddie," said Bunns as he waved his hands. He staggered closer as if completely innocent of such a heinous act. "Great minds like mahself never forget, yer know. Ah just find et hard tae bae diggin' mah paws in filfth when they're meant tae bae slingin' stars and protectin' this here Village! Bandits always bae on the prowl, ready tae attack, an' Ah cannae bae stoppin' 'em 'cause, Roihelm forbid, the plants stay fresh an' in the ground for an extra day."

"No, you make a good point, Bunns," Foxtamas replied with a sly smile, winking at Ruel, "warriors burdened by responsibility can't be bothered by such small and inconsiderable things like, oh I dunno, Tops and all that. I'll go ahead and take your share, then. Don't want to take your focus off those bandits or anything."

The Parcelage couldn't hold it back. His laughter burst, so much so a tint of red flashed over Bunns' cheeks, quickly followed by a punch on the arm of Foxtamas.

"Real, real funny, Scottoh," he added, low and terse. Ruel managed to contain his chuckles and readjust his cap, falling back into the leadership look.

"Oh, you two are too much! I'd love to stay, but we've gotta head out and get an early start to Bridgeburrow. You two take care—and don't kill each other!"

"Can't promise tha'!" Bunns called out to him as Foxtamas began leading him back to the Village.

"I'll keep him in check. See you later!" shouted the fox. Really, he *was* glad to see Bunns. A stickler as he was for work, the kid had heart for what he loved—picking radishes not included.

Village Winthrop stirred into a torrent. With the crisp, cooling air flittering through, bringing along woodland hymns and loose summer leaves, spirits grew flustered with joy as the villagers readied for the Royal Departure. Together as a single unit, with both King Aisar and Princess Acirema prepared and leading the charge, they would venture towards Bridgeburrow and its hosting of the Grammo Day Celebration. Until then, however, things had to get done!

The scrubbed clothes needed hanging on the lines and the dry ones needed plucking off, *especially* if the kids were going to wear the vests their mothers brought out for *the* most special of occasions, Calmas and Tidingsdale included. After that, you of course had to count up just how many Tops you intended to bring (and spend), but not until you picked up the taters you promised to purchase from up the road and the ointment that just came in not even two days ago. Oh, and don't forget the last minute sweeping of the doorsteps and beating out the rugs. The last thing you'd want is to come back from the East to a dirty home!

These thoughts and more consumed the to and fro of the

Winthropians. Amongst such chaos, the boys found themselves a shady spot under the birch grove hugging the left side of the Main Road's bend. Both nestled into the grass and leaned their backs against the pale bark. The breeze practically drowned them.

"Scottoh," Bunns began with closed eyes and a chipper voice, "who yer think weh'll see today? Ah'm bettin' lots of dwarves, whole load of 'em. Oh, and the big fella outta Mikyill."

"President Gniw?"

"Aye, him."

Foxtamas nodded. "Yeah, I'd bet on those too," he added. His mind jumped through the plethora of options while eyeing the bustle shimmying up and down the gravel path. Combined, it worked to keep Foxlaris' words away, and the easy rest alongside Bunns plentiful. "Hmmm, I'll say…Efetes. Lots of them, too."

"And their Lady?"

"Yup."

"Smart."

"And a unicorn or two."

"Oh, tha' would bae a treat!"

"Right? Been *ages* since we saw one. Probably some Northerners too."

"Hah! Missin' home?"

"No, just the sorta people."

"Like what, other foxes?"

"More minks, bears, that type."

"Ah see."

"Heck, I'd even wager Vites."

"Nae! Tae far south!"

"Still could happen."

"Aye, but then yer'd have the whole of Evon showin' oup!"

"They oughta for *this!*" Though he chuckled, Foxtamas swore, further down the road, he could still hear the steady thumps of his brother toiling away.

Bunns hiked himself further up the tree.

"Speakin' of showin' oup..." he started, peeking open an eye with a wicked grin. "Think anyone weh know'll bae there?"

"Hmmm, I dunno," replied the fox, cocking his head. "Reinden? Or...Berry-Don? Pretty sure he went up to Fornrose last year."

"Nae, not them, Aster! Yer girl, laddie!"

Oh, the poor fox! He blushed just hearing that name, even more so with that added adage of "his girl." What a dream.

After Miss Tilly's death a few years back, Asterlyn Carventon decided to head off shortly after the oldest Cammont, journeying up to the grand city of Mikyill to pursue a higher level of botany than her guardian could achieve. Though she wrote back every once and a while, Foxtamas never felt her presence replaced in the Village.

Always a gap in Foxlaris' heart. And his own.

"Oh, shut it antler-ears."

"Wha'! Ah'm just sayin'."

"You know you're not," grunted Foxtamas.

"Fine, laddie, fine," Bunns sighed, "when yer old an' lonely, don't bae complainin' tae meh!"

Another back and forth transpired between the two. It weaved and wove through a couple dozen topics while one by one, family by family, Winthrop readied itself for the day. And, right on time, further up the hill, the golden doors unclasped, and, from them, the procession began.

The blare of trumpets!

The blasting of drums!

Out from the Palace burst the royal entourage. Comprised solely of Watchers in their complete leathers, they rattled out a hastened version of "Valley on the Rise" amongst waving banners and streamers and flags. For Aisar, they carried his royal deep maroon; a lilac, airy and bright, flew for Acirema; and, finally, in remembrance of the late Queen Anlana, a glittering gold floated high.

The opening parade marched forward and split down each side of the Main Road. When in place, the two raccoons entered. Both king and princess came carried on gilded, open-air palanquins. Aisar, burdening ten *awfully* loyal Watchers, was adorned in his overly long, overly billowing red cape. It matched his ruby-jeweled crown and crimson robes, all ornamented by studded gems and silk gold ties. Tying the look together were the springs of aurum ribbon draping from the crown and scepter. How great his grin grew jostling down that white-gravel road. Never mind the fact he'd yet to step there himself in decades; all he needed was the minimal applause dripping out from his subjects—subjects in *such* good heart and health! And from whom did they gain such prosperity?

His breath caught.

A shock ran through his oblong body as the purple carriage of his daughter strutted down from behind (carried by four mere men). Shouts, screams, hollers, cries; they just about deafened him.

Never had the Lady Acirema Feiht made an appearance so gorgeous. Her mauve dress, though gilded and decorated like her father's, felt deserved, dignified and righteous. Ribbons fell like silken leaves upon the wind from her silver tiara, wrapped around her white gloves and shawl hiding her shoulders. Poise and perfection; grandeur and geniality. Every sparkle of her regalia lit a fire in the souls of her onlookers. To them, she was no mere princess, far from it. Acirema Feiht was a *symbol.* One of hope, of faith, and the promise of joy that gave them the voices to ring cheers as boisterous as they could muster.

Down the precession snaked, passing by the shambles and shacks with the marching music playing on. As they passed the birch grove, the smiling, waving Acirema caught a glimpse of two figures, one tall one short. She summoned all her royal training not to openly giggle as her friends, Foxtamas and Bunns, gave overly exaggerated bows with a shout of "M'lady!" At the very least she could always count on them to be loyal.

Eventually, the parade made it to the Village entrance and proceeded out further into Mechmilne. Mr. and Mrs. Cammont locked their door and joined the crowd trailing behind the palanquins. It seemed to them they were the last to do so. Well, besides a certain someone still banging away on a roof...

"Foxlaris!"

A groan.

He sat on the opposite side of the Main Road, careful that no one would spot him. Yet somehow his brother knew. He always did.

"Get down, come on!" Foxtamas shouted from behind him, this time a slight shrill of agony tucked within his voice. "You said you were coming!"

"I said no promises!" he called back down. His head popped over the thatch. "I can visit the Inn anytime. Y'all go on, you'll miss the march."

"Foxlaris..."'"Laddie!" Bunns proclaimed, "do Ah need tae come oup there?"

A long, desperate sigh from Foxlaris. Bunns too? Could they not just leave him *alone!?* All the commotion at Bridgeburrow would drive him insane. His work needed him *here.* So what if it wasn't enthralling? It mattered. Mattered more than...than...

The fox swung his body over and balanced on the roof's center.

"Why do you have to be like this?" Foxtamas said again.

"Ah'll count tae three!"

"Look," Foxlaris started, "they're leaving you both behind. This is my choice, alright?"

"One."

"I need this done."

"Two."

"And I intend to stay."

"Three."

The star flung from the jackalope's hand before the number left his tongue. Foxlaris jumped, practically off the roof He pulled his arm and felt it stuck to the wood, and when he looked down, saw a metal sliver pinning his ragged brown sleeve to the shingles. He darted a tight glare to the snickering Bunns. One full of annoyance, but also fear at how skilled his adoptive brother had actually grown.

"Ah warned yer."

"You really think that's gonna—"

"Aster will be there."

Plainly said.

Both boys turned to Foxtamas. He held his head in his hands, only slightly agonized that he had to spit out the information. Whatever it took to get his brother down.

Foxlaris' ears perked. And a smile hiked up his cheeks.

"Let's get a move on then!"

The trio caught up with the party right on the edge of Mechmilne. Finally, after so long denying it, Foxlaris let himself think about what lay in store at Grammo Day. Would they *really* end up in the East? The first Evoneers in *centuries* to step upon it? Or would that just be the start? What of drinking with dwarves? Eyeing what kingdoms' best smiths and artisans had to offer? Hearing stories and tales told from the mouths of legends themselves? Foxtamas had been right all along—it *did* get him excited. Feeling the leaves compress beneath his boots and light sprinkle through the foliage above, it felt like a classic run to the River.

But before they ventured too far into the forest, the fox took one last glimpse at the Village.

The long, winding road of white.

Plops of brown marring the sunbathed stretches of green.

Overlapping waves of jasmine, lilac, scarlet blooms.

The dazzle of gold mounted on top, gazing over it all.

A part of his heart held Winthrop close, even if his stern exterior hated to admit it. What a shame it would be when he finally had to leave.

"Hurry laddies, hurry, hurry!" Bunns cried, grabbing both brothers and hauling forward through the Winthropian crowd. "Ah ain't gonna waste mah time away at the back!"

The Scottsworths didn't really have a choice. Bunns trampled past the Solberry Sisters, dodged the murderous glare of the Writs, slid between the quiet conversation of Wylhelm Wardenson and Mr. Jillengilch, and scooted alongside Antilik Pinlingshire, an old pal who succumbed to the weight of joining the Watchers.

From afar, one may assume the Royal Departure to be some mass peasant exodus from a failing town. Yet tucked beneath the whistling Mechmilne branches—coated a shade of twinkling green and guiding along the sprinting summer wind—more smiles emerged than any other village, town, or city combined. The trio found that out firsthand as they passed the moles, squirrels, porcupines, fauns, doves, and jackalopes. It seemed nothing could get them down.

"Stoppit, look!" Foxtamas finally protested as they made it to the front. He pointed over towards Acirema and her carriage. Part of them wanted to acknowledge the radiance of her look—the other half pushed for jokes about their friend being so dolled up.

"Ah think weh need tae get ah better look at our ol' pal, eh, boys?" asked Bunns with a sneaky twinge on his face. The jittering of his antlers exposed the antics he had in store.

"Bunns," Foxlaris started, "don't you *dare* go and do anything stupid. Aisar's right in front of her!"

"Nae Rizzeh, this ain't stupid, et's splendid!" Foxlaris yet again had his paw yanked forward. Exchanging glances with his brother, both shook their heads. What else did they expect from Bunns?

"Eh-hem, excuse meh, Sah!" The jackalope strutted alongside one of the Watchers carrying the back of the Princess' palanquin. "Weh shall bae takin' over yer duty, thank yer!"

The Leprechaun, outfitted in his bronze helmet, silver chain, and red

leather tunic stamped by the classic "WW," only provided Bunns a raised eyebrow of confusion.

"You'll be *what?*" he asked, voice snively and high.

"Yer heard meh. Relinquished of all yer duties!"

"*Bunns!*" Foxtamas whispered from behind. "*You just can't say—*"

"My Lady!" the Watcher called forward. "Are we being transferred *already?*"

A confused Acirema glanced backwards with her *own* raised eyebrow. There, she saw not only the worried leprechaun, but the very villager trying to scam him out of his position.

She hid a laugh.

"Oh, um, yes, Midas, you and the others may take your leave. These three will carry me. With the jackalope *in front*, please."

The princess winked, and Bunns' ears drooped back behind his horns. For all his scheming, Acirema *always* had to outwit him. Maybe he could run back and get ol' Gregabbit to share the load, or Antilik, or, um, or...

It wasn't a minute later and the lad was already grunting between the poles. Once the foxes settled in and the troupe beneath dismissed, the raccoon finally let out a billow of her laugher.

"My, you three just *love* nosing about, don't you?"

"Hey, this was all Bunns, not my idea," the stiff voice of Foxlaris replied.

"Of course, Foxlaris. Hardly ever is."

"So, Queenie," the jackalope shouted from the front, nimble white arms slightly struggling with the load, "yer gonna get us them juicy details on Evonian politics, ain't yer?"

"Yeah! Find out all you can on those dwarf lords. The latest books I got barely have anything new them," Foxtamas added.

"You know I'm more than some Ratatoskr with 'juicy details,' yes?"

"Well yeah, but being stuck in a tent with all of them's *gotta* get you something, right?" The fox gave a cheeky smile towards the princess. She returned it with a smirking nod.

"You never know. I may just get to show some of my ruling prowess out here today."

"That so?" asked Foxlaris. "Think you'll take over for the big man?"

"Hush!" his brother whispered.

"It's fine," replied Acirema, "he's too busy talking with those guards up front. But maybe, Foxlaris. If he doesn't lay off the wine."

"Hah! Yer ah shoo in then, Queenie!" Bunns snickered. The princess did too. Foxtamas, though, looked past the laugh and to the princess. Her hands gripped the sides of her carriage until her knuckles popped and faded to a pale alabaster. She tended to look everywhere *but* Aisar's palanquin and the path ahead. All the tell-tale signs of fear.

Even now, that same childhood worry plagued her, only this time it wasn't something to think about "one day." One day was *today*. He saw how the villagers admired her. Those cheers met his ears just as distinctly as they bled hers. Princess Acirema Feiht, the Living Hope, Father-Ridder. One look at her and you could face tomorrow—a tomorrow you *knew* would be better.

For everyone, it seemed, but her.

8

"YES, IT IS SWEET. SWIFT YET RICH

The tree line thinned. Layers of ancient stalks, stumps, and stems parted as the party reached the outskirts of Bridgeburrow. Still set some distance from Nohsis, the newest village of Evon stood a sweeping marvel, aweing the welcomed guests and hugging them within the circle of its opening.

Shops in the image of market stalls ran down lines shooting from the

main square. Such rich colors of bright burgundy and baby blues caught the Winthropian eyes and drew them in, steering them from the permanent homes of the boutiques, blacksmith, tavern, general store, and carriage station. The care given to each was evident. Carvings of waves and rapids rippled through the woodwork, gilded in a sparkling gold and outlined by gems freshly mined from the Fulnoa. The details excelled them past their cabin-like exterior and into a realm of artistry. None more so, of course, than the Riverside Stay.

"See, what'd I tell ya!" Foxtamas jabbed at his brother as the band marched in. They'd been let go of their royal duties just before entering, seeing as the king and princess were needed far and away from where the other monarchs allowed peasantry. "Imagine missing out on that! It looks better than we could have *dreamed.*"

"Y-Yeah," his brother muttered. The three of them had taken up parts on the framing crew. Their hands calloused from the chopping, nailing, fitting the stout northern timber into place. Then, it all appeared so rugged, so…impossible for beauty to come out of some mismatched logs. Now, though, now it *shone.* Had Foxlaris *actually* produced something like that? And if he did, then…what else could he do?

He wasn't given long to ponder as Foxtamas and Bunns scurried off, diving further into the wonder that was Grammo Day.

Traveling up the trail north from Bridgeburrow brought them into lane after lane of pop-up shops. Merchants of every flavor assembled every ware, from handwoven dresses to quilts studded with rubies. The overgrown shade of Mechmilne covering their backs caught them in the perfect spot for ease, relaxation, and profit. The only thing more varied than the vendors were the customers scrambling amongst them.

Evoneers of every kind flooded both the village and streets as the Winthrop crowd pushed through. Within minutes of joining the crowd, they lost all sense of staying together as a single unit. How could they with McGono Kobochaun disappearing beneath the legs of a minotaur and the Rattlys, for all their talents in joke-cracking and hospitality, wobbling hardly more than a good few steps forward per hour.

So, too, did a certain trio break the confines out of sheer excitement alone.

"Laddie! Fulnoa Dwarves! Look 'em, look 'em! Ah knew et!" shouted Bunns, pointing up ahead. Sure enough, a company of armor-laden dwarves cut through the mess of people. All four towered a good head over the other Evoneers. Each bore matching silver pauldrons sitting atop their tunics, a rich blue strapped across with belts of leather and fur around the neck. They kept their beards trimmed and braided, and the hair at their back long yet managed.

"I see, but don't go messing with them!" chided Foxtamas.

"Yer sure?"

"He's sure," Foxlaris added.

"But Ah need ask where their axes went! Lookit, not even ah *dagger* on any of 'em!" The brothers squinted their eyes as the dwarves passed. Always the most picturesque of Fulnoa Warriors were silhouetted with a battle axe or sword hilt brooding over their shoulder. These, however, kept bare backs. All except for the symbol etched into the leather patch beneath the fur lining of their collars.

A simple triangle with a line jutting from the right side.

The emblem of the Blue Mountain.

"Wait, look, that way!" Breaking his rule, Foxtamas pointed to a fruit vendor coming up on their right. Spreading out the last of a blueberry bushel stood an Efete.

It took a good minute for him to fully understand what it was he saw. The creatures hailed from the southern kingdom of Efeters. Supposedly they were of distant kin to the Elves, but folk doubted that *they* even existed, so the lineage never quite settled for certain. Their work was, however, tending their Harvestlands to supply all manners of grains, fruits, vegetables, and other foods for the West. It's said their fields looked like golden waves of a sea and their scythes the glimmers sparkling off the crests.

Efetes themselves were slender, swaying people composed of the very nature of Evon. They grew no bones, held no muscle. The particular vendor before Foxtamas had skin long and formed from pastel pink petals with her sleeves the flowering of tulips. Wheat clung down from her head in the appearance of hair. All at once she looked like a woman mixed with a scarecrow. No Efete ever looked the same. Foxtamas recalled merchants with strawberry seeding across their faces and eyes like the center of a sunflower. Their beauty, complexity…he could never shake himself from it. It was as if all Evon coalesced into a singular, upright spirit.

"Guys, keep walking!" Foxlaris interrupted. He had to shove his brother forward to avoid him from impeding the traffic. "You can stop when we make it to the Bridge."

A fair deal.

Wading further East, the path presented the entire spectrum of the West. Unicorns awed in their capes and jeweled horns while nymphs and fairies flew over gnomes and under bears followed by trails of color sparking off the hems of their patterned skirts. The dust caused sneezes from some doubled-over otter muttering on about the lack of care shown from those eagles and ravens launching in the *middle* of the street. Thankfully the pan flute playing of a faun quartet sapped his focus elsewhere, just as it did families of clurichaun and hedgehogs, foxes and elk.

No soul there dared dawn the sackcloth the Winthropian villagers had become accustomed to, oh no. They wore their best, their brightest for such a day. The longer the trio shuffled among them, the easier it became to distinguish who hailed from the North, with their thick jerkins and hoods, fellow villagers in airy tunics, or the vests and shorts worn by those further West in regions still mysterious to those so close to Nohsis. Amongst it all, another truth emerged: you couldn't miss a Mikyillite.

Whether crow or rabbit, badger or sprite, they sported lavishness. Golden buttons, gilded canes, Top pockets jangling like a dinner bell—all mere accessories to too-tight vests crushed beneath the tailored art of a suit jacket threaded with silver over blues and greens. The worst of them bore mail just beneath their casual garb as if to announce some semblance of multifaceted talents. Writer *and* warrior? Financier by day, fighter by night? Even those of lesser class knew the dress of their city. The sharp, smart-cut style echoed in patched overcoats.

Thankfully, the boys needn't endure the fineries for long (it was hard for them to admit how uncomfortable they found it all.) The packed path finally found its end, pouring out to the long-awaited Bridge Site. It still looked how they remembered it, the riverside playground with its stretches of grass leading to the loamy Western coast. Only now the forest thinned further back, creating more field for the guests to mingle. To the north, tucked tight between the tree line and shore, sat the Royal Tents. The swaying lavender and gold felt twinkled like some overstuffed carnival. Part of Winthrop's caravan had turned that way to bring their royalty to their tent. The rest paid mind to something else.

The Bridge of Evon.

There it spanned. An expanse of umber, aurum, silver. A wooden claw catching hold from one earthen station to another—a hidden beast dwelling beneath. It straddled the bubbling, whipping rapids. No splash leapt close enough to wet it. The bridge looked hewn from a single husk. Its grain, like thin slits of gold, etched from the steps rising from the loamy Western shore to those descending on the pebbled Eastern beach. It held no nails. No bolts. Craftsmen of every Pledged party had converged on the project. Using the northern timber harvested by the Fulnoa Dwarves, it began life far past Mikyill, up near the Guardmont Range where the River Nohsis spanned greatest. Once completed on the Western edge, they sailed it down until it fell snuggly at the Eastern border, a perfect sixty yards in length, wide enough to hold twenty or more from one waist-high wall to the other.

A railing wound along said edge, flowing gold twisted like wild vines and molded into images of maple leaves and roses. More artistry ran along the sides. Symbols spelled the Bridge's history. First of dormancy, then possibility, and ending on the enthusiastic grit that breathed life into the achievement. Beneath them read *Lo Losrym o Evon*—the Old Evonian name for the Bridge.

You could feel the polished edges against your hand by look alone. The gold a cold press into your palm. A whisper from the swaying Eastern trees only a few footfalls away...

Yet not a soul dared to cross. The temptation was there, of course, and palpable as humidity in the air, but the Evoneers knew not to ruin history unfolding at their fingers.

And if they did, an entire brigade of the Mikyill Myriad (the standing army of President Gniw) stood at the entrance.

The trio, as politely as possible, kept their footing amongst the oohing, aweing crowds like stubborn driftwood parsing a stream. Neither one of them could look away.

"This isn't real...is it?" Foxtamas whispered so low it surprised him when his brother replied.

"I'm not sure..."

"Ah thought et'd bae...bigger, somehow."

Foxtamas scrunched his brows and turned to Bunns.

"What?"

"Weh've reached ah brand new era of Evon, one bound tae change our history forever. And et's all on tha'." He lifted a finger. "Ah hunk of wood."

Despite his seeming dismissiveness, with every blink, those wide, brown eyes grew soaked. Bunns pulled his hand back. Balled it up into a fist. Rarely did Foxtamas see him show so much in so little.

"But," he began again with a shake of his head, "weh cannae bae standin' here all day like ah bunch of greasy gophers! Weh gotta whole *lifetime* tae take in tha' beaut, but those knives back there? The roasted nuts? They'll bae gone bae the *hour!*"

Neither Scottsworth resisted his yanking. They swam upstream through the crowds, now mostly devoid of their fellow Winthropians, until Foxlaris slipped himself from Bunns' grip.

"Hey, I think I'm gonna stay back."

The others stopped and glanced back, worried.

"Wait, what, why—"

He cut his brother short with a hand upon his shoulder.

"I'm not *leaving,* I just…Bunns was right. It's a big deal, and I'd rather spend my time taking it all in."

"Yer *sure?*"

"Positive. I'll catch up with y'all before the Crossing, I promise."

Foxlaris spoke those words with direct eye contact to Foxtamas. Those blue marbles jittered when the nerves within started to take over. To ease them, he squeezed the blue tunic over his arm, curling his bottom lip into a smirk. "I won't be gone long."

His brother nodded. Then grinned.

"Fine. Won't be me missing the candied berries though!"

They disappeared beneath the colored banners raised over the endless sea of Evoneers.

Acirema was offered anything but. You would think that, with their prestige and investiture towards such an achievement, the league of Evon leadership, bound together by the Bridge Pledge, would give properly divided time, first to oogling, then ogling, at what had become like the weight of a decade-old child upon their heads. But you'd think wrong.

Instead, they gathered in shadows. Tent by tent, ringed fingers plucked snacks and piecemealed a breakfast together from refreshments served as celebration from the surrounding towns and cultures. The huddles held no more than four or five at a time. Places traded in and out like a game. A Daisy Creek ambassador danced from the Fulnoa tent back down to that of the Kingdom of Sumbellia and the trio giggling inside.

Time slipped away quicker than a morning mist. Never had such a robust gathering of rulers and officials been held in any recent history. Corners of the West, as the Seasonals greeted Efeters as Mechmilian towns greeted Asdatars, were of fiction until today. Thus, talk sparked, especially on matters impossible to share via Ratatoskr letter. Evon's own existed too far apart, too alone for too long. No one missed the opportunity to mingle where they could. Plant seeds in ears. Whisper news, paint an image. Such business always overtook spectacle. It was the nature of ruling. And the poor princess suffered through it.

She plucked at a loose, white thread poking out from the table-cloth. The Winthropian tent kept empty—thankfully. Mikyill had seen to their comforts (as they had to most) with patterned green rugs to mask the grass and banners overlaying the stark, blinding white composing the walls. Acirema found herself a quiet corner beside their bread and cheese table to hide. She preferred it away from the laughter and good talk echoing from the outskirts of the Bridge Site, but she accepted what she could get. It didn't stop her longing, though. Nothing ever did. Not even the brown, seed-topped bread before her, baked halfway across the world.

"Hah! I'll need my own eyes to confirm it—well, the *good* one, rather."

The pompous voice stiffened her back. Decades of royal education took over as her shoulders raised, hands clasped in her lap, ears perked up, and smile landed right between pleasant and happy.

Across the tent the flap opened, and in strutted two figures. One she recognized—gut overhanging a gold belt, skewing his already lop-sided gait. Her father spoke through whatever morsels he had carried from the previous tent. The other, however, was new, and by all accounts of his grandeur, as much the opposite of the raucous raccoon as ever had been devised.

Velvet Gniw deserved the title of President. Standing two heads taller than the King, the owl bore feathers of an ageing yet still earthen brown tipped by gray. His maroon suit, complimented by an obsidian tie patterned with ripples and waves, had tailcoats brushing the ground. They mattered little to his key feature: a golden monocle propped on his cheek. The eye behind was of a striking green and the other, unburned by his bristly brows, a plain, pale gray.

When he spoke, he did so with intention. Command. A bravado few carried all the way to their ascendency in leadership. He knew himself the father of this day. Without his outreach, the Bridge and, in tandem, the East, would still be a dream untouched, the West only half of the land it could be. Yet even with such grandeur palpable from his style and strategy, the pride formed from it was nowhere to be found. When Gniw smiled to the Princess Acirema, he did so with a bow. When he turned an ear to her father, he raised his eyes in genuine interest. What stood before the Winthropains, with mismatched eyes and striking red coat, was all there was to the President.

"Ah, there she is!" Aisar replied, grabbing another block of cheese from the entrance stand, "See, what did I say? All the folk love her. She's as pretty as a lily in their eyes, and right smarter than any of them."

"So it seems!" the owl replied.

"Acirema, this is—"

"President Gniw." The princess cut her father off and stood, offering a curtsy. "It's an honor, especially after all you've done for us and our village."

"Oh, darling, that was all your father—I merely gave him the push!" He chuckled and patted Aisar on the back with a wing before gesturing to Acirema with the other. "And you, very impressive you are, indeed, indeed. To have such support before even taking the throne, I mean. It's a feat!" Despite his sincerity, his words mumbled between the conjoining of thoughts. Age caught him like all the rest. "I assert you must be, oh, quite, quite proud, my lady."

"Oh, um, yes sir, it does make me rather glad," she said. It felt almost impossible to be timid with the President's soft face beaming towards her. "I know not every ruler is offered such support."

"Ah, honest and true. You're blessed to have it. Unlike your father!"

Gniw laughed.

Aisar did not.

His claw stuffed the last chip of cheddar into his dangling mug before responding.

"Love and effective results do not always equate," he started through a swallow. "I've gotten more than enough done with Winthrop than any other here would. And that's honest *and* true." "Yes, yes, well—"

"You take that lot," the king interrupted, "backwatered and down-trodden, and get to work *half* as hard as I have. They'd be sticks in the mud. The whole batch."

"Worth less—"

"Worth less than a Mikyill alleyway, yes."

Gniw nodded, but rolled his eyes over to Acirema as her father interrupted him. She put a hand over her mouth to keep her giggles contained.

"Which is why I *knew* you'd be the first to move the Pact along with more than a supply of Tops. Such a feat shows will, you know, skill. And earned you a few 'privileges,' if I recall."

"I'm sorry, privileges?" asked Acirema.

"Good food, good tent," Aisar answered. "And we get to choose who goes across first."

"The Privilege of the First Easterner, we've been calling it," Gniw added with a wink. "*If* someone is ever decided upon."

"I told you, it'll *be* a Winthropian."

"And which one?"

"You'll know in time," scoffed the king.

"A time that's running out."

"Bah!" He turned to flee the tent altogether. Gniw, however, plated his jab with a deep chuckle. Its warmth helped cool the conversation. "I jest, Aisar, truly. Now's not the time to worry!"

"Come on," the raccoon grunted, "I've still to meet the dwarves."

"Ah, you're right." Before they fully exited, Gniw popped his head back in with another bow towards Acirema. "It was a pleasure, my lady. And please, indulge in the refreshments! More than enough here, I'm sure."

"Of course, sir, will do!" Smiling, she curtsied and picked through her choices of the vast Mikyillian treats before her as the pair left.

The air tasted sweeter after his departure. Perhaps a testament to what pleasantries could come from a caring ruler.

Foxtamas and Bunns swam through the depths of Grammo Day. Strings of gold swung from branch to branch above, filling the sky with flittering pastel pendants. The pair continued in their passing (and aweing) of other races from the Western corners. Leprechauns bobbled about, a few hawks swayed past the merchant stands, and many small clusters of elk were caught divulging in local food wagons. Color burst, talk rang aloud; every step felt like a joining of Evon. At least, the Western half. The East would have to wait a few hours more.

Through their walk, the two started to notice the actual wares being sold as opposed to the sellers. Many sold typical festival trinkets: wood carvings, instruments, toys, and other bobbles. One vendor, however, stacked high her wooden stand with books and loose pages, aged by time but holding within tales that stood against it.

The fox's blue eyes nearly burst from his head. He scanned the

titles quicker than Bunns could throw a star. Oh, so many, so *many!*
Most he'd only heard rumor of, verbal retellings opposed to the literal
text. *Shroth the Ice-Shaper, Teagle's History of Plentis, Buried Beside the
Chinaberry Tree, The Legend of the Light Sea—*

He slapped an arm across Bunns to stop him.

"Laddie, wha—"

"*Look.*"

There, front and center, sat *Gold Shoal*, famed pirate-raving adventure by author C. R. A. Seuq. Painted edges. Gilded place marker.
Its cover of white waves splashing against golden sands made his heart
leap. Was such a place real? Could he, further down the road, visit? Oh,
he just had to know!

Until he looked at the price.

One Silver Top. All he carried were three Green Tops, each a mere
tenth of a Silver.

Foxtamas' poor heart sank.

"Not enough?" asked Bunns.

"Nope," the fox sighed. But, he knew it would be of better use
later, anyway. He promised Mrs. Cammont a gift, after all—and a gift
she shall receive. Though, if he *had* been given enough, maybe both of
them could have shared the read...

He pushed the thought to the back of his mind, and the boys
continued their adventure onward. For an entire seven steps, that is,
until it was Bunns' turn to stop.

"Scottoh, look at those bonnies!" he shouted. The stand in question
belonged to a squirrel, who, based on the quiver hidden beneath his cape
and acorn cap slanted off his head, looked the part of both archer and
Ratatoskr. His sold strings, bows, arrows, bolts, and an odd little item
completely unfamiliar to Bunns.

"What in Evon?" Foxtamas asked as he bent down to examine it.
Sitting on fine velvet carpet, it looked to be a pair of small crossbows.
The bottoms, however, were mounted on finely studded leather that
looped around to form a small belt. Three strings drooped down from
the front. Attached to the ends were little wooden rings, perfectly sized

to fit over fingers.

"Say, laddie, wha' are those things there, them...cross-bow-thingys?" The jackalope asked, in awe at their design.

"Oh, yes!" The seller started, picking them up from their display and giving a demonstration. "*These* lovelies here are crossbawns! Brand new invention making the rounds in Mikyill. All you do is wrap this strap around your arm, load a bolt like any regular crossbow and—" With a close of his fist, the squirrel fired a small arrow into the tree behind him, doing so with the pull of the rings. Such a weapon looked formidable yet simple, sleek in its dark oak and silver accents.

Bunns couldn't look away.

"Ah, um, uh, how much laddie? How much!" he spat out, mesmerized.

"Opal Top."

"For both?"

"Each."

"EACH!?"

Foxtamas ducked down to grab Bunns as he collapsed. The price just about sent him into shock. Why, that would put his entire family in debt! For *life!*

"Um, thank you, sir, but I think we'll pass..." Foxtamas gritted out through a smile, lifting Bunns' dead weight back to the land of the living.

"If you change your mind, be sure to stop back by!" chuckled the merchant.

"Aye," the winded Bunns shouted, "in ah million years!"

The constant rumbling of commotion faded after enough time wading through it, like howling storm winds turning to whispers by the time the rain arrives. Foxlaris found it akin to hammer swings. Background noise as a fertile foundation for his thoughts to grow. And, arriving back at Bridgeburrow, they bloomed.

He didn't enter the Inn. Even if it was all he could think about. He kept thirty feet back, enough for the passersby to flow in and out, admiring the beauty carved into the walls and columns holding up the veranda in front.

Strangely, the building...called to him. He'd heard its rumblings in his admiration of the Bridge, pondering just what it took for the craftsman to excel as they had in their work. Could he have such dedication? Purpose towards a higher goal, one he knew went past himself and gave him...meaning?

The fox stared at the answer. It didn't matter to him that he'd only helped frame it. Every day he made the trek, put in the hours, and created an *accomplishment.* His hands still bore the scars. Mrs. Cammont just about refused to get the last of the splinters out. His hammers became dented, saws and axes bent and dull. The proof was there. How many others could say such a thing? He, Foxlaris Scottsworth, *could* do things. Things *beyond* himself.

Yes.

Yes.

It was settled.

He'd make the move to Mikyill. Leave Winthrop and focus his efforts. No matter the field, the fox would rise in the ranks, squeezing his dreams by the neck until they writhed into reality. Stories were over. *Real* change was coming, and he the progenitor.

Foxlaris Scottsworth wielded passion. And, now, had a place to aim it.

"I knew it!"

His reddish ears fell behind him. He turned, looking for the source of the peppy, giggling voice, and found it. Speeding towards him.

A mistake.

Asterlyn Carventon enveloped him in a hug. She jumped high enough to wrap her legs around his torso, but Foxlaris resisted, too petrified by the surprise.

"Oh, I knew I'd find you here, just knew it!" she proclaimed.

"A-Ast...Asterlyn?" he murmured out, carefully drawing back.

Those bright, emerald eyes still sparkled, smile wide and ears, tufted white, at attention. Mikyill hadn't changed a thing about her apart from her clothes—a tan sundress matched by a flower crown of dandelions.

"Hey to you, too!" She giggled and took in his new features. Taller, yes, and certainly grown. But his once childish face had faded. Gone. Now when he looked at her, a cold glare bore down. "It's been ages! How have you been, what's been going on, with you, Winthrop, Foxtamas?"

He parted his lips, but no words emerged.

What was he *doing!* Here she was after *years* away and he couldn't find a single *sentence* to say!?

Her beauty, her...her smile, tilted head...it felt impossible to take in. Some being of another world sent to steal his voice and...

And heart.

"Good."

One utterance and even that was almost too hoarse to hear. Still, it somehow got a laugh from Aster.

"Really, just *good?*"

"Um...yeah. Real good."

"Well that's uh...good to hear!" Aster chuckled, and Foxlaris matched with a stiff smile.

"And you?"

"Good, too! Mikyill's been fantastic, oh, you'd *love* it! I got a job as one of the Royal Florists there. This has been my longest break in *ages,* especially after preparing all the water lilies for this. It's a *nightmare* to curate so many up there, not without the proper standing water and such, which—"

Foxlaris faded from the conversation. Her words, the crowds, the hammer swings. He numbed and pulled his world within, except for the image of her glowing face. That was all he absorbed.

She'd accomplished his very dream, hadn't she? A genuine sense of pride warmed his chest. Yes, Asterlyn lifted herself from the same parentless beginning and did something. Found *purpose* through the smoke of an upturned life. That crown of flowers made her the queen of a conquered land.

And he just a peasant.

How could he of all people win her over? What skills or tenacity did he possess? Framing? Cutting down a tree? Leave a child with an axe and the same could be done. No, Foxlaris had nothing. Nothing for Asterlyn, for his family, for himself. Looking at the girl only solidified—and amplified—that feeling.

He'd lost everything the night his parents died, and his whole life was a journey back to the moment before the flames overtook their home. He would *not* be that weak little fox dying in the snow. Death wouldn't claim him there. The fox would get up and restore what he—and his family—once had.

And yet, when reality set in, the realization of the truth of his station reflecting in the green of Asterlyn's eyes...

That boy looked right back at himself.

He'd never gone anywhere.

And never would.

"But once we got the rest of the girls carted down here everything became *much* smoother."

"Yeah," Foxlaris replied, face a sullen stone and words crushed beneath it. Where his brother would have stuttered from the fear, he instead grew cold. Too much boiled within. The only way to make sure it wasn't known was to act as its muted, stoic opposite.

"Anyway, you excited about all of this!" Aster asked smiling.

Foxlaris shrugged his shoulders.

"I guess."

She returned a stiffened laugh.

"Well, um, I hope so! I heard they're going to try and get *everyone* across the Bridge today. I *really* hope that's the case."

"Same."

Asterlyn watched him for a moment, noticing his distanced gaze and ears stuck pointed to the clouds. The fox before her was not the same one she left and wrote to. Something felt off and guarded, and her presence was the last thing aiding it.

"Yeah, yeah…well, I'd love to stay and talk some more, but Madam Gillis will be needing me back to take over a stand or two."

"Oh, okay…yeah, go ahead," mumbled Foxlaris as if waking up.

"I'll try and find you at the Crossing! Maybe we can get the old group back together later today."

"That'd be good."

"Great! Good seeing you!"

"You too."

Off she went, melting into the rest of the Bridgeburrow crowds. Her memory, however, lingered. Lingered in the warring mind of the poor, lonesome fox.

"How, *how!* How could I have acted like that!?" Foxlaris whispered only to himself. The bags under his eyes from the early morning had grown worse. To appear so cold, so ignorant! And to Aster, of all people, *Aster!* Why couldn't he just let himself show, even with all that mess swirling in his head? Should he be more like the others? Jovial and boisterous like Bunns, or expressive and genial like…like…

Foxtamas.

A name he heard in Asterlyn's voice.

Of course she'd asked about him. Always he pulled her attention no matter what Foxlaris did to woo her. When Foxtamas saw her, he looked into the loving eyes of a girl. When Foxlaris did…he stared into a mirror reflective of his flaws.

The well-worn fox abandoned any admiration for the Inn. He quested, whether intentionally or not, back towards the Bridge Site and into the twisting lanes of stalls. He moved mindless of the others. The long, rustling wood above gilded by the noontime sun practically glowed and bathed the Evoneers in a kind, kindling warmth—but the darkness inside him hunkered deeper.

Once well-among a group of larger tents, those of minstrels and full-market merchants, his brown eyes spotted two bustling blips up the road. One orange, one white.

"Of *course* they show up now," he uttered.

He took a breath, and Foxlaris regrouped himself as Bunns and Foxtamas thundered at him. The sight of their cheery, breathless faces stirred in him a burst of anger.

"Finally, there you are! We thought we lost you," Foxtamas said, patting his back while sucking in the crowded air. The trio moved themselves over to an oversized yellow tent, doing their best to escape the rising heat. "Where all did you go?

"I, uh...nowhere exciting. Just wandered a bit."

"Yer should have been with us, Rizzeh! We were findin' some real goodies!" the jackalope shot over. He pulled from his star pouch a couple small jars of Harvest Lemon Jam (very out of season for the Middle-Evon region), the exhausted wrapper that once held a scoop of candied nuts, and a cutting knife, the handle etched with the same symbols as the Bridge. Foxtamas too retrieved his haul. Compared to Bunns, he had but one fine ornament: a crystal acorn.

The boys knew the significance. On one hand, it represented potential, a biding seed that, when ready, will sprout and grow into excellence. The other is nurturing of motherhood, encasing, feeding, and forming a beautiful child. Though they will outgrow their mothers, the genesis of their roots will never be forgotten.

"It's for Mrs. Cammont. I reckon she'd like it and can maybe make a necklace or something out of it."

Foxlaris nodded, but not without a hint of jealousy. While he'd been off falling into a pit of his own despair, his brother had gone and found something worthwhile. Because *of course he did.*

"Yeah, Foxtamas. Real great."

"Did you wanna go look some more with us?"

"No, I'm good."

"Sure?"

"Can't. I think I'm ready to get outta here."

Bunns groaned with a roll of his eyes.

"Really? Startin' this oup *again?*"

"Foxlaris," said his brother, aghast at what he'd heard, "you can't say that *now,* we're here!"

The elder fox stepped back and shook his head.

"Just…just stop, y'all just don't get it."

"What's there to get—"

"I said, *stop.*"

"No!" Against his usual demeanor, Foxtamas pulled closer to his brother, a hint of anger riding along his words. "Enough acting like this! I get it you wanna work, that's fine, but you can give it up for *one day.* Why can't you just enjoy yourself? And not be, be *miserable!*"

"Just listen—"

"I'm sorry we left you back there, okay? I knew it wasn't smart, a-a-and I hate it when you're alone—"

"There!" shouted Foxlaris. He pointed a finger right to Foxtamas' chest. *"That's* the issue. You can never let *me* be *me!"* The rage that bubbled within found its exit. It flared out like fire from his tongue. "You purposefully pulled me away from what I wanted to do to bring me *here,* where I'm trapped and embarrassed and away from achieving my *purpose!"*

"What's wrong with you?" Foxtamas fired back. "How is this embarrassing? It's a *festival!"*

"Not with you! It's just another way for you to suppress me like you always do!"

"Stop it, just stop it, Foxlaris! Do you even hear yourself?"

"Yeah, loud and clear!"

Bunns couldn't take the back and forth. Too much of his life had been dedicated to their bickering. One would think it would lessen as they grew older…

Instead, he leaned on the edge of the tent and peaked through the opening, watching as an elderly gnome, dressed in battered overalls and a winter cap, spun a tale to the dozen youngsters circled around his rocking chair.

"So, there the ol' lad was!" the storyteller weaved, "alone, back against the Hardrise Cliffs of the Guardmont Range. Toggybottoms held his axe close as a whole army of bugbears approached. Oh, they were gnarled I say, gnarled! Toggy, like any good dwarf, already whooped them too many a time to count. Their puffy fur had been sheered away, and all they had left was nasty pink skin coatin' their behinds!" His young audience all rolled around in a fit of disgust and laughter. Bunns giggled at the antics. "Thems bugbears was out for revenge. And they right thought they had it. But they was facing Toggybottoms! The lad gripped his axe, and with one last ounce of might, *swung* and *swung* and *swung*! He became a small twister on the cliffs! The bugbears were hit with such force they flew all the way into the East, never to haunt these grounds again!"

"No, just shut up! It's worthless!" Foxlaris spat out. The two were still bickering despite the thrill happening within earshot. Bunns glanced over and found them at his back, close to barging into the tent.

"I've done *nothing* but try and help you!"

"Don't you try and pull that now. Why do you have to be like this? Bunns wouldn't do it! Acirema wouldn't either! No, it's *you,* Foxtamas, *you* have to ruin things by holding me back. Go ahead and take a seat in there and listen to another fake little story, how about that!?"

"F-F-F...Fake?..."

The brothers whipped around. Unbeknownst to them, their ruckus had infiltrated the tent, halting the tale and exposing the hard, harrowing truth. Toggybottom wasn't real. Bugbears weren't either. All just a story.

And oh, did it crush a sweet coyote girl.

Bunns shot his head over to the pair, glaring at them with both disbelief and fear.

"It's fake?" another child asked. His question ignited a wildfire, spreading the worry across them all.

"Nae, nae," said the jackalope, crouching down amongst them. Tears welled, sniffles started. "Ol' Toggy was real as yer bae! Right Scottoh, Rizzeh?" He tried to signal them to agree, but the damage was done. There was no going back.

"You three!" The gnome cried out, raised from his chair, "get your sorry selves out before I get the Myriad on your tails! Out! OUT!"

"I-I-I'm sorry, I'm sorry—" Foxlaris tried to plead despite the shouting. Their eyes all looked at him, and in that moment, his anger, his need for achievement, melted from his mind. Their innocence begged him to be wrong. Curled lips. Rumbled chins. The story *had* to be true. The truth couldn't hurt like that.

It shouldn't.

The dwarf *had* to be real.

The fire *had* to be a dream.

His parents *had* to be alive.

Tears dripped down his cheeks. Snowflakes slain by the flames.

Could he ever do anything right?

9

"LIKE THE TASTE OF RIVERWATER."

G rammo Day lost some of its splendor.

They returned to the Bridge Site in silence. Foxlaris nestled under a tree, wishing to be left alone. Foxtamas and Bunns obeyed, sulking by themselves on the open shoreline.

The passersby beamed at the bright colors, the banners and flags furling overhead. But the younger fox no longer shared their passion. His brother was aching with a pain he couldn't see. Something clawed at Foxlaris' soul and, no matter how hard he fought back or how much Foxtamas tried to help, it wouldn't let up.

Was Foxlaris right? Could it *actually* be him? He wasn't sure, but…but maybe. The thought terrified him. All along was *he* his brother's downfall?

No.

No…

Perhaps his love for work had consumed him, and now Foxtamas only now noticed it. Yes, that worked better. Either way, the issue ran deep. Deeper into the soul of his kin than he'd ever understood.

"Think et'll blow over? With Rizzeh?" asked Bunns. He lay relaxed amidst the warming sands, but his foot continued to jitter.

"I hope so. Something's just eating him up here lately, and I can't figure it out. I just want him to be happy, Bunns. We've been building up to this day for so long, and now I've gone and ruined it for him."

"Come on, don't say tha'—"

"But it's true. Even if I don't see it, I've been hurting him. And he doesn't deserve it. Even if it annoys me, o-o-or scares me to think about. There's gotta be something to help him…right? Make at least this day better?" His head fell back, gazing at the clouds above.

"Ah suppose. Weh already spent our Tops, so weh cannae buy him anything. But et's gotta bae big, eh? Tae take his mind off things?"

"Exactly. Just needs to liven him up, get his spirits going again. But I don't think there's much we can do."

"Ah dunno 'bout tha' one, Scottoh…"

Foxtamas followed his friend's finger. It pointed past the Bridge, past the Myriad, and all the way to Grammo Day's northern edge.

The Royal Tents.

"Bunns," he sighed, "you're *not* going to get Acirema involved in this. Every leader in Evon is over there!"

"An' yer gonna let tha' stop yer helpin' Rizzeh?"

"Don't pull that—"

"But et's true!"

His face scowled. Why did Bunns have to be right? Life (usually) went better when he wasn't.

Still, thoughts of the worst-case scenario bombarded the fox. Sneaking in there could have them strung up by their feet, sent as prisoners to the Allmarsh, forced to forever flee Winthrop, implicated for an assassination attempt on the princess, ran through by one of the Myriad—

He could still see him. His brother. An orange speck curled up beneath a sagging oak tree.

"Fine. But *you're* going in."

This was to be her fifth slice of cheese and bread. If she could get it down. What else was there to do, though? Aisar would welcome in another guest before stuffing his mouth, Gniw following behind to partake in actual, congenial conversation. Acirema would of course bow, then nod, then smile at yet another comment, then sit back in her corner.

And that was it.

For hours.

So, she sat and ate, waiting for the Bridge to finally open.

Maybe turning into her father was inevitable.

"Pssst! Queenie!"

Her ears pricked up. Was this it? Was the boredom of tax gouging and elections driving to her such a level of madness? It had to be, especially with the voice being that of *Bunns!*

"Queenie!"

She glanced down to the bottom of her chair and nearly tumbled out of it. The voice wasn't imaginary—the jackalope was *actually* there!

"Bunns! What—never mind, get out!" She tried to shoo him, but, being as agile as he was, dodged her quiet kicks.

"Nae, listen! Weh need yer help!"

"What now?" Acirema sighed, taking a look back at the front of her tent. Father and Gniw stood engaged with some faun king she'd never heard of. Hopefully the topic engrossed them so that they didn't see the antlers and fluffy ears popping out of the floor. It was useless trying to push him away. At least he *tried* to keep quiet.

"Weh need ah favor for Rizzeh. He's all down 'bout somethin', and we want the laddie tae have a good day. Yer got anything?"

Puzzled, the princess gazed around the room. Nothing stood out as particularly interesting or worthwhile to someone like Foxlaris. Maybe some cheese?

"Nothing. What did you even have in mind?" she whispered back down.

"Ah dunno! Something, eh, like ah favor—"

"Favor? No! How could I even get that?"

"Recognize him."

Her glance shot from Bunns to Foxtamas, his head popping in from the other side of the chair. She read a clear look of distress upon him. This was not the same fox who left Winthrop. Perhaps Foxlaris was in worse shape than she thought.

"What?" she asked.

"Before the Crossing. Have your father, I dunno, commend him for his service and thank him for being a hard-working son of the Village, something like that. Please?"

A fair request. It could work, especially if Father traveled back to the Efeters tent for another sampling of their midsummer wines. But if Foxlaris would already be on the stage, then maybe…

Acirema grinned.

"I'll do you one better. But no guarantee, alright?" She watched his face lift, even just a little. Excitement roared in those blue eyes.

"Thank you, Acirema!"

"Aye, thanks, Queenie!"

"You two owe me!" she called after as they started to slip away.

"Weh'll pay double our tax for ah whole year!"

"Promise!"

And just like that, the heads disappeared, gone as quickly as they arrived.

"Attention! Attention, one and all!"

The sun finally lifted directly overhead, its beams drowning the enormous crowd below in a refreshing warmth. Thousands stood bunched at the Bridge Site. The Royal Tents lay abandoned, and many merchant booths moved from Bridgeburrow to accompany the mass. Most had absolutely no view of the large wooden stage set beside the Bridge. Others, such as Foxtamas, Foxlaris, and Bunns, were close enough to watch Gniw step up and begin the ceremony. Surrounding him, apart from the waving national flags and golden banners, were Evonian figureheads from all over the West. The trio could see the Efeterian Queen, village mayors, forest lords, dukes, ladies—

"Why's there only one dwarf lord?" Foxtamas asked, straining to peek over the heads and shoulders blocking the view.

A chair near the center, positioned close to the Winthropian royalty, held a bold, well-built dwarf. His hair bristled back in the easy breeze. Its colors of bright blondes and rich browns flowed to a gray point in his low, well-mannered beard. Beneath his fur-laden cape he bore royal garbs—a tunic with leather strappings—colored by blacks and golds woven across a blue hotter than a forge fire. He had such vigor, a power pumping through his image. Yet his countenance crumbled beneath it.

He kept his blue eyes pointed to the ground. As Gniw waved for the crowd to calm, motioning for the Myriad to contain the excitement, the dwarf didn't so much as blink. Few took notice. Apart from his admirers, of course.

"No clue. Which one even is tha'?"

"Looks like Enaled based on the blue," the fox replied, a ripple of nerves washing through his words. Just yards away sat a *dwarf lord,* one of the two leading descendants from the Wolverton line. Eobin, Bwayine, Oakwhall, Trobloh, the blood of warriors framed forever in legend beat through him. And he was *there.* Not in his mind, not acted out, as real as the pages that held the words. "But where's Foehn then?"

"Ah'd stay home tae if Ah had tae hear this ol' gob talk all day. Just look ah Queenie, she agrees."

They—Foxlaris included, although he kept to himself behind the pair—watched their friend slip between a polite smile and nodding off. Who could blame her? Gniw's keen nature didn't mean he wasn't long-winded.

He continued with stuttering preambles until the audience settled down. Once only the wind and the rush of the river waters could be heard, he broke the silence and began.

"My dearest Evoneers—or, rather, should I call you now *West* Evoneers—today will be forever etched in the books of our past. Your children, your children's children, shall read of our feat and gasp at the gusto, be blown back by such bravery!

"Today is the day we join together our land. For too long this home has been broken. Evon is missing its other half. Imagine, if you will, the loss of a spouse. Death of a brother. The running away of a child. I know for many here that's not just a thought, but a reality, one true and fiery in the forging of your life. You know, then, that pain and that agony that cleaves your soul. You're left hollow. Broken. And worst, alone.

"Would you wish the same for your home? This glorious land of safety, prosperity, security? No! This land is too precious to feel as such, and yet how long have we let her suffer? If you could, personally, would you not wish to amend the loss of your lives? Heal it, even? Bring everything back to a pure, perfect whole?"

No one spoke.

Foxtamas felt tears wet his eyes.

Behind, the breathing of his brother grew heavy.

"I cannot stand here and let our Evon languish any longer in this pain. We've been given a duty! One to heal our land and, in the same turn, ourselves! Now, my lovely Westerners, we do just that. No more shall we anguish at the gash River Nohsis places on our home, no! We will cross, we will see, and, together, as *one*, we! Will! *Heal!*"

Roars erupted. The sand vibrated. Boughs swung on waves of screams. Shouts drowned out every thought and concern possibly building within the crowd.

The President clapped together his wings, grinning. What a day! So much was ready to change, just dying to! This was his moment. This was *their* moment.

Evon's first step into a new era.

"Think she came through?" the fox asked once the cheering died down. "I don't see Aisar getting up."

Bunns shrugged his shoulders and tried to keep his voice down.

"Ah dunno, but Ah'm hopin'. Maybe bird brain'll do et."

Gniw finished his opening speech with a bow and shuffled in the inside of his vest.

"Now, someone must be the first to start our healing, correct? Cross our dear *Lo Losrym o Evon*, eh?" he asked, chuckling. Hundreds of hands cut through the air, followed by begging, nagging, *needing* to be chosen. "Please, please, settle down! We know the kind of honor that comes with such a choice. This person will be forever tied to glory of this Bridge of Evon, bound together within the annals of our collective history. We the Bridge Council—these leaders here before you—poured laboriously over who should fulfill this position. Names came and went for months, but we wanted a real soul. Someone hardy to take this mantle, someone unknown to you all now but, here shortly, will forever beget heroism into your hearts. And who other to provide that exact person but the precious Acirema Feiht, who I heard is a favorite among certain villagers."

His wing stopped ruffling, and from his jacket he pulled a miniature scroll, stamped tight with a red, double *W* Winthrop seal.

The boys' ears tingled. Their nerves leapt from limb to limb, buzzing lightning leaping across the skies before a storm. She hadn't just gotten him on the stage…

She'd gotten him on *the BRIDGE!*

Foxtamas covered his mouth. Little laughs leaked, but he plugged them up. Beside him, Bunns rubbed his hands together so fast he feared a fire might start. The fox let himself get one quick glance at his brother. Arms folded, he squinted through the crowd, wondering just who it was Acirema picked. Foxtamas grinned. *Wide.*

"So, without further ado, I welcome to this stage, and to the East, Village Winthrop's own son and finest worker, Foxlaris Scottsworth!"

Trumpets blared!
Drums beat to life!
All Evon rang with cheer!

A harmony! One singular song uniting background and body, heart and hearth. Melodious. A taste tongue-sweet, breathtaking. For once, *forever,* all melding into one.

The collective waited for him to make his appearance. The first to touch Eastern soil and usher in healing and hope.

But he made no such choice.

The brown, blurry eyes of Foxlaris stared at Gniw. He watched the owl's smile turn to a hearty laugh. His suit jiggled with laughter. The

President looked onward at him with amusement, but he looked back with fear. A freezing, choking fear.

Everything slowed around him as if barely easing through time. The noise of the audience shifted into the sound of the hammering, the stammering of Asterlyn. Foxlaris felt the push of Foxtamas and Bunns slam against him. Both bounded into the air, faces red, screaming, but stayed frozen. Others behind did the same. Hands pushed him, but he didn't move. He couldn't.

He didn't want this. Not this recognition. Not this…power. No, this was a nightmare. What he'd give to be back on that roof. Or his home. Or dead in the snows of Pradifore. He'd been wrong!

Why had Acirema chosen him?

Why!

WHY!?

"Foxlaris! *Foxlaris!*" The words of Foxtamas finally broke through his stillness. Rushes of unbearable noise flooded back to him as he returned to reality, drowning his senses and pumping in him a choking breath. "Go! I got you up there, now go!"

"W–W–What!?" he tried to mumble out. But the fox was powerless. Foxtamas just kept pulling and tugging despite his obvious refusal. "Stop, stop! Foxtamas!"

Nothing.

The Mikyill Myriad had him on the stage in a matter of seconds. Foxlaris couldn't even remember them lifting him up, only recalling his struggle and terror at the cry of his name. Now, though, he gazed out. Surrounded by the most powerful creatures in Evon, seen by the ocean of people. The endless, unnerving, horrifying waters. So many faces…so many bodies…so many souls staring at him…at *HIM!*

PUH!

Gniw slammed a wing upon his back, knocking the air from his already staggering chest. His cheery grin pricked back his beak and squinted his aging eyes.

"Yes, finally, Foxlaris! Worrying I know, to be the first Westerner into the East," he boomed out. The owl continued, but Foxlaris couldn't follow. The shaking orange sack focused in on Acirema at his left. Her eyes met his and dropped off a small gift: a wink and smile. On any other day, that would be reassuring. But now, it felt like mockery. Hatred. She'd set him up. Foxtamas had done something, or gotten Bunns to do it. It was them, they wanted him up here, they wanted him—

"Foxlaris, are you ready, my boy? To take your first steps into our new life?"

"I, uh, ye-yes, yes." The words burned his dry throat. Even a message that weak still made the cries ring out yet again.

The Myriad formed a strict border towards the Bridge. Shaking, he followed the marked path over to the base, followed by Gniw and his band of rulers. Instruments of all sorts rattled and blurted with each step. Frigid air petted his dark tunic and fur; the branches behind swayed fast, almost whispering and painting the far-off audience in speckles of yellow-tinged light.

As the Bridge grew closer, so too did the dingy, gnarled forest and ridges across the River. The East looked a home with no warm greeting, no band to envelop him as the one that sent him across. It appeared dead. Dim. Just as it always had.

It wasn't long before the fox finally positioned himself. So many thoughts overpowered him that his sole focus became his breathing.

In.

Out.

In…

Out.

Don't panic, don't lose yourself.

His paw gripped the Bridge's gilded railing. Cold to the touch. He couldn't think of that. Only steps, only breaths, only the Eastern abyss ready to swallow him up.

"Whenever you're ready, my boy," Gniw whispered from behind.

Foxlaris nodded. Swallowed. And took the first step.

No creak. The Bridge of Evon's woodwork showed in its strength.

That gave some reassurance. So, he placed his second foot upon the next step up and started on towards the East.

His fears quickly quelled once he faced the final stair and arrived at the Bridge proper. The sheer width isolated him. He looked akin to a single ant crawling across a log. Though still a good distance away, he made out the quiet curvature of the Bridge and and it's end landed on the pebbled shore. Just a short trek and he'd be there. Simple as that.

His steps didn't make a sound. Only the rush of Nohsis below met his ears, the entirety of the crowd behind silent, focused only on him. He took one last look at them. Clearly, Gniw and his fellow leaders would soon follow, along with the rest of the Evoneers dying to make history. Yet when he saw their faces, the light that glimmered upon them was gone. And the wind that wicked through his fur grew strict.

He paid it no mind. His grip tightened on the gold railing and he walked harder, faster. Perhaps, after all, Foxtamas *was* right. This felt historic. He, Foxlaris Scottsworth, stitched the watery wound with every step forward. The thought raised his shoulders, strengthened his stride. He began to practically march across the planks. When those on the shore saw the fox, they'd see a man ready to conquer this new world.

Until a gust of wind blew him back.

The bottom of his boots skirted along the wood as he tried to catch his balance. Another gale roared, but this time he pushed against it. The blow hit him like an invisible wave. He marched on and reached the midpoint despite the incessant whips lashing against him.

For a moment, he thought he heard chaos erupting from the Bridge Site. He turned back to find them equally confused as himself. No, they weren't the ones screaming—the waters were.

Foxlaris looked over the side. The streams once a bubbling azure erupted into sprays and curdles of a frothing, untamed alabaster. Nohsis raged beneath him. The longer he looked, the darker it grew. What little blue remained crept into a sullen black as the clouds above darkened. It became like ivory hands leaping from the shadows.

Above, the sun disappeared behind the dark shroud, leaving Evon in twilight. All at once the gilded accents across the Bridge lost their shimmer, and so too did Foxlaris stop his steps.

Something was wrong. This was no sudden summer storm. The fox tasted a staleness that clung to the air, watched as the trees on either side beat back and forth in the winds. By then the rapids had stirred such that they whipped along the Bridge's engravings, rising to spray him with chilled water.

What was he to do?

He turned back again. Through the darkness, he barely made out the waving hands of those on shore. They begged him to return and leave the fray before it became any worse.

Among the screams, he thought he could make one out specifically. A tone similar to his own, but higher. Younger. Pleading.

Foxlaris!
Get back!
Come on, hurry! Please!
Please!

No.

The East lay too close to turn away from now. If he wanted his brother to cross, to be humiliated and stripped of himself, then he'd see it through. He'd make it. *Proud.* He had to. Through the shame, the grieving, the mistakes, Foxlaris made his choice.

This moment was *his.*

But Evon had other plans.

10
"EVEN IN THE TEMPEST,"

K

C

K

A

A

Z

Z

Z

A

A

K

C

K

C

K

!

!

!

!

Fire fell from the sky.

T he bolt burned the world, a sizzling, crackling flash of blue; a wrapping of crystalline veins weaving downward like a fraying thread. It burst through the Bridge in total silence. Cleaved the middle, inches from the fox. Through the wood. The water. The land. A strike from the top of Evon to the bottom.

The West watched in unified horror. No one could breathe nor speak in the half-second interim. The thoughts, those of terror and confusion, didn't have time to register. They sat static with the rest of the bodies. Taking in the dawn of the destruction together.

BOOROOOOMMM!!!

Time began again as the thunder blew Foxlaris to his back and triggered the Evoneers to screams.

The Bridge!

It was *struck!*

Burning, falling and burning!

The blast shattered the oaken structure and sent it caving in on itself. Foxlaris shrieked. His clothing and fur ignited from the heat and burnt far enough down to singe his flesh. As he fell, pelts of rain launched from the sky. Each stung like a dagger driven thick into his muscles.

He tried grabbing at the stricken planks in panic, but the damage had been done. The Bridge of Evon collapsed. It dove into the raging Nohsis with a *CRASH!* and brought with it the screaming, wailing fox.

Winds, water, and wood swirled.

The darkness of the storm blinded him. He broke the surface for a second until a stray railing bashed him back down under. Foxlaris flung his body, oh, how he flung his arms, trying to raise himself, find freedom from the chaos, but he only sank deeper into the murky hell.

Splinters injected him with at every move. They pierced remorseless. The rapidity of the waves sent nails shredding through his skin, twisting him upside down, unable to orient himself. Nothing he did could stop the thrashing. He opened his mouth and found no air to cry. He opened his eyes and saw red seeping from his wounds and into the shadow of the River.

Foxlaris drank the pain.

Limbs tearing; sinews snapping; bones breaking into dust like the crumbling of rock.

The waters, tainted by the sharp shavings of the Bridge, infiltrated his lungs with each attempt to gain a breath, a second more of life to use to fight towards shore. A sudden slap by a chuck of oak kicked the water out, only for it to refill upon another desperate breath. Foxlaris swirled within a horrid, unescapable cycle. One flaying his insides and sapping his consciousness.

Pain. Surviving and pain. The only two thoughts he spared the energy to grasp.

The broken Bridge of Evon refused to let up. Nohsis held him down to drown. He felt no closer to escaping the rapids or reaching one of the beaches. When he could spare a glance around, it looked no different than the close of his eyes, except for the flaming blue crashes illuminating the water dozens of feet above.

He'd never peek his head above again…would he?

This was it.

Yes.

Yes.

It was settled.

He was dead.

The final thing Foxlaris Scottsworth saw was a wooden scrap barreling towards his head.

The rest of the West too fought for their lives. After the collapse of the

Bridge, the storm and its flares of bright azure lightning attacked and brought the ravaging of an earthquake. It cracked apart the runny soil long caked in the riverbed. Scars formed, racing down from the north and zipping past the Bridge Site. They widened like miniature abysses beneath the waves. As they stretched, they screamed.

It began as a groaning, one to match the quake's rumbling that sent tremors throughout the length of Evon. The sound was of a thousand falling trees or the howl of a storm amidst a midnight rain. Its terror grew as the crack in the River's center widened. Gorges of water, sizzling to the touch, spewed from the depths and flooded the remnants of the Bridge and its crosser. With them came the cry, that wretched, wretched cry!

A child's final shout before sinking into death.

A begging for mercy with cold steel at the neck.

A shriek as sharp as the snapping of bones, ripping of earth.

Judgement forced upon the innocent.

That was the cry. The scream. The overpowering, ear-bleeding screech enveloping the shore as Evon, once more, broke apart.

On that shore, the trees and poles holding up banners and flags toppled into the bellows of hysteria. The bloody mixture of wind and rain flashing to life in the blue blares sent the Evoneers scrambling. Yet wherever they ran, death followed.

The falling trunks smashed skulls into the forest floor. Lightning ignited splashes of fire amongst the trees and, to the horror of those inside the buildings, Bridgeburrow. The once meticulous sculpting and craftsmanship puffed to smoke in the bonfire, one that laughed in the face of the languishing rain. Tents flung up into the gales like the figures of ghosts; vendor stands swung through the open streets and crippled those running down them.

The Bridge Council took to bunkering down against the stage's backside. It held for some time, but the rains sharpened into hail, and no defense apart from full shelter could protect them. One by one they darted away to join the scramble, the terror, the running and going and going out of my way please move now hurry go go go watch out please go run jump move out please please go around hurry watch out duck run run move watch out please please please please *please!*

Foxtamas and Bunns barely avoided a tumbling pine. They ducked behind it once it stilled to put some barrier between them and the winds, trying to center themselves within the chaos.

"Bunns!" The fox's cry was almost drowned out by the commotion. *"Bunns, come on! We gotta reach him!"* He glanced over the log towards the River. Every passing minute it grew wider, almost as if the East was being pushed away. His look didn't last long before Bunns yanked him down to the ground

"Stop et, laddie! Yer gonna get killed!" Bunns spat mere inches from his face. Already the pair had withstood cuts and bruises from the whipping shrapnel. Corpses surrounded them, blood leaking into the sands and congealing them to mud. They needed to push further to Mechmilne and away from the storm. Find Acirema. The Cammonts. *Anyone.*

The jackalope tightened his grip on the fox's shoulders. It was all he could do to hold him in place. To ensure that at least one person in the thousands swarming the Bridge Site kept their life beyond this day.

"No, no, stop it, STOP!" Foxtamas shoved Bunns down. More bites of hail stung him as he did, but he couldn't feel the pain. Fear made sure of that.

The army mounted his walls in a full-scale assault. No part of him was safe from the pillaging, the slaughter, the images flashing in his mind of his brother dead in the river waters, a cold, blue body in his arms.

NO!

He couldn't die, he couldn't die, he *wouldn't die!*

Foxtamas could make it. He had to. He'd been the one to send him out there, and even if it cost him his own life, he'd be the one to bring him *back!*

"Scottoh, yer gotta stop—"

It was too late.

The fox ripped his slickened arms from Bunns and leapt over the log. He heard some yell behind but paid it no attention. That he saved for Nohsis.

Foxtamas pushed towards the waters. Beneath him the quakes still vibrated the earth, blurring what little vision he had left in the darkness. A sapphire strike brightened the sky for a moment. The hail blades glistened like the trees back in Pradifore. His eyes could barely see, his feet barely stable, but he pushed on, step by step by step, grinding his shredded boots into the sands.

"Foxlaris!"

A branch whipped his cheek, sucking out blood.

"Hold on!"

A hole caught his foot, twisting his ankle.

"I'm almost…"

The rest of his battered body gave way, tumbling inches from the waves.

"Almost—"

There.

He spotted him.

A bloodied, crumpled body lying amongst the rocks of the Eastern coast. Mutilated, pricked by splinters and waterlogged. Only his rich orange fur distinguished him from a passing piece of driftwood. His head stirred, and for a moment, his eyes fluttered open.

"FOXLARIS!" Foxtamas clawed at the sand, but the beads passed through his paws. He pushed. Screaming, he pushed. Begging, he pushed.

He gave the last of his strength to grip the sand and bring the tips of his hand to the water. And it was there he stopped.

Worn and ragged, wheezing and beaten.

Yet mortified.

For something moved behind his brother. A large, slinking creature of black eased Foxlaris from the pebbles and further towards the spiked outcropping of roots. The shadow set him aside, then gazed towards the West.

Towards Foxtamas.

Meeting him with a pair of bright, fiery, crimson eyes, made of rage, of fury, of the flaming fear that years ago stole away his family and home.

Now, more than ever, he had to cross.

Foxtamas raised his body against the beating winds. They allied with fear to stifle him, chain him again to the ground, but the determination in his bones, the passion surging through his body like blood, broke apart the fetters.

"I'm...I'm coming, Foxlaris," he whispered through the cacophony of

screams and shouts.

The way forward was too choppy and sliced with wreckage—diving in

would be suicide. Instead, the fox staggered further upstream, looking for a cease in the rapids or some chunk of debris to float across on. If he timed it right, he could be with Foxlaris in less than a minute. That beast would leave him alone, his brother would be saved, back on Western ground, alive, and—

WHACK!

The final thing Foxtamas Scottsworth saw was a limb rushing towards his head.

II

"EVEN IN THE BURSTING BLISTER"

"Folsym…
"whist mekioh…
"Folsym…"

Foxtamas, with heavy care, lifted his long-sat lids. Hazy lights flooded his sight, the brightness fading in and out along a spectrum of heavenly baby blues. He squinted past them to see what called out to him. Only more glows misted into view.

"Lo Fulno, whist. Mek fulno roides," the airy sound spoke again.

"Wh…what?" The fox shifted his head and found himself on a cot, covered in sheets of white. He'd no memory of what had brought him there. And, with it, no other memories at all. He knew himself. But everything else felt empty.

"Foxtamas."

The voice above took the form of a creature looking down towards him. A single remembrance flashed over his eyes. It was one buried in the shadowy halls of his mind, but emerged as he looked over the womanly face, with glowing and floating blue hair and silver eyes glistening like the sun on the sea.

"El…El…Elf" he mumbled. No, it wasn't a memory he found, but a story. The fabled cousins of the Efetes. Long gone from Evon. Illusive. Light-forged. Servants.

The guess brought a smile to the elven maiden. She brought her warm hand to his face and brushed across the bloodied gash near his temple. The fox felt no pain. A cold relief flushed through him. It deadened the wound and all others scarred over his body. His nerves tingled with rejuvenation, a fresh, lively pulse thumping through his veins. Foxtamas took it in. Breathed easy, deep and slow.

His blue eyes eventually looked back to her, trying to focus on her radiating beauty—the curve of her smile bringing dimples to cheeks the texture of eggshell, lashes long, leaving a mist of sparkling blue as she blinked.

"*Your brother. Foxlaris. He lives.*"

"Brother?"

He knew not the word. What was it? Something that was his, it seemed. Had it...died? Was it near?

Behind the maiden a coterie of elves approached. They stepped together, following a unifying hum, and eased close until they fully encircled his bed. All wore long, rich blue dresses woven in the style of feathers flowing down their legs. The garments lifted along the calming breeze of the air before, as they floated past, dissolving into a haze at their ends. Like a sapphire fire trailing smoke, they fluttered. Past the fox's cot. Along the grass. Outside the tent. Beside the River...on...on Grammo Day...

"Foxlaris!" The word finally gained meaning. His brother! Yes, his *brother!* They were there, at the Bridge Site, and he'd been chosen to go and walk and cross and—

The elf's hand once more crossed his face, this time covering his darting eyes.

"*Whist, whist, he lives.*"

"But, Foxlaris, he, he—"

A quiet, dampening sleep grew along the edges of his vision. The fear built inside the fox fought back at the attack, edging on sudden memories of the lightning strike, earthquake, storms, eyes...

Until the sleep silenced it all. Smiling, the elf maiden took back her hand, joining the floating band, but not before seeing the blue sparks settle about the fox's head, keeping his terrorized soul at rest.

12

"OF THE GALE, EVEN WHEN THESE LANDS"

"Hno! Sharpege tool, sharpege!"
"Vor…?"
"Liwez lehg."

Foxlaris awoke to gurgling, gagging voices. All was black besides their words. They radiated from either side of him, spat instead of spoken. They made little sense. He could almost make them out, but the slurry of sounds split, sawed, and mutilated what little he understood. They worked their speech until it became unnatural. Otherworldly.

The slow simmer of thoughts stirred the fox's brain just enough to peer through one of his eyes.

Dark gray stone—the color of dry-rotted wood and ashen grass—composed the tight room. Lanternlight burned near the ceiling and drooped down a faint smell of stale lavender. Along each wall dangled metal objects, the detailing of which his blurry vision failed to grasp. Could they be…knives? Axes?

It mattered little; the voices finally had form. Two beasts darted back and forth through the dimness of the chamber. Both looked to be of the same deformed species: pale of skin, hunchbacked, and hiding a hairy, beastly body beneath black robes dragging to the floor. Together, they studied something outstretched upon a freezing slab made of the same coarse stone as the walls. From the fox's view, it appeared scarred, beaten, bloody, and…orange…

"GAH! AAHH!"

Pain choked any other words from escape. *HE* was that ruined scrap of flesh! The glowing bottom log of a bonfire; an egg cracked and scattered through a kitchen; a sugar sack so worn and torn not a single granule keeps. The torture bathed him. Every corner, every scar screamed in an agony unkempt, uncontrolled, widening in scale the faster his waking heart began to beat.

He couldn't take it! He *couldn't!* His soul *shriveled* inside to *ash* and *dust!* It would never end! This was his eternity—a dying, crying horror not even the darkest of nightmares could conceive!

"Healers."

A new voice. Slick, smooth. Aged, though youthful still to carry snarky wisdom and honest care. Foxlaris felt a cooling cede over his mind as it echoed behind him. "Progress?"

Raucous words passed from the beasts tending the battered fox, but he paid them no attention. His head strained up, catching a clouded look at the approaching figure gaining definition in the dim light.

Tall he stood, shagged with a shimmering silver fur reflecting the lamplight, deepening to black as it flowed down. A long dark robe—similar to those of the healers—outfitted him, though with swirling patterns of red ornamented across the sleeves and back. This was no regular attire. The night must be late, this newcomer keeping long watch. But his face showed no call for sleep. Only laid-back ears, a stout, inquisitive snout, and, shocking to the fox, bright, wide, blistering eyes of red.

Foxlaris forgot all pain the moment he looked upon them. Though blurred, he felt the strength of their gaze, and the horror they revealed when the fox blinked.

"He wakes, you fools!" cried the wolf. He swung back around in a flurry of fabric. "Would you have him feeling your blades!? Hughlich, burn more Stillroot, ease the poor soul back."

The wolf disappeared, and in his place returned one of the brutes.

He shoved a wad of frayed, smoking tendrils at the fox's nose. It overpowered the rest of his senses. The fumes curled black and smelled of thick mold. Foxlaris tried to move away from it, but the wafts pulled him back, holding him tight until the muscles in his neck slackened, and the world once again faded into darkness.

You see him across the chasm.
Your brother,
running for you,
looking your way
He sees you
and the taste of riverwater
leaking from your mouth.
The tears, through riverwater,
leak from his eyes.
You see him
looking the other way,
running from you.
Your brother.
You see him fade across the chasm.

13

"SHAKE AND SHIFT UNTIL YOU CAN'T"

The messy filter of sleep lingered as Foxtamas awoke for a second time. He expected to see his shabby Winthropian walls bouncing back the light of an early workday. Instead, he squinted at the patched, waving white curtains of a tent. He knew they weren't new to him. They'd appeared somewhere before, but...where?

A gap lingered in his mind, one he could almost touch. Something had transpired—important, by the feeling of it. He wasn't supposed to be there.

Carefully, as to avoid straining his long-dormant muscles, Foxtamas slid from his cot. A beige gown, no sturdier than a smock, covered him. He took notice of the many bandaged scrapes along his arms and legs, though no pain lingered beneath them. Once up, he rubbed his eyes and fully analyzed his surroundings.

A tented infirmary. Solely holding him. The rest of the dozen or so beds laid empty, their blankets and covers wet and unfurled.

What was he *doing* here?

The fox found the entrance near the end and pulled back the flap. As he did, a monstrous gale broke into him, sending back his weakened body. He barely grabbed hold of the white felt of the tent to steady himself. Once settled, he ventured out.

The bare bottoms of his feet felt the slop of soggy, withered grass. Beyond it dipped down the shore and the shards of glass, wood, and rock mixed within. The sand had turned to a blotchy brown. But

Foxtamas didn't care for the coast. His focus lay on the River—or, more appropriately, the sea.

The water spanned miles. Its life, that of bubbling ripples and sprays that caught the glimmer of a dawning morn, had died. That River Nohsis faded into memory. One replaced by a murky, gray expanse, solemn and stilled, no different from a man in the final days of a disease. A thin fog billowed over. Lapped far enough in to ebb at the fox. Through it he could make out the distant Eastern ridges, their tops pronounced like the spiked back of a hedgehog. Like a shadow that haunted, but never grew any closer.

And it was in such shadow that Foxtamas finally remembered. The stagnant driftwood and flag scraps reweaved the tale. That of the pain whittled into body, the endless death of Evoneers, the destruction of their home, the horror, the loss, and—

"Foxlaris."

Red eyes seared his skull. They sapped his strength, pushed him to his knees, forced tears to fall, fall and drown the broken ground. Those mythical voices returned to him in their wispy, foreign tongue, but he couldn't trust them, didn't believe what they promised was true.

"F-F-Foxlaris, please, please," he begged in a warbled whisper. "Please be alive. Please…please."

"Foxtamas!"

He whipped his head behind him. The voice he knew, but hearing it again only cemented that this new, twisted world wasn't a dream.

Before he could stand, Acirema embraced her friend in a hug. She squeezed him tight between a sigh of passion and relief.

"Acirema," he sighed. "It's you."

"Yes," she said, almost gasping. "Yes. We thought you were never going to wake." The princess pulled back. The poor fox looked ghastly in his robe, but she was no different in her sodden black dress, long dirtied at the hem. Her eyes stared long at his, noting the deep shadow overtaking him. His body looked healed; his spirit, however, still lay in pieces.

"Acirema, I-I don't know what's going on, what to do, where I am—"

"Shhh, it's alright, okay? Let's get you to camp."

Behind the tent and along the dark edge of Mechmilne, a small fire flickered through the rising mist. Two burlap sacks containing foraged food, blankets, and pans lay near two cots stolen from the infirmary.

Acirema made quick work once Foxtamas took his seat on a downed log by the flames. She wrapped him in a spare sheet, sliced off a few bites of apple, and helped rewarm the fire for the fast-approaching night. Hunched over and hungry, the fox sat. She dared not prod him with a single question.

"How…long was I out?" When Foxtamas finally spoke, he did so almost to himself in a parched tone no louder than a whisper.

"A week."

She sighed even saying it.

"Wow…" he gulped. "Somehow it felt longer."

"Did for all of us."

The evening sky quietly darkened—the grays fading to a duller shade—as the broken bramble beside the camp rustled. The pair glanced and found Bunns emerging. He too had not left Grammo Day unscathed. Bits of loose fabric wrapped around his bruised arms, stalling the power he could put behind his stars. Thankfully, his thumping spirit, though slowed, still beat. Even more at the appearance of his friend.

"Well, hey Scottoh. Been ah bit, eh?"

"Yeah," Foxtamas muttered, taking his time to focus on his words. "Yeah. It has."

"Mum an' Pa' tried tae keep meh back, but Ah couldn't."

Together, the trio sat huddled around the fire, bearing the chilling drafts of riverfront wind. Long, golden lanes of light flickered back and forth among their grim faces. A ballet of shadows to the step of a crackling choir.

Bunns swallowed the last of his bread. "Weh vowed tae stay. Had tae make sure yer weren't gonnae die on us. Tha' hit did you in. Ah've been stoppin' thieves from gettin' tae close while Queenie tended tae yer head."

"I got special leave from Father before the other Winthropians left," she added.

"But I can't tell I was hit," the fox replied. He caressed the area again. Without the bandage, no sign of the impact remained. "The elf said something I didn't catch while she healed me. I—"

"Elf?" The princess squinted in confusion.

"Yeah, in the tent. She and a bunch of others were there humming and floating, and…singing, at one point, I think. It's still hazy," he retold.

"You *would* dream that," Acirema snickered, careful not to break the tension. "The Efetes were the ones tending to the wounded early on. You must have seen them."

"No, these were *elves,* I could tell. I saw them, I *know* I did. They spoke in this language I didn't know and made me…forget. Made me forget…him."

Silence took hold. Both Bunns and Acirema knew what lay heavy on their friend's mind. It shattered their hearts as well, but…they saw the blue bolt. They saw the Bridge of Evon burn and collapse, whip and tear into millions of shredded bits. They saw what no Evoneer could survive.

"Did he show up?"

"Foxlaris?" asked the jackalope, voice low, somber.

"Yes, did he make it back over? At all?" His blue eyes fell on the pair exchanging poor, hopeless glances. "No…no…"

"We checked with the survivors," Acirema began, "hoping to find him. We did our best, searched everywhere. However—"

"No, stop!" A pitiful, raspy rage clung to his voice and trembling chin. Tears welled up, orange ears lying low and soft. "I saw him, Acirema. I saw him get dragged from that mess, by some, some *beast* in the East. Its eyes were this bright glowing red and it scared me and it's all I saw before I went cold. B-B-But Foxlaris got dragged up, okay? I-I know he's alive. He's gotta be." The streams dripped down his face and wetted the blanket. Each individual muscle pulsed to keep them in, but the memory, that elf-hidden, blood-red memory, it squeezed out. It stampeded through the floodgates of fear and worry, and once opened, little good rarely followed. "I-I-If you don't think so, then go. Both of you. Why stay anyway, huh? Are you scared? Scared to go back and see it? Winthrop, it's a mess...isn't it? It's gotta be...it's gotta be..."

What *stupid* things to say! Foxtamas turned his back from the fire the moment they left his lips. He needed to conceal both his tears and shame. These were his *friends*, the only people willing to stay back and guard his almost lifeless body, and he disregarded it. What a fool! What a stupid, scared, worthless little *fool!*

But they saw him in no such light. They knew the fox true. There, alone on the nippy night, life in every corner of Evon frozen in despair, Acirema and Bunns reflected.

Staying was running. She knew the gut-wrenching horror awaiting her when glaring at the empty homes of her people; Bunns already felt the failure mounting inside when passing the graveyard, unable to protect the very neighbors he lived around. Winthrop *was* a mess.

Everything was.

"No."

Their ears perked, eyes wandering from their troubled souls to Foxtamas, blanket off and facing them. "No, I don't mean that. You guys protected me. You cared for me. I don't deserve a lick of it. I'm just—" Without realizing it, shakes of fear rolled through his body. The quakes flashed images of Foxlaris alone; the burning crimson eyes; his hands reaching out at the widening Nohsis. He had no way out. The fear ran cold. Dark. Twisted. It wrapped around his neck, baring fangs of ruination, aiming to strike—

"Easy, Scottoh. Weh gotcha."

The blue eyes opened. On either side of his log sat his friends. They had unfurled their sheets and cloaks and wrapped him, leaning in with a loving embrace. Slowly, the shakes subsided. His thoughts eased while taking in the deep passion shown by those closest to him. A gentle wind of peace drifted along.

Though a deeper, underlying longing failed to leave. The situation's weight fell upon him like a firm raindrop upon a spring flower. Instead of caressing and dripping along one of its petals, it sank down, far into the open and fragile core, softly suffocating it.

Foxlaris was lost.

Evon lay in ruins.

The lives they knew, stable and stagnant, adorned by the same folk, talk, and tales, vanished.

All seemed bleak. Not only for him, but within the heart of every surviving Evoneer. His friends' love was a start, yes, yet it could not quench such a deeper need nor answer the unanswerable. No matter in Mikyill, Efeters, the Fulnoa, or Winthrop, all asked the same miserable question.

Why?

The dawn fared no better than the night. A still, overcast sunrise limped into the sky. The trio were already awake to see it. Sorrow often brings heavy sleep, but sleeplessness stalks right around the corner.

Together, while gathering what belongings remained, they decided it finally time to head for Village Winthrop. Foxtamas still held out hope that Foxlaris survived. If his brother had gone anywhere, it was there. To his home. Acirema and Bunns couldn't argue with the logic. The lost fox meant a massive deal to them, as if he were their own flesh and blood. Hope stirred, even if light. But another issue fell upon them, one Foxtamas' fear blinded him from seeing.

"Yer ready, Queenie? Ah mean, really, really ready?" Bunns asked, stuffing a rough woolen blanket into his makeshift pack.

"I have to be," she said softly. Waves licked the brown shores, coming into tide. So many lives had perished upon those sands—so many of *her* lives. They'd never walk back through Mechmilne or see their home or hug the necks of those too elderly to take the trek. And they'd never see the day they all had hoped for.

The day she'd be their queen.

"My people need me…right?"

"Ah think so. Just like mah family will bae needin' meh." He tried to flash some semblance of a smile. The princess took it to heart, nodding while stomping out the dying flames. A part of her ached to stay with the sharp, bloodied shore. Not because she loved the muted riverside, far from it. Acirema didn't want to leave behind the reality those lost souls would forever haunt. The time and place where she was still free from all responsibility.

Before long, the makeshift campsite lay abandoned, its inhabitants pushing through the ruined shrubbery of Mechmilne Wood. Bunns armed a star in each paw as the friends found their way to one of the roads. Across the way, both up and down, merchant stalls and carts were splintered and overturned. Goods were gone, weapons stolen, and every scrap of clothing long looted. Both bandits and Grammo Day had tidied it up nicely.

"Keep yer eyes out, laddies," commented the warrior. "Them thieves don't like tae give warnin' when robbin'."

Thankfully, the road remained empty apart from the dampened and broken branches, fallen limbs and trees. They stuck out like rusted bones reaching towards the sky.

But nothing compared to the sight of Bridgeburrow. The once prized Inn, ready to hold Evoneers from every Western corner, barely held up two walls. Ashes and oaks had crumpled it during the storm.

Such force blew out windows and doors and totaled the structure. The rest of the village shared a similar fate. They'd cut that wood, those two boys. Foxlaris along with them. Polished it, cut the holes, flushed the nails. And for what?

For thieves, it seemed. In their stopping to stare at the damage, a few shadowy figures bolted from a dilapidated tavern's side.

Bunns hopped into action. Both stars raised, he shouted over and tossed a warning, burying it into the tavern's side. To his surprise, Acirema too readied herself. She put up a measly fist and scanned the forest for danger.

Thankfully, the rustling silenced. The pair lowered their stances and breathed a sigh of relief. Foxtamas, meanwhile, shook a look of fear and confusion from his face. He'd shrunk back when his friends stepped up. What kind of a fighter was he? Or, worse, what kind of *friend?*

Pressing forward proved all the more intense. The thickness of the forest squeezed them into a tighter web of despair. Every leaf and hidden blade of grass sank low; their roots withered with the same fear and disgust that had befallen Foxtamas the day prior. Where far-along snapping branches once began the rhythm for the call of adventure, they now warned of danger, a brief signal, rattling and sharp. The wind tasted sour. The sickly dampness plugged their noses. No beaming rays, no whistling tunes. Only the torture of trudging back to a ruined home.

At noon, the friends finally returned to Village Winthrop. Crossing into the clearing and looking upon the gently sloping hill confirmed every one of their combined fears.

Thick, darkened clouds downcast the mood. Even a week after the terror, the presence of death clung close. The rickety houses had already begun to lose their shape. Thatch had blown away, the structure of the walls bent inward. With no owner to make repairs, they stood as an off-kilter monument to what once was.

The white gravel of the Main Road scattered into the uprooted

garden beds. At its end, the Palace slinked back, cold. Unaware. Un-
caring. The gilding of its roof and columns dulled, the wood stained
dark from stormwater. Not a soul roamed around it, nor at the other
buildings, shops, or homes. All apart from the two Winthrop Watchers
to the left of the friends.

There, near the swaying birchwood grove behind the Cammont
Household, the graveyard lay, growing with each *thud!* of the Watcher's
hammers. Wood crosses popped up like saplings. Dead, lifeless saplings.
Callings to eras now unspoken, lives well-lived. The fox stepped closer
and read the hastily etched names lining the frontmost row.

Samwell Ochet
Elisha Toffelton
Berry-don Mussen
Midas D'lohg
Nore Makin
Seshly Minnel
Foxlaris Scottsworth

"No…"

The face of Foxtamas Scottsworth twisted. His lips snarled. Eyebrows lowered. Fear did not do it, oh no. Its armies had surrendered to
the new sensation, the one dominating the fortress of his mind.

Passion.

"NO!"

His cry blared into the solemn silence. Bolting away from the
others, he pushed past the innocent guard, shoving him into the muddy
piles of dirt. *"NO! STOP! HE'S NOT DEAD! HE'S NOT! HE'S
NOT!"*

Never had the fox moved with such ferocity, such precision. While
the Watcher cowered, Foxtamas slammed his grip upon the cross. He
read it once again.

Foxlaris Scottsworth.

Lies. Utter lies. Stupid, stupid *ruthless* lies.

They had no clue about the life tied to that name. They didn't hug him. Hold him. Know him. Love him. They weren't his friend...they weren't his family...

They weren't his brother.

Seeing his greatest fear realized, the fox let loose the rage. His quivering hands uprooted the marker and flung it into Mechmilne's darkness. Once gone from his sight, he turned the burning gaze to the other Watcher.

The gnome cowered, but Foxtamas' eyes refused to focus on him, blinded by the righteous fury. He *should* be scared! This man painted false truths upon his home! Spread lies! Tried to kill his very *kin!*

But....

Could he be right?

Were the elves truly just a dream? And those red eyes a trick played by the ferocity of the storm?

If so, then...then he, the blood of his blood, had desecrated the only grave his brother would ever have.

No, that's nonsense! It can't, no, he couldn't.

But what if...

He ran. Tears unrelenting, heartbroken and bleeding, he ran, ran away from the shaken guards, the ruined graves, his worried friends. Foxtamas dashed to the Cammont Household. There he broke past the creaky door and disappeared.

Gone.

Gone into pain.

"Scottoh! Wait!" Bunns called after him, darting off while Acirema tended to the troubled Watchers. Both wished to reach out and help their friend but, well, they didn't know how. A deep grief poisoned him now. One that heightened his fear and tainted his passion for the worse.

Mrs. Cammont stopped her son as he ran in. The jackalope mother looked the part of a wraith—tattered white gown long and weary, rings sunk beneath her swollen brown eyes. Tears had carved riverbeds down her cheeks. They seemed to be melting, slowly and surely, drooping and sagging, speaking what her sullen countenance couldn't.

"Bunns! Wha's gone on, wha's the matter?" she croaked through a weary throat. The sight slammed his sprint to a halt. How did she look like this? So stressed, so...broken. What had gone on? What did this to his own *mother!?*

"Mum, uh," he tried to spit out. Clumps of tears already formed over his eyes. "Foxtamas, he was sayin' tha' Foxlaris ain't dead. A-A-An' he got mad an—"

The jackalope was cut off as his mother fell to her knees before him, wailing and staining her apron on the disheveled, unkempt floors.

"Mum!" Bunns dropped down to catch her. Corlawn hardly found a breath between the trembling sobs. "Mum! Please, Mum!"

"Not him, not him, too...Nae, nae!" The tears overtook her, and the dried beds filled up once again, transporting the liquid grief down to the floor, cutting a crater in the dust.

"Mum, wha' do yer mean?" A gaping fear swelled within Bunns. His voice shook, and he hugged tight to his fallen mother, rocking her like she used to him all those years ago.

"O-O-Op-Opel...Opel..."

Who knew if she went on after that name. Bunns couldn't hear it. The throbbing, panging beat of his heart rushed through his ears as his head fell, tears not even dripping, just ebbing away towards the floor.

Opel. His cousin. Wheelchair bound, freedom fighter against the evil the Winthropians faced. Dead. But not just dead.

Dead on his watch.

He, Bunnclar Cammont, proclaimed warrior, was *there!* Right there on that shore where she died, unable to run from the tumbling trees or suffocating tents. And in that horror, what did he do?

Hid.

Hid!

And to think he could protect a single soul.

Not hers. Not Foxlaris'. No one's. And where was he while this grief devoured his household? Father gone to weep for his niece in the shadow of his solitary company?

Pretending to fight. Pretending to be any help against petty thieves. He hid at the Riverside once and he did it again, because how could he not? The truth always trickled out. Bunns would never be the warrior he needed to be. He'd never let his true self show, that scared peasant boy failing to hold together what little family didn't get dragged away. And when the real battle came—the one a star couldn't finish—he'd crumble.

Those were his final thoughts while sobbing against his mother. Both were crying. Crying pain. Crying loss. Crying hurt. Crying need.

Crying.

Crying..

Crying…

Without realizing it, Bunns had left the door strewn open, letting his queen watch the painful scene unfold. Never had her heart been gripped so. These were more than her people. They raised and loved her, cared when it felt like Winthrop and the rest of Evon were ready to burn her real family to the ground.

Now they sat. Crumpled on the ground. Hearts burning and begging for a balm—a relief their princess could not provide.

But it was the sheer scale of it all that sent her flying towards the Palace in a badgering of sobs. This scene was only one example, its pain multiplied by every shack she passed. Each Winthropians felt it. They'd spent their entire lives looking towards their Golden Girl when times fell hard. *She* was their hope. *She* gave comfort. Now what could she give? When their needs surpassed little wages and fresh clothing?

Nothing.

Her heart was but pieces in their already broken pile.

Her pattering up the road added to the Watchers' chorus of nailing crosses into the ground, leaving behind only a name for those who rose that day expecting history, only to fall asleep the victim of tragedy that would forever shape their lives and land.

Hours passed.

Acirema lay drained of tears and the power to stay awake. Her mind drifted around a motionless sleep until a familiar rustling graced her ears. She stirred towards her window and looked down at the trail cutting through the grass.

The princess slid down her old climbing rope she used to use as an escape. Once at the bottom, she shimmied along the Palace's wall, heading towards the back ledge which overlooked the Village. One turn of the corner confirmed her suspicions.

"I'm going to find him, Acirema." Quiet yet determined, hollow but alive. Foxtamas didn't turn away from the ledge. He kept his knees tucked tight towards his chest and eyes lingering on the great gray sea of River Nohsis fading away in the dusk. No lights shimmered below. The wind howled lonely through the empty streets.

Acirema eased down beside him. She studied his orange face as she did, noticing how puffy his blue eyes still were. Hers probably looked the same. "He's out there."

"Hey," she began, rubbing his back, "it's alright. It's alright."

"But it's not." He gazed back at her, doing his best to match her softness. "It won't be until I do something about it. I just can't sit here, Acirema. He's out there with no one looking for him. He's as good as lost. And I'm to blame for it."

"Come on, don't put this on yourself, Foxt—"

"It's true. You know it," he firmly let out. "I asked you to get him up there."

"But it was *my* decision to send him across."

"A decision I started."

She couldn't deny it. The fox had put the idea into her head. Without him, maybe she'd have chosen someone else. And maybe Foxlaris would be sitting there beside them.

"I see," Acirema whispered.

"I did this. And…I can't let it stay this way." Foxtamas lifted his glance to meet hers in the dimming night. "I saw him get dragged out. I know he's alive. It scares me to *death* thinking of going over there, but I have to. He'd do the same for me. And if it takes finding some sort of courage, then I'm gonna start looking. Foxlaris won't be lost out there in that great big scary whatever, Acirema. He won't be."

She had no words left to say. Heavy doubt of the fox's survival ruled her mind ever since seeing the bolt shear through the Bridge. She'd never admit it, but looking for Foxlaris really felt like an unwinnable game to distract from Foxtamas' pain.

But now, transfixed by those deep blue eyes, the doubt eased. Perhaps he was right. Perhaps, in all his worries, games, stories, and fears, he developed a passion that, though buried deep, lay unmovable. She couldn't fault him. The princess knew she needed that same resolve to rule—but it didn't exist. Perhaps it never would.

"I believe you," Acirema said after a pause. She rose and placed a hand on his shoulder. "I really do."

Foxtamas held on to it for a moment before letting go. A way to tell her he needed to be alone.

"Thank you."

With a nod, she crept back towards the Palace. Foxtamas was left to stare ahead at the vast riverwaters separating the civilized from the frontier. Its ridges loomed far back, casting a shadow over the fog, complimenting the heavy gray skies on the verge of dipping into darkness.

Soon he'd be facing that land. Maybe, with a pack stuffed tight enough with food and supplies, he could get past the ridges without stopping. Or just make camp past Nohsis with a lightened load. Whichever choice, he'd be there. No different than Sir Emri Helmstead and his travels around Evon. He could even fashion himself a walking stick, the same way that old cockatrice did when his war wounds worsened. Yes, that would be nice. Exciting, even.

In that moment, the thought turned from a mirage into a reality, and, as it did, the very core of his being shuddered as if left to die in a blistering Pradifore wind.

No, no...no, what was he thinking! Going to the East? After Foxlaris? His brother—no—the last member of his family? Who he *killed*?

What a delusion, what a mess! It was insanity. Not even the going, just the thinking.

Stupid.

Hopeless.

The Red Eyes beat his weary soul. Skinned him, seared him, sapped him of the will to continue. What if he were to meet them face to face? How would he fight!? A few mere thieves he couldn't even *see* stopped him in his tracks, petrified. Would he run away, leaving Foxlaris behind just like he did on that fateful night in Pradifore? Or take him back only to kill him on accident?

How worthless. Worthless! He knew what he was doing, imagining himself some hero on a righteous quest. That's always what he wanted.

"They were dreams, Foxtamas. It's time you grew outta all that."

Those words, those haunting, haunting words, were right. He was no hero. This was no quest. It was another story he couldn't live beyond swinging sticks and flipping pages.

Foxlaris was as good as lost. All because of him. All because his fearful self never learned how to grow up. And he would suffer for it.

Suffer the whipping winds billowing past and the image of a broken Village Winthrop falling into the widening mouth of darkness.

14

"RUN OR WALK OR STAND UPON THEM"

"Easy now, easy. No sudden moves."

Like water quenching thirst. Foxlaris, without realizing, obeyed the calming voice. Again he dragged open his eye, this time with far more clarity than before.

Gone was the dank dungeon closing in on him. He instead lay in a bedroom, outfitted with such lavishness Aisar himself would be jealous. The walls were painted a dark, fine maroon, softly accentuated by trickling candles sprouting warm light at the corners. Wardrobes, shelves, and a desk filled the space. They took on the same crimson color as the walls, only they were carved of a gnarled wood swirled by blood-red knots. Long curtains blocked the semicircle of windows rising from floor to ceiling. From them trickled splashes of moonlight. They soaked the woolen quilts tucking in the fox, warm and dark. Never had a bed felt so complete, nor room so sizable and, strangely, singular. He'd expected to find multiple beds for the others sharing his room, but here it was…just him.

And the wolf.

"I hope you feel comfortable."

He looked the same as in the dungeon, with a simple robe strung over his shoulders and crimson gaze ever so slightly brightening the room. It stared at the fox. He stared back. With his eye. His…

One.

Eye.

Foxlaris blinked and could only do so with his left lid. The right gave no movement, no sight.

Panic sliced across his throat to silence his scream. Shaking, he tried to grapple over the socket with his hands, but nearly fainted from stabs of pain that came from moving. They nearly paralyzed him. But no, he *had* to know. Foxlaris fought through it, grappling at his face, and when he did, felt nothing, apart from the sting of metal rubbing at his gaunt cheek. His good eye glanced down. Instead of his left hand, a rigid metal hook protruded out through an oozing, fleshy wound.

"NO, STOP, STOP!" the fox cried until his throat wheezed. What had happened to him!? What was this, what had gone on!? It couldn't be real, it couldn't be real, please, it can't be *real!*

"Easy, easy!" shouted the wolf. But his demands came too late. Foxlaris whipped and roared his agonizing limbs, twisting them about the bedspread and tossing the sheets to the floor. Doing so tugged against hundreds of splinters threaded throughout his body, no different than the tightening of a woven doll. Each individual bite seized him like a dagger thrusting in and out over and over and over again. The pain, panic, and fear—that deathly fellowship—overpowered him. Without thinking, the fox lurched over the bed with some hopes of freeing himself from another second of the torture.

"Stop, please!" his companion cried. "You'll only hurt yourself more!"

Thankfully, the wolf snagged him in time to stop the flailing fox from hitting the ground. At least most of him.

There, dangling from the bed, hung a wood pegleg outfitted from the same red wood as his room, replacing his right foot.

Foxlaris stopped. Despite the ferocity of the pain, he held himself together. His one-eyed gaze refused to leave the missing foot.

"Please, I know how bad this looks, all of it, but we did *all* we could, I assure you. The second I saw you in the River, I hurried you back and our healers operated immed—"

Foxlaris snatched the wolf's neck. The scarred, ruined hand squeezed deep as the broken remains of his emotions boiled over. His limbs were sawed off; his brain pounded like a drum to the beat of pain. Never would he hurt someone like this, gagging them and shoving nails into their skin. But he had no choice. He had to survive.

Thus, the agony, pulsing through him like new blood, joined by feelings inside just as beaten and disfigured as himself, stirred into a new amalgamation, one that seeped down and wet his soul.

Rage.

Gasping, the wolf pulled at the fox's hand. He watched his singular brown eye twitch, eyebrow even raising over the metal patch screwed into his skull.

"S–S–Stop! *P–Please!* It was to save you! *To save you!*"

THUNK!

The guardian hit the floor. He gulped for air and rubbed at the claw marks scrathed into his neck. Foxlaris stared him down from the bed. An unbridled, untamed madness swirled through his stare, one spurred by the wicked change forced upon his once ripe and youthful body.

However, as the wolf rose back up to meet him, assuring him he meant no harm, the fear, the rage, the very *need* to fight back and defend himself, subsided. Pain swept in to replace it.

"Tell me," Foxlaris began, etching out words through the stings and stabs, "what happ—"

WHOUGH! HOUGH!

Two nasty, roaring coughs flung from his mouth, forcing the fox to hunker over.

"I will, I will," said the wolf with calm melting off his voice. He patted the red smock that dressed Foxlaris and waited for his fiery cough to subside. Thorns and brambles scratched at every breath of air.

Once at ease, the wolf took his seat back on the bed and began his recollection. "Many, many months ago, years now, even, whispers spread of something forming in the West. A coalition, or formation, something along those lines. I'm not sure how it is on your side, but here, we do not treat such rumors lightly. We kept scouts posted and reports flooding in, all until the news arrived of that bridge being floated down the River.

"We suspected invasion—more so than we did already. You can imagine my surprise when, as I scouted at the coast, prepared to send signal of an attack, I spotted ribbon and color floating upon your winds. You Westerners! While we hunkered down quivering with fear you all were *celebrating!* I personally didn't have the wits to understand it, but I watched anyway, all the way up to you taking those first steps..." The wolf held his head down, almost ashamed to meet Foxlaris. "With the distance and the rapids, I couldn't hear much. But to me, you looked some...pawn they pushed across. Sacrificed in some twisted, twisted game—"

Another cough, this one spurting up specks of blood that blended into the quilt. Foxlaris gasped for air. He closed in on choking until the wolf pressed closer, patting his back and guiding his breaths.

"But," wheezed the fox, "they didn't know..."

"No one did. But what a man says with his actions is only spoken in the echo of consequence." Gentle, he placed the fox's hand in his own. "I witnessed them as you drowned in that horror. They *hid.* The only soul they cared to save was their *own.* I've been grateful every day since that I stayed to watch. Had I not, you'd...no. I dare not think it.

"I caught you just before you floated too far downstream. The winds blistered and rain blocked my view, but I pulled you out and into Forguile. Everything here in the East is, well, more cluttered, wilder than the lands Westward. I won't lie and say it didn't strain me physically to haul you. I sustained injuries of my own. But they matter little. What does is I made it back here with you still breathing."

"And where's...here?" asked the fox.

"Vordemohr. Our capital of sorts, our stronghold. Our home."

He *had* been brought to the East. Suspicions grew ever since his first waking. Now, he confirmed it—he'd actually completed the Crossing.

What did it matter, though? Yes his body lay broken, yes he could barely breathe an entire breath, but before any damage had been done, he'd been…abandoned. No one cared enough to save him. His own people. Village. Friends.

Family.

To them he was as good as dead.

"Our healers began work that night and didn't stop for days. They did everything in their power to keep you alive. I must say, it was a rough ordeal as you can, well, attest to. I wish it upon no one. By the end, though, we saved you." He passed the fox a quiet smile, yet found a cold, hardened husk in return. The one singular brown eye looked past him, glazed over. The tale appeared to weigh heavier than he thought.

"Velrick, by the way," said the wolf, extending his hand. "Apologies for not stating it earlier."

"Foxlaris." His working hand eased up to meet the other outstretched.

"It has been well worth the wait to meet you, Foxlaris. You are one strong, strong individual, you know. To undergo that torture and still end up alive? That's a fighting spirit we all can proudly envy. But now, I figure you want to see the rest of yourself, right? What all we had to, um…alter?"

Did the fox have a choice? Slow and careful so as to not inflame any wounds, he rose, aided by Velrick. The peg foot almost sent him toppling. It felt like walking in an oversized sandal, dragging along the carpet and kicking away his balance.

"There, just one step at a time," the wolf encouraged as the pair hobbled. Between two wardrobes along the back wall stood a tall mirror. Velrick steadied the fox next to it and turned to offer a brief warning.

"It *will* be shocking. I'm not sure there's a way around that. Just remember to breathe and don't panic—I'm right here for you."

With that, Foxlaris stepped toward the glass and looked at the reflection. The reflection of a monster.

His left ear was gone while the other lay chipped. Beneath them, deep, jagged scars ripped away the orange fur. They reached his eyes—the good one swelling with tears—and formed an obvious dent under the patch. The metal sheet was attached to his eye socket with a border of small screws. What little the smock showed was enough to upheave whatever lay rotting in the fox's stomach. Gashes spread across him like a field of dead grass. Slices from nails, tears from wood, cuts thick and gushing with puss—his body bore it all. No longer was it that of a fox, but the aftermath of a battlefield. Scarring trickled down his arms and legs, eroding away entire swaths of orange. The metal hook's flange and the wooden peg leg were both screwed into his bone with similar yet larger screws as his patch. His tail was long done away with.

Velrick was right—it shocked him. But the ferocity, the pure *barbarity* of his look, it ever so slowly faded the longer his eye crossed back and forth over his injuries. They clawed at his stomach, shuddered through his shoulders when he glanced at his hook. Yet the fear of what had happened simmered away. In its stead rose a new feeling, one the fox never knew he'd have to face.

Desolation.

This was his body. This horrific mess of jumbled fixes to keep his broken spirit alive. It could never return to how it once was. Neither could he.

His world, as he knew it, had vanished. The days building Inns, living in Winthrop, breathing the Western air with his family…gone. He was deep in the East now, hidden within some room with a figure so mutilated it would fuel nightmares of all the folk back home.

This was Foxlaris.

This was his life.

And what did it amount to…

His eye looked back towards the mirror. He watched as Velrick gathered closer behind and placed a hand upon his shoulder.

"I know I can promise many things in this moment. I can say your hand will regrow, or your tail will appear in the morning. Empty hope. But what I can say, with *certainty*, is that all will be alright, Foxlaris. I am here for you. All of us here at Vordemohr are. The West may have left you, but we won't. We won't."

Velrick ordered a servant to bring in a light dinner once Foxlaris settled back in bed. Within moments, a short, bald, and unfortunately ugly creature slid into the room, two plates of simmering fish and berries in its hand.

"W-What is that..." stuttered Foxlaris, taking his plate. Its ears ended at a sharp point with glittering silver eyes practically bugged out from its pale head.

"Oh, just an alp. Greasy little things, aren't they?" The fox noticed the sharp teeth and red tunic covering its little stature. To him, the alp looked closer to a sickly gnome than anything. "Their kind are incredibly common here along our border. Long ago, they were adamant about serving here in Vordemohr. No one wished to refuse such a generous offer, so they settled and have multiplied ever since. Kyrell here usually tends to me, but I have since assigned him here, with you."

Long ago. To him, everything seemed far newer than the nicest of what he owned in Winthrop. How old was this Vordemohr place?

"But anyway, I am not here to prattle on about *us*, Foxlaris." With a quick bite of fish, Velrick set the plate aside on a nearby table. Kyrell made no work swooping it up and dashing out. "If it's not as nefarious as I had imagined, why did the West send you across as they did? Or, rather, how did you end up being their chosen to begin with?"

The fox pondered the question, but not before inhaling the late meal. It tasted different than what Mrs. Cammont would prepare. More spices, extra flavor stinging the sides of his tongue. He liked it.

"I'm not all that sure myself," he muttered through the last helping of berries. "I wasn't supposed to be. I wasn't even supposed to be there. Heck, really shouldn't have been from my village to begin with—"

"Now *that* is a story!" said Velrick, grinning. "Do share, if you feel up to it. I've nowhere else to be this night and would lend each ear towards it."

For the first time since his awakening, Foxlaris Scottsworth lifted his lips in a smile. Not a broad one, barely noticeable, even. But to hear such enthusiasm about *him,* well. It brightened the room.

Thus, his story drifted along, recounting the events of his parents' death, his miraculous appearance in Winthrop, and the life of poverty thereafter. Velrick watched with deep anticipation. He latched upon every detail and mulled them over. One, however, always seemed to stick out no matter the tale.

"So," he cut in before finishing the events of Grammo Day, "your brother, this Foxtamas. He seems awfully prevalent. Are you two close?"

"Yeah, you could say. I guess more when we were younger. Same with our other friends. We would run around, y'know, play stories and games like kids do. We loved it. But Foxtamas…"

What could he say of him?

He didn't want to slander his own brother. Of course he'd acted foolish in the past, but so did everyone. Foxtamas never *meant* harm, he just…caused it.

"He never could let go of it. It's like he never grew up and, well, it held me back."

"Held you back?" Velrick asked, confused.

"I wanted to leave Winthrop. Get a job somewhere big and show people I was more than just some peasant boy. I could have done it, too."

"We agree there!" chuckled the wolf.

"But Foxtamas couldn't see the vision. He made it seem like I was mad or something to want to leave. Worse, when it came down to it, I mean when I *really* thought I was outta there, I felt guilty for leaving him behind. He's my baby brother. My family, my *real* family. I know how dumb and illogical that is—"

"No, it's perfectly logical," said Velrick. "Those bonds have a truer power than either of us know. My worry, though, is if his holding you back was *actually* a new development. How can you say you only just now felt his intolerance? What if you were merely the victim of such a life together?"

Foxlaris paused a moment and let himself fall back to easier days and brighter nights. He could see him there. His brother. Wading through the shallows of Nohsis. Cheery, giddy, shaking at just the thought of a single Winthrop Watcher catching them in their play.

A new pain seared across his chest.

Longing.

"I...just...don't know," he started, focused on that young vision of Foxtamas. "He was always Momma's favorite, that's one thing. She let him go out foraging with Poppa while I stayed back. They thought I would get too sick out in the cold. I always got sick, but he could do whatever he wanted. The same thing happened in Winthrop." His head sank lower the longer he spoke. Within it, the image of his brother...twisted. Every word and recollection he confessed made the rapids run harder, the sky gray dim, then darken. "Asterlyn...she liked him more than me. He told me it wasn't true, but I could tell. I could always tell.

"Everyone liked him more. Acirema and Bunns did. The Cammonts. All of Winthrop. He made up stories, forced us to play his games. They loved him for that. No one liked the sick one. The quiet one. No, I always had to do my shifts alone while he got to work with Bunns or the others in the crews. He got everything. He got...their love. And I couldn't do a thing about it."

Usually when his feelings for his brother darkened as such, a force pulled him back, reeled him from the depths of that despair. Always he found a light to see Foxtamas in. Truth sought him out.

But here, in the black of his room, only one light came to him.

Lightning flashed, and Foxtamas laughed. The light illuminated him in a blistering of blue, crackling and popping like fire within a shadow. He grew taller as the winds blew colder and the River rose to Foxlaris' knees. The cacophony of sound battled the actual silence of the chamber. In it, Velrick gave a slow nod, careful to not let the tears leak from his eyes.

"Maybe," he said, "you've been lying to yourself. I fear it an easier task than you may imagine. *You* were the one who changed. He stayed stuck in those stories, while you, dear Foxlaris, you took the right steps forward. Now finally separated from it, you can see the truth. Foxtamas was no brother. And for that...you've my utmost sympathy."

Foxlaris couldn't utter a single sound. His brother raised him up, high into the storm blistering his skin with nails of hail and pummeled him back down into Evon. The impact exploded the Bridge beneath him. Walls of water sprayed into his lungs, splinters stabbed and beat his body again. There, in that reliving of the Grammo Day horror, Foxlaris heard it.

"Go! I got you up there, now go!"

The *truth.*

His own brother, flesh and blood, put him on that Bridge and watched as it tumbled down upon him. *He* caused this. He caused *all* of it. The eye, the hand, the foot, the ear, the tail, the scars, the cough—HE did it.

"*He did this to me.*" A whisper at first. Low and rumbling, building higher with every word. "He sent me across. He did this. *HE* did this!" shouted the fox, smashing at his plate and crumbling it under the slam of his hook. Rage again boiled over. "He made me cross the Bridge! *HE* made *ME* into *THIS!*"

"Is this true!?" gasped Velrick. He didn't mind the shards splayed across the covers—he pulled closer regardless.

"He TOLD me! He said it to my face, t-t-to mock me! To *mock me!*" With his words came flashes of the storm, and with the storm the last memory imprinted upon him. There, across the surging, bloody River...his brother.

Foxtamas saw him. He saw him like *this.*

And instead of helping, he ran.

"He couldn't even look at me. He...he *left me.*" The fox's breathing staggered. "He left me *to DIE!*"

More words clambered to explode off his fiery tongue, but another fit of coughing overtook them. This one buckled the fox over. He clawed at his neck to ease them, yet only doubled the pain.

"Breathe, Foxlaris, yes, there you go," guided Velrick. It took an entire minute for the yawping to subside. Once gone, Foxlaris collapsed upon his pillow. Exhausted.

Velrick waited until his wheezing returned to full breaths before striking back up the conversation.

"I cannot say I know your brother, but from what you say, it reads to me of jealousy; fear, even. It's like the killing of a blue rose. Do they have that tale in the West?"

The weakened fox barely shook his head.

"Ah, I figured. It's less of a tale and more of a euphemism. Imagine a rose with petals blue instead of red. Such is a rarity—beautiful, unique, defying all expectations. But it's different. New. And in a world that wants only red, blue cannot be allowed.

"Thus, what should be exalted is instead pruned, snuffed from this world and stomped deep into the ground. There it still may grow, only now stunted. The life it deserves forever out of reach. Sounds to me like you and your brother, is it not?"

"Yeah," he croaked. "It is." The words scraped through his lips.

"And as I've promised you before, you will not be stomped here. You are safe, and more importantly, *wanted*."

With that, he rose and swept the pieces of plate to the ground. "It's beyond time I get going. Tomorrow, if you can manage, I'll show you around Vordemohr. It's quite the place."

Nodding, Foxlaris watched as Velrick went to exit the red room with a bow. "Goodnight, Foxlaris. Thank you for sharing with me your life."

He couldn't make a reply beyond another nod. As the wolf left, Kyrell made one last trip in to clean the mess and pinch out the candlelight. It left their guest in a newly familiar darkness.

Amidst the flickers of light down the blackened Vordemohr hall, Velrick smiled. It cracked back his cheeks like dried mud. How long had he gone without one?

At the end stood a gargantuan door guarded by a cockatrice, armored in a blackened metal with a halberd outstretched like a staff.

"Vorde Velrick," his brassy voice boomed upon seeing his master approach.

"Listen, Getophry," the wolf called out, "gather a patrol and send them to the River, back to where they set up the Bridge. Make sure no one else comes across. The last thing we need is an invasion, especially with the plans finally forming."

"It will be done, my Vorde. I take it he lives, then?"

"More than you know. But hurry—report to me in my study when it's done." With that, the guard took off down the hall and Velrick slipped past the door, descending a stairwell blacker than an abyss.

No sleep came for the fox. Though stilled in a motionless dark, his own mind and body kept his soul stirring. Around and around his vision swirled. Images of Winthrop flashed like the strikes of lightning. Warm and bright, homey and thriving. Within it, the faces of Acirema, Bunns, and Foxtamas looked at him in disgust.

What a *wretched* thing Foxlaris had turned into! They couldn't associate themselves with…*that!*

They must leave him to fend for himself. But when had they not? Were they not constantly scheming behind his back? Trusting in his stupid brother, listening to his jealous, jealous lies!?

Their malicious gaze alone forced open his wounds. Splinters shot and punctured fresh aches across his body. Loud *Whoops!* and *Achs!* erupted with louder coughing fits. The fox flung himself across the bed. Every quilt wove into a knot as he tossed his pillows, begging for one brief reprieve of peace.

Yet, despite the thrashing, his friends appeared every time he closed his eye. Taunting him. Why could they not leave! They had driven him away, driven him to hide his true feelings for purpose and escape. They made him like this.

But now, after finally showing his true colors, Foxtamas forced him to be alone. Broken. Ruined. Mutilated.

He did this.

How had Foxlaris ever loved him? Ever *cared?*

If only he could inflict one missing tail, one sliced ear upon him. Foxtamas deserved this. Not him.

Not him.

Not him!

Not HIM!

WHACK!

In all his unbounded shaking, the fox slammed his head against the backboard of his bed. It cut him out cold. The maddened thoughts of doom and damnation subsided.

It was darker than usual.

15

"WILL THE BEAUTY OF THIS LIFE LAST."

Night finally enraptured Village Winthrop. The few lights that burned had long been swept out as sleep stilled the souls of the sulking villagers. It was the only thing that could. Even if for a few short hours.

Foxtamas took it as his call to leave. He wiped away the tears still clinging near his eyes and set off from the damp grass. Passing by the Palace, Acirema's rope still hung from the side. He recalled for a moment the excitement that once tingled from his nose to his toes at seeing it. Now...now it meant nothing.

His feet crunched the gravel. What was even waiting for him back at home? He knew about Opel. He knew about Mr. and Mrs. Cammont, so grief stricken that, before he left for the hill, they were locked together in their room. It would be depression. A dead, changeless depression. He couldn't stop it any more than he could save Foxlaris. All was lost...wasn't it?

"*Psssst! Scottoh!*"

The fox's head shot towards the birch grove nestled beside the Main Road. There, hiding among the black and white bark, stood his friends, cloaks on and hoods drawn.

Foxtamas diverged from the path and met with them under the darkened branches.

"What are y'all doing here?" he asked, voice creaking as it regained composure from the long tenure of tears. "It's late, y'all need to sleep."

"Nae laddie, not when yer gonna leave tonight. Weh're comin' with yer!" Bunns said, winking. But Foxtamas stepped back in bewilderment.

"W–What?"

Acirema placed a gentle hand on his shoulder.

"To find Foxlaris. I told Bunns about your plan, and we agreed: you're going to need help, and we're here for it. If all goes well, we can leave soon, maybe even before midnight."

"No, stop!" the fox recoiled. "I'm not going, okay! It's hopeless. I'm crazy to think he's still alive and that *I* of all people could save him. I—" His watering eyes glanced at the stunned faces of his friends. Their shock sapped his will to continue the denouncements. "I killed him..." he murmured. "I...killed him..."

"No." The princess squeezed his arm tight, this time pulling him so close he couldn't get away. "*You* said he wouldn't be lost. *You* said you would brave it all to find him. Why say all of that, Foxtamas? Why?" Bunns hopped over and placed his paw upon his friend, smirking. "Because it's *true.* Don't let being scared hide that fact. You *know* Foxlaris is out there. You saw him get dragged out of the river. His life is dependent on you, but that doesn't mean you have to go alone. Together we can find him—I'm certain of it."

"B–But what's in it for you? Or you, Bunns? It'll be dangerous beyond *belief*, and horrifying, and terrible, and you both *wanna* go? Who knows what's out there! Beasts, monsters, thieves! Just like the red-eyed thing! And what about the people in Winthrop? Don't they need you? Why!?"

"Because Ah couldn't save Opel," the emboldened voice of Bunns broke through. He stiffened his back so Foxtamas could see him fully, unable to betray his answer with another string of scared lies. "But Ah can help save Rizzeh. Tha' lad needs us, nae matter how bad things mae look. An' if them beasties are out there..." He lifted the flap covering his star pouch and winked. "Yer need someone watchin' yer back."

"And I—," Acirema broke in, "I can't do a thing for my people. They... need time. Time to grieve, time to grow. I'm clueless on what all I can do for them, Foxtamas, so utterly lost. You and Foxlaris need me more. That's something I *can* do. And maybe, after the end of all this, I may know the answers they need. But Bunns is right. Foxlaris' life is worth being scared for."

His walls fell.

Fear's standing soldiers surrendered to the army of hope surrounding them. They put their hands up to the array of gleaming swords aimed at their sides. As long as the blades stayed in place, the fox had nothing to fear.

Foxlaris was worth more. He was his own blood, his family—he was worth the trial.

Foxlaris would not be lost.

Foxtamas looked back up to the somber yet smiling faces. Nodding, he pushed forward to embrace his friends, new tears—those of joy—welling and dripping down their shoulders.

The hug tightened as removing the shroud of fear unveiled the truth. Foxlaris wasn't dead. Not even by his own hand. Like escaping a vivid nightmare, Foxtamas awoke so eager to taste the reality that he could feel himself ready to bolt towards the East that minute.

Foxlaris was alive.

Alive!

"Thank you," he finally sputtered out on jagged breath despite being crushed on both sides by his friends. "I-I-I don't know what I'd do without y'all."

The trio jumped into action. Acirema made her way back to the Palace where she'd scavenge what supplies she could before meeting the boys back at the grove, the spot chosen as to cloak them from any suspicions. Meanwhile, Foxtamas and Bunns would prepare their own packs at the Cammont Household. Once done, readied, and set, they would depart, travel back down to the Bridge Site, and float across on whatever wood they could salvage. A good plan. Great, even, as Bunns put it.

The boys wasted no time getting back home. Passing through

the dilapidated door made it squeal a nasty squeak, but besides that, silence. Nothing stirred. Usually, they would hear Mrs. Cammont busy herself with some village gossip, something about a Wardenson-this or a Fuanorado-that. The same with Gregabbit. His thundering thumps echoed loud enough to shake the walls, less so than his booming laugh or accommodating grunts at his wife's tales. Yet, in the room lit by a single dying candle melting upon the table, such memories faded. The only ones to make a sound were Foxtamas and Bunnclar finding their haversacks.

"It's, um…quiet," mumbled the fox while making his way to the pantry.

"Aye. They cried themselves tae sleep after yer left. Ah ain't heard ah peep since."

Foxtamas nodded. He tried not to let the sorrow slip back in and sour his unusually optimistic mood.

"Opel was rough, yer know. But Rizzeh…yer two are as much as they're sons as meh an' Rein. Ah…ah cannae imagine wha' they're feelin'…"

"But that's why you're helping, Bunns. To save Foxlaris *and* them."

The jackalope, a bit teary eyed, winked at his friend. That son-of-a-hen knew him too well. More than Foxtamas reckoned, and more than Bunns dared to show.

"Yer right. An' Ah'm the one supposed tae bae keepin' *yer* spirits high. Go start gettin' yer clothes, Ah got the food," he shot back.

"*You* getting the food? You sure about that?"

"Ah'm ah master class cooker an' eater, Ah can pack ah meal like one of Aisar's royal cooks."

"You know that doesn't mean much. The man'll eat anything."

While Bunns gathered an assortment of spare fruits, breads, and flasks, Foxtamas picked about his wardrobe, putting on the best outfit he could match together. He chose his nicer blue tunic, outlined in threads of silver, matched by his dark trousers and muddy brown work boots. He tied it together with his cloak. Years ago, during the "thief era" of their adventures, Acirema pulled a few strings to make three black, matching cloaks as gifts for the Night of Calmas. The three boys soared about Mechmilne with hoods up and capes to the breeze. Wonderful times. Now, outfitted as a true adventurer, those stories and games were coming true. Just dressed as a thief stealing his brother back from the East, not Cherry Sugar Fizz from the royal cellars.

Once finished in the kitchen, Bunns bounded in and readied himself. His outfit paired well with his friend's, though he went for his maroon tunic, the one "fashionably" dotted with gold that Corlawn bought moons ago. Yet it fit him like a child wearing a smock. Thankfully, with cloak on, belt tightened, and star pouch fitted, the lad made the look fearsome in a way only Bunns could.

Foxtamas hiked up his half-full haversack and turned from his room to go. Acirema would be meeting them soon. But a pull, one that never leaves your mind until you address it, one that stays and barks and bites until you inevitably answer, struck him.

He was leaving Village Winthrop. He was leaving the Cammont Household. His home, his life, his entire world was, without question, changing and being left behind. It could…be the end. It could also *not* be, but to step away and embark into the wide world of Evon required closure. Every good story had it, when the hero ventured out upon his quest, leaving behind those he loved for the sake of the greater good.

Thus, he declared his promise to return—and Foxtamas would do just that. If not for the whole village, then for the two poor jackalopes that took him and his brother in all those years ago.

The fox leapt back into their room and pulled out an old blank leaf of paper from his shelf. With a nearby lead piece, he scribbled down a note, one of thanks and admiration, hope and reassurance. Foxtamas wished to believe his own words of being gone a day or two and returning perfectly safe. What mattered, though, was that the letter gave the *Cammonts* relief about their disappearance. If not, Mrs. Cammont may reach Foxlaris before they could. Once done, he lay it on the table and, beside it, the acorn he bought on Grammo Day.

"Ready?" Bunns asked, smirking at the letter and gift.

"Yeah. Guess I have to be."

The usually punctual princess was running late. Perhaps Aisar had held her up, or Watchers questioned her sudden need for light, filling food. Or, as Foxtamas worried, she was caught, nailed, and hanged in the dungeons to die. A dumb fear, and one easily disproved as her silhouette sneaked past the streaming moonbeams filtering through the birch branches.

"Sorry for the wait, decided we may need a few more things than anticipated."

Bunns perked up and turned to his friend, taken aback by the massive sack she dragged by her side.

"Wha' yer got there?"

"Something you'll like." Acirema had dressed herself nicely, picking from her vast wardrobe a look fitting with the peasant duo. Her tunic was dyed a rich, royal purple. It wound around her slim shape, showing slips of her silver undershirt. She had tied it at her waist with a small belt and threw on her black leggings and gilded dark hood. The shimmer of the gold would out her as royalty eventually, but her bet lied on no one in the East knowing enough to care.

The raccoon set aside her pack—stuffed with proper dried trout, pears, berries, breads, and Butterswath—and opened the lopsided sack.

"Weapons! Really!?" Foxtamas exclaimed. "What are we gonna do with those? Only Bunns knows how to use them."

"That's why I got these for you."

Out she pulled two fresh, never fired crossbawns, just as gorgeous as they were on Grammo Day. Both boys gasped at the sight.

"Crossbawns! For Scottoh? An' not meh?" protested Bunns. He pawed at them, but the princess pulled them away to hand to the fox.

"Yeah, Acirema, I dunno—"

"No, they're perfect for you. Father purchased sets for the recruits that were supposed to come in after Grammo Day, so I assumed you could work them easy enough. They're so new I had to pry them open from storage crates—not even the *Watchers* have gotten their hands on them."

"Well, yeah, but won't I run out of bolts?"

A sly smile eased across her face, and her hand went back digging into the sack.

"I have you covered." To the boys' shock, Acirema pulled out a bow. One   slender and curved without crack, the wood the color of a dark, crimson sunset. With it came a full quiver of arrows that bore an ornate crown on the side. "I can cut down a few of my spare arrows to make more."

"*Yer* spare arrows!" Bunns could hardly believe his eyes—no, he couldn't believe them *at all.* Queenie…with a bow? A *weapon*? "How in *Evon* did yer get tha'!"

Smiling, the princess threw on her quiver and felt the bow in hand. It would take some getting used to after a lull in practice.

"Oh, just ol' Gregabbit. You two know him?" She smirked at their rolling eyes. "He hated seeing me defenseless and worried what might happen one day if no Watchers were near. So, he petitioned father to fund me this here set and, when you three started off to work, I did so as well. Just…secretly."

Her smile was contagious. Foxtamas and Bunns beamed *just* a bit to see their perfectly primmed princess a little rough and rowdy for once. It fit her oddly well. But she could never be a better shot than Bunns; he reassured himself of that.

"Um…wow, alright then. I'll take your word for it," the fox replied, baffled.

"Yeah, yeah, Queenie's gotta bow. Wha' yer got in tha' bag o' goodies for meh, eh? New stars or somethin'?"

"Not really…"

His heart sank. No star emerged, no sword, no bow. Just a fat mallet, worn down at the edges from its daily work on the grave shift.

"Yer kidding meh…"

"Listen, it's hard to pick something for the self-proclaimed 'warrior.' I thought a hammer like that could do you well. What if that Red

Eyes wants to get close and personal and all you have are some stars?"

Oh, why did Acirema have to be *right*. The jackalope couldn't admit it, though. Instead, he shrugged and tucked the weapon into his belt, satisfied with its look at least. "Oh, and Foxtamas, one more thing."

The last, and perhaps grandest, object emerged, this time reflecting the pale moonlight illuminating their exchange. She presented a dual-headed axe, its thick wooden handle woven with blue leather and upper frame bejeweled by a shimmering sapphire on either side. This was no Winthropian weapon. Someone, decades ago, must have brought it as some trophy or treasure from a distant Western land. One could feel the sharpness of the blades even at a glance. No Watcher dared wield it, that was for certain.

"This is, um, a bit more than the crossbawns," he said upon taking the axe. To his surprise, it swung across the air with ease, needing only a slight heft.

"Mah mah, Scottoh, yer sure yer can handle tha'?"

"Oh, *easy*," he snarked back. "It's lighter than the axes we used inn-building, that's for sure. I can get the hang of it. Crossbawns...they may take a bit." The fox had already adjusted them across his wrist and lower forearm. Both had in fact never been worn as the leather held firm and the strings pulled tight by the clenching of his fist. Deep down a simple thought sprouted, one that brought a quiet smile to his face: Foxtamas Scottsworth was finally looking like an adventurer.

"Father kept it on display near the barracks. I figured it could do with some use," Acirema explained while the fox fitted the axe across his back with an extra belt.

"Let's hope it doesn't get any," he replied.

"Aye, unlike *this*," said Bunns, patting his hammer.

"Do I need to go back and get you something else?" Acirema asked, sighing.

"Nae, nae Queenie, Ah appreciate et. Worried yer might bring back ah fork or spoon, and Ah know those'll bae *more* than used!"

Below their feet, the fleeting gray gravel fizzled into the welcoming sprigs of grass and ancient layers of leaves. After finalizing their supplies, they'd come to the border of Village Winthrop. No one dared to speak. No one wanted to. As Foxtamas had meditated on earlier, this could very well be their last time at their home.

And what were they leaving behind?

Bunns? His parents.

Acirema? Her people.

And Foxtamas…

He glanced back at the rising slope of a town. His gaze studied each and every house, noting the people who built their lives there, how they had shaped his own, and what destiny had befallen their final days. The Kobochauns. Jillengilches. Hilsks. Quivers. Rattlys. Ochets. All of Winthrop held a story. Connected, they made him into the fox he was. And now he had to leave them all behind.

But he would not return empty handed.

In his final glance, Foxtamas made a vow—unbreakable, resolute. He would not return to Village Winthrop without Foxlaris. He would not be lost. All of Winthrop shall ring out when the Scottsworth brothers bound back in together, restoring hope to every desolate denizen. Oh, the beauty of that moment. So vivid to him he could almost touch it. To do so, however, Foxtamas had to leave.

And that he did.

Turning around, Foxtamas followed Bunns and Acirema down the Mechmilne trail, stepping into the wood's thicket and letting the thrill of adventure course through him.

After so long, his own quest had finally begun.

The midnight sky kept still while the trio marched towards Nohsis. Little talk met the open air, the hard-pressed thoughts of their departure still heavy on their minds.

Mechmilne lay damp and dreary, foreboding when pressed against the starry sky. Trickling lanes of ferns and brush looked akin to the darkened alleyways of Mikyill. They trailed off deeper into the unknown; passageways walked only by wandering souls. Slim flickers of moonlight barely brushed the crisp floor beneath. It made each trample forward like a step into an abyss. Bugs, of course, were nonetheless noisy, though chirped at odd times, jumping from limb to limb as if to scare the passersby. Long had the forest been a creature of its own. One of good and comfort, despite what ferocity lay in its mystery.

And Foxtamas *did* feel that warmth, yet the more logs they crossed and looming branches they ducked under, the more he felt fear slithering back in, this time entering not through the gate, but a hidden crack unrepaired.

"G–G–Guys, you sure no one followed us? Or will?" he mumbled. The blackened greens creeped towards a haunting gray, glimmering into forms of beasts and creatures at bay between the starlight.

"Ah'm sure. Everyone seemed tae bae sleepin', an' the Watchers were pinned oup." Bunns did his best to reassure the fox. Leading the pack, his senses were far too keen to let something as noisy as a Winthrop Watcher trail them.

"Yeah, yeah, I know. Just kinda, um, t–troubling out here, it being so dark and all."

"You used to love playing out in the dark," Acirema cut in, "you'd sneak out just to go."

"It's different for a game. Now, n–now…"

Acirema stopped in front of the fox and turned towards him.

"Foxtamas, we're not even to the River. Things will be okay."

He nodded. Slowly but surely, he placed each thump of his boot down with an ease of confidence. This was for Foxlaris. He could do it. He just had to drop his fear, not listen to the noise, avoid the dark forest corners, not ramble in thought…

Luckily for him, Nohsis lay not much farther away. But in his recollection of himself and his worry, out of the corner of his eye, he swore up and down, left and right, that something shadowy moved between the long lanes of trees. What was it? He dared not look. The thought alone was enough to pause his heart and kick his tail forward.

The River Nohsis lay just as they had left it, almost untouched from their morning departure. Long streaks of mist carried the moonlight across the sullen gray surface. They formed a cloudy wall that hid anything beyond a few feet in.

"Right," said Bunns, rubbing together his hands. No one wanted to stay on shore long. The debris of banners and merchant stands were testaments to the horrors they didn't wish to revisit. "Ah think tha' stage'll bae our best bet as ah raft. Bet weh can carry et over here, eh, Scottoh?"

"I hope, it looks heavy. Sure it'll float?"

"Ah'm countin' on et."

The large wooden pallet in question had been flung far from the riverside, smashed and shredded upon the tree line. Despite the scarring, it was wide enough for the trio to ride on, and would serve them well enough for the half an hour or so it would take to cross.

As the boys hobbled over debris towards the platform, Acirema stared across to the East. She was meant to be searching for paddles, but the sight transfixed her.

The ridges still loomed. Dark, towering rolls like an island drifting at sea. The land clawed deep at her heart. Never before had she considered anything living within the East, not creatures, not people. It was just…the East. No different than an ocean or mountain ending her view of the horizon.

Now it had become more. *Much* more. If Foxtamas was right about Red Eyes, who knows what forces they may have awoken. "They" meaning her Father, of course. His hubris—spurred on by that of Gniw—planted these seeds. That thought sent more chills down her spine than any imagined ghoul or monster.

She began gathering spare scraps of wood strewn among the sands. They'd only need three or so, but she picked up all she saw so Bunns could have his options. Her hand reached down for one last piece when the waters pushed it forward. Behind it, the River stirred.

Nohsis rippled.

Choked by the realization, Acirema peddled back further on shore. Something sailed within the fog. Silent, it drifted towards her motionless, its dim shadow growing past every second and bated breath.

Her eyes adjusted and looked deeper. The mass sharpened, turning into a stout, pointy form riding upon a small vessel.

"HIDE!" The princess didn't know whether to whisper or shout. She flung the spare wood away and darted to the others, waving her hands as she did. *"HURRY! GET IN THE WOODS!"*

The pair let go of the stage and squinted at her in confusion.

"Wha'? Why?" asked Bunns.

"Something's coming *across!"* Acirema snatched both their capes and dragged them further inland. Both tried to protest, but she smacked their cheeks as they tried.

All three clambered behind one of the fallen posts. It hid them well enough while giving a clear view of the water.

"What did i-i-t l–look like?" quivered Foxtamas. By now, the light *plip…plip…* of paddles against the murky water sounded. With each, Bunns drew a star.

"I couldn't tell, just *keep down!"*

As the shadows grew closer, Foxtamas covered his mouth to quiet his stammering breaths. Was this the beast he noticed in the shadows earlier? If not, who was it? *What* was it? The Red Eyes, ready to take more helpless foxes across? Foxlaris, sailing back after a lengthy escape? Whatever it was, he approached, coming, closer, closer, closer, *closer…*

TWING!

The fox clenched his fist.
A whistle flicked through the air.
And a gurgled scream followed.

16

"FOR TO REJOICE IS TO TURN THE PAGES"

Rapol was dead. In front of his other alpian scouts, their leader and honorable comrade had flung back and spurted blood across the canoe. The wound leaked a black slick from his pale neck until the spark behind Rapol's eyes, dark and bulbous as a bubble of tar, faded.

What lay on this Western frontier?

The scrawny soldiers looked away from the scene and towards the shore. There, behind a pole of fallen wood, popped three heads.

Murderers. Scouts of the enemy.

If they could slay such a valiant commander, any of their lives would be at risk. Battle, it seemed, was a must.

"Ta zore!" a gurgled voice cried, dropping his paddle and replacing it with a sword.

"Ta zore!" the other seven joined in. Together, the Eastern scouts, adorned in the lightest of armor patched together with strings of leather, jumped from their vessel and waded to shore. One stayed back with bow in hand to cover his fellow fighters.

"Another fox!" sounded his distant cry. Arrow knocked, he fired for the beasts. Perhaps the West was worse than Vorde Velrick's legends.

❧

"Yer bug-brained loon!" Bunns yelled, bunkered behind the post. Arrows zipped overhead; hideous, impassioned creatures ran up the beach; and his stupid, *stupid* friend had incited it all. "Look ah yer mess!"

"I-I-I flinched, I gripped my fist, I didn't know, I, I—"

"*Gah,* nevermind et. Just listen tae meh." Reluctantly, he patted his shaking friend and tossed a stare of disbelief to Acirema. But now was *not* the time for anger to cloud him. "Ah counted eight, one still in the boat. Ah need yer two tae cover meh. Yer shoot, Ah'll use mah stars, got et? An' when they surround meh, Scottoh, yer gotta come swingin' with yer axe."

Fear pounded its way across the muscles of his face, making even the hairs upon his brow quake.

"No, n-no, I can't do that—"

"Yer must. Et'll bae either yer or them makin' et outta here, an' Ah dinnae think Rizzeh wants some beastie like *tha'* savin' him."

"But—"

Bunns gave him no time to retort. Stars in hand, he leapt from behind

the pole and darted for the approaching mob.

"*TETELESTAI!*" Gregabbit's old saying at the end of a long day, or the final word of a story. The Evonian Word for *finish*. And, now, his son's battle cry. Long had it been since any Cammont dared label themselves a "fighter," but Bunns changed that. With every scrape through the grass and fling through the sand.

"Foxtamas," started the princess, grabbing an arrow for her attack, "try to keep low—and calm—as best you can. It's my first time in a fight as well. Same... same with Bunns..."

But you could hardly tell.

Twin stars cut the air in two. They sank so deep within the first alp that his lifeless corpse erupted the sand around him as he fell. The swift eyes of Bunns sought out the next victim before the grains sprinkled the ground. He flicked out a third star right as the full wave of the creatures met him, tossing it and taking down the one closest. Easier than expected.

That was, until a dagger brushed his cloak, swiping inches from his skin. Training logs never did *that*. Nothing beats the surprises of a real battle, he figured.

Another cut came from the front, and Bunns narrowly avoided it. All the creatures appeared to use short swords swung wild and random. Such ferocity made it difficult to create enough distance for a star to cut deep enough when thrown. As Bunns kicked back, trying to exit the circle formed around him, one of the monsters tackled him from behind. Both crashed into the sand. The bug-eyed, sunken expression of his attacker gave him the needed fear to recoil and squirm away. What *were* these things!?

"Yer ugly rat, hop off!" His threat went nowhere. The slick-skinned alp tugged at his legs. Bunns rattled off kicks, but the claws wouldn't dislodge from his boots. It gave the other three enough time to pile on. Their swords crept closer and closer to his neck. They forced Bunns to wriggle about like a fish until a victorious *ZIP!* flew overhead, nailing one beast in the shoulder.

"Got one!" Acirema shouted while re-knocking the string. "Took me long enough."

Foxtamas nodded and swallowed, hard. His crossbawns shook every which way. Each of his shots kept firing past Bunns and plopping beyond into Nohsis. Finally, however, one bolt flew true and knocked back the Eastern archer, making their lives a tad easier.

"M-Me too!" he shouted. Until his "kill" rose back up. "Or...not..."

"I'll take him and give you cover, just go get to Bunns!"

He turned his attention away from the boat and towards Bunns wrestling the alps. The jackalope finished off the one Acirema hit, but due to the three others holding him down, he couldn't grab another star to slice back with.

"I can't, Acirema! I'm not a fighter! I'm gonna *die* out there!"

"No, you won't! I have your back, Foxtamas. Go, before he gets hurt!"

So, so, *so* much sprinted around his mind. It felt as if Evon had stopped. No River flowed, no monsters invaded their shores.

What would he do? Every speck of fear—not just panic, or worry, or a buzzing uneasiness of the future, but a literal terror stalking his soul as to freeze his very heartbeat—consumed him. He was back. Back to Pradifore, back to the frozen tree stinging his breathless back, back to Foxlaris dying at his side, back to the stalking black figure seeking to slit his throat and let his warm spurts of blood run cold.

Was his choice then not now the same?

Bunns lay pinned and in need. Foxtamas could save him. Acirema had his back. All would end well.

But what if it failed…all of it, crumbling down, their dead bodies plundered and left to dye the waves of Nohsis red—

No.

Bunns needed saving, and Acirema had his back. That's all that he could count on. It was all that *mattered.*

Thus, he held firm his axe and hopped upon the beach. This, unlike his childhood kitchen knife, would *not* be an accident. For the first time in his life, Foxtamas Scottsworth would turn to face the threat. Even if his legs quaked beneath him.

The fox charged. Confused at the sudden scream, the alps turned to the tree line and saw the crazed Foxtamas swinging their way. His strokes came backed by genuine strength, built off the work of fallen trees and repaired roofs. They tried moving back, but it was too late. Foxtamas caught the central villain pummeling Bunns. His axe blade twinkled in the moonlight before slamming down his exposed back. Black, droopy bile squirted out—Foxtamas pushed the sight far from his mind. All that mattered was Bunns finally being able to breathe.

"Ahah! See, wha' did Ah tell yer!"

"N-Not n-n-now," the fox sputtered back. Worry began building within, but the rage of battle, the constant looking, frantic fighting, and dizzying dance with death, controlled his attention. Without even thinking, Foxtamas took another swipe and caught his second creature by the side. Its sharp, spindly teeth whipped around at the fox, smile suddenly snapping into a bite. Had not it been for Acirema's random flinging of arrows, Foxtamas would have suffered a hole in his neck. He lived either way. The same could not be said for those fighting Bunns.

He was *back*. Flashes of silver sparked across the beach like embers. Two more attackers fell victim to his flurry of stars. He took one down, dislodged the metal piece, then slammed it through the leather of the other's jerkin and between his ribs. Both crumbled into screams that pierced the night like a squawking of birds.

One fighter remained—the archer. He'd broken off the bolt Foxtamas landed in his arm and swam to shore. Bunns was too busy to notice. They met with the alp socking the jackalope from behind and wrapping an arm around his neck. He squeezed hard, catching him off guard. The breath puffed from Bunns' lungs. In return, Bunns kicked back with equal force. The boot launched and cracked into his knee.

That did the trick.

Gasping, he pulled away from the archer and put his back towards Foxtamas, loading another pair of stars as he did.

"Get back, Scottoh!" he warned before dashing at the alp. It too, rushed, this time with one of his fallen comrade's short swords. He swung it as if to cleave off Bunns' entire head. Seeing this, the jackalope punched forward and hit a perfect point in his stride.

The enemy reached close. Inches from his antlers.

But Bunns jumped.

And his stars fell.

SPLUNGE SPLUNGE SPLUNGE!

It fell dead at the fox's feet. Bunns crashed into the sand and rolled to see the finale. Three stars rose from the alabaster back of the creature. Like a sickly baby dragon.

The trio regrouped within their new-found silence. Fallen streamers and broken tents lay joined by lost weapons and lifeless husks.

"What just…happened…" Acirema's remark resounded in their heads. Slowly, not daring to draw close, she slinked around the fallen. Many of her shots fell far from target. Those were easy to find and re-holster. As for those buried deadly deep within the creatures…

"Ah dunno," replied Bunns, picking up his stars and taking a closer look at the foe. These were not fighters. Not close. "They dinnae look tae bae comin' here tae fight. Look, lil' armor, small weapons."

"Then what are they here for? Who…who are they?" Obviously, Foxtamas let sadness mix into his words. The battle-frenzy and duty that had pushed away his grief faded, leaving his eyes open to the truth. *Real* blood coated his hands. Never did he think he'd watch so much life slip from so many individuals. How quickly did it happen. Entire memories, both past and potential, slipping away into that darkness. Horrible. Horrible, and from *him*.

"Easterns tha' wanted us dead," Bunns said.

"Because I shot one of them?"

"Nae, Ah doubt et. They mae not bae meant for battle, but they did look trained for et."

None of it made sense. Foxtamas took to finding his bolts, needing some task to clear his mind. How many questions could possibly swirl within a head? The course led him back to the enemy boat, now washed ashore with the first body flung to the back. The fox sighed. How could he have done that? He never *wanted* to kill, of course, but…well, it was better that…thing…than him. Right? *He* was a real being. The creature was just that—a creature. No different than a fish, or eel, or spider.

…right?

Holding his breath, he stepped in for a brief moment to collect the ammunition. *Not* to dwell on the death before him. He tried not to, at least.

Thankfully, the bolt was already slick by the oily blood and slipped out with ease. Foxtamas looked away as he wiped it off. He wasn't *that* much of a warrior.

He couldn't help notice that this beast was dressed differently than the rest. It bore a leather cap and silver pauldrons belted to his tunic. The outfit was like of the higher-rank Watchers, with added armor to denote their status. Was this the same? Had he slain a leader of sorts?

Foxtamas gently rolled over the corpse, scanning it for any other details. Bunns would want to know more. Before he could look, however, his boot fell victim to the grip of a cold, blood-soaked claw.

"For...Vorde Velrick..." croaked the body.

"GAH!"

Scrambling, the fox tripped his way to the canoe's front. He turned back and saw the alp raising up its black-metal sword. Yet no matter the ambitiousness of the attempt, it fell, taking with it the creature's final breath and toppling next to the face-down body.

Foxtamas hugged himself. Tight.

It took him a moment to calm himself, ensuring that the reanimated body was *actually* dead this time around.

"Vorde...Velrick?" Foxtamas muttered. His words met only the boat, body, and fog once again rising above the river. "Who in Evon is that?"

His eyes waded through the deepened night to allow his thoughts free range. Vorde Velrick? The name rang no bell. Not in old stories, fables, or yarns. Not from a printed book nor fireside chat. What kind of a figure could it be? A commander, perhaps, by the looks of the attire. Or a king, or an idol, or a god. Foxtamas had no way of knowing.

In his meandering, he came upon a disturbance in the River. His fumbling inside the canoe had caused some ripples, yes, but those pushed away. These, they were ebbing *towards.*

From the mist emerged more boats, all longer, wider, and deeper, carrying across the River beasts of ghastly proportion compared to those slain by the trio.

"*Nonononononono,*" Foxtamas huffed. He rolled from the vessel trembling and darted back up the sand.

"There's more! There's more!" he shouted. Bunns and Acirema pulled away from their inspection of the bodies, confused.

"Where?" asked the princess.

"Coming across right *now*. They're bigger and there's three boats of them, and, *gah,* just *go!*" The fox pushed them both forward, nearly tripping them. Together they made it to the tree line. Before heading in, Bunns glanced back and witnessed firsthand the next arrival of invaders. First, they looked shocked to see the slain littering the beach. When they saw him watching from the trees, they looked worse.

Livid.

17

"OF AN ENDLESS BOOK, ONE WHOSE STORY"

The direction Foxtamas chose sent them flying northwest of the River, skewing away from Bridgeburrow and Winthrop. Such thoughts bothered them little, of course, for the terror of facing yet another round of fighting flung their already tired limbs through the shadowed foliage and deeper into trailless, unkempt woodland.

The interlaced branches of endless oak and ash made the escapees practically blind. Neither of the three knew how far they had gone, where to they ran, or even if those trailing them still followed. If they could put another foot forward, they would. Bunns kept in his spring with ease. Training and the rush of a real battle strengthened his calves to a point where his mind faded back, allowing his reality to form into a game of hopping over roots and dodging thorn patches sprouting deep within the shade. Foxtamas and Acirema, however, felt the pain. Each breath proved a new challenge. Still, they didn't dare stop.

Weakened, the trio pushed further until reaching a slow-rising ridge. Seeing no way around, they grappled up its face, composed of thick chunks of rock. The stony juts became to them small footholds amongst the leaves and shrubbery. Once near the top, the ground leveled out, easing them back into pace. Sprints started and gasps heaved, yet all three failed to look beyond the next step in front of them.

"Ah! Wait, stop—" Bunns tried to warn, but to no avail. He flung off the top of a rocky landslide. The ridge's opposite side had been wiped clean from steady erosion, giving out and piling the bottom with dead branches, fallen logs, and withered bushes wedged between them.

The trio tumbled down together as one.

Bumps, bruises, scrapes—all left their mark upon the villagers. Stark stains of brown coated their clothes. With the moon hidden by the thicket, none of them took notice.

The rotten brush had thankfully acted somewhat as a cushion for the fall. Nothing too severe, but not something you wish to take on every day.

Foxtamas squeezed his way from the sharpened edges of the branches and found footing on top of the central foliage.

"Y'all alright?"

"Mostly," coughed Acirema, helping Bunns up. The poor jacka-lope felt his whole world spinning. "Think we lost them?"

"I hope so," gasped the fox. "Here, hide deeper in the brush, just in case they stumble down. That fall was bad enough; I don't need them squashing us too."

His friends obeyed. The three bundled up under a nearby stretch of lengthy pine branches, creating a canopy to hide beneath. It felt almost like a fort from their childhood—only this time, the threat they safeguarded against wasn't imaginary

"Yer were right, Scottoh," Bunns finally peeped up, whispering to stay quiet. The only other sounds were the scratching of the needles above, pecking each other in the midnight breeze. "They *were* bigger."

"How big?" asked Acirema.

"*Huge.* Like three of the pale beasties stacked together."

"I still don't even know what those things were to begin with." She shook her head and scrunched her knees tight to her chest. "Surely some legend or tale speaks about scrawny…monster-looking things."

"Not one I know," replied the fox, "They almost didn't look real. One of them—the one I, um, shot first—was still alive by the time I made it to the boat. He grabbed me and said something about a 'Vorde

Velrick.' I couldn't place it to any story either."

"Well, yer heard wha' they said when they started tae attack, dinnae yer?"

Foxtamas and Acirema exchanged confused glances before turning back to Bunns.

"I could barely focus on *myself*, Bunns. What did you hear?" the fox quietly pressed back.

"He screamed somethin' 'bout 'another fox.'"

"Wait, what?" "On mah heart. Ah heard et in both ears."

His blue eyes widened to a worrying degree. The rest of the world faded around him into the darkness.

Another fox…

Another…

Fox!

"He's alive…"

Though slow, each syllable passed from his starved lips with assurance, power. "Foxlaris, he's alive then, right? Right!?"

BUUUUURRRRRRMMMMM!!!

All three whipped their heads back towards the ridge. A trumpet—loud and dangerous and powering out a sound like metal grinding rock—blasted just a short distance from their fort.

"They found us!" the princess shrieked.

"Must've seen our trail. Hurry laddies, move!"

"Where!?"

Bunns hiked up his haversack, pointing past the darkened trunks to a moonlit field a ways beyond.

"There, tha' way! Hurry!"

Grunts and jeers sounded from atop the ridge as the trio darted for the valley. Before, the focus lay on the aches their bodies sustained from the sprints; now, with brutes yards behind, it mattered little how they felt, only that their feet kept moving.

Breaking into the field unveiled just how deep they'd traveled into

Mechmilne. Clear from leaves and debris, the field itself spread both long and wide, stretching from their broken ridge behind to the start of an older one ahead, denoted by sporadic trees on the forest line. The length traveled north and south quite a ways, carrying the shaggy, short grass beneath the moon's silver river of light. They caught no twinkling glimmers of civilization, only the rich open air of unclaimed wilderness.

The valley gave heart to the escapees, letting their bodies soar across. Soon the Easterners would cross this green river, and by then, their trail could be anywhere. The beasts could turn south or head north or, just maybe, march on back home across Nohsis. Either way, hope fueled their flight, not any amount of food or sleep. Yet such freedom changed upon reaching the other side.

This beyond wished no disturbance. Trees grew fat and close; thorns replaced the grass; branches sank low like spears blocking what lay ahead. Trying to traverse this Mechmilnian blockage let the full weight of weariness fall upon them, even Bunns. Slinking around would be a challenge, taking all remaining effort. But, as was on the shore, it was either push onward or fall victim to the monsters.

The deep groves of trees lay fast asleep. Among them the nightly bugs and insects whispered and pranced about. Their hushed melodies concocted an otherworldly symphony unheard by many, if not most. Floors of fallen leaves kept cool in the darkened hour, daring only to move at the silent beckoning of their airy master. That frigid force walked its way through the rugged bows above and cozied sprouts below. It stirred little sprigs of life. Ants trotting along roots; elder bark chipping and falling and sweeping to the ground. This was a home all its own. Far from folk, further from their daily dilemmas.

It was this delight—finding home among the darkness—that the three companions stumbled through. Little by little they slowed enough to take it in. Behind, their pursuers fell to whispers, then to the rattle of leaves. They found themselves lingering in their breaks and leaning against the rotund trunks. It felt almost like a new land entirely. Wherever they'd reached, it was plenty away from Winthrop.

After what felt like hours mingling about the lost groves of Mechmilne, the trunks drifted apart and the foliage slinked back. Needles, scented by their distinctive sweet earthiness, bunched at their feet and hung overhead. They finally broke through the thicket and into a wide pine grove. Not just any, however—one with a sight at its center.

"A...tower?" Foxtamas tried but failed to fully look it over. His lungs ached and needed his attention lest he perish then and there. He bent over and let the chilled wind sweep through his sweat-soaked tunic.

"Looks...very...very old..." Acirema added, equally out of breath. She too could hardly stand. "Good place...to hide."

"An' sleep."

Bunns? Winded? A bit, maybe, but not enough to *not* gawk at the tower.

It rose high, breaking the surrounding brush to reveal the clear night and moon. The top was sheered at an angle with jagged rocks cut like ill-formed battlements. It must have been taller, once. The powdery gray stone showed decent wear, long faded from its original glory. Thick mosses now covered the sides and trickled inwards, all the way up to the broken third floor. The tower, like the surrounding forest, felt lost. Or hidden.

It was agreed: no one wished to run anymore, and they felt far enough away from the monsters anyway to keep the running up. Thus, they entered the building and explored where it was they were to spend their night.

"Ah ain't certain weh're the first tae bae discoverin' this place..." Bunns' voice echoed along the walls as they passed beneath the sunken doorway.

"I think you're right," Foxtamas said, almost too stunned for words. Bones littered the wide, open floor. Covering ingrown attacks of grass and moss were shredded rugs and blankets, dirtied in a pale dust from the crumbling bricks above. Torches hung along the walls in rusted wire sconces. The husks of wood, while dry rotted, had fresh ash still burned along the tip.

"Not happening," Acirema boldly, yet shakily, demanded, starting her way up the stairs that wound up along the wall. "I'm *not* staying here. Something *clearly* dangerous has already made its home here, and I'm not keen on invading it."

"Et'll bae *fine*, Queenie," protested Bunns, following her up. "Weh'll only bae here 'till the morn."

"Foxtamas, back me up here."

To her dismay, the fox bit his lip, unable to agree. Sleep *did* sound nice, and those bones, they technically weren't *fresh...*

"Fine. You two stay here and get eaten first. I'll be up here."

Bunns rolled his eyes towards the fox before chasing after her.

"Nae, *Ah'll* bae the one eatin' *et!*"

Like the first, the second story was barren apart from old, faded banners and daggers rusted far beyond their prime. Foxtamas couldn't stop himself from inspecting every little bit of debris. It suited him better than bickering of the other two.

He dusted off one of the flags and held it up towards a gap in the stone, illuminating it in moonlight. At one point it may have been colored a burgundy, but now, crisp and tattered in the fox's hand, it barely came off as pink. A symbol was once stitched in the center. Maybe a...tree? Or off-centered crown? He couldn't tell. Only the holes and afterimage of the threading remained. Still, it gave him just enough to ponder.

What had this banner—this *tower*—been in its glory days? Some watch post for traveling scouts? A self-proclaimed prince's fortress, claiming this pine grove his own? The symbol of an army that people gave their lives to, now forgotten all these years later in the future they forged?

Giddiness trickled through him. What *possibilities!* Thousands of stories in one mere glimpse. Oh, to be there, to witness this history and watch every line of it connect in one massive web. It eased him away from the worries of the night.

But his companions were already hiking up, and he had more important business to settle than ruffling through dulled knives and dilapidated crates. He promised to be back in the morning, though. The night's light couldn't compare to that of a fresh dawn.

Reaching the third and final story revealed a lookout across the vast landscape of Mechmilne. The sheered stone reached only to their chests. It was rounder here, weathered by the elements and ground down to the structure's bones. Leaning over the edge, they found what once would have been above them crumbled into an overgrown pile of rubble.

The view beyond it, however…

Bunns scampered back down to find a spot to cozy up, but Foxtamas and Acirema couldn't find it in themselves to leave. The darkness did little to diminish the raw beauty. It was akin to how the stories described the ocean—ridges rising and falling, bursting through the surface and rippling the rest of the waters, moonlight sizzling upon their crests. The further it stretched, the more it became like a painting melting into the horizon. If they were a smidge closer they could reach out and feel the strokes of the brush.

"I can't even see the River," whispered the fox. "It's just trees for leagues."

"I didn't realize how far we ran…" Acirema tried to speak with an air of calmness, but the warble in her throat betrayed her and caught Foxtamas' glance. "Almost too far."

"You think so?"

The princess sighed and leaned upon the smoothed stone. "It just worries me where we're going to head now. We're far off from Nohsis, and for all we know the monsters will be in the way both on our side *and* the East. Who knows when we'll be back home at this rate."

Nodding, Foxtamas joined her on the edge. Despite the vivacity of his eyes, the stars still somehow reflected within them.

"You're not wrong," he sighed. "I never asked before, but…how long did you think this was all gonna take?"

"My honest answer?"

"Mhm."

"Maybe a few days. You?"

"Worse. I figured by the morning." Acirema giggled to herself as Foxtamas shrugged his shoulders. "I guess I was being a bit of an optimist."

"Which some say is a good thing."

"Yeah...but I don't know how to be one about this." He let himself linger on the forest. Those rolling trees *were* like waves to him. He'd swim through them and explore every shadow, every secret if he could. If this quest kept going as it had been, perhaps he would. Fear retreated against the protection of unkempt passion. "I figure we might just need to rest. Give it some time. If all's clear in the morning this might just be a little detour. Foxlaris'll understand...probably." To his surprise, the raccoon laughed, rubbing her eyes at the mention of heading to bed. "What, *too* optimistic?"

"No, no, it's perfect. Just sounds so much like me!"

Chuckling, Foxtamas turned back to the stairs.

"Looks like *you* were the bad influence all along. I'm going to see where Bunns ran off to. You coming down?"

"I'll see, might try and sleep up here."

"Very monster-proof."

With that, he slid down the steps, leaving Acirema alone at the top, a smile still pressed to her lips. How had she ended up with such strong friends? She should've ended up the same as her father. But, well, maybe without them she would have.

The thought of Aisar sent her looking south. Nothing even hinted at being familiar to Winthrop's territory. She'd watched those ridges all her life. Even though these still coated the far reaches of her vision, they lacked the same dips and points as the ones fencing in her home.

That wasn't a necessarily *bad* thing. Good always came from seeing more of the world, even accidentally. They'd be back to Winthrop in a few days anyway, so the time to enjoy this new country was now.

Yet the thought of return squeezed her stomach. Dried her throat.

Only sadness waited there. Death clung to the homes like a heavy snowfall, bringing with it the same shivers and wails. Her people mourned, at first individually, then as one. A singular beckoning song of loss, of aches, drifting up the hill and towards the Palace. Towards her.

Her hands squeezed the stone as all the thoughts of failure yet again pounded against her skull. A new one emerged, however.

What if...she never went back? How much easier would life be then? How...*free?*

No no no. A silly thought. A foolish one. She couldn't be thinking like that. If anything, it was a sign she needed sleep *soon.* Any longer and delusions like that would creep up stronger.

Finger by finger, she let go of the tower and pulled away, joining the boys below. Her body thanked her for the choice. After a hellish twenty-four hours, an ounce of peace and quiet was *quite* deserved.

And an ounce they would get. Nary three hours after laying down, Acirema shot, up awake.

The tower was shaking.

Always the light sleeper, her visionless dreams rattled about her brain, finally bringing her to the dizzying reality of the early dawn. They'd chosen the third floor after all for the position and protection it gave them over their pursuers. Even so, the quakes at the base trembled as fiercely as if they were on the ground. Something below grunted and snorted in unkempt fury. After each resounding *THUD!*, it pulled back, regained composure, and thrust again.

"Hey, hey!" she shook the sleeping boys, keeping her voice to an inaudible whisper. *"Wake up!"*

"Mmm?" moaned Foxtamas, cracking open a single eye. "Do you hear that? The thudding against the walls?"

"Do I hear *what?*" he asked again, this time as loud as his usual timbre.

GRRRUUUAAAHHHH!!!

That fully woke him.

He bolted up in terror as, after the bloodcurdling war cry, a final

BOOM! erupted throughout the tower. Dust exploded from below and shot upwards. The thick powder reached the third floor and began to choke their breath and cloud their vision. Seconds after the blast erupted, the entire structure groaned. Those awake felt it begin to lean, tilting to the right and veering on the edge of collapse.

"WE GOTTA GET DOWN!" Foxtamas shrieked, pulling Acirema up from her blanket. "BUNNS!"

Nothing. Sound as a babe.

"BUNNS GET UP!"

The jackalope felt them fling him up by his hood and drag him to his feet. What was…happening? Why did everything look so gray? And that taste…gah, like chalk, or…that bread Rein burned.

Little by little his senses returned until the ground beneath his feet shifted, sending the trio sliding towards the exposed side of their floor.

"Wha' in Evon!" he cried, suddenly awake. He joined the flight without thinking.

Foxtamas and Acirema still clung to his arms. With that added weight, he steadied himself and kicked away from the broken stone and fell backwards, dragging the others with him. All three tumbled down the stairwell. The second floor, too, was falling over, more grunting and roaring beneath it, only now loud enough to damage their hearing.

"Are we going down more!?" Acirema frantically threw out to Foxtamas, the first to find his footing.

"I-I dunno, I think—"

Too late.

After standing for perhaps hundreds, if not *thousands* of years, the moss-blanketed, grove-hidden tower of old gave out. The bottom portion collapsed in on itself while the top half toppled backwards, first into a splintering of the pines, and then an endless, airless cloud of gray.

"I can't see! I can't see!"

Wiping his eyes did nothing. Everything looked a milky shade of white blinding him from the darkness before the dawn. Some stones he made out. He scrambled at their rigid backs, rough sides. He to felt the wounds scored down his legs. All his digits still wiggled—an easing thought to balm the pain of the cuts. Somehow, he'd avoided being crushed by the rock, but the shock, the *fear* did just the same. The weight of the situation suffocated the fox.

As the dust settled around him, small bits of vision returned. It stung worse than a wasp, of course, but he squeezed his eyes until he caught flashes of sight. The field of ruins expanded around him, the blocks like miniature mountains. The pines, scarred, splintered. The sky easing into morning, its black running out of ink. The figure, a bulky dark mass, huffing and snorting and standing but a few feet away…

Foxtamas gagged as it inched closer. Heavy were its horns, cutting out from his furry head and marred with chips and cracks. Golden chains dangled their way down from his necklace to silver cuffs. They paired well with his loincloth and belt, extenuating his powerful build and twitching muscles empowered by every breath. Doom lived in his eyes. Hollow, empty eyes. Robbed of a thinking life, bound to one of eternal anger.

A minotaur.

The embodiment of death.

Foxtamas yelped. He'd already been spotted by the beast. It began easing back and aiming his horns towards him. It would be an easy kill.

Scrambling, tossing limb after limb over and around the rubble, the fox tried to escape the minotaur's path.

"HELP! HELP!" he hollered until his voice, caked by dust, ran hoarse. And fell on deaf ears. He leapt his aching legs over a semi-standing piece of wall right as the minotaur huffed and charged his way, tearing apart the stone littered across the grove.

One hit would end the fox. A single brush of a single horn could crack his skull and rip the sinews from his neck. What a pitiful end.

The pain of both his frantic thoughts and bleeding cuts caused him to trip. He flew forward, splattering against another jutting piece of wall. That did him in.

The worn, mortified Foxtamas cowered up against the ruined tower. Doing so squared him directly in front of the face of death. He watched, dizzied, as the minotaur advanced in leaps and bounds, eyes narrowed on his prey. Oh, how the fox wanted to stand tall in his last moments, but he couldn't. He couldn't.

Instead, he tightened his body into a ball. Maybe that would ease the pain. Maybe even give him a chance. Slim, if at all.

And maybe he shouldn't have squeezed his fists.

FLUNK! FLUNK!

Two accidental bolts flung from the crossbawns, flashing through the night and imbedding themselves deep into the thickness of the minotaur's chest.

"*GRRAAAHHH!!*" roared the beast. The sudden shock disengaged him. His claws grappled at the wounds and veered him off course. He swerved, missing the fox by the breadth of his hair and crippling both the wall and himself. What remained of the standing stone fell upon him, exploding more dust into the air.

It took a moment for Foxtamas to fully grasp his actions. Again he'd pulled the loops of his weapons in terror, only this time *not* to his detriment. The minotaur had passed so close that he felt the waft of his foul musk. But now wasn't the time to linger. The second chance at life pushed him from the rubble and towards the safer side of open trees and easier breath.

Already Bunns and Acirema had made their way over, waving to him from beneath the pines.

"You're alive!" shouted the princess, but Foxtamas shook his head with maddened fury.

"M-M-Minotaur, Minotaur!" he gasped as if biting the air. "That's the beast, a-a-and we gotta move, go, it's o-over…over th-there." It was all he could mumble before his legs finally gave out. Thankfully, Bunns caught him in time and led him to the forest line.

"Keep yer calm, laddie. Sit down next tae Acirema, Ah'll handle et."

"You, you…you can't," sputtered Foxtamas. "We have…to run."

"If tha' beastie took down the *tower,* then et's got the strength tae chase us tae the *sea.*"

"Bunns, he's right," said Acirema. She rested her hands on both boys. Dust had thickened in her fur, blurring her stripes. "You've never taken on something like *that.*"

"First time for everything!" He winked and turned towards the ruined scene of the tower. Slowly, the cloud where the minotaur clipped the wall faded, revealing his silhouette cutting through the white of the dust like an abyss. Even from their distance, the trio heard his strained, eager, *forceful* pants.

He wasn't finished.

"Bunns." Acirema squeezed his arm and met his eyes. "I'm *serious.* We need you alive. Your *mother* needs you alive."

At her words, his expression ever so slightly shifted. The blacks of his pupils tightened. His nose wrinkled up and brow furrowed down. For some reason, Bunns…darkened.

"An' Ah need yer alive *tae.*" He pulled his arm away and whipped back around, reaching for enough stars to fill the spaces between his fingers. But the pouch wasn't there. "Where'd yer put mah stars?" he asked, frantic.

Acirema shook her head. "I don't know, you left them with the packs." The packs that lay buried beneath the field of rock.

Part of her hoped that would deter him, and the three of them could start a trek through the forest before the creature realized where they'd gone—but the other part of her knew better.

For the first time since Grammo Day, fear pounded in the chest of the jackalope. Something a minotaur's size could be brought down with a good round of well-placed stars. But without them, and with his two friends downed, begging for escape…

His paw trembled over the empty spot on his belt. His foot rattled against the ground.

"Nevermind et. Ah got ah plan."

He did not.

But he could *never* be seen without one. Bunns was the fighter. The defender. He *had* to defend them.

He had to.

He had to.

Foxtamas dragged himself through the pine needles and closer to Acirema. The princess' left arm had been cut down the back, perhaps on the rusted daggers he found earlier. She'd gathered leaves and random cloth from her tunic and did her best to dress it, but the red seepage still bled through. The packs probably had enough supplies, even just some random rag tossed in. Until the minotaur left, however, finding them was hopeless.

"Is he...really going?" the fox asked. He didn't have the courage to turn back and watch.

"He wouldn't listen," sighed the princess. To her surprise, Foxtamas pushed out a chuckle.

"Has he ever?"

Bunns did in the moment, even if it was just to his own rattled heartbeat. He sped from the forest haven and rounded to the other side opposite his friends. Once there, he clambered up the broken stone and leapt his way to the middle. A plan still had yet to form. He'd know what to do when he met his foe, though. He had to.

He had to.

He had to.

He had to.

The hopping landed him right behind the minotaur. The beast stood as a tower unto itself. Coated in gray, the powerhouse no longer looked like its kind. Bunns almost mistook it for an ancient spirit raised from the ashes, damned to haunt Evon with soulless gaze and bleeding chest.

"Lassie!" Bunns shouted, skirting back in shock when it turned, "Aye, this away! Yer pal Bunnclar, here!" The minotaur lowered its beady gaze in annoyance. "Wha' ah stick in the mud yer are! Yer open yer doors, let us start tae sleep, then *destroy* the place! Did yer momma skip out on manners or—"

"*YOU!*"

The single word blasted throughout the grove like the falling of a tree. It rumbled the rocks at Bunns' feet, sent his ears back behind his head.

"*YOU INVADED MY HOME!*"

"Aye, perhaps, but Ah dinnae *tear et down!*"

That didn't help.

The minotaur leaned forward, and Bunns forced himself to think. Making him hit the rubble could be an option—really his *only* option. Foxtamas somehow pulled it off and dazed the thing. But looking around, no remnants of wall still stood. Maybe…he could trick him into a chase instead. If so, then he'd need to find a thick enough tree he could get him to hit it and—

"*GRAAAAHHH!*"

The pursuit, it seemed, had begun.

Bunns squeaked as the minotaur raced his way, horns pointed at his hide. *Why* must he have lost his *stars!* He'd have the beast begging for mercy by now! It mattered little in the moment. He centered his focus on jumping from rock to rock, luring the beast back towards the forest.

Once at the tree line, he found the thickest pine and turned around to face the predator. One hand stayed pressed to the rugged bark. The minotaur barreled towards him, a shadow of thundering grunts. Bunns waited until the horns were mere inches from him, and when they were, he pushed off into a jump from the tree and over the beast.

But he didn't get high enough.

In a single thrash of his neck, the minotaur caught the jackalope between its horns and *slammed* him into the ground.

The air within Bunns' lungs vaporized. The beast's forehead crushed deep into his ribs, and the scarred ivory on either side squeezed him like a berry in the hands of a child.

"*Ugh...*" he gasped, only to be drowned out by the snorting over him, undulating almost into a laugh.

Bunns tried to wriggle free. He beat upon the horns despite the pain burning through his chest with the movement of his arms. As he did, the minotaur lifted him again, whipping him up and into the tree.

The wood splintered against his back. Groaned, to the point of collapse.

Consciousness waved over the jackalope. Ebbing to darkness. Pushing back towards reality. The world around him a swirling black.

Finally, drained of breath, his insides screaming, blood sprinkled across his lips, Bunns came to. This time, however, he didn't fight. His body fell limp.

Feeling it, the minotaur grunted and flung him loose to the ground. He slid back into the forest along the needles and cones, pinpricks of pain peppering his bruising wounds.

Nothing within him stirred to get up. He barely found it in himself to stay awake. Through his fluttering vision he caught a glimpse of the minotaur, back upon the rubble, eyeing him with a grin.

In that moment, he thought as Foxtamas had—would this...be his end? Flayed like some fish, toyed with no different than a babe with her rattle? It wasn't how he pictured it. The ruined tower looked little like a real battlefield. It lacked the fanfare. The *heroics.*

No, this...this couldn't be it.

It couldn't be.

If he didn't get up and finish the fight, he'd fail. Oh, how he *begged* himself not to think on such a truth, but in that state, black and blue, he felt the sting to admit it. Bunnclar Cammont. *Failure.*

Who was he without a star in his paw? People to protect? What happened when the warrior mask slipped, and everyone saw the crying kid beneath it?

The thoughts suddenly subsided as the minotaur turned away from

Bunns and back towards the rubble. Towards his *friends*.

No.

No.

He hadn't failed yet. And as long as he breathed, he *never would*.

Coughing on the powdered air, the jackalope rose. His vision spun, and his muscles hardly afforded him a step, but he took it anyway, dragging his beaten body forward. He instinctively reached down to where the star pouch usually clung.

Nothing.

He swiped his paw to the other side.

Nothing.

His search just about stopped until he brushed past the beaten wooden mallet tucked behind his cape.

"Aye...lassie!" Bunns coughed out. The beast turned back, a hint of shock glimmering over his soulless eyes. "Knockin' meh out ain't...good compensation...for ruinin' mah sleep!"

The shock faded to anger, and the anger surged into another charge, this one akin to the power of an avalanche.

Bunns tightened his choke around the hammer. It didn't fit right, but it would have to make do. His feet stumbled forward. The ground beneath them trembled. If he missed his mark, he'd be sent *through* the tree this time, if not the grove itself. The thought made his dried throat gulp.

The monster, that shadowed tower of power, closed the gap.

Inching. Inching. Inching. Inching. Inching.

A full breath.

Then half.

Then an exhale.

Bunns made the move.

He reached back his arm and slung out with everything still beating inside, every passion, hope, and dream dripping through his veins, everything to prove he was the warrior he claimed to be.

C

R

A

C

K

!

He was hit.

18

"WILL LAST FOREVER AND ALWAYS.

"Uuungghh…"

Foxtamas' ears perked up. He sat atop the fallen staircase, taking in the refreshing midday breeze and near-cloudless sky. At the moan, he turned back towards their makeshift camp and found Bunns lifting his dizzied head.

"Acirema! He's awake!" the fox called, hobbling down the steps to help up his friend.

"Grab him water and the bread," she replied. Despite her arm now wrapped in both spare pack rags and torn strips of her purple tunic, she worked to prop Bunns up as he awoke. "Good morning, Bunns. Sleep well?"

"Real…funny…" he groaned. His lids fluttered against the light. The sun shone too bright, and the thickness of the pine aroma, which the others had been enjoying all morn, overpowered him. But he tried not to care. Bunns pooled his strength and craned up his head with an almost unnatural series of pops. He twitched to either side, scanning over the rubble. "Where's mah pack?"

"They're up over where Foxtamas was," said Acirema, "but don't worry about it. You need to eat and—"

The jackalope refused to listen and hopped up instead. The second he made it to his feet, the entire length of his body froze. Breathing hurt. Moving stung. The *thought* of taking a single step forward cut him down with a wave of pain. His watery eyes glanced down to see his chest, open from tears in his tunic, painted a rich purple, brown, and blue, the same pattern as an impending summer thunderstorm.

"We don't know how you made it," the princess added. Bunns detected the slight disapproval in her tone. "So, it's best not to push it. Sit back down, I'll get the pack."

"N–Nae, Queenie, Ah got et. Ah'm sure," he replied between clenched teeth and failing confidence. Acirema tried to race him, but even in his beaten state, Bunns still squeezed ahead. He climbed—crawled, really—across the rock until reaching the three haversacks, one royally crafted, the others hardly sewn together. His smile returned. "There yer are!"

He undid the drawstring and rummaged through until a tinge of cold steel pressed against his paw.

"Ah," he sighed. The star settled into his palm. A babe in the crook of a mother's arm. "Yer ain't *ever* leavin' mah sight again. *Promise.*"

He reoutfitted his star pouch, but before heading back down, took with him one last item. A little surprise he'd been saving.

"You are *kidding* me..." mumbled Acirema. There, held high above Bunns' head like a trophy, was his Banjalope.

"You brought it!" cut in Foxtamas, returning with food. He tossed down the plates and met Bunns clambering down the hill, looking over the instrument as he did. "I can't believe it!"

Acirema's eyes rolled. "*Why* did you bring that along?" she sighed.

"For travelin' songs! Yer cannae bae makin' yer way Eastward an' *not* sing ah few ditties. But Ah also figured weh could celebrate this historic victory with ah smatterin' o' fanfare. Celebrate us all still *breathin'* after last night, eh?"

Foxtamas rubbed his hand together in excitement; Acirema, quite ostensibly, hid hers behind her back.

After Bunns strummed out a few melodies to fully wake himself up, the group fed their bruised savior his lunch of water, berries, and almond bread, relaying the events of last night as they did.

"We didn't know what happened, all we heard was a loud crack. I thought he knocked a tree over on you," said Foxtamas.

"Must've been when Ah slammed tha' hammer square on his nog!" giggled Bunns between mouthfuls. "Tha's the last thing Ah remember. He ran off after tha' then?"

"Yep, and hollered the whole time, too. We ran over to you once we knew he wouldn't be back and set up camp."

"Speaking of that hammer, however..." Smirking, Acirema glared over at Bunns, his ears already pulled back in embarrassment. He knew what was about to hit him. Nagging wasn't *usually* part of the princess's customs, but in this case, after all his hemming and hawing...

"Yer don't have tae tell meh," the warrior sighed.

"Oh, I know. Just seems like the hammer wasn't the *worst* of choices now, was it?"

Foxtamas withheld a snicker.

"Yer right, Yer Majesty, yer all-seein', all-powerful wisdom helped meh beat back tha' beastie. Where *ever* will Ah bae without yer!?"

"Oh goodness, who *knows*. Perhaps...eaten alive by the minotaur? Antlers hiked back Eastward as a trophy of his easiest kill to date?"

"I don't think he was from the East, though," the fox added. "He acted alone. Surely the band that chased us would've brought everyone they had."

"Aye, Scottoh, yer might bae right. Ah don't remember seein' ah minotaur on those boats."

"So then that thing..." A chill tingled through Acirema's spine. "It left the bones we saw?"

"Probably so," said Foxtamas.

"But no minotaur I've met has done...*that*."

"I don't know what to tell you. Maybe he went insane or something. It's not *common*, but..."

"I just don't like the implications."

Bunns nodded in agreement. He chomped down on his final bite of bread and leaned back against his haversack, spinning a star around his finger to focus his thoughts. What was *happening* to Evon? Was it always like this? Monsters seething on *both* sides? You saved conflict like that for stories, not trips through the woods.

Maybe something had changed. Fundamentally. Grammo Day could have stirred it up—wouldn't be the most bizarre explanation. But whatever it was, Bunns homed in on the singular truth shining amidst the chaos of questions: this journey was going to be more perilous than the trio first anticipated.

He squeezed the star until it left an imprint upon his palm.

The excess food was put away, Acirema redid her bandages and the few Foxtamas needed for his legs, and Bunns practiced slowing his breaths so as to not irritate the bruise. The peace comforted them. It had been too long without a bright day or moment to sit in a reflective silence.

In that quiet, Foxtamas' mind brewed. Had since laying eyes on what the minotaur did to Bunns. Or, truthfully, since he'd awoken to the desolation of Grammo Day.

Were his actions—his *choices*—ever his own? Bunns and Acirema pushed him to leave Winthrop. Now, actually out on such a journey, their skills in battle, observation, and preparation kept the fox afloat. *They* took the brunt of the scars *he* deserved. And what did he give back in return? What did he do to propel them forward? To ease the load they bore because of *him?*

Both boots beat a hasty rhythm against the stone. He had an idea. One of his own determination. The longer he lingered on it, the heavier the *crunch!* of the marching armies in his head. Their count outpaced the shake of his legs. What if it led them even further from the East? What if they encountered *more* danger like the minotaur? The spindly white creatures? What if they wound up lost in a thicket and entangled in thorns so dense and sharp that the mere brush of the wind pushes them close enough to slice their necks and *that* ends up leaving Foxlaris forever alone in the East thinking no one was *ever* coming to save him or help him and he'd spend the rest of his days captured and alone and angry and hurt and—

"So, where tae now, eh?"

Bunns' voice broke through the fog of his brain like a ray of dawn. Slowly, Foxtamas' rattling settled, and he leaned in towards the pinpricks of developing conversation to calm himself.

"Eastward, preferably," replied Acirema, repeatedly stretching her arm to avoid any possible soreness. "But that's hopeless."

"Aye, aye. Best tae not fight any more of them beasties for ah bit."

"What's our best bet then? Heading back to Winthrop?"

"Nae! Weh're tae far in this tae turn tail."

"I don't mean giving up, more like…regrouping. Resting and then starting out again. If Father's in the mood, he may be able to lend us a squad of Watchers as protection, or—"

At the mention of the village militia, Bunns folded his ears in half and looked the other away.

"Tha's the *last* thing weh need tae do!" he scoffed. *Intentionally.* Another set of fighters when they already had *him?* A lesser jackalope would've been offended.

Annoyed, the princess glared at him. "What do you propose then?"

"Ah say we head west," said Bunns, "an' keep puttin' as much distance between us an' them ghouls. Once weh're rid of them 'em for ah bit, weh can head on back tae Nohsis."

Acirema mulled it over with a rocking of her head.

"True, but how long could that take? It'll at least double our journey length. And what if the monsters keep appearing? Won't leave us alone?"

"Then weh'll keep feedin' them ah taste o' steel 'till they don't!"

"You think you're in a condition to do that?"

"Better than those Watchers would bae!"

"Goodness, here we go…"

"Hey, *Ah* ain't the one who had tae bring them oup!"

"No, but you're *perpetuating* it."

"An' tha's worse?"

"In some circles, yes."

"How 'bout this one?"

"*Extremely.*"

"We're going north, a-a-and that's the end of it."

The bickering between Bunns and Acirema ceased. Both turned towards the fox, his legs stammering, heartbeat rattling up his throat.

"Wha', Scottoh?"

"I've been thinking," he said beneath a breath. His words croaked out in such a way both friends thought he had to be choking. "And it's time I do my part. Y'all are the reason I'm here after I couldn't drag myself outta Winthrop, and all y'all've gotten out of it is getting hurt. I can't ask any more of you. I mean, we're only a day in, and, well, look at us."

That they did, Bunns specifically poking at his chest and wincing.

"Foxlaris is our friend through and through, but...but he's my family, and *my* responsibility to bring back. So I have to be the one to call the shots. Y'all know I hate that kind of pressure, and yeah...yeah I do, but it's what I *can* do, so I'm saying we go north. At least until we find some place to lay low, refresh ourselves, and plan out a *good* strategy. It'll get us away from here and hopefully throw off the monsters if they're still prowling. I know it's not foolproof, but..."

His words faded there. It was a miracle he made it that long. Thankfully, he'd been helped by smiling faces and, to his relief, assuring, agreeing nods.

"North it is!" beamed Acirema.

"Ah don't think Ah can argue with tha', but Ah *am* glad tae give yer the leader title, Scottoh. Yer see what et did tae meh!" Bunns quipped out with a laugh (that subsequently curled him into a ball of pain). Acirema scooted over to side hug him, grinning ear to ear.

"We will follow wherever you go. You know that, don't you?"

"Yeah," he said, voice low and somber. "Just worried. That's all."

"That's why we're here, Foxtamas. That's why we're here." She squeezed him closer.

The midday sun started its descent. It didn't take long for the fellowship to repack their little belongings and wave a few final goodbyes to the desolate watchtower. Perhaps the heaping of stone knew it would be its last day to stand tall and gaze at the wider Western world. Perhaps not. But it did know as the trio disappeared within the pines that where its days finished, the fresh start to an unforgettable journey began.

Trekking back into the lush harmony of Mechmilne, the friends felt an air of relief, of momentary peace. Their traveling would always be overcome by the woodland's beauty whether they fought it or not.

Long, rolling waves of lilac and penny rose swayed between the grand roots of elden oaks. Bees, crickets, ants, ladybugs, all rode atop the flowery seas. The golden sunlight flittering through the midday breeze sprayed such as foam, dousing them in a bright gilding. Beneath the earthen ocean swam fallen fruits of an accidental harvest. Their skeletal husks were no more reminders of the legends that haunt the deep than the gnawed bones which wash upon shore. Bushes, isolated like luscious islands, rustled thick in the wind, which itself blew heavy with leaves like salt upon the breeze. It shook over and past and through the branches of the trees, beating out sounds of a sailor unfurling the sails.

Awe returned to the trio. The same heart-thumping, soul-stirring beat they found in the deep part of Mechmilne the night before. Such a feeling encapsulated the joy of an overdue hug, the firm press of two clasped hands. It promotes glee if not careful, a tantalizing lure to wonder, wander, and explore even more so. But for Bunns, it stirred within him the need to *sing.*

While hopping from one protruding rock to another, he fiddled with his pack and pulled out his precious heirloom Banjalope.

"Ah think et's bad luck tae start ah journey without ah lil' ditty. Wha' do yer tae think?" the cheeky voice abounded, booming against the thick trunks and shaking branches.

"Bunns—"

"Yeah! Play a good one, though. A classic," Foxtamas cut off Acirema, already giddy at singing a *traveling song* while actually *traveling*!

The jackalope nodded and tuned the strings. This would be the
performance of a lifetime.

Aye, laddies, 'tis the wind,
By which we start this travelin' march.
The same which makes the birds ascend
and sees the seasons start!

Yes, oh! Yes, oh!
'Tis the wind at last!
Off we go, off we go,
with it at our backs!

Aye, laddies, 'tis the wind,
It'll be our journey's guide.
A pal to freeze your coldest ends
and heat you high and dry!

Yes, oh! Yes, oh!
'Tis the wind at last!
Off we go, off we go,
with it at our backs!

Aye, laddies, 'tis the wind,
who's seen the past fair and true;
when great ol' Roihelm, land he split,
blue wings right cuttin' on through!

Yes, oh! Yes, oh!
'Tis the wind at last!
Off we go, off we go,

with it at our backs!

Aye, laddies, 'tis the wind,
Who leaves our venture now.
But the wind itself will never end—
It blows to keep its vow!

Yes, oh! Yes, oh!
'Tis the wind at last!
Off we go, off we go,
With! It! At! Our! *Backs!*

Foxtamas beat his hands together with a holler as Bunns strummed out the final note. Together, the pair had blared out the old tune, practically dancing and stirring up piles of leaves as they went.

"Ho ho! Wha' ah jig, eh, Scottoh?"

"Perfection! And what a choice! What did you think?" he asked the princess, regaining a breath as he did.

"Eh."

Nothing more. Nothing less. Just a flat line lost between her monotonous step forward.

"EH!?" Bunns shrieked. His hand clasped over his chest in horror (like Mrs. Cammont grabbing at her apron strings when appalled by his behavior). He hopped to the front of the line to stop the group's pace and her *blatantly* wrong opinion. "Wha' yer meanin' *'eh'?*"

"Just awfully noisy and loud. Mismatched schemes. Not enough grace."

The poor jackalope felt himself on the verge of death. He tumbled back in shock, shaking his head in pure distilled disbelief.

"Noisy? *Loud!?* Not even wha'? *Grace!* Wha's been gettin' tae *yer*, lassie? Ah reckon the ol' Palace is rottin' yer head dry of all an' any good tunes!"

"I highly doubt that, Bunns," retorted the princess with confidence. Yet, the more she thought on it, the more he...wasn't exactly wrong.

When the boys had gone off to work, and their long days of play ended, Aisar wasted little time regimenting her efforts towards political training, spanning all forms of royal etiquette from the arts to communication. Many days were spent entirely in the confines of the Palace. Only Mr. Cammont and the occasional dinner with her father provided her company, but even that didn't last long once Gregabbit reached the end of his service. Her world became the Palace and the teachings, posing, and writings within. Often, she longed for the days back with her friends in the Cammont Household. Pure times, peaceful and powerful. But now...how much had her days locked away distorted her? What had she lost? Bunns and his traveling songs were *legendary*, highlights of her childhood! They begged him to sneak one into each of their stories. Now, after all she and the rest of her friends had endured...what touch could she keep with anyone?

"Come on, you liked it when we learned it. Heck, you were *there.* Don't you remember?" asked Foxtamas.

"Uh, um...sort of, I guess," came her hasty reply. "It was...before the Night of Calmas, correct? With the merchants?"

"Yes!" Foxtamas chuckled a bit and looked to Bunns who, despite still fuming from the feedback, started to turn an embarrassed shade of pink. Perhaps his outburst was a *tad* too furious. "The Walking Village from Efeters was coming in, and this one vendor had the best-smelling thistlecakes in all Evon."

"Aye, an' the petal-head wouldn't give us a lick! Laddie looked like ah rotten core of corn an' didn't budge on the price for ah few peasant kids," Bunns added with seething distaste.

"And we weren't gonna take that behavior, So—""So you three planned to steal some!" Acirema cut in, memory flooding back, pausing her in her tracks. "I warned you against it and offered up every Top I could find to try and put a stop to it."

"But we wanted *revenge*," Foxtamas chuckled. "We set Bunns to talk with the vendor while me and Foxlaris sneaked around back. Thing was..."

"Bunns was too busy learning the song to leave!" She had it! Her cheeks rattled with chuckles and glee, both at their childhood antics and Bunns puffing out his chest as if having accomplished such a noble pursuit.

"Tha' Ah did! Yer heard the words, yer can feel the meanin'. Ah wasn't 'bout tae let somethin' tha' precious slip out of mah hand! An' now look—Ah can sing et for yer lovelies without ah lick o' help."

All three laughed. It was rather nice to think on fonder times, stealing included. The cakes *were* rather tasty. Thankfully, for the sake of their souls and rears, Mrs. Cammont never found out. If the long, outstretched oaks or flimsy young ashes could speak, their secret would spread like wildfire.

As they press onward, Bunns glanced back at Acirema and called up to Foxtamas.

"Yer know, there mae bae hope for this one yet!"

The sun drooped lower, the forest grew thicker, and the ground below the six traveling feet began rose higher. Their aimless, simple trek north had led them upon yet another ridge, this time sturdy enough to hike up the side. Going around would push them too far off course. The only way forward was up.

Exhaustion quickly set in, even for Bunns (which he, of course, blamed entirely on the bruise). Such weariness often brings out the melancholiest of thoughts, and, for one Acirema Feiht, things were no different.

"Why," she asked between breaths, "do you think this all happened? The Bridge and sorts, the earthquake. Why any of it?" The sudden death, destruction, and turmoil that had consumed both Winthrop and Evon alike had shielded her from tackling the question. Now, pacing up a ridge lost in the middle of Mechmilne Wood, the guard was lowered, allowing the true questions to hit their mark. "Suppose it could be Roihelm?"

"No."

A brisk answer from Foxtamas.

Still leading, he shook his head and leaned against a tree for a sip of air. "It's not his nature."

"What do you mean?" she replied.

The mention of the Phoenix sent the fox back to the warmth and care of Omaya, his mother. Poppa would always be gone during the long, seemingly endless Pradifore winters when no tree bunkered bare. He could almost feel the fireplace licking his frozen hands after climbing about their house with Foxlaris. Momma would bring them in, cozy them up in handstitched blankets, and tell stories of Roihelm. Good stories. Loving stories.

The truths of them never strayed far from his heart. Roihelm was their Author, and he was good. He loved all four of those foxes. He made them. What went down on Grammo Day was anything *but* love.

It was evil.

But...wasn't Roihelm over all? Creating, making, writing all into existence? If so, then would the disaster not too be under his control? Or maybe—

No.

He was good.

He *is* good.

And that was that.

"He wouldn't do those things to people he created," Foxtamas replied with a sullen tone, "it doesn't make any sense. He made Evon and he'd sustain it. Now come on, we're just about to the end of this ridge."

The other two didn't dare push him. He was their myth master—what he said about ancient, auspicious figures like Roihelm didn't go challenged. From what he and Foxlaris spoke of their original family, they were devoted to the Phoenix, more so than many others in Central Evon. With that came a reverence few saw these days. Most, however, viewed him the same way they viewed all legends: a story.

The ground leveled out gently. Before they realized it, they were back among the rest of the forest which, once again, obscured their view of the wider landscape. Foxtamas wondered if keeping to higher ground would help spot some place to stay or recuperate; after all, he *was* taking charge.

He pondered the thought as he trekked. Until his eyes fell on an…*unruly*…sight.

"Um, guys…we might not be going this way…"

The others made their way over and froze behind the fox. A trail of madness broke through the woodland and intersected their path. Trees were ripped up from their roots. Dirt lay overturned and flung free. The underbrush looked like the aftermath of a tornado.

Gulping, they looked to their right and saw the desolation extend beyond their line of sight, like a fresh scar across Mechmilne pointing towards the East. That alone worried them witless. The hoofprints slammed into the upturned earth, however…

"Is this from…the beastie?" asked Bunns. Despite the minotaur being long gone, he instinctively rested a hand over his star pouch.

"Has to be," Foxtamas replied, bending down to look closer at the tracks. "You know anything else that could have done this?"

"Nae."

"So, where now then?" Acirema asked with a hint of fright in her voice.

The fox—clearly harboring the same nervousness—moved out into the trail. It opened into the sky for him to see another ridge rising close enough for them to reach. It didn't follow a strictly northern path as he hoped, but it would give them a height advantage and, more importantly, a place *away* from any potential raging minotaur.

"Let's start up the next ridge," he replied. Foxtamas motioned for the others to cross the trail with him. "We should be far away from him by then and closer to…something." Together, they began yet again, doing their best to stay quiet in case, to their horror, a certain minotaur had ears like a hawk.

Ridgetop foliage grew airier than the mangled yet flourishing flora below. Trees of ash and birch bunched themselves across patches of tall grass and jutting, mossy rocks. Walking among it all was a dream. And for Foxtamas, in more than one way.

The brush gave way to a clear, perfect view of the wider West Evon landscape. It put what little he could see from the tower the night before to shame. The blanket of forest, drenched in a viridescent hue so vibrant it sparkled in the setting sun, rolled far and wide from him to the horizon. Ridges soared like the scales of a massive dragon guarding the sacred ground. Some hardly bumped the green spread whilst others, fading to a pale periwinkle the further back they flowed, rose with an unknowable yet unmistakable power.

Sublime passion could easily swallow any and all who gazed too long. The slumbering beast would snatch them up and hold them captive in his wooded belly forever. Had the sky not begun to melt into a glittery pastel pink, and if the sun avoided lying down for a well-deserved rest, Foxtamas Scottsworth would have been gobbled up in heartbeat. Oh, how Evon called to him. Every bone begged, every tendon tugged, muscle moved, nerve nagged. So much of his own will was taken over by the sheer beauty and excitement one look, one glance, one fleeting, fleeting glance gave.

Both Foxlaris and his friends fled his mind; what use had he for them? Was *this* not the truest form of freedom, away from every fear, every pain, every hardship, every heartbreak? He knew his life could be transformed walking under the boughs and exploring their endless routes. A sink for his worries. An alleviated chest. A clear mind.

His salivating mouth could almost taste the relief. Cooling water poured over his thumping, rattling, roaring anxious soul.

Yet...

"Look!" Acirema cried out. She pointed to a cluster of gray smoke rising a short ways away from their lookout. "That *has* to be a village! Come on, we should head there before it gets too dark."

Red Eyes.

Foxlaris.

Pain.

Fear.

It all came back like a wound tearing open its stitching. Away went the Mechmilne mysteries, the endless roads, the people and places destined to never meet his wide blue eyes. He welcomed back reality with a nod. And a sigh.

"Yeah...yeah, I bet so too. Let's hope they have a place to stay, it's getting later than I thought," he chimed back in, shaking his head from the mental journey.

By the time the three descended (taking special care to avoid any uprooted path), darkness once again enveloped Evon. The trio hopped over a few brooks and prickly brushes before finally seeing the small twinkle of lights sparkling in the distance.

"Scottoh, Queenie," Bunns whispered with their destination in sight. "Ah know et mae seem like ah village, but yer never know." In saying this, he drew out two stars, one for each paw, and crouched low as to not be seen.

Acirema could hardly believe her eyes. "Are you serious?"

"Hey, you never know."

She whipped around and found, just like Bunns, Foxtamas, crouched, hood up, and fumbling to load a bolt into the Crossbawn.

"Only a day in and you two have already lost it," she sighed, ducking down herself. It was one thing to avoid Eastern monsters; it was another to walk into a village looking like thieves!

They crept together with a careful gait. Before long, rough sounds of strings, hollers, and merriment erupted up ahead. All that from...a village? No one settlement could produce such bustling banter. The closer they crawled, the more sense the sudden noise made.

There, far away from the start of a few well-kept hamlets, sat a tavern. It was large for being so isolated. Hefty Northern timber made up the walls and columns supporting the roof, itself a mix of wrapped hay and shingles. The building stretched high enough to house at least two or three stories. Large windows, arched and designed to mimic clattering tankards, were placed evenly on all sides. From them came mild lantern light and the ceaseless clamoring heard yards away. Everything looked like a tavern should. Though oddly isolated from the rest the of town tucked further back into the wooded thicket, it would do for the night. It was either that or another sleep bunched up between sticks and stones.

Foxtamas and Bunns peeled back their hoods, and Acirema inspected the sign hanging above the door.

"*Hucksubtle Tavern.* I don't think I recognize the name."

"Same here," said the fox.

"But et's lookin' like ah ripe ol' time tae meh!" Bunns winked at the others and pulled the brass handles. The princess and the peasant, however, just exchanged defeated yet accepting glances, following their friend into the hustle and bustle of Hucksubtle Tavern.

19

"REJOICE IN IT, THEREFORE,"

Bristled with the beaming flickers of lantern light, the tavern's inside felt grand in the way a childhood home does in midnight memories. The room was L-shaped, with half leading to tables, chairs, booths, and a stage on the far wall, while the other funneled to a staircase rising to some secret second-story. A bar ran along the bend. Shelves layered with bottles sat behind, creating a display of blue and silver amongst the wooden interior.

Everything within sat well-furnished and clean. Tables, long and stout, crafted of hardy wood, supported a mixing of patrons and drinks alike. The guests too were…furnished, some may say. Foxtamas immediately picked out the oddities: otters, legs and rudders crippled; mice hardly tall enough to reach their mugs; gruff eagles eyeing only their drinks. Many were normal, mind you, fair, upright folk. But Hucksubtle seemingly held few boundaries. All were welcome into the fray.

The fox turned away as a call of welcome shouted towards them.

"Evenin' folks! Welcome on in to Hucksubtle!" cried the peppy voice. Behind the bar, dressed in the finery of a brown suit, slacks, and suspenders, a coyote bartender waved over. His bright green eyes lit up as he slid an overflowing glass of ale down to a happy hand. He had a hop and a skip in his step while mixing and filling drinks, letting a bright and wide smile overcome him. It only grew as he motioned for the newcomers to settle at the bar.

Bunns smiled back and offered up a wave. As he did, he felt

Foxtamas start to wobble, slinking back towards the door.

"Scottoh," he whispered, "yer alright?" Bunns moved back towards his friend to steady him, matching the worried glance of Acirema.

"There's just...people, Bunns...people—"

"Ah know et, laddie, but wha' about 'em?"

"I–I haven't seen this many since, since...Grammo Day." How his voice wheezed out the words. His body dropped lower, now firmly back against the door. The fox was on the verge of making a scene.

"Hey, laddie, Scottoh, *listen,*" Bunns began to reassure, lifting him off his wobbling orange knees, "tha' days long gone. Et *ain't* comin' back, got meh? Yer gotta leave et alone. All tha' fear, right here, at the door. Leave et. Tonight, weh'll relax for the first time in ah while. Yer dinnae want tae bae missin' tha', right?"

"Y–Yeah, yeah, I guess not," he replied, shaky. He knew Bunns was right. Something about the confidence in those brown eyes helped ease the fox's struggle. Today wasn't Grammo Day. Foxlaris wasn't dying right before him. They were here, in a tavern, ready for a night of calm. He could do this. He had his friends. They had him.

"There yer go! Come on, tae the bar!"

Bunns marched on ahead past the tables of squirrels and fauns while his companions lagged behind. Foxtamas, still breathing away the worries, felt the cooling rub of Acirema's hand upon his back. She bore that classic warm, welcoming smile. They got this. And it was time to show it.

As they hopped up to their barstools, the bartender slid down towards them.

"Howdy howdy! Welcome on in to our fine establishment. Name's Teardic Yotesman, tavern's owner always, but tonight I got the delight of bein' y'all's here server. Anything I can get y'all swallowin' right quick?" The coyote spoke with a drawl thicker than honey left out in a snow storm. He asked amidst cleaning out a mug and sliding two more down the bar. Never once did he step out of motion, flowing marvelously in his work and beaming a smile no battle could break.

"We are, um, new around here," piped up Acirema. Teardic

whipped up his head and met the princess with his blazing green glare.

"Course! Silly me, miss, knew I didn't recognize y'all folk. How 'bout that menu, eh?" He put away a newly cleaned glass before reaching below the counter. The trio readied themselves to scan over the approaching list; instead, the coyote shot out three fresh mugs and began reciting the Hucksubtle selection.

"Let's see here, I got stocked Pickety Ale, Roistlind Rush, and an Asda Fresh for starters, the heavy hitter duo of Rutstur Whiskey and Bytuk Beer, Slimrun Wine, Chewger Wine, and Drumdedge Grog are the ol' folk favorites, and, for our specialty and Evon-renowned drink, we 'course carry *the* Hucksubtle Mug.

"But, let me warn ya' three, ya' won't be findin' a *lick* of alcohol in this here joint. My Pops made that rule a ways back, and I ain't got a plan on changin' it." He ended his show with a dazzling smile, waiting for the orders to come through.

"Um..." Foxtamas tried to begin. He fished through his mind to remember what sounded pleasant enough to drink. "Pickety Ale, please."

"And a Slimrun Wine," Acirema followed.

Teardic nodded and picked up two of the mugs. His buzzing eyes whipped to Bunns, awaiting his order, when he noticed a look on his face he'd seen too many times in his tavern: bargaining.

"Well, yer *sure* yer cannae add just ah *touch* of help tae the drinks?"

"Sorry sir, no can do—" Teardic slowed as Bunns pulled back his tunic to reveal his chest. The massive Minotaur-induced bruise had melted into a hideous blotch of blacks, yellows, and blues. Had some of the fellow patrons taken a glance, their drinks would be splattered across the floor, followed shortly by whatever else floated in their stomachs.

The coyote flinched. No words passed his lips as he held the third and final mug under the counter for a few moments. He pulled it up once done and slid over to Bunns, sloshing some of the foam down the mug's side.

"That there's a *special* Hucksubtle Mug, ol' son. Keep quiet, sip it slow, an' don't think 'bout no refill. It'll give the kick ya need." With a wink, he flashed back around and prepared the other orders. Bunns just chuckled and slurped.

Foxtamas stared down his mug before giving it a taste. Huh. Fairly good, but nothing compared to Butterswath. Just the thought of that childhood delicacy eased his mind, reminding him what Bunns had said. Tonight was not one of worry, but *rest*.

"Say, Mr. Teardic," the fox asked after a few more sips, hoping to start some conversation, "Is—"

"Oh, no misters for me, friend! Just Teardic'll do." The coyote once more winked and tossed another full mug down the bar. "What's it you were sayin'?"

"Oh, um, just that it seems awfully busy tonight. Is it usually like this?"

"Not one bit. It's more than I've ever seen in all my life workin' here, and I've been workin' here my whole life!"

Once again, his smile lit up; but it didn't stay long. Teardic threw his cleaning towel over his suspenders and leaned against the bar, close to where only the trio could hear him. "No, friend, Hucksubtle ain't been the hit it was for some time. Y'all saw that village comin' in, didn'tcha? Well, used to it came right up to our door. Place is called Hucklebee, or *was*, anywho. We was a big ol' community way back when, 'till ol' 'Granpa' Subtle—named as such 'cause you couldn't get more than a word or two outta him atta time—started this here joint. It was on the edge of town, ya' know, not causin' no ruckus or nothin', but it attracted the lonesome of Hucklebee. All them rascals that passed through, or the ones with no love or no home. The ones them townsfolk saw as filth.

"The town kept growin', but not thisa way on t'wards us. They built their new homes and such further West. Time swept on through, and the ol' stores shut down, folk moved on to new places, and what began to wear an' tear away got tore on down. Things've changed so much ol' Hucksubtle's left standin' all 'lone these days. But we still draw a crowd. Not anyone from Hucklebee, *that's* for certain."

"So yer get tae run this whole ship bae yerself?" asked Bunns between the stings of the drink.

"Yessir! Well, as of recent, yes. After Pop's death, it was me and my sister that was 'sposed to run it, but she wanted a break an' started up her own place over yonder in Mikyill. Ever since the Grammo Day though? Well I'll *be!* I bet she's regrettin' *that* choice!" Teardic giggled and started to fill a mug for himself. "Sorry for the life story, friends, but you're right, mister, it's been real busy. I take it as grief, ya' know. People'll try an' fill that hole any way they can, and it's the games and drinks that's a quick fix. Been thata way since we were in Hucklebee. Now, well...seems everyone's feelin' somethin'."

For a single moment, a faltering look of sadness blew past the coyote. He raised his mug, took a swig, and tossed it back down, smile climbing back to lips place amongst the foam left behind.

"No, no, I think you're right. It has been...hard...since all of it started," replied the fox, trying to produce a smile of his own. "And the story was nice. It's a shame what happened, though."

"Oh, always will be, friend, ain't nothin' changin' that. Say, ya' from these parts? Just don't really see many foxes this far south."

"Um...yeah, moved when I was young. Past Pradifore there aren't too many of us."

"Is that right! A real travelin' soul then. Where ya' from now? Or—" The tavern owner shook his head and halted his words. "Forgive me, folks! It's awful rude to ask where ya' from without even knowin' ya' *names!*"

The trio smiled at his antics with Bunns, slamming down the last of his drink, accepting the invitation to introduce the crew.

"Name's Bunns Cammont! The lady bae Acirema, and mah foxy friend bae Foxtamas." Bunns held a beaming grin. Jovial? Yes. Feeling the effects of the Hucksubtle Mug? Slightly.

"Lovely to meet y'all's company, Mister Bunns!" Teardic replied. "Where do you three travelers hail from?"

"Village Winthrop. It's...*somewhere* near here," Foxtamas answered.

"Ah." A cold, stilled reply from Teardic. His green eyes darted

across their faces, picking up the notion they knew the village's reputation preceded them. "Word is Winthrop ain't the best. Poor, small,
solemn, right?"

"Sadly…" Acirema cut in. Her wine was barely sipped; her leg
rattled against the bar. "My people are…wounded. Or, better put, mis-
treated. It's the only place around that takes them in. Our community is
strong, but…" She shifted her gaze to Foxtamas. Without even moving
his mouth, the princess knew his message. He was hiding the grief of
Grammo Day; this was her time to do the same.

Acirema whisked up her mug and gulped down the wine. As she
eased it back upon the bar, Teardic chuckled.

"Sip all ya' want, m'Lady! It's on the house. Didn't realize I'd
welcomed *royalty*!" Bounding back, the bartender bowed, half in jest
and half in truth.

"No, Mr. Teardic, it's nothing, truly—"

He paid no attention. Instead, he swiped away her glass and refilled
it. Teardic glanced back with a wink. "Seriously," she continued, "I'm
hardly a ruler in Winthrop. I just sit, a-and read, and—"

"Queenie," Bunns whispered while pushing up his own mug to be
topped off, "Yer *might* should let this one bae." The coyote twisted back
to her, sliding down a glass brimming with the rippling of a rich purple.
As for Bunns'…he pushed it down with a glare.

"Oughta listen to Mister Bunns, m'Lady. Our ol' blue bird put you
in that spot, and I ain't deservin' of this here joint if I don't honor it. I'd
do the same if ol' Gniw himself done dropped by." A small smile and
quiet blush awoke on her face. Nodding, she raised the glass and took
a cheerful sip.

Bunns scoffed. He turned around on his seat, taking in the sights.
A game of some sorts had been set up at one of the tables. Light cheer
erupted as a dwarf, burly in nature, rung out a hand, somehow soaked
in ale. What had he been doing? The growing crowd of rapscallions
blocked Bunns' view and any information he could grasp. Intrigue
pulled at him with no remorse.

"Wha' are them laddie's playin', eh?" the jackalope asked.

"Oh, just some Flapdragon, an ol' tavern timewaster. You can go on and join if ya' like. If they don't let ya' in, send word and I'll handle it. They know the rules," said Teardic. His wink this go around felt surprisingly forceful. Bunns nodded back with a wink of his own and headed over.

The coyote swiped up his mug and looked down into its empty belly. "Gah, good one. Keep watch I don't give him a refillin'," he snickered to the fox and raccoon. "Mister Bunns is in for a rough one tonight!"

The jackalope looked on from the crowd's outer fringes. He hopped up and down to glance at the action before finally just nudging his way further in. Between the gaps, he found the dwarf from before seated at the table. His hand waved over a flaming mug of ale, fingers prickled by the rising licks. The anticipation squinched his dark-bearded face. With a thin exhale, the lad dashed his hand beneath the flames, splattering the table and the onlookers with drink. He whipped it back out in a flash, holding between his fingers a small, sweetened blueberry as his prize.

The circle's roars shook the table. Burling out a laugh, the dwarf popped the berry into his grinning mouth. He rose and emptied the seat for the next contender, a giddy squirrel, to have a go. Bunns rushed over to meet him as he worked on drying his arm at the next table over.

"Aye, laddie," Bunns called, catching his attention with a quick tap on the shoulder, "how do yer play this, uh, Flapdragon mess?"

The dwarf turned and looked down, meeting the jackalope with warm, honey-colored eyes. It was apparent he was unlike the rest of the Hucksubtle crew. He wore a large, blue, fur-lined overcoat that hid a warrior's tunic and small single-bladed axe tucked beneath his belt. Though long, his curly black hair and beard stayed trimmed and upkept. Of the few dwarves Bunns had seen, he felt the most important.

"Oh, it's nothin'!" His voice had the pips and nasal most Northern folk did. "The goal's to grab what's at the bottom of the mug as quick as y'can. If you miss it or get y'hand burned, you're straight outta luck. Keep it going though and the mugs an' prizes an' whatnot get bigger and bigger. Although..." His eyes darted back to the table. No one was close enough to hear. The dwarf leaned down closer to Bunns, whispering, "don't be puttin' a single Top on any of it. The tender back there be a real stickler 'bout bettin'. I say he's in his right to do it. Up where I'm from, it never leads anywhere good. Torchings, hangings, just the worst."

Bunns nodded, carefully. What was he getting himself into? The crowd seemed a wild bunch, but the game itself was worth it.

Speed. Skill. Danger. Reward.

All his desires rolled up into one scramble of cheer and applause. Utter perfection! Oh, the tavern goers of Hucksubtle would see his glory tonight!

His thoughts must have revealed themselves in his face, for the dwarf chuckled before shouting over his shoulder, "Mosho! Hop on out lad, we got a newcomer wantin' to have his go."

With a scoff and curse beneath his breath, the squirrel obeyed. Had it been anyone else's call, he may not have been so willing.

The seat nestled Bunns like a throne holding a long-lived king. An older gnome, twisted gray beard and hair twirling beneath his leather cap, prepared his mug of Summer Swallow and ignited it with a flick of flint. The flames danced high and wide on the jackalope's eyes; the smells of apricot and soured lime flavored his mind. Hundreds of tingles ran through his fingers as he readied them over the fire. His hand would dash through like the flick of a star. Never had the folk around him seen such speed; and never again would they after tonight. Now was his time. Now was—

"Steady now bunny boy. Don't 'urt y'self."

Bunns shot his focus from the drink to the hoarse voice across the table. Some eye-patched badger, too lanky and wrinkled to resemble his own kind, chuckled to himself at the comment.

"Aye, Yotesy's got salve on deck!" came the cry of another too nestled in the crowd to be seen. The cadence felt...familiar. Nostalgic.

They sounded like the mocking Winthrop children of years past. They sounded like the Watchers peering into every corner of life. They sounded like the thoughts of a boy, a boy without his brother, a boy without his father, a boy—

No. They sounded like taunts from good-for-nothing outcasts.

He refocused on the mug. With a nod, the gnome tossed a blueberry into the mix of froth and flame. The moment was now, he reminded himself. The moment was now.

Hand up.

Breath out.

Eyes closed.

All stood still.

The crowd blinked, and the feat was over. A sudden *Plop!* rang aloud, and the jackalope was chewing the ale-soaked berry.

"Tasty!" he shouted to break the silence.

How…how in *Evon* were they supposed to react!? They looked closer and, indeed, he'd plucked it straight from the mug's bottom. But…but *how!*

The dwarf, obviously shocked, clapped and hollered, inviting the rest to follow. Bunns slipped him a wink as the applause finally rose. He'd been right: now *was* his time.

The gnome spared no second lighting the second pour, this time a bubbling Daydream Draught. Pops of fizz sent sparks into the air, singeing the table below. He tossed in the prize, a single Blue Top, and let it sink to the bottom with a foreboding *Clank!*

"Whenever you're ready, bud," grunted the gnome, backing up so as to not be hit by the fiery spray.

"Eyes open this time, laddies!" Bunns snickered. In all honesty, the fizzing spray did sting a tad. But not enough to keep the Top from being his.

Down his hand shot, drenching itself in the drink. The fire would start leaping at his fur within the second. His fingers cracked against the mug's end, and he scooped like digging a star from his pouch, snatching a mix of draught and gold. Already the heated licks were starting to wrap themselves around his wrist. But before they could attack, their prey vanished. Bunns ripped out the coin and tossed it against the table, again in a flash all too quick to fully take in. This time, however, the right kind of rush and cheer followed.

"Bring the bowl! Bring the bowl!" cried Mosho the squirrel, long past his disdain for the warrior.

"Aye, grab it!" another howled.

Confused, Bunns turned around to his dwarven friend.

"The *bowl?*"

"Aye," replied the dwarf, "hardest Flapdragon challenge here. Looks they figure you can beat it."

A dangerous smile sprouted along Bunns' face.

"Seems weh have ah couple prophets here tonight!"

While the bowl was off being prepared at the bar, a long-aged clurichaun, held together by dirtied rags and a cane, tossed a roughened bag of Tops upon the table.

"I-I-I'll wager on 'im."

Silence.

Gulps circled the table. Eyes darted away from one another. No one dared so much as breathe.

They knew the rules.

"No one touch it!" screamed a crippled, tattooed otter, "The rat's a cheat. Can't take a damned loss. Done lost half me savin's to tha' filthy hand o' his!" The angered brute pushed his way closer to the gambler, a small shimmer of silver rising from his pocket. "I oughta show ya' what happens to no good brigands like you—"

THWACK!

Whistling through the air, a dagger jammed into the table, stopping the otter in his tracks. Behind it came the blade's owner and last person the players wanted to see.

"I *know* my ears ain't lyin' to me, Klack. What was it I heard over here? Somethin' 'bout a...wager?" asked the Teardic with a dark, parental sneer. The clurichaun tried to reach for the purse, but the tender slid it away.

"No, just listen, l-listen—"

"I had it handled, Yotesy," the otter cut in, putting himself in front of the bumbling Klack. "I know the rules." His furrowed brown eyes met the glowing green of Teardic's.

"If you knew 'em, Grale, you'd let me handle it. I done showed ya' mercy once after your last 'incident.' Don't ruin it playin' savior." His gaze tightened, and so, too, did Grale's. For half a second, he broke the stare and caught a glimpse of the otter's hidden blade edging out of his pocket. This was headed to the one place he hoped to avoid.

Teardic threw himself back and dodged Grale's sudden swing. With a leap, he bounded over the table, picking up his knife on the way and whipping behind the attacker before his lumbering body could catch him. A cold sting of metal met the rugged, tattooed skin.

"You just can't listen," the coyote whispered. He threw him down, tumbling upon Klack and towards the door. "Out! Both of y'all, out! Show ya' rotten faces 'round here again an' you'll be leavin' a *lot* worse for wear!"

The pair bolted. They scrambled over one and another and swung open the door, letting the late summer air suck them out.

Teardic smirked, tossing the bag of Tops back on the table right as Mosho returned with the readied bowl. It was the size of a long, deepened pot. Diving for a Top in it would be closer to nabbing a fish in River Nohsis than simply looking for a berry in the mug.

As the onlookers grappled for a piece of gold, the owner took a Silver Top from his pocket and plopped it in the passing drink.

"Besta luck, ol' son," he winked to Bunns. Grinning.

The confused, anxious faces of Foxtamas and Acirema awaited him when he returned.

"What was all that?" asked the fox.

"Gamblin'. Scourge of Evon if ya' ask me. Them tales of what happens to folk who get caught up in it freeze my soul still. I don't need boys like these messin' with games like those. Same with the drinkin'.

They've done got it bad enough; don't need 'em any worse."

The duo slowly nodded. Acirema chewed on the barkeep's works, taking in the wider scene of Hucksubtle as she did. The scrapes and scars on the outside of the patrons matched what they held within. The abandonment of being an outcast became palpable aura. One that reminded her of a similar place. A place…called home…

"But," Teardic broke through, "y'all might wanna go watch Mister Bunns over there. He's takin' on the *bowl*."

Foxtamas shook his head.

"Goodness, what kinda mess is that word for?"

"Oh, no mess, Mister Foxtamas. If I allowed bettin' here, I'd wager the whole tavern he'll make it through this one squeaky clean."

The friends tucked themselves tight beside the dwarf. Once settled with the rest of the crowd (or, more specifically, the entirety of the tavern), the gnome flicked his flint and sent flying a single spark.

How the flames soared! The whips of white and gold jumped higher than Bunns' antlers and invited a unanimous *woah!* from the eager audience. Maybe the bowl shouldn't have been next…

Bunns thought the opposite. Seeing the fire tingled every nerve in his small body, readied the synapses to fire with a frightening flash.

"Ready lads!?" he cried. Instant cheer surrounded him. Oh, what a stupid grin grew on his face. It told the fox and raccoon in attendance that their friend had gone beyond the point of saving. Instead, he'd finally reached his moment.

Hand up.

Breath out.

Eyes closed.

"Tetelestai," he whispered, and plunged in his paw.

The difference struck him immediately. Thick, heavy heat began to attack not only his wrist, but high up his arm and to the frays of his tunic. Worse, the bowl sank deep and wide; reaching further only brought the flames closer. Time allowed a single thought, two if quick enough. It was either barely scrape the bottom, maybe picking up the Top but avoiding the fire, or dive deeper, securing the gold and risking the impending burns. Too much pride and glory pumped through his veins to select the route of possible failure. He'd jump into the ale if he had to.

The jackalope popped from his seat to fully reach the bottom. Once there, he flung around his paw with unthinkable speed until he nicked the side of the Top.

He had it. Inches from his grip.

But the heat resisted.

Would the flames *actually* let this *thief* take their precious Silver Top? Steal from them with ease to impress a rowdy crowd?

No. And they would *not* be going without a fight.

Thus, with a gripping force, they wound around the arm of Bunns and bound it tight. The white of his fur smoldered to a charred brown. It started to lap at the skin beneath until the warrior saw the game at play. If the flames burnt any further he'd lose, leaving only with a bandage and salve. But that would *not* be his fate. He had the Top in his sight. He had the drive to snag it. He had everything he needed.

Out shot the arm and away broke the orange snares. The rush splashed a wave of ale across the table and patrons, but no one gave it a second glance, for Bunnclar Cammont stood tall, arm soaked and Silver Top gripped within it. All of Hucksubtle Tavern shook with glee and cheer, shouts and roars.

He'd done it! He'd beaten the bowl! A new champion stood amongst them!

Bunns!
Bunns!!
Bunns!!!

Once the celebration died down and other contenders gave their own go at the game, the Winthropian trio quested back towards the bar for another round of drinks to finish off the night.

"So," Teardic asked, looking behind while shelving the tankards, "y'all here on some big ol' political mission? Seems ya' got quite the talented guards for the job, m'lady." He flashed a grin towards Bunns, but the champion paid no attention. His focus was downing the last sips of his Hucksubtle Mug—a *regular* this time.

"Oh, no, Teardic, these are just my friends. Our reason for travel is, well, personal in nature."

"Well golly, in that case don't let me be 'trudin'. Ya' business is ya' business."

"Well..." Foxtamas piped up. The fox set aside his glass and glanced up to Teardic. "They're doing it for me. And my brother. It's kind of a long story, but—"

"No, Mister Foxtamas, I'd love to hear it!" replied the bartender, nodding with an ease of compassion. The fox returned the gesture, took one last swig, and retold the tragic tale.

Once finished, Teardic tossed his towel over his suspenders and leaned against the bar. "Goodness, goodness me, Mister Foxtamas. My heart breaks for ya'. Tales like that, they stir a soul into changin'. If I lost my sis Selida like that, I ain't sure I'd have the bravery y'all three have. But 'bout them, er, Eastern beasts..."

The trio perked up. Leaned in closer to the coyote's words that dropped towards a whisper.

"I done heard stories just like 'em right 'fore y'all made it in here tonight. Straight from the mouths of Ruel and his Ratsy boys."

"Ruel was here!?" The fox's question broke the silence and pushed Teardic back in surprise.

"Course! Ol' Nuthead loves this place, uses it for them quick breaks he and the boys get."

The friends knew exactly what he meant and couldn't help but smile at the thought. The squirrel's stops had to be brief; however, when it came to Winthrop, he seemed to always stay a *tad* too long.

"Even made 'em their own brew, the Ratatoskr Rush, quickest

concoction I can whip up. Anywho, Ruel was tellin' 'bout his scouts seein' carnage at the Riverside. They traced it inland this mornin' and found some merchant an' his cart upturned and killed right in the middle of the road. Terrible business, even just hearin' it. Then word came one of his older lads ambushin' a beast that got lost from the party. Claimed he was all gnarled an' ugly, just like the ones y'all fought." Teardic took a moment to wipe his head with the towel. "I ain't one to speculate, friends, feels a tad too close to gamblin' for my like. But I tell ya, somethin' ain't right out there, an' I don't want a *lick* of it."

His audience nodded in agreement. The same thought wore heavy on their minds, ever since the sky darkened above Foxlaris. But before they could respond, the twang of a banjo and rasp of a drum bleated from the tavern's back corner. Their attention turned towards a one-faun-band starting a tune on the stage. The Flapdragon games ceased, and the crowds fell into place to give the musician his due.

Bunns shot around to Foxtamas with wide, bloodshot eyes.

"Scottoh! He's playin' 'Creek Water Wilds!'" slurred the jackalope. Between a mess of motioning for his friend and pointing at the performer, Bunns slumped from his seat and waded back to the Flapdragon table. It didn't seem to matter all that much whether the fox joined him or not.

"Oh, I feel bad," sighed Acirema. "I ought to join him, to make up for what I said earlier about his songs. Are you coming?"

"No, I'm, um, I'm good. I'll listen from over here." Foxtamas added a grin to his words to ensure her he'd be more than alright at the bar. The princess replied with a wink, then set off to find the drunkard.

But Teardic saw through the stunt. Up went the fox's mug, suddenly refilled with another round of Pickety Ale. The bartender slid it back down with a smile.

"I've lived too lil' life, but I know a look like that 'un when I see it, pal. Still on them beasts and ya' brother, ain'tcha? Even when ya' tried leavin' it all at the door?"

Foxtamas gulped.

"Y-Yeah, that's it. How'd you know?"

"Ya' don't deal with these rascals all day and not learn nothin'."
Although a smile was starting to sprout, Teardic uprooted it, choosing
to lean in closer to his guest. "But bein' honest, Mister Foxtamas, I've
heard more than just what Ruel told. I figured you'd like a share in the
secrets." His whisper carried the cold chill of a haunted night, the flashes
of terror and intrigue that sneak in when one dwells on a mystery.
Whatever knowledge he held, with it came a tantalizing urge that so
fully engrossed the fox all else faded from view.

"Yes, yes, I'm all ears," Foxtamas responded, voice faltering.

"Well, folk have been bringin' in...*explanations*...of all kinds.
Some are sayin' Grammo Day was just an earthquake. Me and you were
both there, Mister Foxtamas. That wasn't no earthquake. The sky? The
storm? All too much for that. Others said the Efetes was up to it, bein'
kin to them ol' elves an' all. My take? Whole buncha scared folk pointin'
fingers tryin' to make themselves sleep a lil' easier at night. All 'cept this
last one, though. It's the real kicker." Eyes wide and readied, the fox
scooted closer, scared to miss a single syllable. "Word is, the scholars up
in the Fulnoa are claimin' this is all comin' down from *Roihelm*. Every
lick of it."

Fear seized the fox. The same doubts he denied earlier that day
arose from the dead and haunted over him. His worries, that the Author
of Evon, the person his *parents* worshipped and prayed to, caused all of
it...could be real.

The idea sent his thoughts spiraling. It would mean that Foxlaris
had been taken by something nefarious, that the deaths and monsters
and mayhem had been planned, orchestrated for some, some goal, a
divine one, formed not from justice but wrath and—

"Who told you all this? Did they say anything more, l-l-like they
were certain or something, or what it meant?" stuttered out the fox. It
was clear by his hot, rapid breaths how deeply the shock choked him.

"Nothin' too deep, just gossip from the few Blue Patrols that stop
by. Shame, the dwarf Mister Bunns was talkin' up was the one who first
broke the news to me, but he just headed out. I'd like to think they're still
puttin' somethin' together up there. Folk need the answers, ya' know?

But Roihelm…seems a stretch to me, but who knows 'bout these things these days."

Foxtamas surely didn't. Didn't know what to think about the news at all. His head spun, dizzied at the flashes of his brother, childhood, and faith crushed beneath a tsunami of riverwater. It had to be a stretch. *Had* to be. The implications, why…why…

Why.

"Aye laddies! Et's mah turn!"

That shook the fox awake. He turned back towards the stage right as Bunns wobbled upon it, feet dragging and head bobbing too far forward then even further back. His appearance must have disturbed the plans the faun had, seeing as how he drew a small crowd of confused guests once back amongst the tables. From them spread a wind of whispers.

"The win already done got to that horned head of his."

"Thinks he's rich 'cause he got those two ruffians kicked out."

"Probably got a special somethin' from Yotesy."

The last rumor came with uneasy looks tossed at the bar. But right as the worry sparked, Bunns himself stomped it out with an original "song."

'Ow bout et mates, ah toast!
Ah toast tae yer all.
Yer mums, Yer paws,
yer lil' brother tha' stumbles an' falls.

Ah toast tae yer wives,
yer friends 'an yer foes,
ah toast tae yer all,
and the journey here tae go!

Ah say weh give ah toast!
Tae all the things in life,
good, bad, sad, nice,

wha's et matter?
Here, take ah toast tae life!

With his words exhausted and eyes glazed over, Flapdragon Champion Bunnclar Cammont smiled. Then collapsed.

Both friends rushed to action. They sprinted from their sides of the tavern and lifted up the drunken jackalope, heaving him off the stage.

"Bunns, Bunns! Wake up!" Acirema shouted through clenched teeth. With her free hand, she slapped him back and forth. Nothing shook that stupid grin from his cheeks.

"Why didn't you stop him from going up there!" asked Foxtamas.

"I told you, I felt bad from earlier!"

The fox could only sigh before hauling the limp body up and over his shoulder. A loose hiccup escaped him.

Amongst the crowd's applause for their Champion, the pair brought him back to the bar, a slight panic rising through them.

"Teardic," said Acirema, "where can we take him? Is there a place in town?"

"Oh no, m'Lady, y'all don't wanna head over there. Y'all can take the ol' Yotesman suite for the night. Here, follow me on up." The coyote whipped around the bar's bend and took to the dark, steepened set of stairs at the corner. As Acirema went up with ease, Foxtamas grunted before starting, best friend in tow.

So.

This was his punishment for his mistake at the River, huh?

20

"AND THEREFORE, REJOICE."

The Yotesman Suite was *more* than the trio needed. Well-organized and spacious, it usually held a tired Teardic during the early hours of the morning. A bed, wide enough to hold an entire family and thickened by ridges of quilts and covers, took up one side, nestled by an already blazing fireplace. Across it sat a reclined couch with recipe-ridden bookshelves guarding it. The entire wooden loft was illuminated by an open window on the far wall, letting the windy summer air drift in and bathing the homely scene in milky white. There was little wondering why the coyote never wanted to venture far from his home.

Foxtamas slumped Bunns upon the bed. The slightest of smiles passed over his face, and the frivolous blankets below molded to his drunk, bruised form.

"Sleep tight, antler-ears," he whispered.

"Are you certain we can have your room? We will be fine elsewhere, surely—" Acirema did what she could to barter, but Teardic put up his hands and started out the door.

"Trust me, m'Lady, ain't a hair off my back. I've got ol' Selida's room to work with, an' if that ain't comfy, I'll snuggle up on the bar. Y'all just take it easy, y'hear? An' don't be scared to stop on back down!" He smirked as the fox and raccoon nodded, slipping out the door and away from view.

"So…" Foxtamas raised his eyebrow at Acirema, then back to the motionless shadow of Bunns. Her cheeks rose into a grin. It was contagious. "You didn't tell Teardic he was a lightweight either, huh?"

The pair burst into a fit of laughter. Of course, a day after battling away a minotaur and aweing the Flapdragon world, he would end the night in a show like this. Typical.

Foxtamas made his way over to the window and took a seat at the small breakfast table beside it. The view stretched northward, high enough like the tower and ridge previous to take in the sloping, waxy landscape of Mechmilne. The speckles of moonlight reflecting across the leaves flittered in the wind. Shimmers of brightness in the dark.

"Hey, Foxtamas." Her voice broke through the fox's nightdreaming. He shook his head and turned her way, finding the princess near the door. "I, um…am going to go back down for a bit. They said more shows were going to start, and it's not often I get to see things like that, and, well—

"Acirema," Foxtamas said with a stirring chuckle. "Go! You don't need a reason. I'll watch over Bunns, you go have a good time, alright?"

The princess beamed.

"Thank you, Foxtamas. I'll try not to stay too long." Although at the room's other end, the fox picked up the slight gleam of happy tears in her eyes. Like all her exits, hardly a footstep was heard.

The fox shuffled back towards the window. Something about the scene provided him the space to simply…be. The serenity. Isolation. Being alone in an unknown corner of the world, staying the night in a place you never knew existed and, after the break of day, will never see again.

A breath in, a breath out. Steadied to finally face the real questions he avoided between breaks and drinks.

Where *would* they go from here? Foxlaris somehow survived in East Evon. Probably. No, *certainly.* How then were they supposed to reach him? Eastern threats now lurked within the West. Just making it to Nohsis would be dangerous enough. What would they encounter on the Riverside? Or after they crossed? Bunns and Acirema could only take so many. He'd be dead weight one way or another.

A quiet assault by fear began. His thoughts left their Eastern demise and worried about the wider issue. What of Roihelm? Knowing of his good, gracious presence had often been enough to steady the fox. It kept his parents calm, at least. It kept other Evoneers firm in keeping on with the toils of their lives.

Now…that foundation felt shaken. Maybe gone *entirely* if he listened to the notion that the Phoenix had his own wicked plan for the very world he created.

Evil thoughts, fearful and menacing thoughts, *powerful* thoughts, all thrummed and drummed and *pounded* the walls of the fox's head.

Hope fled.

The room spun.

All the questions and thoughts and fears and worries were too, too much. He needed to leave. This world. This state of being.

With one last glance at the Mechmilnian ridges, Foxtamas faded, eyes drooping and slumber close at hand. He tucked his head between his arms and nestled upon the table.

Sleep gave him escape.

You're back there.
In Pradifore.
In the tree.
The flames are licking your walls,
the smoke clouding all vision and view.
Just the sight,
nay,
smell
lets the fear in, doesn't it?
Choking. Smoldering.
Unable to move, only able to hear the screams.

But wait...
> *there*
> *aren't*
> *any.*
Everything is...
> *quiet.*
> *Odd.*
But no...
I hear it too.
It's his scream.
The one when he fell while you two climbed;
the one when Momma refused to let him go out because of his cough;
the one when he realized there was no leaving Village Winthrop
and going back home.
It's your brother.

It's Foxlaris.

You must get to him! Hurry, before it's too late!

You look around at your childhood nightmare.
There's only one exit you can recall:
the window.
Amidst the silent flames
you find the gaping hole,
outlined by broken glass.
The memory of cascading into the snow strikes you.
Do you really want to feel
that pain again?

But when you look out, the fear retreats.
It's never done that.
A...bridge...of sorts, glowing a bright blue, stretches from the window and down into the blistering white below.

Huh…that wasn't there before.

But no matter, you don't have time to trifle with bridges.

Foxlaris doesn't either.

Without hesitation, you scramble down with a much more graceful landing than before. The scream still echoes, now deeper into the frozen forest of Pradifore. For a moment, before you sprint off down the trail, you take a look around.

No Momma.

No Poppa.

No fiery raiders on the verge of slaughtering your parents.

Seeing the scene in such a way shakes you. Was this the only way you remembered Pradifore? With the fighting and flames?

What are you doing!?

Stop thinking and start running!

Aren't you hearing his cries!!

He'll be dead by the time you reach him

There you go,

finally,

into the woods,

right where Momma sent you.

Your steps are bigger now; you'll find Foxlaris in no time. All the lanes, however, are starting to look the same. All tall. All dark. All frozen. Still, his scream is louder. Where did you two go?

That's right. The ruins. You remember.

You make that turn into the forest and find it. But no, no, this isn't it. There were flowers, right? Of blue and purple? And the massive stones with all the markings—

Now there's…a void.

An endless abyss stretches out before you.

A scratch of darkness clawed into the forest.

Across continues the screams of your brother.

They're gurgling now,
begging for air.
Like the screeches of some beast.

You look up over the trees for some way around, but only see, looming in the distance, breaking through the snowy sky, their shadow. That shadow that shouldn't be there, was never there, like the chasm, like the missing ruins, flowers.
The Twin Mountains.
The Fulnoa.

Rising up,
hiding your brother,
your kin
behind them.
How could two brothers
do that to another pair!?

Before panic can seize you, the blue light returns. It unravels itself across the endless void, creating yet another bridge. But not just any bridge.
The bridge.
The Bridge of Evon.
Go on now, cross it! Run over, reach the Fulnoa and beyond. Don't you hear him, he's worsening by the minute!

But you can't,
can you?
You remember what happened the last time
a Scottsworth stepped foot upon it.
Those moments are fresher than the one you're in now.
It broke.
The world ripped apart.
Foxlaris fell
and endured

whatever torture rallied beneath the torrents.
How is it supposed to hold now!?
What kind of trust does it require?
Will it even lead to Foxlaris
or take you directly away from him!?

Keep calm, the fear is rising in you.

No, you can find another way.
The void's not that long.
You don't need the Bridge
and all its troubles, it's too much.
You grew up in these woods, right?
It's your home, your world.
You can find the way.

Don't listen to those thoughts.

But…what if you can't?
And the Bridge is the only way?
What then?
Will you go back?
Back to the tree?
Hide underneath the fallen bunk just like you did?
Where you should have died?

Stop!
You can't take any more!

There's no way out, is there?
You'll die because of this.
You can't trust the Bridge.
It's all too much to even consider
placing a single foot on those blue planks,

to have the ground beneath you not be your own
but someone else's.
Both you and Foxlaris will be dead because of this.
Because of your fear, your inaction.
The raiders thought the Scottsworths were dead that night;

turns

out

they

were

RIGHT!

"NO!"

Foxtamas struggled to swallow, his tongue and throat dried and aching. Sweat dripped down his forehead, clung to his nose. The nightmare fought but eventually eased itself from his mind. What...what had that been?

He eased up from the table and struggled to recall what he'd been witness to. Nothing showed. Only feelings of distress, his heart thumping quicker and quicker to the point of collapse.

No, there *was* something. A single word, an image cloaked in shadow, framed in midnight light.

Fulnoa.

Slowly, he rubbed out the sleep from his eyes. The night must've reached an early morning. Acirema had returned and taken residence upon the couch; Bunns still slept exactly as he was placed. Foxtamas snickered, then turned his back to the window, yet found within it the image of the rising twin mountains burned to his vision. No matter the blinks, they tainted the horizon.

The longer he pondered the stone brothers, the more a...realization of sorts entered his mind. One tempting. One...that when placed in the wider context of his worries…fit.

They needed to go to the Fulnoa.

All suddenly clicked together, a puzzle scattered now reforged. What better aid to fight back the Eastern beasts and journey into the unknown lands of East Evon than the dwarf warriors, the Guardians of the North? Even just a small party to travel alongside them would be enough. Better, the trio could talk with the scholars Teardic mentioned. The two parties could trade information, one about the cause of Grammo Day and the other about the creatures. Perhaps the two were linked.

To his surprise, a soft, sleepy smile nestled upon his face. But not because of the Fulnoa.

No, the thought of Roihelm once more rattled his brain. This time, the picture was not one of potential malice and vile intent; the image instead simmered down into a mystery. A curious comfort. It was probably just his mind relaxing after the sudden relief of stress, like a parched throat gulping its first sip of water. How could one hold hate when their journey *finally* had a destination?

"Hold out just a little longer, Foxlaris. Help's on the way," Foxtamas whispered to his brother. He pulled his hood over his tired eyes, giving one last look northward. They were doing what the young fellowship of four had dreamed about in all their stories, all their games—they were journeying to the Mountain Fortresses of Evon, the Twin Mountains, the Gateway to the North.

They were going to the Fulnoa.

This life: how sweet, how sweet.
It will bleed like tears that cling
close to a mother's cheek as she holds
her baby before he journeys home.
Too will it heal, as wishes blossom
into a throng of heartbeats gathered
around the union of two lost loves.
Yes, it is sweet. Swift yet rich
like the taste of riverwater.
Even in the tempest,
even in the bursting blister
of the gale, even when these lands
shake and shift until you can't
run or walk or stand upon them
will the beauty of this life last.
For to rejoice is to turn the pages
of an endless book, one whose story
will last forever and always.
Rejoice in it, therefore,
and therefore, rejoice.

"Psalm from the Riverside"
— Written by Princess Acirema Feiht.
on the banks of River Nohsis.
after the Desolation
of Grammo Day.

The story of the Foxtamas, Foxlaris, Acirema, and Bunns continues in Book II: *To Walk Where Mountains Sleep.*

Available early 2026.

About the author

Marshall Cunningham grew up in the woods of Arkansas but lived in the castles of Narnia and mountains of Middle-Earth. He began *The Bridge of Evon* in fourth grade, writing and re-writing it multiple times before its four-part publication across 2025 and 2026. He holds a BA in English and Creative Writing from the University of Central Arkansas and owns Bean's Books in Pickles Gap Village. He resides in Conway with the store's titular schnauzer, his reading and writing buddy, Bean.

You can keep up with him, Bean, his books, and his store at the following:

beans-books.com
@beansbooksconway
@thebridgeofevon

www.ingramcontent.com/pod-product-compliance
Lightning Source LLC
Chambersburg PA
CBHW020536020726
47494CB00006B/1790